BETTY N

THE ULTIMATE C

Betty Neels's novels are loved
by millions of readers around the world,
and this very special ***12-volume collection***
offers a unique chance to recapture the pleasure
of some of her most popular stories.

Each month we're bringing you a new volume
containing two timeless classics—irresistible love
stories that belong together, whether they share the
same colourful setting, romantic theme, or follow the
same characters in their continuing lives...

As a special treat, each volume also includes an
introductory letter by a different author. Some of the
most popular names in romance fiction are delighted
to pay tribute to Betty Neels; we hope you enjoy
reading their personal thoughts and memories.

We're proud and privileged to bring you
this very special collection, and hope you enjoy
reading—and keeping—these twelve wonderful
volumes over the coming months.

Volume Two

—with an introduction from award-winning author

Liz Fielding

An enchanting duet of classic romances:

THE MOST MARVELLOUS SUMMER
A SUMMER IDYLL

We'd like to take this opportunity to pay tribute to **Betty Neels**, *who sadly passed away last year. Betty was one of our best-loved authors. As well as being a wonderfully warm and thoroughly charming individual, Betty led a fascinating life even before becoming a writer, and her publishing record was impressive.*

Betty spent her childhood and youth in Devonshire before training as a nurse and midwife. She was an army nursing sister during the war, married a Dutchman and subsequently lived in Holland for fourteen years. On retirement from nursing Betty started to write, inspired by a lady in a library bemoaning the lack of romantic novels.

Over her thirty-year writing career Betty wrote more than 134 novels and was published in more than one hundred international markets. She continued to write into her ninetieth year, remaining as passionate about her characters and stories then as she was with her very first book.

Betty will be greatly missed, both by her friends at Harlequin Mills & Boon® *and by her legions of loyal readers around the world. Betty was a prolific writer and has left a lasting legacy through her heartwarming novels. She will always be remembered as a truly delightful person who brought great happiness to many.*

THE ULTIMATE COLLECTION

Volume Two

THE MOST MARVELLOUS SUMMER

&

A SUMMER IDYLL

Two full-length novels

Harlequin Mills & Boon Limited,
Eton House, 18-24 Paradise Road, Richmond, Surrey TW9 1SR

ISBN 0 263 83644 4

Set in Times Roman 10¾ on 12½ pt.
141-0802-96905

Printed and bound in Spain
by Litografia Rosés, S.A., Barcelona

Dear Reader

Nearly twenty years after it was published, I still remember my first '**Betty Neels**'. *Polly* was published in 1984 and began for me a love affair with Betty's determined, strong-hearted heroines and wonderful doctor heroes who have the wisdom and character to recognise true virtue and value its worth.

More, she inspired me to write my own romances so that I became, in time, not just her fan, but her colleague.

Betty, however, will always have a special place in the hearts of her readers. Uniquely amongst 'bestsellers', she needed no violence or bad language to hold her audience. Her stories take us all back to a more innocent age and their appeal is enduring.

She remains an inspiration to all who believe in the power of love, all who seek to reach out and touch their readers' hearts, and the world is a poorer place without her.

Liz Fielding

THE MOST MARVELLOUS SUMMER

by

Betty Neels

CHAPTER ONE

MATILDA had fallen in love. She had had no intention of doing so, but there it was. She first saw the stranger during the reading of the first lesson by Sir Benjamin Fox, whose pompous voice, pronouncing biblical names with precise correctness, always set her thoughts wandering. She glanced along the pew at her two brothers, home for the half-term holidays, her two sisters and her mother and then allowed her gaze to wander to the manor pew at the side of the chancel, where Lady Fox sat with various members of her family. They all looked alike, she thought, with their fine beaky noses and thin mouths. She turned her head very slightly and looked across the main aisle and saw the stranger sitting by Dr Bramley. He appeared a very large man with broad shoulders, fair hair which she suspected had a sprinkling of grey, and a splendid profile. A pity that he didn't look round... Sir Benjamin rolled the last unpronounceable name off his tongue and she fixed her eyes on him once more—green eyes, shadowed by sweeping black lashes, in a lovely face crowned by a wealth of copper hair.

Her father announced the hymn and the congregation rose to sing it cheerfully, galloping ahead of the organ when it had the chance, and then sitting once more for the second lesson. The headmaster of the village infants' school read it in a clear unhurried voice and this time she listened, until something compelled her to glance across the aisle again. The stranger was looking at her and he was every bit as handsome as she had expected him to be; unsmiling—it wouldn't have done in church if he had smiled anyway—and somehow compelling. She went faintly pink and looked away from him quickly, feeling all at once as though she were in some kind of blissful heaven, knowing with certainty that she had fallen in love. It was a delightful sensation, and she pondered over it during her father's sermon, taking care not to look across the aisle again; the village was a small one and rather isolated, so that everyone was inclined to mind everyone else's business and turn a molehill into a mountain, preferably a romantic one, and that if a girl so much as glanced twice at the same man. She was aware that the village was disappointed that she hadn't married. She had had three proposals and although she had hesitated over them she had declined them kindly and watched her erstwhile suitors marry without regret. Twenty-six was getting on a bit, as Mrs Chump at the general stores so often reminded her, but she had waited. Now here he was, the man she wished to marry, dropped as it were from heaven into her path. He could of course be married, engaged or a confirmed bachelor—she would have to find out, but, as she was great friends with Dr Bramley, it would be easy to ask him.

The last hymn sung, the congregation filed out, stopping to chat as it went, and since the rector's family were well liked their progress was slow; they arrived at the church door just in time for her to see the stranger, still with the doctor, talking to Sir Benjamin, and even as Matilda looked Lady Fox tapped him on an arm and pushed Roseanne, her eldest daughter, forwards. Matilda watched him being swept away down the tree-lined avenue which led to the manor-house from the churchyard.

She watched him go, already planning to ask who he was when she got to the manor-house in the morning. Esme, her younger sister, fourteen and as sharp as a needle, tugged her arm. 'Hey, Tilly—come on,' and then, 'I bet you've fallen for him—I have. A bit old for me I suppose, but he'd do nicely for you.'

'Rubbish, love. What nonsense you do talk.'

'You went all pink when he looked at you—I expect it was your hair—it kind of glows, you know, even under a hat!'

They started to walk along the narrow path which led to the rectory garden and Esme said, 'Hilary's seen him too, but of course she's engaged…'

'Let's forget him,' said Matilda cheerfully. 'We'll probably never see him again.' She uttered the remark with the heartfelt wish that it might not be true. However could she marry anyone else now that she had seen him and knew that she had fallen in love at last? She would have to stay an old maid, if there was such a thing these days, helping with the parish and wearing dreary hats and worthy undateable clothes.

She sighed heavily at the very idea and Esme said, 'I bet you'll meet again—I dare say he's your fate.'

'Oh, what romantic nonsense,' said Matilda again and hurried to the kitchen to help her mother dish up the Sunday lunch.

Her mother had her head in the Aga oven, and was prodding the joint with a fork. 'Put the apples on for the sauce, will you, dear? I wonder who that giant was in church? Did you see him?' She didn't wait for an answer. 'He seemed to know the Foxes. I must keep my ears open in the village tomorrow.'

She emerged and closed the oven door, an older version of her lovely daughter although the hair was streaked with grey. 'That was a frightful hat Lady Fox was wearing—I wonder where she buys them?'

'Probably makes them herself.' Matilda was peeling apples and biting at the cores.

She was up early the next morning and while her mother cooked the breakfast she sorted the wash, got the machine going, made sure that Esme was up and had everything she needed before catching the bus to Sherborne where she was having extra coaching for her O Levels, and then roused the two boys. Hilary, her other sister, was going to stay with her fiancé and was already up, doing the last of her packing. They all sat down to breakfast presently, a meal taken with the minimum of conversation since everyone there had his or her plans for the day. Esme was the first to go, then the boys on a fishing expedition, the rector to visit a parishioner in hospital at Salisbury and then Hilary, leaving Mrs ffinch and Matilda to clear the table and leave the dishes for Mrs Coffin, who came three times a week to help in the house.

'Don't be late,' warned Mrs ffinch as Matilda got Nelson the cat's breakfast. She sighed as she said it—it irked her that her beautiful daughter should have to go to work each day. Not that it wasn't a suitable job for the daughter of the rector—social secretary to Lady Fox—even though it was badly paid and covered a multitude of odd jobs which no social secretary cognisant with her normal duties would have countenanced. But, as Matilda pointed out, it paid for her clothes, and the fees for Esme's coaching, and helped towards the upkeep of the rectory, a large, rambling house with out-of-date plumbing always going wrong, draughty rooms and a boiler which swallowed coke by the ton. All the same, it was comfortable in a shabby way and the family was a happy one.

It was only a few minutes' walk to the manor-house; Matilda nipped smartly through the light rain and went in through the side-door—not that she wasn't expected to use the front entrance, but the polished floor of the wide hall showed every mark from damp feet and she was aware that Mrs Fletcher from the village, who obliged each day at the manor-house, would have just finished polishing it. She went along the passage to the kitchen, wished Cook and the kitchen maid good morning and made her way through the baize door into the front of the house. Lady Fox was coming down the staircase, holding a handful of letters.

'Good morning, Matilda.' She glanced at the long case clock in the hall, but since Matilda was exactly on time and she had no cause to find fault she went on, 'Such a number of letters this morning; really, my days are so busy...'

Lady Fox gave Matilda a faintly disapproving look; there was nothing wrong with her appearance—the striped shirt, navy pleated skirt and sensible shoes were, to say the least, not worthy of a second glance—but dowdy clothes couldn't dim the brightness of Matilda's hair or the sparkling green of her eyes, and those allied to a delightful nose, a curving mouth and a complexion as smooth and fresh as a child's. Lady Fox frowned slightly, remembering Roseanne's regrettable spots and unfortunate nose. 'I have guests for lunch,' she observed. 'I had better see Cook at once while you deal with these.' She handed the letters to Matilda and hurried away kitchenwards.

Matilda, sorting out butcher's and grocer's bills from invitations to dinner and requests from charities, reflected that Lady Fox wasn't in a very good mood and, since there was no sign of that lady, she put the letters on the desk in Lady Fox's sitting-room and went along to the chilly little room where she arranged the flowers. The gardener had brought in early tulips and daffodils and some rather overpowering greenery and she was trying to decide what to do with them when Lady Fox's voice, high and penetrating, reached her. 'You might do a small centre-piece for the table, Matilda—go into the garden and see what you can find.'

Matilda, well brought up as she had been, allowed herself the comfort of a childish grimace; if it hadn't been for the useful money needed at the rectory, she would have liked to flounce out of the manor-house and never go back.

The garden was soothing, if chilly, and she took a basket with her and picked primulas and grape-hyacinths, late Christmas roses, lily of the valley and a handful of brightly coloured polyanthus and bore the lot back through the garden door and into the hall, intent on fetching a particular bowl which would look just right on the dining-room table.

Lady Fox was in the hall, talking animatedly to the stranger. She paused to look at Matilda and her companion looked too; Matilda, her fiery head a little untidy, her pretty face glowing from the fresh air, clutching her basket of flowers, was worth looking at.

'There you are,' observed Lady Fox with distinctly false *bonhomie*, 'but shouldn't you be arranging the flowers?' She turned to the man beside her. 'My companion-secretary, you know—I couldn't manage without help and Roseanne has her painting—quite talented.'

He gave her a grave, enquiring look and she went on hurriedly, 'This is Matilda ffinch, the rector's eldest daughter—Matilda, this is Mr Scott-Thurlow.'

Matilda transferred the basket to her other arm and held out a hand, to have it engulfed by his large firm grasp. Now that she could look at him face to face, she was even more certain that this was the man she had been waiting for. She beamed at him, full of delight, and he smiled a little in return. A firm mouth, perhaps a rather stern one, and his eyes were blue, heavy-lidded and cool; he would be at least thirty-five, perhaps nearer forty.

His polite 'How do you do?' was uttered in a deep quiet voice and her smile widened. Her 'hello' sounded like that of a little girl who had just been offered something she had longed for.

Lady Fox spoke in the voice she kept for recalcitrant children on those occasions when she had been asked to give away the Sunday school prizes.

'If you would see to the flowers, Matilda—and since I shan't need you for a few hours you may go home for your lunch.'

'Back after lunch?' asked Matilda.

'Half-past two.' Mr Scott-Thurlow would be gone by then; Roseanne on her own could be quite charming, reflected her fond parent, and there would be no competition...

'Very well, Lady Fox.' Matilda turned an emerald gaze upon Mr Scott-Thurlow. Her goodbye was cheerful; having found him she didn't for one moment expect fate to lose him again for her. She would have liked to have stayed for lunch—usually she did—but one lunch more or less would make no difference to the future.

She nipped smartly to the back of the house, arranged the flowers and then took herself off home. She passed Roseanne as she left the house, and since she was a kind-hearted girl she was sorry to see that she was wearing an expensive two-piece in the wrong shade of green—it showed up the spots.

Roseanne stopped when she saw her. 'I hate this outfit,' she declared, quite fiercely for her. 'Mother says it's elegant but I feel a fool in it.' She cast an envious eye upon Matilda's person. 'You always look right—why?'

'I don't know. You'd look nice in the greeny blue...'

'There's that man coming to lunch,' went on Roseanne unhappily. 'Mother says I must exert myself...'

She hurried indoors and Matilda went back to the rectory to give her mother and father a hand, prepare the lunch and then sit down and eat it.

'You aren't usually home at this time,' remarked her father, ladling shepherd's pie into exact portions.

'Got the sack?' asked Guy, and Thomas added,

'Shouldn't be surprised with that hair.'

'Visitors for lunch,' explained Matilda, ignoring her brothers. 'I'm to go back at half-past two.'

'You usually stay there even when there are visitors,' mused her mother.

Matilda turned limpid eyes upon her parent. 'Probably I'd have made the numbers wrong, Mother.' She handed out the plates. 'Is it Esme's evening for dancing class? Do you want me to collect her?'

'Well, that would be nice, dear; the bus takes so long to get here.'

Matilda went back to the manor-house after lunch and found Lady Fox and Roseanne arguing about the green outfit. They both looked cross and Lady Fox said at once, 'This silly girl has been invited to stay in London and she doesn't want to go...'

Matilda had collected the second post as she went in, and she sat down and began to sort it. 'Why not?' she asked, pleasantly. 'I should think it would be the greatest fun.'

'I don't know anyone,' mumbled Roseanne.

'Well, you don't expect to until you're there,' said Matilda reasonably, 'but think of the theatres—you know, *The Phantom of the Opera* and *Aspects of Love* and *Cats* and there'll be exhibitions at the Tate and the National Gallery. You might meet some artists.'

Roseanne brightened. 'Well, yes—I suppose that I might; perhaps it wouldn't be so bad.'

Matilda went home again after tea, taken off a tray while she added up the household accounts for Lady Fox. It was a fine evening and the drive to Sherborne would be pleasant. Abner Magna was only a few miles from that town, but the roads were narrow and winding and the evening bus which Esme sometimes took stopped whenever someone wanted to board it or get off, making the journey twice as long. Matilda got a thick knitted jacket, poked at her hair and went to tell her mother that she was about to leave. There was no one in the kitchen but there were voices in her father's study. She opened the door, stuck her head round it and cried, 'I'm off to fetch Esme, we shouldn't be—' She came to a halt; Mr Scott-Thurlow was standing beside her father, surveying the rather untidy garden.

He said at once, 'Good evening, Miss ffinch,' and her father said mildly, 'John Bramley asked Mr Scott-Thurlow to bring a book over which he had promised to lend me. You have met?'

'Very briefly,' observed his guest. 'I mustn't keep you, sir. Do

I understand Miss ffinch to say that she is driving into Sherborne? I'm on the point of going there myself and shall be glad to offer her a lift.'

A delightful prospect, which she had to refuse with regret. 'I'm going to fetch my sister—she's at dancing class, and we've no way of getting back here—the last bus would have gone...'

'I shall be coming back; I have to take something to the hospital for Dr Bramley, a matter of five minutes. We could collect your sister and I can stop at the hospital on our way back.'

'Oh, well, yes—thank you very much. Do you want to go now?'

'Certainly.' He said all the right things to the rector and then stopped in the hall for a moment to bid Mrs ffinch goodbye before ushering Matilda outside.

He opened the door of the car standing there and she skipped inside. 'What a treat,' she declared happily, 'a Rolls-Royce—wait till Esme sees it.' She added the information that such a vehicle was seldom seen in Abner Magna. 'Of course Sir Benjamin has a Daimler, but it's a bit worthy if you know what I mean.'

He made some non-committal answer, but since she felt strangely at ease with him she enlivened their short journey with odds and ends of information, all of them good-natured, about the village and its inhabitants. 'I dare say you live in London?' she wanted to know.

Mr Scott-Thurlow was sitting back, not driving fast; he said idly, 'Yes, I do. Your village is delightful.'

'Well, I like it, but I was born here. Have you known Dr Bramley long?'

'Er—he and my father knew each other in their youth...'

'Oh, well, I didn't think you were all that old,' said Matilda kindly. 'Dr Bramley is always saying that he'll retire so he must be getting on a bit.'

Her companion allowed himself a faint smile. 'I am thirty-eight,' he told her. 'And how old are you, Miss ffinch?'

'Me? Oh, twenty-six.'

'And heart-whole?'

A difficult question to answer. 'Well, I was... Are you married?'

They were in Sherborne now and he asked, 'Which way?' before saying, 'No, but I'm engaged.'

Matilda knew exactly how a balloon must feel when it was pricked. She said in a rigid voice, 'I expect you're looking forward to getting married. Here we are.'

He stopped the car and turned to look at her. 'Do you know, Miss ffinch, I cannot remember when I was cross-examined so thoroughly?'

She stared at him, stricken. 'I'm sorry, I didn't mean to pry—I just wanted—I was interested...'

He smiled then and her heart turned over. 'I rather enjoyed it. Is that your sister waving to us from the other side of the road?'

A snub, a gentle one, but still a snub. Matilda went a delightful pink and frowned ferociously, remembering the string of questions she had flung at him; he probably thought her a dull country woman with nothing better to do than poke her nose into other people's affairs. Her daydream had been shattered by a few well-chosen words on his part and life would never be the same again. The quicker he went away and she never set eyes on him again the better. She said in a sober voice, 'Yes, that's Esme.'

It was a good thing that Esme elected to sit beside him and chatter non-stop so that Matilda had no need to say much; she thanked him rather primly as he stopped at the rectory gates but it was Esme who urged him to go in with them. An invitation he declined pleasantly enough.

He had gone the next day, or so it seemed from a remark her father made the following evening, and it was then that she realised that she had no idea what he did or who he really was. He had the calm self-assured manner of a solicitor and she had heard him discussing a point of law with the rector during his brief visit. Solicitors, she had always supposed, earned themselves a good living, good enough to run a Rolls—she allowed her thoughts to wander—he might have to get a cheaper car when he married though; his wife would want clothes and the children would need to be educated. She made a resolution then and there not to think about him any more. That she had fallen in love with a man who was on the point of getting married to some other girl was a trick of unkind fate, and there was nothing to do about it.

A week went by, the boys went back to school and so did Esme, and Hilary was home again. Matilda's days were full: Lady Fox each day, choir practice on Thursday evening, Sunday school, driving her father to one or two of the more distant farms; the pattern of her future, reflected Matilda, indulging in a rare attack of self-pity, and then forgetting to be sorry for herself when she went for a Sunday afternoon stroll through the woods above the village. It really was a delightful day; the sky was blue, the trees were turning green even as she looked at them and there were lambs racing around the fields, and when she sat on a tree stump to get her breath a squirrel came and sat within a yard or two of her. There were compensations, she told herself stoutly.

She was surprised to find Lady Fox waiting for her in the hall when she went there on the Monday morning. She wondered uneasily if she had done something really dire, like sending a letter in the wrong envelope, but from the smile on Lady Fox's face she thought that unlikely.

'There you are, Matilda,' said Lady Fox unnecessarily. 'Come into the sitting-room, will you? I should like a word with you.'

She nodded to a chair and Matilda sat down, wondering what to expect.

'Roseanne,' began Lady Fox, 'has consented to pay a visit to London—her godmother, you know, the Honourable Mrs Venables. I am delighted; she is bound to meet people.' Lady Fox really meant young men free to marry. 'There is simply no one of her age and class here.'

Matilda said nothing, although that was difficult; the ffinches had been in and around Dorset for centuries and were as good, if not better than the Foxes, and what was more her mother was distantly related to a peer of the realm—so distant, it must be said, that her family name was a mere dot on the outskirts of the lordly family tree—all the same, it was there.

'Such a pity,' went on Lady Fox in what she considered to be a confidential voice, 'that Mr Scott-Thurlow is engaged to be married, although of course he would have been rather old for Roseanne—a pity that I wasn't told.'

'You were telling me about Roseanne's visit,' prompted Matilda while she thought about Mr Scott-Thurlow.

'I am coming to that. She will go only on the condition that you go with her. The visit is for a month and you would go as her companion. Her godmother has no objection, and I shall of course pay you your usual salary. In a week's time.'

'I'll talk it over with my mother and father,' said Matilda in a quiet voice which her nearest and dearest would have recognised as the first sign of rage coming to the boil. 'I shall want to consider it myself.'

Lady Fox looked astounded. 'But my dear girl, it is such a splendid opportunity for you to see something of the sophisticated world—you might even meet some suitable young man. If you are worried about clothes I'm sure—'

'No, I'm not worried about clothes, Lady Fox. I'm not sure that I want to go to London. I really must have a day or two to think about it.'

Lady Fox's formidable frontage swelled alarmingly. 'Well, really, I don't know what to say. It is most important that Roseanne should go—she is so—so countrified and gauche. Vera and Mary are so much younger and already quite self-possessed.'

Matilda, who disliked the two teenagers, agreed politely; Roseanne was dull and had no backbone worth mentioning, but at least she wasn't rude.

Lady Fox rose. 'Well, since you seem to want time to think over this splendid offer, perhaps you will let me know as soon as you have decided? Now, will you see to the post and wash the Sèvres? I have to go in to Sherborne. I shall be back for lunch—Sir Benjamin is out so there will be just myself, Roseanne and yourself. Tell Cook, will you?'

She hurried away, looking cross, and Matilda wandered off to the kitchen where she discussed lunch with Cook and had a cup of tea before going through the post.

She was in the china pantry washing the precious Sèvres china when Roseanne wandered in.

'Matilda, you will come with me, won't you? I won't go unless you do. Mother keeps on and on, if I don't go I won't stay here either, I'll run away.'

Matilda eyed her carefully. Roseanne meant it. The worm had turned, and, let loose on an uncaring world, Roseanne wouldn't stand a chance...

'I'll have to discuss it with Mother and Father but I don't think they would mind, just for a few weeks.'

'You'll come? Oh, Matilda, I'll never be able to thank you enough—I'll do anything...'

'No need,' said Matilda prosaically, 'I dare say it will be quite fun.'

Her parents raised no objection; she told Lady Fox the next day that she was willing to go with Roseanne and listened to that lady's monologue about the benefits of London to a girl like Roseanne. 'Of course *you* may not get invited to the dinner parties and dances her godmother will arrange, but I dare say you will be glad of that.'

'Why?' asked Matilda with interest.

Lady Fox went an unbecoming red. 'Oh, I have no intention of being rude, Matilda—what I mean is that you will need time to yourself occasionally and there will be no need to attend all the parties Roseanne is bound to go to. I rely upon you to see that she buys only suitable clothes, and please discourage any friendships she may strike up if the—er—young man isn't suitable. She is very young...'

Twenty-two wasn't all that young, thought Matilda, and it was high time Roseanne found her own feet and stood on them.

At home, she inspected her wardrobe and decided that there was no need to buy anything new. She had two evening dresses, both off the peg and by no means new, but nevertheless pretty. She had a good suit, blouses and sweaters enough, a skirt or two and a rather nice jersey dress bought in the January sales. She climbed the narrow stairs to the attic, found a rather battered case, hauled it downstairs and packed it without enthusiasm. London in the spring would come a poor second to Abner Magna.

Each day she was taken aside and lectured by Lady Fox about

the London visit; she must do this and not that, young men were to be scrutinised and Roseanne wasn't to go gallivanting off...

Matilda forbore from pointing out that the girl was the last person on earth to gallivant, and anyway with those spots and that unfortunate nose she wasn't likely to get the chance. Let the poor girl have her fling! However timid, she was a nice girl and perhaps with her mother out of the way she might even improve enormously.

She made suitable replies to Lady Fox's remarks and that lady, looking at her, wished for the hundredth time that it could have been someone else but Matilda ffinch who was going with Roseanne; the girl was too pretty—more than that, that hair and those wide eyes weren't to be ignored. She would have to drop a word in Roseanne's godmother's ear to make sure that Matilda attended as few dances and parties as possible; no one—no man—would look at the dear girl while Matilda was there, although give the girl her due she wasn't a young woman to push herself forward; she knew her place, Lady Fox reflected, happily unaware of the superiority of the ffinches over the Foxes.

They were to travel up to London in the Foxes' Daimler driven by Gregg the chauffeur and gardener. Matilda got up early, made a tour of the rather untidy garden, ate a good breakfast and presented herself at the manor at nine o'clock sharp.

Roseanne, wearing expensive mud-brown tweeds, quite unsuitable for the time of year, looked as though she would change her mind about going at any moment; Matilda bustled her briskly into the car with the promise that they would telephone as soon as they arrived and they drove away.

It was a pleasant morning, chilly still but the sun shone and Matilda, chatting bracingly about the pleasures in store, wanted very much to get out of the car and walk or get on to her old bike and potter off for the day. She listened sympathetically to Roseanne's uncertain hopes for the next few weeks, bolstered her up with the delights of London in store for her and whenever she had a moment thought about Mr Scott-Thurlow.

The Honourable Mrs Venables lived in Kensington, in a massive red brick flat, furnished with splendour and a regrettable tendency to overdo crimson velvet, gilding wherever possible and dark, heavy furniture. She received them graciously and somewhat absent-mindedly, since she was holding a lengthy telephone conversation when they arrived. They sat while she concluded this and were then handed over to a dour-looking woman who led them down a long corridor to two rooms at its end, overlooking a narrow garden and more red brick walls.

'There's the bathroom,' they were told. 'You share it. My name's Bertha.'

'I'm not going to like it,' declared Roseanne when they were alone in her room. Her lip quivered. 'I want to go home.'

'We've only just got here,' Matilda pointed out. 'At least let's give it a try. It's all a bit strange—you'll feel better after lunch.'

She was right; Mrs Venables had a great deal to say over the meal, laying out for Roseanne's approbations the various entertainments she had arranged for her. 'We shall have a quiet evening here today,' she said, 'but tomorrow we might go shopping and there's an excellent film we might see in the evening. I shall leave you two girls to amuse yourselves during the day—there is plenty to see and do. I have arranged a dinner party or two and there are several invitations for you.' It all sounded rather fun so that when Roseanne telephoned her mother after lunch she said nothing about wanting to return home.

They spent the next day or two finding their feet. The mornings were taken up with shopping; Roseanne had plenty of money and urged by Matilda bought the clothes she had always wanted and never had the smallest chance to since her mother had always accompanied her. It was a surprise what a difference they made to her appearance, especially when Matilda, given *carte blanche* at the cosmetic counters, found a cream to disguise the spots and chose lipstick, blusher and eye-shadow and applied them to her companion's face. 'Don't you want to buy anything?' asked Roseanne. 'Clothes?'

Matilda assured her, quite untruthfully, that she didn't.

It was their third day there and they had been shopping again. It was Matilda who stopped outside an art gallery with a discreet notice, 'Exhibition Within', and suggested that they might take a look.

The gallery was a series of rooms, very elegant and half filled with viewers, and the first person Matilda saw there was Mr Scott-Thurlow.

CHAPTER TWO

MR SCOTT-THURLOW wasn't alone: there was a tall, willowy girl beside him, a fashion-plate, so slim that she might have been cut out of cardboard. She was exquisitely made up and her hair was a teased-out halo, lacquered into immobility. She was beautiful but there was no animation in her face; indeed, she looked bored, far more interested in arranging the pleats of her long skirt than viewing the large painting before which they stood.

Matilda, after the first shock of delight, wanted perversely nothing so much as to get as far away from Mr Scott-Thurlow as possible, but Roseanne had seen him too. She darted up to him and caught his sleeve.

'Fancy seeing you here, Mr Scott-Thurlow—' for once she had forgotten her shyness '—and Matilda's with me...'

He took her hand and shook it gently and his voice was kind. 'How delightful to see you again, Roseanne. Are you staying in town?' He turned to his companion. 'Rhoda, this is Roseanne Fox; we met in Dorset a few weeks ago.' He smiled at Roseanne. 'My fiancée, Rhoda Symes.'

He looked past her to where Matilda was waiting and his smile faded, indeed he looked angry but so fleetingly that watching him she decided that she had imagined it. There was nothing else to do but to join Roseanne, greet him politely and be introduced in her turn to the girl with him.

Rhoda Symes was everything that she wasn't, reflected Matilda sadly, thinking of her own pleasant plumpness and kind of knowing that in the eyes of this girl she was just plain fat, size fourteen, wearing all the wrong make-up and with the wrong-coloured hair... All the same she gave the girl a friendly smile—if she was going to make Mr Scott-Thurlow a happy man, then she, Matilda, would make the best of it; she loved him too much to think otherwise.

The girl was lovely. Matilda supposed that in all fairness if she were a man she would undoubtedly fall for all that elegant beauty.

They stood and talked for a few minutes until Matilda observed that they still had almost the whole of the exhibition to see and since Roseanne was interested hadn't they better get started?

She bade Mr Scott-Thurlow a colourless goodbye and smiled without guile at Rhoda Symes, trying not to see the very large diamond on her left hand—a hand which that lady flourished rather too prominently.

'I say,' said Roseanne excitedly, 'isn't she absolutely lovely? I wonder if we'll get asked to the wedding?' She added, not meaning to be rude, 'Not you, of course.'

Matilda, contemplating a large oil-painting which she thought privately looked as though the artist had upset his paint pots over the canvas, agreed cheerfully to this remark; wild horses wouldn't drag her to Mr Scott-Thurlow's wedding—he was, as far as she was concerned, a closed book. Or so she told herself.

Roseanne's godmother gave a dinner party on the following evening; just a few friends, the Honourable Mrs Venables had said, most of them unattached men of suitable age with a complement of safely married ladies; Roseanne must have her chance and a dinner party was a very good way of getting to know people. Matilda was to attend too although her hostess would have been happier not to have had the competition; she consoled herself with the thought that men didn't care for such bright red hair.

Matilda did her best to look inconspicuous; she did her hair in a severe french pleat, wore an unassuming gown—grey crêpe and several years out of date—and stayed in the background as much as possible. Nevertheless she attracted the attention of the company, and since she was a nice, unassuming girl the ladies of the party liked her as well as the men. She did her best to see that Roseanne was a success and her godmother had to admit that Matilda hadn't made any attempt to draw attention to herself. All the same, an excuse would have to be found for Roseanne to go without her to the dinner dance later that week, and Matilda, being told on the morning of that day that she looked poorly and perhaps it would be wise if she didn't go out that evening, agreed for

Roseanne's sake that she had a very bad headache and an early night would do her the world of good.

Of course, during the days she was expected to accompany Roseanne wherever she had a fancy to go, leaving her godmother to pursue her own busy social life, and it was a day or so after the dinner dance that they found themselves in the National Gallery. It was while they were admiring some splendid examples of the Netherlandish school that the young man standing close by spoke to them, or rather to Roseanne.

'Forgive me,' he began, 'I overheard you discussing this picture—you know something about it, do you not? Are you interested in oil-paintings of that period?'

When Roseanne nodded, her beaky nose quivering with the unexpectedness of it all, he asked, 'You paint yourself?' Then when she nodded again, 'Then let me explain…'

Which he did at some length, taking her from one painting to the next with Matilda, intrigued, keeping discreetly in the background. He seemed all right; he had a nice open face, not good-looking, but his gaze was direct, and he had introduced himself and shaken hands. 'Bernard Stevens,' he told them, working as a picture restorer for a famous art gallery and painting when he had the time. Roseanne had to be prised away from him after half an hour or so but only after she had promised to meet him there on the following morning, ostensibly to discuss more paintings but Matilda, studying her face, thought that was only partly the reason.

'You won't tell Aunt Maud?' begged Roseanne.

'Roseanne, you're twenty-two, old enough to decide whom you want to know. Of course I shan't breathe a word.'

All the same she played discreet gooseberry the next morning, and again on the following afternoon, only now it was the Tate Gallery. She had been reassured to hear him mention the names of several people whom Roseanne's godmother had talked of from time to time and he appeared well dressed and had good manners; she was no snob, but just supposing the gentle little flirtation turned into something more serious—she would have to answer to Lady Fox.

They were to go to the theatre on the next evening, quite a small party and Matilda found herself paired off with an elderly man, a widower who told her at great length about his late wife's ill health, and during the interval, when she had hoped to escape him for a short while, he led her firmly to the bar where he fetched her a tonic and lemon without asking her what she would like. 'I don't approve of pretty young ladies drinking alcohol,' he told her and, because she had a kind heart, she accepted it nicely and sipped at it. She really needed something strong. Vodka? She had never tasted it. Brandy and soda? She looked around her—everyone there appeared to be drinking gin and tonic or champagne.

She took another sip and while appearing attentive to her companion's remarks—still about his wife too—glanced around her. There were some lovely dresses, and the grey crêpe was drowned in a sea of silks and satins. There was a vivid scarlet gown worn by someone with her back to Matilda and standing beside it, looking over the silk shoulder, was Mr Scott-Thurlow, watching her.

She went pale with the strength of her feelings at the sight of him and then blushed. It seemed impossible for her to look away but she managed it and she hadn't smiled because he had looked unsmilingly at her.

She tossed off the tonic and lent a sympathetic ear to her companion's description of his late wife's asthma, murmuring in all the right places and not really hearing a word.

She went to bed later, feeling unhappy, longing for a scarlet gown in which she might dazzle Mr Scott-Thurlow and at the same time wanting to go home then and there. She even wept a little and then her common sense came to the rescue; scarlet would look hideous with her hair and no way could she go home and leave Roseanne just as the girl was beginning to find her feet—perhaps she would find romance too.

And it seemed likely; two days later, attending a preview of an up-and-coming portrait painter and this time with their hostess, Matilda was intrigued and delighted to see Bernard Stevens. He was with a friend of Mrs Venables and naturally enough was introduced, and presently he bore Roseanne off to make a tour of the rooms while Matilda stood between the two older ladies and listened with interest while Mrs Venables asked endless questions about Mr Stevens. The answers seemed to satisfy her and Matilda reflected that their month in London would make one of them happy, at least. That night after they had gone to bed Roseanne came along to her room, brimming over with excitement. She should get excited more often, thought Matilda, sitting up in bed, lending a sympathetic ear; it added a sparkle to Roseanne's plain face; even the unfortunate nose seemed less prominent and her mouth had taken on a softer curve.

Bernard, Roseanne told her, now that he had made the acquaintance of her godmother, was going to find a way to meet her parents; her godmother was one of the few people her mother listened to, and Mrs Venables liked him. 'Isn't it wonderful?' breathed Roseanne. 'Our meeting like that? He thinks I'm pretty, only my clothes are wrong—you always said that too, didn't you? He's going to meet me one day and go with me to choose an outfit. I wish we were staying here forever.'

'Well, if you want a super wedding you'll have to go home to get ready for it, and the sooner you do that the sooner you can get married. Big weddings take an awful lot of organising.'

Which started Roseanne off again until she gave a final yawn and said goodnight, but on her way to the door she stopped. 'I'm ever so glad it's happened to me—I wish it could happen to you too.'

'Nothing,' declared Matilda in a falsely cheerful voice, 'ever happens to me.'

She was wrong; fate had a testy ear tuned in to that kind of remark.

They had been for a morning walk and now they were hurrying home as rain, threatening to be heavy, began to fall. There was a short cut to the house through narrow streets lined with small, rather shabby shops and used a great deal by drivers avoiding the main roads. They were turning into it when they saw half a dozen people standing on the edge of the pavement looking down at something.

'I'm going to see what it is,' said Matilda and despite

Roseanne's peevish reluctance went to look. A small dog was lying in the gutter, wet, pitifully thin, and also obviously injured.

No one was doing anything; Matilda bent down and put out a gentle hand. 'Leave it alone, miss,' said a large untidy man roughly. ''E'll bite yer—'it by a car, 'e'll be dead in no time.'

Matilda flashed a glance at him and got on to her knees, the better to look at the little beast. It cowered and showed its teeth and then put out a tongue and licked her hand.

'How long has it been here?' she demanded.

''Arf an hour...'

'Then not one of you has done anything to help it?' She turned to look at them. 'Why, you're nothing but a bunch of heartless brutes.'

''Ere, that won't do, lady—it's only a stray, 'arf starved too.'

No one had noticed the car which drew up on the other side of the street; Mr Scott-Thurlow was beside her, bending his great height, lifting her to her feet before anyone had spoken again.

'Oh, dear, oh, dear,' he said softly, 'Miss ffinch helping lame dogs...'

'Don't you start,' she warned him fiercely. 'This poor creature's been here for half an hour and no one has lifted a finger.'

Mr Scott-Thurlow wasted no time. 'Get me a piece of cardboard,' he ordered the man nearest him, 'flat, mind you, and please be quick about it.'

The people around suddenly became helpful; suggestions filled the air, even offers of help, unspecified. The cardboard was brought back and everyone stood aside watching; they weren't unkind deliberately, only indifferent—if the big gent liked to get bitten by a dog that was going to die anyway, that was his lookout and they might as well be there to see it.

He wasn't bitten; he slid the cardboard under the dog, lifted it with the animal trembling on it and carried it across the street to his car, closely followed by Matilda and Roseanne. Matilda turned back halfway across to address the untidy man.

'Now you know what to do next time an animal gets hurt,' she told him, and added kindly, 'I dare say you didn't think, did you?

Standing and looking at something that needs to be done is such a waste of time.'

She smiled at him and he smiled back, mostly because he hadn't seen green eyes like hers before.

Roseanne was already in the car, sitting in the back. 'Get inside beside me,' ordered Mr Scott-Thurlow, 'and I'll lay the cardboard on your lap.'

'A vet?' asked Matilda. The little dog looked in a bad way.

'Yes.'

He had nothing more to say until he turned into a side-street and got out. 'Stay there, I'll be back,' he told her and opened a side-door in a long brick wall. He came back almost at once with a burly, bearded man who nodded at Matilda and cast an eye over the dog.

'Let's have him in,' he suggested, and lifted the cardboard neatly off her knees. 'Coming too?'

Matilda got out of the car, but Roseanne shook her head. 'I'd rather stay here…'

Mr Scott-Thurlow held the door open and they went in one after the other down a long passage with the surgery at its end. 'You wait here,' the vet told her. 'I'll do an X-ray first—you can give a hand, James.'

Matilda sat in the waiting-room on a rather hard chair, cherishing the knowledge that his name was James. It suited him, though she doubted if anyone had ever called him Jimmy or even Jim. Time passed unheeded since her thoughts were entirely taken up with James Scott-Thurlow; when he joined her she looked at him mistily, shaken out of her daydreams.

'The little dog?'

'A fractured pelvis, cracked ribs, starved and very, very dirty. He'll live.'

'May he stay here? What will happen to him? Will it take long? If no one wants him I'm sure Father will let me have him…'

'He'll stay here until he's fit and he'll be well looked after. I should suppose he'll be fit, more or less, in a month or six weeks.' Mr Scott-Thurlow paused and then went on in a resigned voice, 'I have a Labrador who will be delighted to have a companion.'

He was rewarded by an emerald blaze of gratitude. 'Oh, how good of you; I'm not sure what kind of a dog he is but I'm certain that when he's well again you'll be proud of him.'

Mr Scott-Thurlow doubted this but forbore to mention it. 'Were you on your way back to Kensington? I'll run you there; Mrs Venables may be getting anxious.'

'Oh, I don't suppose so,' said Matilda airily. 'We may do as we please during the day, you know, unless there is some suitable young man coming to lunch. Do you know Mrs Venables?'

They had reached the door but he made no move to open it. 'I have a slight acquaintance. Rhoda knows her quite well, I believe.'

'Oh, then I expect you will be at the dinner party next week—a kind of farewell before we go back to Abner Magna.'

He had categorically refused to accompany Rhoda when she had told him of the invitation. Now, on second thoughts, he decided that he would go with her after all.

He opened the door. 'Then we shall meet again,' he said as they reached the car. Before he drove off he reached for the phone and said into it, 'I shall be half an hour late—warn everyone, will you?'

He drove off without a word, leaving Matilda guessing. Was he a barrister, defending some important client, she wondered, or someone in the banking world, making decisions about another person's money? It would be a clerk at the other end, middle-aged, rather shabby probably with a large family of growing children and a mortgage. Her imagination ran riot until he stopped outside the Kensington house, bade them a polite goodbye and drove off.

'He doesn't talk much, does he?' Roseanne wanted to know. 'I think I'm a bit—well—scared of him.'

Matilda looked at her in astonishment. 'Scared? Of him? Whatever for? I dare say he was wrapped up in some business transaction; of course he didn't want to talk. Anyway you'll change your mind next week—he's coming to your godmother's dinner party, so we shall see him then.'

She saw him before then.

The days had passed rapidly, too fast for Roseanne, not fast enough for Matilda; she wanted to go home—London, she felt, wasn't for her. True, while she was there there was always the chance that she would see Mr Scott-Thurlow, but what was the use of that when he was going to marry Rhoda? A girl who was undoubtedly beautiful, clever and wore all the right clothes regardless of expense. She and Roseanne had gone shopping, gone to more exhibitions than she could count, seen the latest films and plays and accompanied Mrs Venables on several occasions when that lady, an enthusiastic member of several committees, introduced them to their various other members, mostly middle-aged and not in the least interested in the two girls. Roseanne found them a waste of time when she might have spent it in the company of her Bernard.

There were only a few days left now and preparations for the dinner party that night were well ahead. They were finishing their breakfast, which they took alone since Mrs Venables had hers in bed, when the dining-room door was thrust open and the kitchen maid—who should have known better, as Roseanne was quick to point out—rushed up to the table.

'It's Cook—cut herself something awful and the others down at the market getting the food for tonight. Whatever shall I do?'

'My dear good girl,' began Roseanne, looking alarmingly like her mother, but she was not allowed to finish.

'I'll come and look, shall I?' suggested Matilda calmly. 'If it's very bad we can get her to the hospital, but perhaps it looks worse than it is.'

Cook was sitting at the table, her hand wrapped in a teatowel. She was a nasty green colour and moaning faintly. Matilda opened the towel gently, making soothing noises the while. There was a lot of blood, but if it was a deep cut she could tie the hand up tightly and get a taxi to the nearest hospital. Since both of her companions were on the edge of hysteria she told them bracingly to close their eyes and turned back the last of the towel. She would have liked to have closed her eyes too; Cook's first and second fingers had been neatly severed just above the second joints. Matilda gulped and hoped her breakfast would stay down.

'Milly—it is Milly?—please go and ring for a taxi. Be quick and say that it's very urgent. Then come back here.'

'Is it a bad cut?' asked Roseanne from the door. 'Should I tell Aunt Maud?'

'Presently. I'll go with Cook to the nearest hospital and perhaps you'll tell her then.' She glanced at the girl. 'Would you get a shawl or something to put round Cook?'

'There's blood everywhere,' said Roseanne, and handed over a cape hanging behind the door, carefully looking the other way.

Matilda hung on to her patience. 'Thanks. Now find a table napkin or a scarf and look sharp about it...'

'No one speaks to me like that,' declared Roseanne.

'Don't be silly! I dare say you'll find a cloth of some sort in that cupboard.'

Roseanne opened drawers in an aggrieved manner and came back with a small teacloth. It was fine linen and beautifully embroidered and Matilda fashioned it into some kind of a sling, draped the cloak round Cook's shaking shoulders and propelled her gently out of the kitchen across the hall and out to the waiting taxi. They left a trail of red spots across the floor and Matilda heard Milly's gasp of horror.

'The nearest hospital,' urged Matilda, supporting a half-fainting and sturdily built Cook, 'as quick as you can.'

The cabby drove well, taking short cuts, cutting corners, beating the lights by a hair's breadth. At the Casualty entrance they got out and he got out too and between them they got poor Cook in to Casualty.

There was a young man standing talking to a nurse near the door. Matilda paused by him. 'Would you please pay the cabby? I'll let you have the money as soon as I can leave Cook.'

He looked astonished, paid the man while Matilda offered hasty thanks, then took his place on the other side of Cook.

'She's cut off her fingers—two of them—they're there, inside the towel. Could someone get a doctor?'

'That's me. Casualty officer on duty. Let's have her in here.'

The place was half full, patients on chairs waiting to be seen, nurses going to and fro, several people on trolleys and a fierce-looking sister coming towards them.

'Well, what's this?' she wanted to know and with a surprising gentleness turned back the towel. She lifted Cook's arm and pressed the bell beside the couch and, when a nurse came, gave her quick instructions and then glanced at the young man.

'Shall I get her ready for Theatre? Nurse is taking a message—the quicker the better.'

Matilda was holding the other hand and Cook was clinging to it as though she would never let it go. Her skirt and blouse were ruined and her hair was coming down but she didn't give them a thought. She felt sick.

The shock of seeing Mr Scott-Thurlow in a long white coat over an excellently tailored grey suit dispelled the sickness. He was coming towards them with calm speed and fetched up beside the couch. He gave her a cool nod and she said in a wondering voice, 'Oh, I've been wondering just what you did...' and blushed scarlet as he gave a faint smile as he bent over Cook. The casualty officer was doing things—a tourniquet?—some kind of pressure so that the bleeding wasn't so bad any more and Sister was handing swabs and instruments to Mr Scott-Thurlow. Matilda, feeling sick again, looked at the curtains around the couch.

She heard him say, 'Right, we'll have her up right away, please, before I start my list. Warn Theatre, will you?' He bent over Cook. 'Don't worry too much, my dear, I'm going to stitch your fingers on again and you can stay here for a few days while they heal. Nurse is going to give you a little injection now to help the pain.' He patted her shoulder. 'You're very brave.'

He spoke to Matilda then. 'What did she have for breakfast?' he wanted to know.

'I don't know, but she would have had it quite early—about seven o'clock. She was slicing bacon with one of those machines...'

Matilda felt cold and looked green; the thought of the bacon had been too much. 'I'm going to be...'

Mr Scott-Thurlow handed her a bowl with the manner of someone offering her a hanky she might have dropped or a glass of water she had asked for. He was just in time.

There was someone beside her, a young nurse being sympathetic and helpful, and when Matilda lifted a shamed face everyone had gone.

'Don't worry,' said the nurse, 'there's somewhere where you can wait and I'll get someone to bring you a cup of tea. Mr Scott-Thurlow is going to operate at once so you'll know what's happening quite soon. Do you want to phone anybody?'

'Yes, please, only I haven't any money.'

She was led away to a rather bare room lined with benches with a kind of canteen at one end and two telephones on the wall. The nurse gave her twenty pence, patted her on the shoulder in a motherly fashion and hurried away.

She phoned Mrs Venables. 'How could she?' cried that lady in an outraged voice. 'When we have the dinner party this evening and absolutely no chance of getting a cook at such short notice. What am I to do? She must have been careless—'

'She's cut off two fingers,' said Matilda. 'I'll stay here until I know what is happening to her. She's been very brave.'

She didn't wait for Mrs Venables's reply.

She sat for an hour, revived by a cup of hot strong tea, thinking about Cook and Mr Scott-Thurlow. She shouldn't have blurted out her silly remark in Casualty—she went hot again just thinking about it—and then to have been sick... She wriggled with humiliation. He had been kind to Cook; she hoped that he would be able to sew the fingers back on—surgeons were clever and she supposed that he was very experienced.

The kind little nurse who had lent her the twenty pence came into the waiting-room and she got up to meet her.

'She's going to be all right,' said the nurse. 'Mr Scott-Thurlow did a good job, and her fingers will be as good as new—well, almost. He's a wizard with bones. Sister said will you arrange for Mrs Chubb's clothes—nighties and washing things and so on—to be brought in? She's to stay a few days.'

Matilda nodded. 'Yes, of course. Which ward is she in?'

'Women's Orthopaedic, second floor. You'll be able to see her.'

'I'll go and get everything now and come back as soon as I can. Thank you, you've all been awfully kind.'

She was back within the hour, Cook's necessities in a case, with a couple of paperbacks she had stopped to buy and a bunch of flowers, Mrs Venables's unfeeling, complaining voice still ringing in her ears.

'The woman will be of no use to me,' she had said impatiently. 'Now I shall have to get another cook.'

Matilda had turned a thoughtful green gaze on to her hostess. 'Has she worked for you for long?' she asked.

'Oh, years,' said Mrs Venables. 'I must say it is *most* inconvenient—'

'I dare say Cook finds it inconvenient too, and very painful.'

She had received a very cold look for that; a good thing they were going home in a few more days.

Cook was in a small ward, sitting up in bed, looking pale. Matilda put everything away in her locker, fetched a vase for the flowers and offered the paperbacks—light romantic reading which she hoped would take Cook's mind off her problems. She parried the awkward questions she was asked, skimming smoothly over the future, and invented one or two suitable messages from Mrs Venables. 'I'll pop in some time tomorrow,' she finished, 'just to see if there's anything you would like.'

'That's kind of you, miss. We all said in the kitchen what a kind young lady you were, and so very understanding.'

Matilda said goodbye and found her way out of the hospital, trying not to wish that she might meet Mr Scott-Thurlow. But of course she didn't.

She got back to the house to find Mrs Venables raging up and down the drawing-room floor while Roseanne sat in a corner looking obstinate. She had intended to spend the morning with Bernard and she had had to put him off. Her mouth was set in a thin line and she looked very like her mother.

Mrs Venables, pacing back to the door, saw Matilda. 'I've telephoned every agency I can think of,' she declared. 'There is not a decent cook to be had at a moment's notice. I am distraught.' She wrung her hands in a dramatic fashion and glared at Matilda.

'You will be relieved to know that Mrs Chubb's operation was successful and that she is comfortably in bed.' Matilda glared back. 'I can cook—I'll see to dinner this evening.'

Mrs Venables's glare turned to a melting sweetness. 'Matilda! Oh, can you really cook? I mean cordon bleu? My dear girl, however can I thank you—what a relief, you have no idea how worried I've been.' She reeled off the menu: consommé royale, poached salmon, roast duck with orange garnish and brandy, straw potatoes and a selection of vegetables, some sort of a salad—she had left that to Cook—and then peach *condé* and coffee mousse. 'Can you manage that?' She patted Matilda's arm. 'So good of you to do this for me.'

'I'm doing it for Cook,' said Matilda.

She didn't wait for Mrs Venables's outraged gasp but took herself off to the kitchen, where she explained matters to the domestic staff and sat down at the kitchen table to get organised. She had plenty of willing help, and, satisfied with the arrangements, she went away to tidy herself for lunch, an uncomfortable meal with Mrs Venables suppressing her ill temper in case Matilda should back out at the last minute, and Roseanne still sulking.

Matilda spent most of the afternoon preparing for the evening. She enjoyed cooking and she was an instinctive cook, quite ordinary food turning into delectable dishes under her capable hands. She had her tea in the kitchen, which rather upset the butler and the kitchen maid and certainly upset Bertha, who had disapproved of the whole thing to start with. 'Ladies,' she had sniffed, 'don't belong in the kitchen,' a remark to which Matilda didn't bother to reply.

Everything went well; as the first guests arrived and the butler went to admit them, Matilda gave the ducks a satisfied prod, tasted the consommé and began to make a salad. There was half an hour before dinner would be served and she enjoyed making a salad.

The Honourable Mrs Venables greeted her guests with an almost feverish eagerness. She had planned the evening carefully and if anything went wrong she would never recover from it. She cast an anxious eye over the laughing and talking people around her. Bernard had come and she sighed with relief, for Roseanne had stopped sulking at the sight of him and even looked a bit pretty.

There were two more to come, Rhoda Symes and Mr Scott-Thurlow, and they entered the room at that moment. A handsome couple, she conceded; Rhoda looked magnificent, but then she always did. Mr Scott-Thurlow looked much as he usually did, rather grave; always courteous and lovely manners, though. She went forward to welcome them.

Mr Scott-Thurlow had seen Roseanne as soon as he entered the room but there was no sign of the bright head of hair he had expected to see. He listened politely to one of the guests trying to prise free advice from him while he glanced round the room. Matilda wasn't there. He caught Rhoda's eye and she smiled at him. She was looking particularly beautiful, exquisitely made up, her hair a blonde halo, her cerise dress the very latest fashion. She would make him a very suitable wife; she was a clever woman as well as attractive, completely at ease against a social background, cool and undemonstrative. The uneasy thought that her charming appearance hid a cold nature crossed his mind and he found himself wondering why he had asked her to marry him. He knew the answer to that: she made no demands upon him and appeared quite content with the lack of romance between them. He had been an only child and had lost his parents in a plane crash when he had been a small boy. He had gone to live with his grandparents, who had loved him dearly but had not known what to say to him, so he had learned to hide his loneliness and unhappiness and had grown up into a rather quiet man who seldom allowed his feelings to show, channelling his energy and interest into his work. It was his old nanny, Mrs Twigg, who kept house for him, who had begged him to find himself a wife and he had acknowledged the good sense of that; his friends were all married by now and despite his absorption in his work he was sometimes lonely.

He and the man to whom he was talking were joined by several more people and the conversation became general until they were summoned to dinner, where he sat between two young married women who flirted gently with him.

It was someone at the other end of the table who remarked loudly upon the delicious duck. 'You must have a splendid cook,' he remarked, laughing.

'I've had her for years,' declared Mrs Venables. 'She's a treasure,' and Mr Scott-Thurlow, happening to glance at Roseanne across the table, saw the look of surprised rage on her face and wondered why.

It was some time afterwards when they were all back in the drawing-room that he made his way to her side. 'Nice to see you, Roseanne, and you look charming. Is Miss ffinch ill?'

Roseanne said softly, 'No, of course not—she never is. She's in the kitchen. She cooked the dinner.' She smiled suddenly. 'We'll go and see her if you like.' Before he could answer she said loudly, 'It's rather warm—shall we go on to the balcony for a minute?'

There was a small staircase at one end of the balcony and she led the way down it and round the house and in through a side-door.

The short passage was rather dark and smelled vaguely damp. Roseanne opened the door at its end, revealing the kitchen.

Matilda was standing at the kitchen table, carving slices off a roast duck. She wasn't doing it very well and there was a large pan of rather mangled bones and bits beside her. She looked up and saw them as they went in. She was flushed and untidy and swathed in one of Mrs Chubb's aprons, many sizes too large for her, and despite that she still contrived to look beautiful. When she saw them she smiled and said, 'Oh, hello...'

'What the devil do you think you're doing?' asked Mr Scott-Thurlow with a good deal of force.

She chose to misunderstand him. 'Well, I never could carve—the bones will make splendid soup and there's still plenty of meat...'

His tone was measured. 'That is not what I meant, and you know it. Why are you working in the kitchen when you should be in the drawing-room? That abominable woman...' He stopped, mindful of good manners. 'Do you mean to say that she asked you to cook dinner?'

'No. I said that I would—to help Mrs Chubb; you know she was in such a state. They tell me that you did a splendid job on her fingers. Are you a consultant or something?'

'Yes. Let us keep to the point, Matilda.'

She looked meek, but her eyes sparkled because he had called her Matilda and not Miss ffinch. A tiny step forwards perhaps?

She picked up the knife again and started on the other side of the duck and he stepped forwards, took the knife from her, carved the rest of the bird with a practised hand and laid the knife down on the table.

'Is there no one to help you?'

'They're having their supper. I'll stay down here until you've all gone home.' She selected a slice of duck and popped it into her mouth.

It was Roseanne who spoke. 'Look,' she sounded worried, 'we must go back—they'll wonder where we are.'

'Very well. Have you had your dinner, Matilda?'

He looked as cross as two sticks, she thought lovingly. 'I shall take a tray up to my room. Goodnight, Mr Scott-Thurlow, or is it goodbye?'

CHAPTER THREE

MATILDA, packing the remainder of her things ready to leave in the morning, reflected sadly that it really had been goodbye and not goodnight. From upstairs at the landing window she had watched the dinner guests go home and it seemed to her that Mr Scott-Thurlow was quite devoted in his attention towards his fiancée as they left the house. Rhoda had really looked quite stunning.

She was glad to be going home; Mrs Venables had thanked her for her services rather coldly, remarking at the same time that she had no idea how she was going to manage with the temporary cook whom she had engaged. Matilda, who had been to see Mrs Chubb again, had observed rather tartly that she would appreciate Mrs Chubb's services all the more when she returned, 'Because, of course, she will be coming back here, will she not? After all these years?'

A remark which received no answer save a non-committal murmur which could have meant anything or nothing.

Gregg fetched them soon after breakfast and the two girls bade their hostess goodbye. She embraced Roseanne warmly and begged her to visit her again very soon, but when she shook Matilda's hand she observed rather distantly that she supposed that the daughter of a rector had much to occupy her and that they were unlikely to meet again.

Matilda, who had no wish to improve her acquaintance with the Honourable Mrs Venables, assured her that the likelihood of her visiting London in the foreseeable future was indeed remote.

Gregg obligingly stopped at the rectory and deposited Matilda and her case in the porch while Roseanne hung out of the car, calling to her to come up to the manor as soon as she could. 'Mother will want to know about Bernard...'

Matilda nodded and smiled, thanked Gregg and opened the door of her home to hear her mother's voice from somewhere upstairs and a moment later her father's deeper tones from his study before both parents converged in the hall to hug her warmly.

'We've missed you,' said her mother. 'It's lovely to have you back...'

'You're glad to be home?' enquired her father.

'Oh, Father, yes.' Her eyes shone with tears. 'I missed you all too.'

They went into the kitchen and presently sat down round the kitchen table to drink coffee.

'You enjoyed yourself, dear?' asked her mother. 'When you wrote and telephoned there was always a party or a dinner or something.' She added causally, 'Did you meet anyone you liked?'

Matilda cut herself a slice of the cake her mother had taken out of the oven and bit into it. She wiped the crumbs away from her mouth before she answered. 'Yes, but he's going to be married to a very beautiful woman.' She went on steadily, 'I met quite a few people I liked too but not many young ones. They went to the dances and Roseanne mostly went with her godmother.'

Her mother nodded and smiled a little; she could imagine the Honourable Mrs Venables's disquiet when she had first set eyes on Matilda—Roseanne wouldn't stand much chance...And this man? She wondered who he was and where Matilda had met him and whether he had been aware that her darling daughter had lost her heart to him. She longed to know; instead she asked, 'And Roseanne, did she have a good time too?'

'Oh, yes—we met a young man, Bernard Stevens—at one of the picture galleries, and he fell for her. Luckily he knows friends of Mrs Venables so I can't see that Lady Fox could possibly object—Roseanne wants to marry him and she can be as stubborn as a mule. He'll be down for a weekend soon, I expect, and you'll meet him or at least see him in church.'

'What a relief for Lady Fox,' observed Mrs ffinch. 'There are three daughters and those unfortunate noses... Did you enjoy the big dinner party before you left? Did the grey crêpe do?'

Matilda took another slice of cake. 'Well, I didn't go...' She paused, smiling a little, remembering Mr Scott-Thurlow's visit to the kitchen. 'The cook cut herself,' she began and recounted the happenings of that eventful day, leaving out Mr Scott-Thurlow of course.

Her mother was indignant. 'Well, really—it was one thing letting you do the cooking but she could at least have told her guests and thanked you.'

Mrs ffinch looked quite fierce and the rector said, 'Now, now, my dear, Matilda had the thanks that mattered—the poor woman with the cut hand will remember her with gratitude, while Mrs Venables is to be pitied for her lack of charity.'

His wife cast him a resigned look; sometimes she wished that he would get really annoyed about something or someone, but he never did. She smiled suddenly at him. 'You're quite right, of course—you always are.'

Matilda went to the manor the following morning to resume her usual duties there. Roseanne met her at the door and said eagerly, 'You will tell Mother what a splendid man Bernard is, won't you? She's sure to ask you. If you could persuade her to invite him for a weekend...'

'I'll do my best,' said Matilda doubtfully. Lady Fox wasn't the kind of person one could persuade easily.

As it happened her task was made easy; Lady Fox had already had a good report of Bernard from Mrs Venables. All the same she cross-questioned Matilda about him at length. 'I should like to meet this young man,' she concluded.

Matilda was catching up on the household accounts. 'I expect you have already thought of a way to do that,' she suggested. 'A weekend here would give you the opportunity to get to know him.'

'That is true, and I had of course already decided to do so. I cannot have one of my girls throwing herself away on some unsuitable young man.'

Matilda murmured. She was of the private opinion that Roseanne intended to marry the young man whether her mother approved or not.

Lady Fox got up from her desk. 'Yes, I shall certainly do so,' she said in a voice which suggested that Matilda had begged her not to.

'How very wise of you, Lady Fox,' said Matilda, looking as meek as red hair and green eyes allowed her.

Life settled back into the quiet routine which had been interrupted by their visit to London. Matilda, soothed by the comparative leisurely progress of her days, was able to think about James Scott-Thurlow in a sensible way. She was in love with him and always would be, there was no gainsaying that, but she had known her case was hopeless when she had set eyes on Rhoda. It was now just a question of forgetting him, she told herself firmly. Unfortunately she soon discovered that this was impossible.

They had been back for ten days when Bernard Stevens was invited for the weekend. Roseanne was almost sick with excitement and despair as she examined her face. 'Look at the spots,' she said pettishly. 'What am I to do?'

'I'll come early tomorrow and do your face—some of that cream you bought in London. I know your mother doesn't like you to use make-up but if I'm careful I don't think she'll notice.'

So that, when Bernard arrived, Roseanne presented a passable face to him, skilfully made up and made almost pretty because she was in love. Anyway, he wouldn't have noticed because he loved the girl...

Matilda made herself scarce once she had greeted him; there were the flowers to do for the dinner table that evening and then she would go home for the weekend. Not, though, before Bernard and Roseanne came looking for her.

'I've a message for you—do you remember Mr Scott-Thurlow? He asked me to say that the little dog is doing well—oh, and the cook—Mrs Chubb?—is staying with her sister and then going to a new job where there will be plenty of help.'

Matilda bent over her flowers. 'Oh, what splendid news—thank you for telling me.'

'You're awfully red,' observed Roseanne. 'It is rather hot in here.'

'I've almost finished. Are you going to show Bernard the garden?' Then she added, unable to help herself, 'I didn't know that you knew Mr Scott-Thurlow.'

'Well, I don't—just an acquaintance really. Nice chap, but I don't like that girl he's going to marry.'

Matilda stopped herself just in time from agreeing with him.

There was a splendid congregation in church that Sunday—the village knew all about Bernard Stevens by now and everyone was agog to take a look at him; he sat in the manor-house pew with Lady Fox in one of her terrible hats on one side of him and Roseanne on the other with her sisters and Sir Benjamin. He looked quite at ease and happy; presumably Lady Fox had given him her blessing, which meant that Sir Benjamin, who did what he was told, had given his too.

Going out of the church, Matilda bumped into Mrs Chump. ''Er ladyship will be pleased,' she breathed, lowering her voice since they were still in the porch. ''E looks a likely young man. Not a patch on that there friend of Dr Bramley's—now there was a gent for you, Miss Matilda. Happen 'e'll come visiting again some time.'

'Unlikely, I should think, Mrs Chump. What a lovely day it is…'

Bernard left on Monday morning and Matilda was met by an ecstatic Roseanne with the news that they were to become engaged. 'Isn't it marvellous?' she wanted to know. 'I'm going up to town tomorrow to meet him and choose the ring.' She danced away, calling as she went, 'I've been so afraid I'd get left like you and be an old maid!'

What a good start to a Monday morning, thought Matilda gloomily as she went along to Lady Fox's sitting-room and started on the post. That lady joined her almost at once and spent the next hour expressing her satisfaction at her daughter's engagement. 'Quite a good family,' she conceded of Bernard, 'related to the Crofts of Norfolk, and he has good prospects.' She glanced up from the bill she was frowning over. 'Why does the butcher send this account for the second time?'

'It wasn't paid, you said that he could wait for his money.'

Lady Fox went an unbecoming red. 'You must have misunderstood me, Matilda—see that it is paid at once.' She added, 'What a pity you can't find yourself a husband.'

Only by reminding herself that no ffinch would lower herself to answer such a vulgar remark from the inferior Fox family did Matilda manage to remain silent. It was becoming obvious to her that she would have to give up her job at the manor-house; the money was useful but there was a limit to what a girl could stand. She wasn't trained for anything but she was a good cook and she liked children; there must be something...

Roseanne came back the next day with a diamond ring on her finger; it wasn't as large or as brilliant as that of Mr Scott-Thurlow's fiancée, but it was worth the unstinted admiration Matilda gave it.

That evening, sitting round the supper table with her mother and father and Esme, Matilda told them that she wanted to give up her job. It was a relief that no one asked why.

Her mother answered at once, 'Yes, dear, I think that will be a good thing. Lady Fox leans on you far too heavily,' and her father nodded his head in agreement, and as for Esme she gave a crow of delight.

'They'll never get anyone to do the chores like you do, Tilly, and they'll have to pay the earth too. What are you going to do?'

'Well, I don't know, I'll have to think about it.' Matilda looked anxiously at her father, who observed placidly,

'I should miss you helping around the parish, my dear, but Esme can take your place and Hilary will be back home in a week or so and will be here until the wedding. We must put our heads together...'

So Matilda went to the manor-house with a speech carefully prepared and all the answers likely to be needed as arguments as to why she wanted to leave. She was going in through the side-door when she heard the sound of breaking glass, bumps and screams.

She ran along the passage and into the hall and saw Roseanne lying in an untidy heap at the foot of the staircase, an excellent example of the Tudor period, wide, its treads worn smooth with age. It was obvious that the girl had missed her footing and hurtled down its length, scattering the contents of a tray of china and glass as she went.

Matilda bent over her and, as she did so, Roseanne opened her eyes and started to scream. Lady Fox, who had come hurrying to see what was the matter, started to scream too and Sir Benjamin, taking his time, joined her, only he didn't scream but swore. Various members of the staff had arrived by now and the noise was considerable.

'Phone Dr Bramley,' said Matilda briskly. 'Lady Fox, please stop screaming so that we can hear where Roseanne hurts.'

That was going to be difficult, for Roseanne was making a great deal of noise. 'My leg!' she shouted. 'My arm! I can't bear it, I'm dying.'

'No, you're not,' said Matilda firmly. 'Try and be quiet and tell me exactly where the pain is.'

Roseanne glared at her. 'My leg, I told you—above my knee, of course, can't you see for yourself? And my arm, it's my wrist...I'm in agony.'

Sir Benjamin, who had gone to telephone, came back and Matilda sent him for a cushion which she tucked carefully under Roseanne's head.

'You can't leave my poor girl like that!' bellowed Lady Fox. 'I'll get Gregg in to lift her.'

'Lady Fox, if there are broken bones they'll be even more broken if we move her.'

'Nonsense, I'm her mother and I know what's best for her.' She glared at Matilda. 'You have no idea...'

Matilda had prudently taken up a position by Roseanne which would fend off any efforts Lady Fox intended to make. It wasn't much use saying anything—poor Roseanne was screaming her head off, Sir Benjamin stood there looking useless and the housemaid together with the cleaning lady seemed rooted to the spot. If only Mr Scott-Thurlow were here, thought Matilda.

Dr Bramley came instead, nodded to everyone and got down on his knees beside Roseanne.

'No one moved her?' he asked, running gentle hands over arm and leg.

'I told them to fetch Gregg and have her carried to her room,' said Lady Fox loudly, 'but of course Matilda disobeyed me and left my poor girl lying there.'

'A very good thing too—more damage done by people moving injured people than you'd believe.' He was opening his bag and getting out a syringe. 'First we will stop the pain then she must go to hospital.'

'Certainly not, Dr Bramley. Roseanne is a sensitive girl; to be in a ward with other sick patients would do her a great deal of harm.'

He drew up an injection and gave it into a shrinking Roseanne. 'She must be X-rayed as soon as possible and the bones set by an expert.'

Sir Benjamin and Matilda spoke together. 'There's King's Hall…'

'Send her there. Matilda, go and phone for an ambulance, will you? Then pack whatever Roseanne will need for a short period there.'

Roseanne opened her eyes again. The injection was already doing its good work but she was rather vague. 'I won't go unless Matilda comes with me—and stays there.' And when no one said anything, 'You heard what I said—I won't go, I won't.'

'My darling child,' declared Lady Fox dramatically, 'of course she shall go with you. Matilda, pack her things and then pack some things for yourself—it's the least you can do.'

Matilda's eyes and hair seemed to glow with rage.

She caught the doctor's eye and he winked and nodded his head, knowing exactly how she felt. 'Please, Matilda, until Roseanne has quietened down.'

'I'll go because you asked me to,' said Matilda and marched off to phone for an ambulance.

By the time the ambulance had arrived she had packed a bag for Roseanne and gone home, packed one for herself, given a brief account of what had occurred to her mother and presented herself, outwardly calm and inwardly fuming still, at the manor-house again.

She would have liked to have flung her resignation at Lady

Fox's head there and then, but Roseanne needed someone with her until her arm and leg had been put to rights. It should have been her mother, thought Matilda, casting that lady an accusing look.

Lady Fox interpreted it correctly for she said defensively, 'This has been a tremendous shock to me; my sensitive nature cannot face up to it.' She embraced a drowsy Roseanne gingerly. 'Dearest child, you will soon be better. Matilda will let me know what is to be done.'

Dr Bramley, supervising the patient's disposal in the ambulance, heard that. 'I shall phone you as soon as it's been decided what has to be done, Lady Fox, then you can make your own arrangements concerning Roseanne.'

Matilda got into the car beside him as the ambulance pulled away. 'Someone should let Bernard know,' she pointed out tartly as Dr Bramley started the car.

King's Hall was twenty minutes' drive away, a private hospital set in pleasant surroundings and with a high reputation. Roseanne was conveyed into it and taken straight to the X-ray department with no delay while Matilda sat patiently in the comfortably furnished waiting-room. Someone brought her coffee after a time and told her kindly that once the specialist had seen Roseanne someone would be along to make whatever arrangements were necessary.

Matilda drank her coffee, ate all the biscuits and speculated about lunch, and not only lunch; Lady Fox had told her to stay with Roseanne but perhaps the hospital wouldn't approve of that—perhaps she ought to phone...

There was a small stir in the hall and a moment later the half-open door of the waiting-room was thrust open. Mr Scott-Thurlow, looking calm, grave and unhurried came in.

'Ah, Matilda, I felt in my bones...' He didn't go on. 'Be good enough not to go away—I'll see you presently...'

She sat staring at him, awash with delight. She should have known—Lady Fox would have demanded the very best treatment for her daughter and he was undoubtedly the very best. Suddenly the annoyance she had felt at being sent with Roseanne melted away; fate had very kindly thrust her in his path once more, which was delightful—probably he felt no delight at all though. A pity she couldn't have thought of something to say instead of gasping at him like a stranded fish.

She heard one o'clock strike somewhere and a moment later a smartly dressed domestic came in carrying a tray which she set on a small table. She smiled at Matilda. 'Your lunch, Miss,' and hard on her heels came a dignified lady in a grey dress and a fetching muslin cap.

'They're in Theatre now,' she explained, 'and it may be some time. Please make yourself comfortable in the meantime.' She smiled and went away and Matilda, a girl with a healthy appetite, lifted the lids covering the dishes on the tray. Soup in a pitkin, piping hot, fish and creamed potatoes, broccoli and carrots and a baked custard.

She sat herself down and ate the lot and the domestic came back with a tray of coffee just as she had finished. She went back to her easy chair then and since there was nothing else much to do she closed her eyes and dozed off.

Mr Scott-Thurlow, coming silently into the room, paused by the door. She made a delightful picture, her glorious fiery hair against the soft green of the chair in which she was sprawling. He stood for a few moments looking down at her and then bent and touched her shoulder gently.

She woke at once and smiled widely and sat up. 'Is everything all right?'

He sat down opposite her. 'Yes. Roseanne's arm is in plaster, a simple fracture which should knit quickly. Her leg is rather more complicated: a double fracture above the knee—rather unusual; it will have to be in extension for some weeks. She has come round from the anaesthetic but is asleep now. I've spoken to her mother—I gather that you are to stay here with her until such time as she feels she can cope without you.' He smiled faintly. 'An arrangement which I hope doesn't inconvenience you at all?'

'Well, as a matter of fact, it does. I was going to tell Lady Fox this morning that I wanted to leave, but before I could do that Roseanne fell down the stairs.'

'But you will stay here as long as you think it necessary?'

'I suppose so. Perhaps Lady Fox could come and stay here. I'm not necessary here; there must be plenty of nurses.'

'There are.' He looked up as Dr Bramley came into the room and sat down.

'Hello, Matilda. They're bringing tea and presently you'll be taken to see Roseanne and then shown your room. James, what had Lady Fox got to say?'

'I had to refuse her—er—request to remain here. I have patients to see this evening and a list in the morning. I'll be down again in a couple of days and we'll take another X-ray but I foresee no complications.'

Tea was brought in then and Matilda was invited to pour out.

'I've had a talk with Matron,' said Mr Scott-Thurlow, 'and explained the position with regard to you, Matilda; I'm sure that you will find her and the nurses most kind and helpful. I have also asked her to allow Bernard Stevens to visit at any time—he seems to have a great deal of influence with Roseanne.'

'Thank you. How long do you suppose I must stay here?'

He raised his eyebrows. 'That is something I am unable to tell you. It depends on Lady Fox, does it not?'

'Well, yes, of course it does. But she will listen to you because you're an—eminent surgeon.'

'I'll do my best.' He spoke gravely but she had the feeling that he was laughing silently. 'I saw Mrs Chubb this morning. She is doing excellently—she sent her love. So did that little rascal of a dog...'

'He's still at the vet?'

'For another week. Can you suggest a name for him before I introduce him to my household?'

'He was in Theobald Avenue. Could you call him that?'

This time he allowed his amusement to show. 'I don't see why not.' He glanced at his watch. 'I must go. I'll take another look at Roseanne first.'

He went away with Dr Bramley, leaving Matilda to sit and dream. They didn't come back; presently she heard voices in the hall and then the sound of cars being driven away and when a nurse came to fetch her she asked if she might telephone. 'I told

Lady Fox I would let her know if Roseanne was feeling more herself. Mr Scott-Thurlow has already talked to her, hasn't he? And I'm sure Dr Bramley will go and see her. And I'd like to ring my mother, if I may. I had to leave rather suddenly...'

Roseanne was awake now and fairly free from pain. She was also irritable and tearful. 'Now I'll never get married,' she wailed, 'with a broken arm and leg.'

'I can't think why not,' said Matilda hearteningly. 'In a matter of weeks you'll be as good as new and you weren't planning to marry for a month or two, were you?'

'No. Why doesn't he come? He should be here, comforting me...'

'Well, he'd have to be told first, wouldn't he? He might be out of town; you know he travels around to various museums. He's got to get here too, you know.'

'Do I look awful?'

Matilda examined the rather cross face on the pillows. 'No, if you could smile just a little you'd look pretty. It's not so bad, you know—this is a nice cheerful place and the nurses are awfully kind, and you had Mr Scott-Thurlow to put you to rights and he's one of the best, so I've been told.'

'Who told you that?'

'Someone at the hospital where I took poor Mrs Chubb when she chopped off her fingers.'

'Oh, her...Mr Scott-Thurlow is stern, isn't he?'

'I don't know him well enough to say,' observed Matilda, rather at a loss as to what to say and relieved when a nurse came in with a basket of red roses.

'Just look at this,' she begged them. 'Here's the card.'

'Open it, Matilda,' ordered Roseanne, and added 'please' at the look of surprise she got. It was from Bernard, of course—she read the card Matilda handed to her, cried a little and then, to everyone's relief, smiled. 'He's coming to see me; he's going to stay with Mother and Father until I feel better. Now I don't mind any more—not much, anyway.'

Matilda stayed with her until supper was brought, a very small light meal because of the anaesthetic, but she ate most of it and, when a nurse came to make her ready for the night, Matilda was free to be shown her own room, next to the patient's. There was TV in one corner of it and she sat eating the supper which was brought to her, watching a film while she did so.

Lady Fox had been vague when Matilda phoned her. She would come to see Roseanne in the morning, she had said, and then they could discuss what was best to be done. 'Roseanne needs all the support she can get,' she had observed. 'Fortunately you are there with her.'

Matilda had frowned fiercely at the phone. She had said with asperity, 'I should be glad if you or one of her sisters will take over from me as quickly as possible—that is if she needs someone. I need to go back home, Lady Fox; you must realise that I have to help my father in the village.'

Lady Fox had snorted angrily. 'Surely you realise that Roseanne is more urgent than anything else.'

'Yes, I'm sure that she is, but if you feel it's so urgent that someone is here with her, should you not come yourself?'

She had put down the phone before Lady Fox had caught her outraged breath. Tomorrow, she thought as she got ready for bed, she would be sent her notice and a good thing too. It would make it awfully awkward for her father, of course, and she was sorry about that, but she was sure that Dr Bramley would back her up. She got into her comfortable bed and put out the light and a second later someone tapped on the door. A nurse came in. 'I'm so sorry, Miss ffinch, but Miss Fox is being rather difficult. Perhaps if you came…'

Matilda, muttering under her breath, went.

Morning came and with it Lady Fox, in a nasty temper too, made worse since she had had to wait until the matron was free to see her. By the time she got to Roseanne's room she was rigid with annoyance because the matron had suggested that Roseanne would do much better if she had several days quiet, without visitors.

'I am her mother,' Lady Fox had said grandly.

'In that case,' Matron had replied smoothly, 'you will wish to co-operate in every way, will you not?'

Matilda was reading one of the more gossipy newspapers to Roseanne when her mother came into the room. Her eye lighted upon it at once.

'Gutter Press!' she cried. 'How dare you read that rubbish to Roseanne?'

'It's not my cup of tea either,' agreed Matilda cheerfully, 'but it takes her mind off herself. I mean *The Times* or the *Telegraph* don't print titbits, do they?'

Lady Fox gobbled, bent to embrace her daughter, who burst into tears for no reason at all, and then sat down heavily by the bed.

The visit wasn't a success—mother and daughter were too much alike for that. Matilda, who had prudently skipped away, could hear their raised voices and presently the quiet, severe voice of the sister on duty, and later Lady Fox was ushered into her room.

'And what was all that rubbish on the phone last night?' demanded that lady. 'I must say I was amazed at your rudeness, Matilda.'

'Do please sit down,' said Matilda, 'and I wasn't rude, Lady Fox, only stating facts. Now that I have the opportunity I should like to give up my job with you. I really only stayed because of Roseanne, you know, but she will be getting married soon. Let me see, it's Thursday...I'll stay with you until Saturday week if you would like that; that gives you time to find someone to take my place.'

Her companion looked thunderstruck. 'But what am I to do? I shall never find someone who will come each day...'

Not from the village you won't, reflected Matilda naughtily—the salary Lady Fox paid was a pittance compared to other jobs. Matilda, who had been unnaturally meek for far too long, felt a surge of delight at the idea of being free from her petty chores at the manor-house. She would be free to choose what she wanted to do. Mr Scott-Thurlow's handsome features imprinted themselves behind her eyelids; what she wanted to do was marry him...

She was aware that Lady Fox was speaking rather loudly in a cross voice, to stop abruptly as the door opened once more and Dr Bramley and Dr Scott-Thurlow were ushered in.

'Interrupting a little chat?' asked Dr Bramley and winked at

Matilda. 'Mr Scott-Thurlow has come to see Roseanne and then perhaps something can be arranged...'

Mr Scott-Thurlow wished Lady Fox good morning and then turned his attention to Matilda. 'Roseanne is more herself today?' he wished to know.

'Oh, yes. Rather a ragged night, though, but Bernard telephoned early this morning. He is coming down this afternoon.'

'In that case I suggest that we examine the patient.' The men went away and Matilda and Lady Fox sat without speaking until they returned.

'Quite satisfactory,' declared Mr Scott-Thurlow. 'I leave Roseanne in Dr Bramley's capable hands. I shall, of course, visit from time to time. It will be necessary to take further X-rays to monitor progress. Physiotherapy will be started as soon as possible.

He stood just inside the door and Matilda thought how distinguished and handsome he was and so sure of himself... She heaved a sigh which he noticed with amusement. That there had been some kind of disagreement was obvious—the air was thick with it. Matilda had probably spoken her mind...

He went on gravely, 'I am of the opinion that Roseanne will make better progress if she is without constant companionship. Visitors by all means, and certainly Mr Stevens should be allowed to call at any time. The nursing staff here are excellent; she will not lack for sympathetic treatment.' He went to the door. 'You must forgive me if I leave now—I have a busy day ahead of me. This is an unfortunate accident for your daughter, Lady Fox, but I can assure you that within a very short time she will be fully restored to normal health and strength.'

He bade her goodbye and turned to Matilda. 'Thank you for your help,' he said and smiled and took her hand, and was interrupted by Lady Fox.

'Your bill, Mr Scott-Thurlow...'

The eyes smiling down at Matilda became icy. 'You will receive my account from my secretary in due course, Lady Fox.'

Matilda, who had done her best on several occasions to be sympathetic to Lady Fox, and failed, felt sorry for her; Mr Scott-

Thurlow's voice had been courteous and straight from the North Pole, implying delicately that there had been a breach of good taste on her part.

When he had gone and Dr Bramley had gone to speak to the sister looking after Roseanne, Lady Fox spoke. 'Well, you had better get yourself back home,' she said crossly. 'It seems you're not needed here. I shall have to come over every day, I suppose. I shall forget all this nonsense about your leaving, Matilda, and expect you tomorrow morning as usual.'

'Certainly, Lady Fox, I did say that I would stay until Saturday week, but it was no nonsense. I shall leave then.'

CHAPTER FOUR

DR BRAMLEY gave Matilda a lift back home after a stormy ten minutes with Roseanne, whose threatened hysterics at the idea of being left on her own were curtailed by Matilda's timely reminder that Bernard when he arrived to visit her would expect to see a bravely smiling girl, looking her best and wearing the lacy bed-jacket her mother had had the forethought to bring with her.

On the way back Dr Bramley asked cautiously, 'Have you and Lady Fox fallen out, Tilly? I detected a distinct coolness in the air...'

She explained. 'Anyway, it's time I found something else to do—Hilary will be home for some months and Esme's awfully good helping Father. I'd quite like to get a job not too far away from home, so that I could pop in regularly. I've no idea what. I don't suppose there are many people who want someone just to see to the post and the flowers and so on.'

'I'm given to understand that you are a splendid cook among other things. I don't doubt that something will turn up. Go and see Roseanne from time to time, won't you? She needs someone to stiffen her spine; she never could stand up to her mother. This chap she intends to marry seems nice enough.'

'Oh, he is—she's a different girl when he's with her.'

'It amazes me how love can alter a person.'

Matilda said yes, doesn't it and wondered if it had altered Rhoda Symes. She thought it unlikely. Perhaps that was because she didn't love James Scott-Thurlow, or even that he didn't love her. Wishful thinking.

She enquired after her companion's bees, a passionate hobby of his, and they were still discussing them when he stopped outside the rectory and, when invited to go in with her, followed her inside for a delayed cup of coffee.

The next ten days were a bit difficult; Matilda went to the

manor-house each morning, obeying Lady Fox's beck and call without outward rancour although her feelings inside didn't bear scrutiny. Her successor had to be found—no easy task, for no one who knew Lady Fox and the miserable salary she paid was prepared to work for her.

Lady Fox was reduced to asking Matilda what to do.

'Well,' said Matilda thoughtfully, 'if you were to offer a bigger salary and advertise in the Salisbury or Yeovil papers...and there's room enough to offer a bed-sitting-room, free, of course.'

'Well, really,' observed Lady Fox indignantly and did so. There was one applicant, a middle-aged lady, rather stolid, who obviously would stand no nonsense, expected a good deal of free time and a month's holiday and showed not the least timidity towards Lady Fox. On the other hand, she had splendid references, a pleasant voice and manner and her typing, after Matilda's home-taught efforts, was excellent. She was engaged and Matilda sighed with relief for she had known all along that, if no one had been forthcoming to take her place, she would have felt compelled to stay until someone turned up.

She had gone to see Roseanne several times, driving herself in her father's elderly car, and found her much improved. Bernard had gone again but had promised to return each weekend and, since he had the good sense to take a pile of magazines with him, Roseanne was quite happy sitting up in bed, looking at soft furnishings, tables and chairs and the like, planning their home when they married.

Dr Bramley had been quite right, thought Matilda on her way home after a particularly cheerful visit; love worked wonders. Which thought, naturally enough, led her to Mr Scott-Thurlow.

She wished that she could see him again, but although he had been back to the hospital to see Roseanne she had never been there at the same time. Perhaps it was just as well. A job, she told herself firmly, something else to think about, new people to meet and occupy her mind.

She left Lady Fox's employ ostensibly on good terms with that lady. Her father saw a good deal of Sir Benjamin and it would never do to have ill feeling between the manor-house and the rectory. On Sunday, Miss Twisk, who had taken her place, was to be seen sitting where Roseanne usually sat in the family pew and Lady Fox, on her way out after the service, bowed graciously towards the rectory pew—on the surface at least bygones were to be bygones.

It was delightful to be free of her various little tasks at the manor-house; over the weeks she helped her mother make rhubarb jam, poked around very happily in the large untidy garden, painted one of the numerous sheds which were dotted haphazardly around and then, since the weather was warm and sunny, she embarked on the drawing-room curtains, well worn and faded. Mrs Chump had rummaged around her stock and found a dye in a pleasant shade of old rose and Matilda set to. It was a messy business but she was pleased with the result as she hung them up to dry. Still in a serviceable pinny, she went back into the house and sat down in the kitchen to drink her coffee with her mother and Mrs Coffin. The old fashioned bell, first in the row ranged beside the dresser, disturbed their casual gossip.

'Front door, drat it,' said Mrs Coffin. 'It'll be Postie, and why 'e 'as to make such a din...' She got up. 'The dear knows what 'e'll be up to next.'

She went away and Matilda kicked off her sandals and lolled back in her old basket chair. She said, 'Today I shall go to Sherborne and look for a job.'

Mrs ffinch put down her coffee-mug. 'Darling, but what will you do?'

'I've no idea—something will turn up...' She smiled at her mother and turned round to see what Mrs Coffin had been given by the postman.

Not a parcel and not the postman either. Mr Scott-Thurlow came through the door behind Mrs Coffin, bending his handsome head so as not to knock himself out on its lintel.

Matilda, to her great annoyance, blushed at the sight of him; her mother beamed a welcome and got to her feet. 'Good morning, Mr Scott-Thurlow—you're just in time for coffee. Do sit down. Have you been over at the manor-house?'

She patted the Windsor armchair beside her and Matilda, glad of something to do, got up to get the coffee-pot from the Aga.

'You must forgive me for calling at such a time, Mrs ffinch. Yes, I called at the manor on my way back from seeing Roseanne. She is doing well now.'

He took the mug Matilda offered him and Mrs Coffin said, 'Well, I'll get on with the bedrooms, me loves,' and took herself off.

Before she left the kitchen Matilda, strangely reluctant to be with Mr Scott-Thurlow, asked, 'Do you want any help with the beds?' and had actually got out of her chair again, intent on escape, when he said quietly,

'Please don't go, Matilda; it was you I came to talk to.'

'Me?' She sat down again. 'Whatever for?'

He smiled a little, and Mrs ffinch said briskly, 'Oh, well, I must get on—such a large house, you know, always something to do…'

'Please stay, Mrs ffinch. I have a suggestion to make to Matilda. I understand that she no longer goes to the manor and I wondered if she would be interested in a temporary job—not far away—between Sherborne and Montacute. An old gentleman whose wife is in hospital for a few weeks. There is a housekeeper and plenty of help in the house but he needs companionship, someone to read to him, play cards, potter in the garden with him, listen while he talks… You would of course need to live there but there is no reason why you shouldn't come home at the weekends. There is no hard work involved but it may be dull and perhaps at times demanding. The salary…' The sum he mentioned made Matilda's eyes open wide.

'Too much,' she said roundly.

'Indeed not,' he told her seriously, 'taking into account the fact that you will have very little time to yourself save at the weekend.' He didn't smile. 'I hope that you will consider it very seriously, Matilda.'

She loved him very much, but at the same time she was aware that she was just a little in awe of him; he looked and spoke exactly how an eminent surgeon should—courteous and impersonal and remote. She had no idea what he was thinking behind that calm face. She frowned. 'When do you want to know?'

'Now.'

She looked at her mother and found that lady smiling. 'You were only saying, Tilly dear, that you were going to look for a little job in Sherborne today.' Her parent gave her a guileless look.

'How would I get there? Is there a bus? And how do I get home for the weekend?'

'You would be driven there. You drive, do you not? I believe that there is a car you might use at weekends.'

'When would this gentleman want me to go?' She looked down at her pinny. 'I've been dyeing curtains...'

Mr Scott-Thurlow, who knew nothing of dyeing curtains, let this pass.

'Tomorrow afternoon?' he suggested gently. 'Try it for a week—if you aren't happy then the matter can be arranged.' He got up. 'I must get back to town—may I pick you up about three o'clock tomorrow?'

Matilda heard herself say yes as her mother went out of the room with him. It was only as she heard the front door squeak when it was opened that she realised that she didn't know the name of her new employer. She ran through the house, swept past her mother about to shut the door and raced down the garden path to where Mr Scott-Thurlow was getting into his car. He was in it by the time she reached it and she poked her head through the window, her bright hair all over the place, her lovely face inches from his.

'His name?' she demanded urgently. 'What's his name, this old gentleman?'

He allowed himself the pleasure of studying her face before he answered. 'Scott-Thurlow—Mr Charles Scott-Thurlow. My grandfather.'

A man of reserve, not given to impulse, he kissed the face, so temptingly close, raised a hand in grave salute and drove himself away.

Matilda stood staring after the car, a prey to mixed feelings: delight, surprise—and why had he kissed her? He was engaged, wasn't he? To a beautiful woman, and what would she say if she knew? Or perhaps in her particular social circle the odd kiss didn't count for anything. But it hadn't been an odd kiss…

Mr Scott-Thurlow was having mixed feelings too. After years of knowing exactly what he wanted, and that included a suitable marriage to someone who would make no demands upon his dedicated life, run his house well and take care of the social side of his life, he was experiencing an overpowering wish to see Matilda again and as often as possible. She would wreak havoc in his orderly life, she was impulsive, quick-tempered, given to speaking her mind upon occasion and, from what he had seen of her, uncaring about her appearance.

He shot past a busload of people who waved but he didn't notice. He must uproot the girl before she became important to him… He regretted now that he had offered to drive her to his grandfather's house, reflecting with his usual honesty that he had thought the whole thing up in the first place because he had wanted to see more of her. It was true that his grandfather was in need of company but he could have called upon any number of suitable middle-aged ladies to fulfil that office. He could of course take a few days off; a change of scene would help. Perhaps Rhoda would go with him. He viewed the idea with no enthusiasm.

He had a list that afternoon; he thrust Matilda out of his mind and concentrated upon pinning and plating a shattered leg, a laminectomy for the removal of a spinal tumour and a meniscectomy to relieve a torn cartilage. These done to his satisfaction, he drank the tea Theatre Sister had ready for him, bade her a courteous good day and repaired to the consultant's room where he found an urgent message from his secretary asking him to telephone her.

There had been a mine disaster in Spitsbergen and he was asked to go there to advise upon several cases which might require his particular skill. He accepted at once and spent the rest of the day making arrangements for his registrar to take over from him, booking a flight for the next day and then telephoning the rectory. Mrs ffinch answered.

'You want to fetch Matilda in the morning? Of course that's all right—she's out at the moment but she's quite ready to leave. I'll tell her—ten o'clock? She'll be waiting.'

Mr Scott-Thurlow put the phone down with a sigh; circumstances, unhappy for some, had dealt with his problem very nicely. He whistled the dogs, and with Theobald under one arm—for he was still something of an invalid—he walked to Regent's Park, which he strode from end to end and then back again, much to the dogs' delight. Despite the exercise he had little appetite for the excellent dinner Twigg, his man, served to him.

A circumstance which made that faithful servant observe to his wife, 'It's not like him, Mavis, not like him at all. Something's up and it's nothing to do with going to Spitsbergen; he's always off here, there and everywhere and never turns a hair.'

'That Miss Symes?' suggested Mrs Twigg, who didn't like her.

He shook his bald head. 'Can't be—he was on the phone to her, saying he couldn't go to some concert or other with her, quite affable too.'

Matilda was quite ready when he arrived at the rectory the next morning. She had dressed carefully in a wide flowery skirt and a plain cotton blouse with a matching cardigan, and she had taken great pains with her hair and face. Mr Scott-Thurlow took one look at her and then wished her a coolly detached good morning. She supposed that he had had a busy time of it since she had seen him last, and at the thought blushed. She hadn't expected him to refuse the coffee her mother had ready. Pressure of work, he explained pleasantly, and ushered her out to the car without loss of time.

There was no need to go into Sherborne; country roads skirting round the north of the town took them to Mackrell Cantelo, a small village between the A303 and Yeovil and as remote as Abner Magna. Throughout the short journey Mr Scott-Thurlow had had little to say. Matilda had essayed a few remarks, to be met with pleasantly non-committal replies. She had been looking forward to the trip, longing for it, in fact, but now she felt uneasy; her companion having withdrawn behind a bland face and manner. They were almost there when she hit on the answer. He was letting her see that his interest in her was purely superficial; a chance acquaintance who most providentially could fill a needed job. The kiss had been sheer relief on his part—well, he need have no fears that she had imagined otherwise. She lapsed into a dignified silence, studying the scenery as though she had never seen it before and smouldering inwardly.

They swept through Mackrell Cantelo, turned in between stone pillars and drew up before a nice old house, eighteenth century, with stone mullioned windows and a red tiled roof and set in grounds planted with rhododendrons, ornamental trees and shrubs of all kinds and boasting a small lake to one side of the house. Mr Scott-Thurlow stopped before the front door, got out to help Matilda and crossed the gravel sweep with her beside him. He didn't ring the ancient bell-pull beside the door but opened it and without delay walked in. The lobby opened into a large square hall, very pleasant and light with a polished wood floor partly covered by Persian rugs, its walls, panelled in some light wood, hung with paintings and across which hurried a spruce middle-aged man, neatly dressed.

'Ah, Slocombe, how are you?' Mr Scott-Thurlow turned to Matilda. 'Slocombe runs the house for my grandparents and is a tower of strength. You will find him the greatest help. Slocombe, this is Miss ffinch—you already know that she will keep my grandfather company until my grandmother returns home.'

Slocombe bowed his head gravely at Matilda, who stepped forwards and offered a hand. 'I'm sure I shall be glad of your advice,' she told him and Mr Scott-Thurlow watched the older man succumb to her friendly smile and green eyes.

'Your grandfather is waiting for you, Mr James,' said Slocombe and led the way across the hall, into a large room with windows back and front.

The old gentleman who got up as they went in must have been as big a man as his grandson when he was younger and even now, in his eighties, he was upright and remarkably handsome with a fine head of white hair and the blue eyes his grandson had inherited. Matilda, as usual, allowed her imagination to go to work; in fifty years' time James would look exactly like that, it would be their golden wedding anniversary and they would be surrounded by children and grandchildren... She was suddenly aware that both gentlemen were looking at her, wearing the same half-smile, their eyebrows tilted at exactly the same angle.

'Matilda, this is my grandfather. I'm sure you will be able to help him pass the time until my grandmother comes home again.'

Matilda shook hands with the old gentleman—she liked him at once, but of course she would; he was James's grandfather and therefore to be cherished. 'I do hope so,' she said and smiled widely.

'You'll stay for lunch, James?'

'Regretfully, no. I must be on my way—I've a plane to catch.'

Matilda had an instant and vivid picture of him boarding Concorde with Rhoda, off to some exotic island.

'Ah, yes, of course, the mine disaster in Spitsbergen. Several in your line, no doubt.'

'I fear so.' He shook his grandfather's hand. 'I'll see you when I get back.'

'Taking Rhoda with you?' asked his grandfather.

His grandson looked astounded. 'Rhoda to Spitsbergen? I doubt if she knows where it is.'

'A very beautiful woman,' observed his grandparent. 'I wish I could come with you.'

'So do I.' The two men smiled at each other and Mr Scott-Thurlow turned to Matilda, standing so quietly beside them. 'Take care of him, Matilda,' he said pleasantly and had gone before she had even nodded her head.

'Now, my dear, shall we have a drink just to get to know each other? Slocombe will have taken your things upstairs and Mrs Slocombe will take you to your room presently. A pity James couldn't stay, but of course it's quite a longish flight to Spitsbergen.'

'You said a mine disaster—is that the one I read about in the paper this morning?'

'Yes, they're well equipped there for accidents and so on, there's an excellent hospital at Ny Alesund, but when there's a disaster of any sort then they need extra help. James has been before of course. A good chap—told me when he was quite a small chap that he would be as good a surgeon as his father, and he is. Bones, of course—it runs in the family.'

Matilda sipped her sherry. 'Your wife…' she began tentatively.

'Having a prosthesis—hip joint, you know. A colleague of James's did it last week. Normally she would come home but she's an independent woman, doesn't want to be an invalid in her own home, so she will stay at the nursing home until she is fit—three weeks or so, so she tells me.' He added, 'I do miss her.'

'I'm sure you do, but how nice to look forward to having her home again in a week or two with a new hip.'

'Yes, yes. She's a keen gardener, you know, able to name every flower she's ever grown.' He sighed, 'Never got over James's father dying like that. His mother too—a nice little thing she was, and quite devoted.'

He closed his eyes and was all at once asleep and she sat there quietly, her thoughts with Mr Scott-Thurlow driving himself to the airport, going hundreds of miles at a few hours' notice because he was needed. His grandfather had called him a 'good chap', which from that rather austere gentleman was probably high praise—she thought of him in warmer terms; he was everything she had ever hoped for in a husband, only there was no chance of his being that…

'Do you play chess, Matilda?'

Mr Scott-Thurlow senior had opened his very blue eyes and was watching her.

'Me? Chess? Well, in a manner of speaking—I'm really bad at it, so my father says.'

'Splendid. I shall beat you each evening after dinner. Now tell me all about your family.'

Which she did until Slocombe came quietly into the room to remind them that lunch would be in half an hour and would Miss ffinch like to go to her room first?

Matilda was led up the curved staircase by Mrs Slocombe, stout and friendly. Her room was at the side of the house, overlooking the gardens, and was rather charmingly furnished with white-painted bed and dressing-table, an easy chair or two, a pretty little lamp table and carpeted in a soft blue, echoed in the curtains and bedspread. There were flowers and books too and a small bathroom leading from it.

'Anything you want, my love, just you ask,' said Mrs Slocombe in her soft West Country voice. 'There's Alice the housemaid lives in; she'll bring you tea in the morning. Mr Scott-Thurlow eats his breakfast early—eight o'clock sharp. Miss Symes, when she's visited here, has hers in her bed—don't like to rise before ten o'clock or thereabouts.'

'If it's all right I'd like to come down for breakfast—I'm used to getting up early. That is if Mr Scott-Thurlow won't mind.'

''E don't hold with lying in bed of a morning, miss. You come down and welcome.'

She trotted off, leaving Matilda to explore her room, hang out of the window and finally sit down at the dressing-table to tidy her person.

They both enjoyed lunch; they discussed a variety of subjects, arguing happily and at length until they parted company for the afternoon, he to take a nap in the library, she to explore the house at his invitation.

'Tea at four o'clock,' he told her. 'I enjoy my tea, and if you have nothing better to do you can go through the post for me and deal with anything that needs looking into. And we might have that game of chess...'

It was that evening, after he had beaten her soundly and declared that he would go to bed that he observed, 'James will be in Norway by now.'

'How will he get to Spitsbergen from there?'

'Well, he will have flown to Oslo and then taken a plane to Tromso, that's in the north, and from there he'll get a light aircraft to Spitsbergen. Or perhaps a helicopter.'

'It will be late when he gets there.'

'Or early morning. I dare say there is other stuff being flown out—tools and so on.'

'He'll be tired,' said Matilda.

The old man agreed quietly, his eyes suddenly alert, but all he said was, 'Well, I'm for bed. Do I see you at breakfast?'

'If you would like that, yes.'

'My wife has never been one to languish in bed until all hours. Until she needed to go to hospital we breakfasted together every morning. We will visit her tomorrow. I go each day in the morning. James tells me that you drive. Slocombe will be delighted, for it has upset his morning's routine having to take me there and wait to bring me back.'

'Is the hospital far away?'

He mentioned a private hospital on the road to Bath. 'Half an hour or so, and it's a good road.'

Matilda slept soundly, ate a good breakfast in the old gentleman's company and then, a little nervously, got behind the wheel of the Daimler Slocombe had brought to the door, but she soon forgot to be nervous—the car ran like a dream and the roads were quiet. At the hospital Mr Scott-Thurlow broke the silence. 'Very nice, my dear. My dear wife does not drive, but of course all young women should do so nowadays—shopping, children to school. You will find it useful when you marry.'

Matilda said bleakly, 'I don't expect to marry…'

'But you will.' He smiled at her and looked exactly like his grandson, so that her heart lurched.

Mrs Scott-Thurlow was sitting in a pleasant room full of flowers. Her husband kissed her tenderly, told her that she looked beautiful and introduced Matilda.

'Ah, yes,' said Mrs Scott-Thurlow, 'James was quite right.' She smiled brilliantly. 'He told me that you were beautiful too. My grandson, you know.' She nodded her head so that the silvery hair danced around her pretty elderly face. 'He seldom notices women. It's time he took his nose out of that hospital and looked around him…'

'I fancy he has done so,' observed her husband and Matilda, turning the knife in the wound, said brightly, 'His fiancée is very beautiful; I met her once.'

'Ah, yes—you were in London, were you not? Did you enjoy your stay there?'

'Well, it was most interesting,' began Matilda carefully, 'but I'd rather live in the country.'

A nurse brought a tray of coffee and presently Matilda sauntered out, having said that she would like to look at the garden if no one minded, leaving the two old people together.

They were a delightful pair and they were fond of their grandson, but she suspected that they shared a life which they had made their own. For a small boy who had just lost his parents that had been a barrier, and he had sensed it and never overcome it although he must have come to terms with it now that he was a man with a well-established life of his own. 'But no roots,' said Matilda, talking to herself, and since there was no one else to talk to she added, 'He needs a home and a wife and a clutch of children to warm him and that Rhoda will never do that. He'll get more and more remote because she won't expect him to be anything else, and the children, if they have any, will see him for a few minutes each day and he won't know how to talk to them, just as his grandparents didn't know how to talk to him.' She plucked a weed with a good deal of unnecessary force. 'Something must be done.'

The choice wasn't great; even if she had been an unscrupulous girl it would have been difficult to divert Mr Scott-Thurlow's affections from Rhoda, who was beautiful, amusing and shared his background. Matilda, aware that she was very pretty was none the less not conceited about it—besides, he had demonstrated clearly enough that he had absolutely no interest in her. Here she paused to mull over the kiss he had given her. It had been done on the spur of the moment; probably he had been thankful that she had agreed to stay with his grandfather... She dismissed the occurrence, although she would have like to linger over it, and returned to the vexed question of Rhoda. Perhaps if she got to know her? Persuaded her that James needed to be loved and teased a little and even annoyed a bit from time to time, made aware of the fact that there was a good life outside his working world? In ten years' time, thought Matilda unhappily, he would be so wrapped up in his world of surgery that he might just as well not have married.

She started to wander back, deep in thought. Why on earth had he decided to marry the girl? Rhoda liked a social life and, granted, she would be a splendid hostess and no doubt run his house admirably—would she like waiting up if he got called out in the evening, or getting his slippers when he got home or making sure that he had enough to eat? It would be easier if she knew more about his personal life—and Rhoda's too. 'I am an interfering busybody,' said Matilda softly to herself, 'and I want him for me not her, but I can't have him so I'd better try and help.'

A depressing thought struck her; perhaps he liked Rhoda like that, cool and undemonstrative and slightly bored—at least she had appeared so to Matilda, but who knew what she was like when she was alone with James? It was a sobering thought; perhaps she would do well to hold her tongue and forget him, but she would have to wait until Mrs Scott-Thurlow was back home again and she could go home herself and wipe him clean out of her mind.

Mr Scott-Thurlow was ready to leave. Mrs Scott-Thurlow gave her a kind smile. 'I feel so much easier in my mind now that you are at home, my dear. The Slocombes are old servants and friends but it is company my husband needs. Do let me know the moment you hear from James.'

He telephoned that evening. Matilda happened to be by the phone in the sitting-room when it rang and Mr Scott-Thurlow, unable to get out of his chair with any kind of speed, asked her to answer it.

She said, 'Yes?' in a wispy voice, sure that it was James. It was; his voice, very clear from all those miles away, sent her heart racing.

'Matilda? I should like to speak to my grandfather...'

That was that as far as she was concerned. She went out of the room once the old gentleman was settled by the phone and went upstairs to her room and hung out of the window, looking at the late spring evening. He could at least have said how are you, or even hello. She went downstairs again and out of a side-door into the garden and stayed there until Slocombe opened the french window in the drawing-room and reminded her that the drinks had been poured.

Mr Scott-Thurlow was chatty. 'What a blessing the telephone can be,' he observed happily, 'although I suppose it must be complicated between here and Spitsbergen. A clear line though. James is busy, but he expected to be. He won't be back for a week—

there were some bad injuries and the hospital is full. He will be ringing again in a few days' time. I let my wife know, of course—he sent a number of messages.'

None for me, thought Matilda peevishly. Out loud she said, 'I expect it's difficult telephoning all that way. I expect Miss Symes is anxious, but I dare say there's a way in which she can phone him.' To make it sound more casual she added, 'There's a time difference, isn't there?'

'Yes. I don't imagine Rhoda will telephone him; I believe that she leads a very busy life.' His voice was dry.

'I should think she would—she is so beautiful, and attractive too.' She spoke sincerely; she didn't like Rhoda but that was no reason to be spiteful about her, especially to this nice old man who would shortly be her grandfather-in-law.

The days passed pleasantly; chess, strolls in the garden, listening to Mr Scott-Thurlow talking about every subject under the sun. Matilda found that there wasn't a dull moment. They went each day to see Mrs Scott-Thurlow, although Matilda only stayed in the room for a few minutes, tactfully absenting herself for an hour or so. She got to know the grounds of the hospital rather well and she would stroll up and down thinking about James.

She would have liked to know so much more about him but his grandfather rarely spoke of his private life and she couldn't ask. He didn't talk about Rhoda either but Matilda was after all a stranger, filling a gap until his wife returned home. That wouldn't be too long, she was told, as it was now only a question of finding a suitable nurse to stay with her for a week or so until she felt quite able to be independent.

Matilda went home at the weekend, glad to see everyone again and tell them about her job.

'Sounds cushy to me,' said Esme. 'How long will you be there?'

'Not long, another week or two at the most.'

'It will be nice to have you at home again, Tilly,' said her mother.

'Yes, Mother, but I shall find another job as soon as possible. I can ask for a reference...'

She was welcomed back warmly. 'I missed you, Matilda,' said

Mr Scott-Thurlow. 'The house seemed very quiet. We seldom have visitors, you know.'

One came the very next day—Rhoda Symes!

CHAPTER FIVE

RHODA drove up in a Porsche just as they were getting ready to visit Mrs Scott-Thurlow. It was a bright red car and she wore a scarlet suede jacket over a black dress, not suitable for the country but very eye-catching. She got out of the car slowly and came towards them as they stood poised to get into the Daimler.

'Hello,' she called, 'I've been at Brooke House for the weekend and it seemed a good idea to come and see you on my way back to town.' She kissed Mr Scott-Thurlow's cheek. 'I've had a marvellous time—a pity James couldn't have been with me.' She looked at Matilda then. 'Haven't I seen you before? Of course, at that boring picture gallery with Roseanne Fox, and aren't you the girl who cooked the dinner? James told me about it—what a joke.' She turned back to the old gentleman. 'And where is Mrs Scott-Thurlow? Is she—' she nodded towards Matilda '—the new cook?'

Matilda admired Mr Scott-Thurlow's nice manners. 'My wife has had an operation; Matilda is most kindly staying here to keep me company until she is back home. Did you not know?'

'Oh, I believe James did say something about it—but I've got the most awful memory, especially about anything unpleasant.'

'Have you heard from him?'

'I told him not to bother to phone or write, he'll only be away for a week or so. Why he has to go to these awful God-forsaken places...! He can take his pick of all the private patients he wants in town.' She looked at the car. 'Are you going somewhere? Am I keeping you?'

'We're going to see my wife. Perhaps you would like to come along too?'

'Love to. Is she in that nice place outside Bath? A friend of mine went there to have something or other done; wildly expensive too.' She gave Mr Scott-Thurlow a charming smile. 'You tootle along, I'll follow.'

Matilda drove silently, afraid that if she spoke she might say something she would regret afterwards. She was on fire with rage and a strong wish to tear Rhoda's hair out by the roots and then take a pair of sharp scissors to that red jacket. She kept these reprehensible thoughts to herself with difficulty and was relieved when they arrived at the hospital. Mr Scott-Thurlow hadn't spoken either, only as they got out of the car he gave her an understanding smile.

The visit wasn't a success. Rhoda was charming but Matilda saw Mrs Scott-Thurlow bristle with anger when she was referred to as a poor old thing. Old she might be, but poor she certainly was not, and it was doubtful if anyone had ever dared to call her that before. She couldn't be faulted in her manner towards Rhoda; she listened to Rhoda's high and very clear voice, recounting the fun she had had over the weekend, and her plans for future entertainment. 'When James gets back I'll see that he gets out and about,' she declared. 'There are several good parties and it's months since we went to the theatre together.'

Matilda, after a decent interval, said that she would take her usual stroll in the grounds and, mindful of the old people's wish to be alone for a time, invited Rhoda to go with her.

'Whatever for? Gardens bore me unless they're spectacular—besides, whatever should we talk about?' She gave a little rippling laugh. 'Cooking?'

Matilda kept her pretty face smiling although her eyes darted green fire. 'About half an hour?' she asked, and, receiving a nod from Mr Scott-Thurlow, wandered off. Trying to walk off her temper she reflected that if Rhoda was staying for lunch she herself would have a bad headache. 'What can he see in the girl?' she asked the hospital cat, sitting in a sunny corner. 'But perhaps she never talks like that when he's with her.'

They drove back presently and Rhoda, after the briefest of goodbyes and declining coffee or lunch, shot away in the Porsche.

Mr Scott-Thurlow led the way into the house as the car disappeared into the lane and there was no mistaking his air of relief although he said nothing, merely asking her to see if Slocombe would bring them some coffee. 'I know it's almost time for lunch, but a cup would be nice. Have one with me, Matilda.'

So she sat with him, drinking first coffee and then a glass of sherry and then going in to lunch, all the while chatting about nothing in particular and never a word about Rhoda, sensing that he was upset.

The days went by, pleasantly enough. Mrs Scott-Thurlow was to return home in a week's time, accompanied by a nurse, a placid little woman who didn't fuss. She was already at the hospital and her patient liked her. She joined Matilda on her morning strolls in the grounds and they got on well together.

'I shall go home as soon as you get back with Mrs Scott-Thurlow,' said Matilda. 'I came just to keep Mr Scott-Thurlow company. I've enjoyed every minute of it too; they have been so kind and really I've had nothing to do.'

'Well, there will be precious little work for me,' Nurse Watkins said. 'A couple of weeks, perhaps less, and I'll be off again.'

'Oh, don't you work at the hospital all the time?'

'No. I work for an agency but I take Mr Scott-Thurlow's—that's the grandson's—patients. I wouldn't want to work for anyone else; he's marvellous. I've been with him for years now. He's in Spitsbergen, operating on the bone injuries from that mine disaster, but, just fancy, he found time to telephone the agency asking for me to come and look after his granny. He's a wonderful man. Have you met him?'

'Well, yes, but I don't know him well...'

'He's engaged, you know. To a hoity-toity piece—well, I shouldn't have said that, I dare say she's all right, just not my sort. I don't think she's his sort either, but that's neither here nor there.'

It was the following morning that Mrs Scott-Thurlow, after greeting her husband, told him to take Nurse Watkins for a walk round the grounds. 'I want to talk to Matilda—all we ever say to each other is good morning and goodbye and she will be leaving us soon.'

As the door closed behind the other two she said, 'Come and

sit down here beside me, my dear. I have to thank you for being such good company for Charles; it has been the greatest help to him during this tiresome time. I told my grandson that when he telephoned me yesterday. It was a splendid idea to ask you in the first place. He tells me that you were actually going to a job when he asked that you should come to us, and reminded me to allow you to leave just as soon as I am home again, so you must make your plans. Slocombe will drive you to your home.' She leaned over and patted Matilda's hands, lying idly in her lap. 'We shall miss you and I hope that you will visit us from time to time. And now that is settled tell me something of your family and your life.'

'There's not much to tell,' observed Matilda, and embarked on a description of life at Abner Magna while she seethed silently. James Scott-Thurlow didn't deserve to be loved—he was a nasty cold-blooded creature who, as soon as he had got what he wanted from someone, ignored them; got rid of them just as he was getting rid of her. He deserved Rhoda—in fact the girl was too good for him!

She was finishing a light-hearted account of bingo in the village hall when the others came back, and she said goodbye to Mrs Scott-Thurlow and tactfully went out to the car with Nurse Watkins.

'A very nice girl,' declared the old lady to her husband when they were alone, 'and such a charming voice and manner. I wonder what is worrying her...?'

'Worrying her? What should be? She seems content enough.'

'Yes, dear, I am sure that she's as happy as possible with you. All the same I must find out.' She added casually, 'I suppose she has met James?'

'Of course—he fixed her up with us, didn't he? Besides, I remember her saying that she had met him at some exhibition or other. Anyway, he drove her down, didn't he? So of course they've met even if that was for the first time. You can't count that exhibition—I dare say they were introduced and didn't speak. Why do you ask?'

'No reason, my dear,' said his wife airily. She bade him goodbye and, when she was alone, sat in deep thought, frowning a little.

The day came when they were to fetch Mrs Scott-Thurlow back home. The Slocombes had polished and cleaned and, with Matilda helping out, put flowers in every room, and a festive lunch had been arranged. She got into the car and drove it for the last time to the hospital. She was packed and ready to leave that very afternoon; Slocombe was to drive her home, and although she didn't want to go in the least she could see that it would be much easier for Nurse Watkins if she wasn't there. 'Too many cooks spoil the broth,' said Matilda, which wasn't quite what she meant but near enough.

They were met in the hall by the matron, looking apologetic.

'There is a slight hitch,' she began. 'Nurse Watkins had severe toothache during the night and she is even now at the dentist. I phoned just a few minutes ago and he tells me that he has taken the tooth out but recommends that she should have a day's quiet before resuming her work. Shall we keep Mrs Scott-Thurlow until tomorrow, when I'm sure that Nurse Watkins will be well enough to accompany her home, or would you be able to manage for a day?'

Mr Scott-Thurlow didn't hesitate. 'Miss ffinch here will look after my wife until Nurse Watkins can join us—we cannot disappoint her after our plans have been made.'

Matilda opened her mouth and then shut it again—there was no point in making an awkward situation more awkward—and when he turned to her and said, 'You don't mind, do you, Matilda?' she shook her head meekly and murmured that of course it didn't matter at all.

So they drove back again with Mrs Scott-Thurlow sitting in the back with her husband, so delighted to be going home again that she was on the verge of tears.

Everyone in the house came to welcome her home. She was led tenderly into the sitting-room, sat in a suitable chair, offered coffee and fussed over while the old gentleman watched with a delighted smile.

There were enough people there, Matilda decided, so she got

the luggage from the boot and carried it upstairs and unpacked it and put everything away in what she hoped were the proper cupboards and drawers, and then went down to the kitchen to tell Mrs Slocombe what she had done and offer to give a hand with lunch. Mrs Scott-Thurlow was quite comfortable, talking quietly with her happy husband—they would have a lot to say to each other before they sat down to the splendid meal which Mrs Slocombe had prepared, and after that, Matilda reflected, she would suggest a little nap until teatime.

Mrs Slocombe was standing at the table beating eggs. 'There you are, miss. Madam would like to go to her room to tidy herself and won't take no for an answer…'

Matilda and the old lady went very slowly up the staircase, watched by her anxious husband from the hall. 'You see,' said Mrs Scott-Thurlow triumphantly when they reached the gallery above, 'I knew I could do it.'

All the same, Matilda persuaded her to sit down for ten minutes while she combed the pretty white hair and powdered the haughty little nose. Mrs Scott-Thurlow was impatient. 'We will go back now and sit for a few minutes, and we will have a glass of sherry, my dear.'

So they trundled downstairs, which wasn't as easy as going up had been; all the same, they reached the drawing-room safely and Matilda sat her down in the chair again.

'I would like a shawl,' said Mrs Scott-Thurlow, 'just for my shoulders. Matilda, will you go to my room and get one? There should be several in the commode drawer, and when you come back we will all have that drink.'

Matilda closed the double doors behind her and started across the hall. She had taken herself half a dozen steps when the house door was flung open and James Scott-Thurlow strode in. He saw her at once and she gave him a delighted smile and started towards him.

'What in the name of the almighty are you doing here?' he demanded, his voice as cold as the Arctic regions he had just left. 'I arranged for a nurse…'

Not even a hello, thought Matilda crossly, and however did she allow herself to fall in love with such a rude, bad-tempered man?

'Arrangements go wrong sometimes,' she told him waspishly. '"There's many a slip," you know. Nurse Watkins had to have a tooth out, and I'm to stay until she gets here tomorrow. Too bad, isn't it? But I'll go the very moment she has put a foot inside the door.'

She turned her back on him and went up the staircase. She was in the gallery before she heard the drawing-room doors open and shut.

She took as long as possible finding the shawl; she had no wish to go back to the drawing-room, but on the other hand if she didn't show herself he would think that she was feeling awkward about their meeting in the hall.

'Bother him,' she told her reflection in Mrs Scott-Thurlow's dressing-table mirror. 'I don't care if I never see him again.' Upon which heartening lie she took herself downstairs once more.

He was sitting between his grandparents but he got up when she went in. 'Ah, Matilda, come and sit down and have a glass of sherry.' He pulled a small armchair forwards for her and went to the drinks tray. 'It is most kind of you to stay until Nurse Watkins gets here. Have you had time to phone your mother?'

No one could have been more polite or easy-mannered. She accepted the sherry, muttered that yes, thank you, she had already phoned home, and lapsed into silence. Presently Slocombe came to tell them that lunch was ready and she went into the dining-room with the old gentleman behind his wife and grandson.

'Splendid to see James back, my dear. His grandmother is delighted. We must get him to tell us something of his work on Spitsbergen; I'm sure it will be most interesting. So delightful that he will be staying the night.'

Matilda agreed with him, her feelings mixed.

The conversation at table was general; the old gentleman asked about the weather in Spitsbergen, the local amenities and the scenery, but he asked no questions as to his grandson's work, nor did James mention it. Matilda, speaking when spoken to on such topics as the habitat of the wildlife there, the plants to be found and similar sidelights on life in the Arctic Circle, found it strange that no one was agog with questions about James's own life and work there. Now, if she had been at home, she reflected, just returned from some place or other, everyone would have wanted to know everything concerning her, never mind the flora and fauna. The three people at the table with her were all so polite and detached; she had no doubt that they were fond of each other but they seemed unable to show it. She wondered if they had been so detached when he was a small boy, thrust into their lives at a moment's notice, and if that was why he was so reserved. She made up her mind there and then to find out.

It would be difficult. She remembered James Scott-Thurlow's somewhat acid remarks when she had asked him rather a lot of questions in his car. He had called it a cross-examination; he wouldn't take kindly to any prying on her part.

She coaxed a rather tired old lady upstairs to have a nap when they had finished lunch and then went to her room and sat in a chair by the window. It was a splendid day and she would have liked to have gone into the garden, but she wanted to avoid Mr Scott-Thurlow: besides if he and his grandfather wanted to talk she would be a nuisance. She poked her head out into the summer sunshine and was accosted from below.

'Come on down, Matilda,' said old Mr Scott-Thurlow. 'James is going to tell me something of his stay in Spitsbergen.'

'Later perhaps?' She thought wildly for an excuse. 'Mrs Scott-Thurlow is a little unsettled; I thought I might read to her for a while.'

'A good idea. Please come down when you can.'

She withdrew her head and sat down again and since she had said that she was going to read aloud she had better go and suggest it. The old lady was sound asleep.

For the rest of that day Matilda contrived to keep in the background, and since Mrs Scott-Thurlow had had strict instructions to go to bed in good time she was able to accompany her to her room to help her to bed. This took some time so that, beyond polite regrets, neither gentleman appeared put out when she bade them goodnight and went to bed herself. It was a lovely evening—just right for a stroll in the gardens. With James Scott-Thurlow, of course; such a pity that she was forced to go to bed instead. If she had been Rhoda... Matilda had a very hot bath and, as pink as a lobster, got into her bed and lay listening to the drone of the men's voices coming faintly from the open windows of the drawing-room below. Old Mr Scott-Thurlow's rather slow voice, and his grandson's, deep and deliberate. She closed her eyes and slept.

It was pouring with rain when she woke in the morning, dressed and went down to the dining-room. It was barely eight o'clock and she hoped that she would be able to eat her breakfast, or at least most of it, before anyone else came down. She was doomed to disappointment—Mr Scott-Thurlow the younger was already there, reading *The Times* newspaper and consuming bacon, mushrooms and eggs. He got up when she went in, gave her a polite good morning and begged her to help herself. She noticed that he folded the paper and put it on the table beside him with a faint air of annoyance, so that she said in a voice she strove to keep amiable, 'Don't stop reading for me; I don't mind in the least.'

She poured coffee, filled a plate with bacon and egg and began to eat. There was a slight edge to her voice as she went on, 'So unfortunate that I should still be here, isn't it? I'm going immediately after I've seen to Mrs Scott-Thurlow.'

It was disconcerting when he didn't answer, and, quite reckless because she wouldn't be seeing him again, she added sharply, 'Well, has the cat got your tongue?'

He leaned back in his chair and looked her over. 'What an abominable girl you are, Matilda; I'm not surprised your hair is so fiery for you have a temper to match it.' He poured himself some more coffee. 'And why should you suppose that I should object to finding you still here?'

'The look on your face when you saw me,' she said, not beating about the bush. She glanced across at him and all her ill humour evaporated at the sight of his weary face. 'Heavens, you're worn out; was it very busy at Spitsbergen?'

His eyebrows rose. 'Why the volte-face? But yes, I was kept busy.'

'Then you should take a holiday,' said Matilda, 'and have some fun. Miss Symes was here, you know, and she said there were several parties she would take you to when you got back.'

'And is that your idea of fun?'

'Parties? No, well, I'm different, aren't I?'

She didn't hear his, 'Indeed you are.'

'I mean, I don't fit in awfully well—with your kind of people. I like dining out and dancing and going to the theatre, but there's no conversation at parties, is there? Or, if there is, I can never hear it.' She gave him an almost motherly smile. 'But I expect you will enjoy yourself.'

'I am touched by your solicitude, Matilda, but you have no need to concern yourself with my way of life.' He spoke gently in a cold voice so that she went very pink and blurted out,

'I'm interfering—'

Old Mr Scott-Thurlow coming into the room at that moment saved her from uttering whatever she had intended; she wished him good morning, murmured that she would go and see how his wife was and took herself off.

Beyond giving his grandson a good look, the old gentleman said nothing and it was James who spoke. 'The matron phoned soon after seven o'clock to say that Nurse Watkins should be here by half-past nine.'

'Good. I'll tell Slocombe to drive Matilda back.'

'No need, sir. I must call in on my way and see how my patient is getting on. She was taken to King's Hall. Matilda lives only a few miles further on—I'll drop her off.'

'Splendid. Have you told her?'

'No. Did grandmother have a good night?'

By mutual consent, they began to discuss his grandmother's health.

Nurse Watkins arrived soon after nine o'clock, by which time Matilda had got Mrs Scott-Thurlow out of her bed and into a comfortable chair while she got a bath ready and put everything in order so that she might dress. She was wondering just what she should do next when the nurse joined them and the following ten minutes were taken up with apologies, regrets and goodbyes. Mrs Scott-Thurlow put up her face for a kiss and pressed a small box into Matilda's hand. 'You have been so good, my dear, and we shall both miss you. You must come and see us again soon—and that isn't an empty remark, I really mean it. Now run along and I hope this job you're going to will be a pleasant one.'

Matilda kissed the elderly cheek, shook Nurse Watkins's hand and fetched her jacket and case from her bedroom. She still had to say goodbye to old Mr Scott-Thurlow and, although it broke her heart not to see James just once more, she was determined to avoid him.

He was in the hall with his grandfather and stood quietly by while she bade that gentleman goodbye. It was impossible to avoid him now; she gave a brief nod in his direction. 'Goodbye.'

'I'm driving you back.'

'Oh, but there's no need, thank you. Slocombe is taking me.'

He shook his head. 'No, I am—'

She didn't give up easily. 'But I saw him only a short time ago and he never said—'

'I told him not to. Come along; I have no time to waste.'

She was aware that his grandfather was standing there looking amused and at the same time thoughtful. She said with dignity, 'Very well,' gave the old gentleman a delightful smile, handed James her case with a scowl and a flash of her green eyes and marched out of the door. The Slocombes had come to wave goodbye so she changed the scowl to another smile, got into the car while her case was put in the boot and then waved until the group by the door was out of sight.

They drove for several miles without speaking until he asked, 'Still sulking, Matilda?'

'I don't sulk. I have no reason to do so.'

'Good. In that case let me talk sensibly…' He ignored her cross mutter. 'You will find your fee waiting for you at your home. What do you intend to do next?' He added, 'And don't tell me to mind my own business.'

'I had no intention of saying any such thing,' said Matilda, who had been on the point of uttering those very words. 'I have no idea what I shall do next; certainly I shall stay at home for a short time. I cannot think why you should want to know.'

'Nor can I.'

The conversation seemed to have come to an end, such as it was. But presently he said, 'Theobald should be quite recovered; he is a splendid companion for my Labrador, who mothers him relentlessly. He loves it.'

'It was kind of you to take him in,' she said stiffly.

'You have no dog of your own?'

'No. Our dog died last year. I would love to have another one, but if I get a job away from home it's hardly fair on the rest of the family.'

'And you intend to leave home?'

Now who was cross-questioning? 'I haven't decided.'

Mr Scott-Thurlow allowed a small sound to escape his lips—it could have been a chuckle or a grunt—and he said smoothly, 'I'm sure that you will find something worthwhile to do. But why not get married?' He gave her a quick sideways glance. 'I'm surprised that no man has snapped you up.'

She said fierily, 'And I am not a bargain—what a horrid thing to say.'

'Not a bargain—a prize. Once you have been tamed a little and have lost your prickles and your impulsiveness—but that, of course, is the fault of your hair—'

'If you weren't driving this car, I would box your ears—you're more than horrid, you're deliberately baiting me. I hope I never see you again.' She was being childish but she didn't care.

He went on talking just as though she hadn't spoken. 'And yet you were splendid when Mrs Chubb severed her fingers; I don't know of anyone else who would have dealt with the situation with such good sense, nor can I think of any woman I know who would have retired to the kitchen and cooked a meal to cordon bleu standard. And Theobald—you made it your business to help him and you didn't stop to think, did you? The men could have turned nasty; you had no idea what to do with him, had you? Yet you rushed to his aid—and you have been kindness itself to my grandmother and Roseanne. I am forced to the conclusion that it is I who rub you up the wrong way.'

'This is a pointless conversation, Mr Scott-Thurlow.'

She peeped at him; his profile looked grim. He had looked so tired… Her ill humour evaporated, she said, 'I'm sorry if I annoy you—you must be tired. Mother will have coffee ready; perhaps you would like a cup before you go to King's Hall?'

His stern mouth relaxed. 'Why, thank you, Matilda.'

Her mother flung the door open as the car stopped. 'There you are—how nice to see you, Mr Scott-Thurlow; come on in, both of you. There's coffee ready and I made a lardy cake.' She embraced Matilda and shook hands with Mr Scott-Thurlow. 'Dr Bramley told us that you had gone to Spitsbergen to help those poor men in that frightful accident.'

She led the way to the kitchen. 'Sit down, won't you? You don't mind having your coffee here? The sitting-room's being cleaned.'

Mr Scott-Thurlow sat down facing Matilda, made polite small talk with the rector and then said that he must go.

'I expect that you will take a little holiday,' said Mrs ffinch chattily. 'You must need a rest and a change. I dare say it's rather different at Spitsbergen.'

He agreed pleasantly. 'But I hear from Matilda that my fiancée has several parties lined up for me.' He bade her goodbye, shook the rector's hand and paused by Matilda's chair. 'I'll give Theobald your love,' he told her. 'Goodbye, Matilda.'

The rector went with him to his car and Mrs ffinch poured more coffee. 'Such a nice man,' she commented. 'He looked tired—he should go somewhere quiet for a few days but I dare say he won't get the chance; Lady Fox was telling me that his fiancée has been to visit Roseanne at the hospital and told her that she had planned dinner parties and theatres and I don't know what else; she said that he needed to be taken out of himself, whatever that means. I don't think she should be his wife—he needs someone more suitable.'

Matilda said slowly. 'But she is suitable, Mother: she comes from a similar background, she's lovely to look at and dresses marvellously and she'll be a perfect hostess…'

'I should have thought that what he needed was a perfect wife and mother of his children.' She saw the look on Matilda's face and went on quickly, 'Now do tell me about this nice old couple you've been staying with, and is Mrs Scott-Thurlow quite well again?'

Matilda listened to the gentle purr of the Rolls going down the drive—she would never see him again; she didn't want to believe it but it was true. She began to tell her mother about her stay. She looked unhappy but her mother pretended not to notice that. Her dear Tilly would tell her why in time, although she could guess very well who it was that had taken the happy look from her eyes. She frowned a little; Mr Scott-Thurlow had paid scant attention to Matilda—in fact he had behaved with the scrupulous civility of someone being polite at all costs towards a person they disliked. She had been very stiff too. They must have quarrelled. Somehow the thought cheered Mrs ffinch; at least they weren't indifferent to each other. He was of course engaged to marry that other girl but she dismissed that with a maternal single-mindedness. Tilly would make him a good wife. When Matilda had finished her disjointed tale, Mrs ffinch said brightly, 'There's a letter for you, Tilly. It's in the hall.'

It contained a cheque and a short businesslike note stating what it was for; it was signed 'J. Scott-Thurlow'. Or, at least, that was what she supposed it was; it was almost unreadable.

'Isn't it funny,' she observed to her mother, 'that someone who can put bones together again is unable to write legibly?'

'Yes, dear, but we can't excel in everything. I'm told that Roseanne is doing very well. I didn't realise that he was so well-known until Lady Fox waylaid me the other day—she has a new hat, dear, tweed and floppy, quite terrible—where was I? Oh, yes—well, she kept on and on about his brilliance and then told me what his fees were for the operation on Roseanne. Not that I wanted to know; she is sometimes vulgar, you know. I must tell you something else, though; Dr Bramley told me that Mr Scott-Thurlow refuses his fees when he is asked to give his aid at some disaster. The trip to Spitsbergen must have left him very out of pocket.' She added thoughtfully, 'It's a pity that Lady Fox doesn't know that.'

She glanced at the tell-tale face Matilda turned to her and went on cheerfully, 'It's lovely to have you home again, Tilly. They missed you in Sunday school, thought I must say Esme does very well, your Father did say.'

'It's grand to be back, Mother.' Matilda studied the cheque; it was quite a nice sum of money. 'I'll pop into Sherborne tomorrow and pay this in, and at the same time I'll poke around and see if there are any jobs going.'

She had friends there but none of them knew of any likely job; she had no qualifications, but they were full of suggestions as they sat over coffee at the café opposite the abbey. None of them very practical, though; Matilda parted from them presently and went off to do some shopping for her mother. That done, she wandered into the bookshop in Cheap Street and thumbed through the magazines. The *Lady* had pages of adverts, too many to skim through in the shop. She bought a copy and took herself off to the restaurant in Denners where she sat down with a pot of tea and a plate of sandwiches and began to search the pages.

There were dozens of jobs, mostly for trained nannies and married couples, and she had nearly given up when her eye lighted on a lengthy advertisement under the heading 'Educational'. A young lady was needed for the rest of the school term—barely a month now—and the week subsequent to that, to take the place of a junior matron to work under the school matron, and to be in charge of the youngest girls—all boarders. No teaching would be required, but a sense of discipline and common sense were essential. The salary, from Matilda's point of view, was adequate, and to crown everything the school was situated in a small town north of Sherborne, a few miles on the other side of the A303, a mere matter of fifteen miles or so from her home.

Never one to beat about the bush, she gobbled her sandwich, drained the teapot and went off to find the nearest phone box.

The voice at the other end of the line sounded severe but faintly desperate. There had been several applicants but none of them had been satisfactory—the voice gave Matilda the strong impression that she wasn't expected to be satisfactory either, but she persevered. Having a rector for a father, once she disclosed this fact, was the turning-point in her favour. She was bidden to attend an interview on the following morning.

The occasion warranted recognition of some kind; she had paid her cheque into her bank account, put aside a good deal of it to give to her mother for Esme's fees, and went on an impulsive shopping spree. She didn't dare spend too much, though—probably the owner of the voice wouldn't think her good matron material—all the same she bought chocolates for Esme, tobacco for her father's pipe, a bottle of perfume for her mother and a charming little teapot from the china shop in Cheap Street for Hilary—it would do very nicely for her to use when she was married. The boys could have money—she would send it to them at school.

She bore her gifts home, told her family what she had done, handed over the presents and went to select an outfit for the interview. Something sober, she decided, suitable for a junior matron. Eyeing her rather basic wardrobe she found herself thinking about Mr Scott-Thurlow—probably at one of the parties Rhoda had lined up for him. A pity she couldn't tell him that she had found something worthwhile, and in record time. Being Matilda, of course, she never doubted that she would get the job.

CHAPTER SIX

MATILDA, soberly clad in a jacket and skirt, borrowed her father's car and drove herself to her appointment. It was for eleven o'clock and she allowed plenty of time. She knew where the school was; it was fairly well known, taking mostly boarders, children whose parents were overseas and, unlike most schools, it was for girls only.

She got there too soon and parked the car some distance from the wide gateway, thinking up suitable answers to the likely questions she might expect, but this palled after a time and she allowed herself to think of Mr Scott-Thurlow. What would he be doing? she wondered. Sitting in some handsome consulting-room, she supposed, behind an imposing desk, listening courteously to some wealthy patient complaining about his bones. On the other hand, he might be doing one of those ward rounds which always looked so impressive in films. He might even be spending the day with Rhoda...

Mr Scott-Thurlow was bending his large person over his patient on the operating table, meticulously piecing together bits of a bone in a boy's leg, wiring them together and fitting them into a whole with all the care of a jigsaw puzzle enthusiast. Unlike Matilda, he wasn't allowing his thoughts to wander...

Matilda glanced at her watch and started the car, turned in through the gates and stopped neatly in front of the front entrance of the school. It had at one time been the country estate of a member of the eighteenth-century nobility, a point stressed in the prospectus, and any necessary additions and alterations which had been done had been prudently carried out at the back of it and its imposing Georgian front had been left in its original state. Matilda got out, rang the bell and waited composedly to be admitted. The maid who came to the door was rather wooden-faced and dressed in a print frock, white apron and cap. A nice touch, thought

Matilda, suitable for a school which had a high reputation for the educating of girls. She gave her name, was shown to a small room at the side of the hall, and sat down, still composed. She wasn't kept waiting long; the maid returned and led her across the hall, knocked on a door and opened it for her. The room was light, high-ceilinged and well furnished rather severely, a fitting background for the stern lady sitting behind the desk.

She didn't get up but said, 'Good morning, Miss ffinch. Please sit down.'

Matilda got to her feet fifteen minutes later—she had got the job. Her quiet answers seemed to satisfy her questioner; her references, from Dr Bramley and her godfather, who was a bishop, were impeccable. She was asked to start in two days' time and to remain until one week after the end of term. 'You must understand,' said Miss Tremble, 'that this is a temporary post only. You will have one day a week free, that is from directly after breakfast until ten o'clock. It will be one of your duties to get up at night should you be needed. There is a head matron, who will direct you in your work, and another assistant matron who looks after the older girls. Be good enough to come with me so that you may see the school.'

The classrooms were on the ground floor, hives of activity into which she wasn't taken. 'You will have nothing to do with the teaching of the girls, of course,' said Miss Tremble in a quelling voice and led the way up the handsome staircase. The dormitories were airy and comfortable, with four or six beds in each of them. 'The small girls sleep in these four rooms and your room is at the end of the corridor.'

She was shown a small, nicely furnished room with a bathroom leading from it. 'You share this with the assistant matron,' she was told, and, 'There is a small kitchenette where you make tea and coffee if you wish. Your free time will vary from day to day and you will be responsible for accompanying any child who needs to go to the dentist or doctor's surgery.'

She was led downstairs again, bidden goodbye in a voice only slightly less severe than earlier, had her hand shaken with the brisk reminder that she would be expected by ten o'clock on the second day from then, and was ushered out by the wooden-faced maid.

Matilda drove herself home, occasionally breaking into song and uttering little yelps of delight between mental calculations as to how much exactly she would earn. She would have to wait a month, of course, for her cheque and there would be only the extra week after that; all the same, it would be a useful sum. She drove the car round to the garage and went in through the kitchen door.

'Did they give you coffee?' her mother asked, shucking broad beans at the table. 'And did you get the job, Tilly?'

Matilda chucked her jacket over a chair. 'No to the coffee, and yes to the job.' She went to the Aga and fetched the coffee-pot and a mug. 'I start the day after tomorrow...'

'Sit down, darling, and tell me all about it—no, wait a minute, I'll get your father, he's in the study, and Hilary's somewhere...'

They gathered round while she told them and then sat back listening to their pleased remarks. How different from the polite talk when James had visited his grandparents; she felt sorry for him never to have had the simple pleasure of sitting in a loving family circle, knowing that everyone there was as pleased as you were, hanging on every word and then all talking at once. She mustn't think about him though. She was doing what she had said she would do, making a bid for independence. The job was temporary, but it was a first step in the right direction, and the money was three times what Lady Fox had paid her.

Hilary drove her to the school. 'Very impressive,' she observed as they arrived. 'Do you want me to wait?'

'No, love.' Matilda got her case off the back seat and stuck her head through the window. 'Thanks for bringing me. I'll phone as soon as I know when I can have a day off. Someone will have to fetch me and bring me back.'

'Oh, Max is down for the weekend to discuss the wedding—he'll come for you if you're free.'

The same maid opened the door and this time she said, 'Good morning, miss,' and when Matilda asked her name told her it was Winnie. 'And I'm to take you straight to Miss Tremble, miss.'

Matilda put her case down and, following her across the hall, went in to Miss Tremble's room. This time Miss Tremble smiled as she entered. 'I hope that you are prepared to start work at once, Miss ffinch? Winnie will take you to your room and my senior matron, Mrs Down, will tell you exactly what your daily routine will be.'

Mrs Down was comfortably middle-aged and pleased to see Matilda. 'We've been run off our feet, me and Joan—that is, Miss Willis. We're making beds, as you can see, but now that you're here I shall be free to see to the sick-bay, check the laundry and inspect the dormitories. You'll need an overall. Come with me and I'll see if I can find one to fit you.'

Matilda was a girl of noble proportions and it was only after a good deal of searching through various linen cupboards that a garment was found that fitted more or less. 'There are two, thank heaven,' breathed Mrs Down. 'They belonged to a rather stout matron we had for a time. Not that you are stout, my dear. On the contrary, you have a lovely figure—such a small waist too.'

Matilda enveloped herself in the garment, belted it firmly and was led away to inspect the dormitories, where the assistant matron was making beds on her own. She looked cross and Mrs Down said, 'Supposing you give Miss Willis a hand first? Then we'll have a cup of coffee and explain the routine to you.'

When she had gone, Miss Willis said, 'Call me Joan—what's your name?'

'Matilda, and do call me that. Do the little girls call us by our Christian names?'

'Lord, no, Miss Tremble would never allow it. This isn't a free-and-easy place—the children have to behave and there's no familiarity allowed. They're happy enough though.'

The beds made, they went downstairs to a small sitting-room next to the kitchen. 'This is our room,' said Mrs Down. 'Not that we get much time to sit in it. We're supposed to have three hours off each day but it doesn't always work out that way—we take what we can get. You get a day off, of course, but Miss Tremble won't let any of us sleep out.'

'Yes, she told me that, but I don't live very far away—Abner

Magna. Someone will fetch me after breakfast and bring me back in the evening.'

'That's nice. Now, Matilda, I'll explain your work...'

A busy day, thought Matilda, listening carefully, especially mornings and evenings, when a score of small girls would have to be readied for their day and bathed and bedded each night.

'Quite often at weekends parents come down and take them out for tea—that's allowed. We don't get our days off at weekends, by the way.'

Mrs Down bustled away and Matilda was led off to be shown the dining-room, the cloakrooms, the changing-rooms and the room where the children could play in their free time. Despite its imposing appearance and Miss Tremble's rather severe demeanour, the place seemed comfortable and homely and the girls she glimpsed looked happy as they hurried from one class to another.

After that first day she enjoyed her work. She had some twenty small girls in her care but over and above them there were a number of chores she was expected to do so that her days were filled. The food was good and her room, though small, was comfortable. She liked the little girls and they loved her; she tucked them into their beds each night, listened to their small worries, admired pictures of Mummy and Daddy, plaited hair, inspected fingernails and cuddled the tearful victims of bruises and grazed knees. At the end of a week she was given her day off and went home, fetched by Hilary. The day went too quickly—there was such a lot to talk about—and when she had exhausted her descriptions of her work at the school there was plenty of village gossip to be discussed.

'One shouldn't listen to gossip,' observed her mother, 'but one does hear things, you know... They say that Lady Fox has given the new secretary a week's notice, but I don't believe it; she looked very firmly entrenched in church last Sunday. Roseanne is still in hospital, of course. Her arm plaster is to come off next week. Lady Fox is fussing because Mr Scott-Thurlow hasn't sent in his account. I did point out that he wasn't likely to do that until Roseanne is on her feet again and he can discharge her. After all, he's not the butcher or the baker, is he?'

Matilda had gone a little pink at his name but all she said was, 'I wonder when Roseanne and Bernard are going to marry?'

'September, I believe. Dr Bramley told me that Mr Scott-Thurlow is working too hard. That fiancé of his tries to get him to go out in the evenings and spend the weekends with her friends in the country but he almost always refuses.' Mrs ffinch sighed. 'She seems so very unsuitable for him...'

'Well, he doesn't have to marry her,' said Matilda, and just for a moment her eyes shone at the thought. 'But I expect he will,' she added soberly.

Her father drove her back that evening and before she got into her bed she trod softly through the dormitories, making sure that the children were sleeping. Only one little girl was awake. One of the youngest there, Lucy Phelps, almost seven years old, whose parents were somewhere in South America where it wasn't wise to take children. Her father was head of a medical team sent out to get a new hospital started and her mother had gone with him; they wouldn't be home again for months and Lucy was homesick.

Matilda sat down on her bed, put her on her lap and cuddled her and let her cry quietly. 'Three months will go very quickly, darling. Where are you going for your holidays?'

'To my godfather—he's nice but he's not Daddy or Mummy.'

Matilda offered a handkerchief to mop at a small red nose. 'Of course he's not, but aren't you lucky to have him? When you come back after the holidays your mummy and daddy will be coming home in just a few weeks.'

She popped the moppet back into her bed and tucked her up and bent to kiss the wet cheek.

'I like you,' said Lucy, 'I like your name too. Do they call you Tilly at home? Have you got a mummy and daddy?'

'Indeed I have; brothers and sisters too.'

'Mummy promised me that I can have a baby brother or sister when they come home. I shan't have to be a boarder then.'

'Now, that is something nice to look forward to, love. Do go to sleep now.'

The days slipped away, filled with monotonous jobs which seldom varied, but the little girls were fun, she got on well with Mrs

Down and Joan and seldom saw Miss Tremble, and between them they mostly contrived to get an hour or so to themselves each day. On her next free day she had got Hilary to drive her to King's Hall on their way home and went to see how Roseanne was getting on. Her arm was out of plaster now and she was sitting up in bed, her leg still in extension. She was pleased to see Matilda and began at once to talk about herself and Bernard. 'You see my arm is quite all right now, but I've got to stay like this for weeks until my leg's all right. Mr Scott-Thurlow says it will be perfectly sound by September so we shall get married then.' She paused to eye Matilda. 'Mother said you'd got a job at a school. Do you like it?'

'Yes, I do...'

'Are there any men there?'

'Two gardeners and an odd-job man.'

'Don't you want to get married?'

'Not to a gardener or an odd-job man. I must fly; they're expecting me at home.'

The last few days of term came and Matilda was busy packing trunks, finding lost garments, writing labels and washing small heads of hair. Mrs Down was going with the children who had a train journey. The school bus would take them to Yeovil and it was her task to get the little girls into the right trains before boarding the London train herself. Joan was to leave next, to go home to her mother in the Midlands, leaving Matilda to see that the remaining children were collected by parents before beginning on the hefty job of stripping beds, getting the dormitories ready for the maids to clean, tidying the playroom, checking that nothing had been left in drawers or cupboards and then putting out clean bed linen by each bed ready for the beds to be made up before the new term started.

'A pity you won't be here,' commented Mrs Down, 'for you've fitted in very well, Matilda, and you're a good worker, but Joyce will be back—Miss Tremble told me this morning.'

The children were excited, getting them ready for their various journeys took all her time, and it was a relief to see the busload drive off. Joan, with the two little girls she was escorting to Manchester on her way home, left next and that left a bare dozen children, waiting more or less patiently for their parents to fetch them. Most of them were older girls with whom Matilda had had little to do and they went off in ones and twos until she was left with four of the smallest, Lucy among them.

They sat on a wall in the sunshine, hardly moving because they wanted to look their best, and Matilda, sensing their impatience, started a game of 'I spy with my little eye' to keep them occupied.

A car came up the drive and one of the children rushed to meet it; that left Lucy and two sisters. Their father came next, made polite conversation for a few minutes, scooped them up and bore them off. That left Lucy.

'He's not coming...'

'Of course he is, love. Perhaps he's got to drive miles and miles to get here.' As she spoke they both heard the car and stood up expectantly.

'It's here—it's Uncle James!' screamed Lucy as the Rolls came to a quiet stop and Mr Scott-Thurlow got out. He caught the little girl in his arms and hugged her but his eyes were upon Matilda, standing there in her outsize overall, her hair, as usual, rather untidy.

They stared at each other for a long moment until Matilda said inadequately, 'Hello.'

'You do pop up in the most unexpected places,' he said, 'just when I think...' He stopped because someone else had got out of the car—Rhoda, dressed as for a garden party and quite breathtakingly lovely.

She put a gloved hand on Lucy's head. 'Don't blame your uncle because he's late—it was naughty me; I couldn't find the right clothes to wear.' She glanced across to where Matilda was standing. 'The cook—how we do keep meeting, don't we? Is this your latest job?'

Matilda took no notice. She said, 'You're Lucy's godfather...?'

He had an arm round the little girl's shoulders. 'Indeed I am. And you, Matilda, what are you?'

'A school matron—you see, I found a job.'

'Permanent?'

She was so delighted to see him that she didn't stop to think. 'No, I finish at the end of the week...'

'So you will be out of work again,' drawled Rhoda in a sugary voice.

Matilda hadn't heard her. Somehow she and Mr Scott-Thurlow were in a world of their own—not for long, she knew that; he would make some chillingly polite remark and go away again.

She wasn't sure if she could bear that, but she would have to.

'Do you know Uncle James?' piped Lucy. 'You could come and stay with us, Miss ffinch.'

Matilda saw the look on Rhoda's face; she didn't dare look at James. 'Lucy, dear, I have to be here for another week and then I'm going home, but it's very kind of you to think of it.'

Lucy wasn't to be side-tracked. 'Will you be here next term? I won't come back unless you are.'

'Listen, love, your mummy and daddy will be home again in just a few weeks after you come back here and I expect you won't need to be a boarder then.'

'You're not coming back?'

'No. I came for a week or two while Miss Tring was ill. She's better now.'

'But I'll see you again.'

The conversation had gone on long enough. Matilda gave her a hug and kissed a round pink cheek. 'Won't it be fun if we do?' she admonished.

Mr Scott-Thurlow had remained silent; now he took Lucy's hand and started towards the car. His 'goodbye, Matilda' sounded very final.

Rhoda lingered. 'All this fuss over a child—and what are you hoping to get out of it, buttering her up like that? It's nauseating.'

She had lowered her voice, but it had a piercing quality which made it possible for Lucy to hear her. James heard her too.

Matilda put her clenched hands behind her back for fear she might slap Rhoda and turned her back. She stayed like that until she heard the car's engine. She turned round then and waved and called goodbye to Lucy sitting beside her godfather.

The big house was very quiet now that everyone had gone. Miss

Tremble was still there but she would be going on holiday herself on the following day and several of the domestic staff had already gone, leaving the housekeeper, one maid and the gardeners to mind the place. Matilda took herself upstairs and started the beds, glad to have something to do, trying to dismiss from her thoughts Mr Scott-Thurlow's indifference. Yet when he had got out of his car and seen her she could have sworn that he had been pleased to see her. 'Oh, well, no good moping,' muttered Matilda, bundling up sheets as though her life depended on it.

Contrary to her expectations the week went quickly; there was a lot to do but there was the odd hour when she was free to roam the gardens or even, greatly daring, sit down at the piano in the assembly hall and thump out a few tunes. The housekeeper was kind, making sure that she ate the good food she got ready and not complaining when Matilda took her cup of tea and slice of cake out into the garden, to sit under a tree.

She hadn't been paid and she was a little worried about that, but on the day before she was due to go the postman left a letter for her. Miss Tremble had written her a kind note, promising a reference if she wanted one and enclosing her cheque. Matilda sat and admired it for quite a time, thinking of all the things for which it could be used.

Hilary came for her on the last morning and she bade goodbye to the remaining staff, quite sorry to go, but once in the car, exchanging news, her regret was soon forgotten.

'Roseanne knows you're coming home today; could you bear to see her for a few minutes on our way home?'

'Yes, all right. How is she?'

'Waiting impatiently until she's on her feet again. She's having physio so it shouldn't be too long now.' She added, 'She wants you to be one of the bridesmaids.'

'Me? Oh, no—anyway, I doubt if Lady Fox will allow her to invite me to the wedding.'

At the hospital Matilda got out of the car. 'Are you coming in?'

Hilary shook her head. 'I'll give you ten minutes.'

Roseanne was in good spirits and greeted her with delight. 'Only another few weeks,' she began at once, 'then I can get up on crutches. But I don't want to go home until I'm quite well, Mother will only fuss...' She studied Matilda's face. 'You must have been working awfully hard—you're pale or sad or something.'

Matilda let that pass. 'How are the plans for the wedding going?'

Roseanne launched into a detailed and rather muddled account of the plans; the ten minutes was up but there seemed no way in which to stop her. Matilda was searching in vain for a chance to stem the flow when the door opened and Sister came in and, with her, Mr Scott-Thurlow.

Matilda said, 'Oh, lord,' and then blushed scarlet.

Mr Scott-Thurlow, never a man to dissemble, looked surprised in a manner which appeared genuine, which, considering that he had gone to a good deal of trouble to ensure that he should visit Roseanne when Matilda was with her, did him credit. He had taken a lot of trouble to engineer their meeting, suggesting to Roseanne that since Matilda would be going home that morning it would be nice if she called in. 'I'm sure whoever fetches her won't mind suggesting it,' he had said offhandedly and had left the rest to kindly fate, telling himself that he only wished to see Matilda in order to let her know about Lucy and Theobald.

His 'good morning' was suave; he said politely, 'There is no need to leave the room; I merely wish to tell Roseanne that her latest X-ray is most satisfactory. I think we might start the crutches at the end of next week.'

He waited while Roseanne enjoyed an outburst of delight. 'You'll be here?' she asked anxiously.

'Yes, and I shall bring Dr Bramley with me.' He gave her a kindly smile and looked at Matilda, who was quite pale now. 'You have finished at the school?' he asked blandly.

'Yes.'

His small, mocking smile annoyed her, and she wished that she could think of something clever to say to him but she couldn't. Instead she told Roseanne that she really had to be going. 'Hilary's waiting in the car and they are expecting me at home.' She conjured up a smile. 'I'm so glad you're doing so well.'

'You'll come again?'

'Oh, yes, of course. Goodbye.'

She said goodbye to Sister too and, since there was no way of avoiding Mr Scott-Thurlow's elegant bulk leaning in front of the door, she made her farewells to him too. She looked him in the eye as she did so but most annoyingly he had dropped the lids over his eyes and, since his face still wore its bland, pleasant mask, she was unable to discover what he was thinking. Why am I worrying? she mused as she made her way out to the car. He isn't thinking about me, anyway.

She was wrong of course.

'Mr Scott-Thurlow's here,' Hilary told her unnecessarily as she got into the car.

'Yes, I saw him.' Matilda busied herself with her safety-belt and her sister gave her downbent head a thoughtful look. There had been a forlorn note in Matilda's voice. She decided not to pursue the subject and began to talk about her own forthcoming wedding.

At home, once more, Matilda was engulfed in her family; the boys were on holiday, so was Esme, and the house was full. There was no question of a holiday of course although later on in the autumn, when the younger ones were back at school, her father and mother would be going to a small seaside town in Cornwall, exchanging with the vicar of the parish there for two weeks, and shortly Hilary would be going to stay with her future in-laws again.

'Have you any plans?' asked her mother. 'There's your Aunt Penelope, she would love to have you, and you've enough money to enjoy yourself there.'

'I'll think about it,' Matilda told her, anxious to put her parent's mind at rest and not disclose that most of her cheque had been given to her. 'It's nice just being at home.'

She was sitting outside the back door stringing beans with Nelson on her lap. It wasn't very convenient but he had insisted on climbing up, pleased to see her back home again.

'Well, dear, you do just what you want—only it's rather dull for you.'

'Never dull, Mother dear. But I did enjoy that job at the school and I think I'll see if I can get something similar for the autumn term. There are dozens of schools around this part of the world.'

Her mother glanced at her. She was such a lovely girl, and nice-natured into the bargain; true, she had a temper when roused and she was impulsive, but her heart was warm; there must be a man somewhere in the world who would want her for his wife. A pity the world was such a large place and Abner Magna was so remote. Mrs ffinch cast a mental eye over the village; there wasn't a man around who would do for Matilda. Only Mr Scott-Thurlow, and that was a closed book never to be opened.

Matilda found plenty to do now that she was home again; doing the flowers in the church, taking over a class in Sunday school, driving her father around the parish, which was a scattered one, helping in the house and taking her mother into Sherborne to shop, but there was still time to wander off into the country around, sometimes with Esme but more often than not alone.

Two weeks went by, and Matilda, despite her hidden unhappiness, became nicely tanned, which made her eyes greener than ever and her hair even more fiery. She had a sprinkling of freckles too which did nothing to detract from her prettiness, and only when she was alone did she allow her charming mouth to droop and then not for long. She had plenty of good sense; crying for the moon wasn't going to help but a job would. She went into Sherborne to an agency and put her name on their books, and scanned the local paper each week as well as her father's *Telegraph*. Something would turn up, Esme assured her, coming upon her poring over the vacancies column.

It did, the very next day, in the elegant shape of Mr Scott-Thurlow, getting out of his car with the air of a man who knew what he wanted and intended to get it. Matilda was on her knees, grubbing up weeds from the rose-bed under the drawing-room windows, and since she hadn't intended to go out that day she had tied her hair back with a ribbon and put on a wide cotton skirt and a sleeveless top, neither of them either new or fashionable. All the same she looked delightful.

Esme, perched on the steps outside the french window, saw him first. She went dancing to meet him. 'Look who's here,' she called, 'just in time for coffee.'

Matilda turned to look over her shoulder. Mr Scott-Thurlow was strolling towards her. He had abandoned the drive and was crossing the lawn with Esme skipping beside him. She sat back on her heels and waited until he had paused beside her, looming above her head so that she got to her feet quickly. She had become rather pink in the face but her 'good morning' was cool and faintly questioning.

He smiled down at her. 'Good morning, Matilda. I have come to ask a favour of you. Can you spare the time to listen to me?'

She dusted the earth off her hands. 'Of course. Won't you have some coffee? Mother is indoors...'

She led the way into the house, going through the french window into the drawing-room. 'Do sit down,' she said in what Esme called her hostess voice. 'I'll fetch some coffee and tell Mother.'

'Er—might I not have my coffee in the kitchen, if your mother is busy? What I have to say is for everyone to hear.'

Her already warm cheeks glowed. He had made it sound as though she was expecting to have a tête-à-tête with him. The very last thing she wanted, she reminded herself.

Esme had gone ahead, and Matilda opened the drawing-room door without a word and ushered him through, but he paused in the doorway. 'It would be so much easier if we were on a friendlier footing,' he said blandly, and at her indignant little snort, 'Yes, I know I have not given you reason to be friendly, have I? But if you could believe that what I am going to ask of you is not for myself?'

She looked at him then. He appeared severe and remote, but then he smiled slowly, his eyebrows raised.

'All right,' said Matilda gruffly and opened the kitchen door.

Mrs ffinch had the coffee-mugs on the table; a cake, warm from the oven, sat fragrantly on a plate at its centre and in some mysterious fashion the two boys, her father and Mrs Coffin, unnecessarily busy at the sink, were all there with her mother and Esme. Mr Scott-Thurlow was welcomed with what Matilda considered to be unnecessary warmth, bidden to sit down and offered coffee and a slice of the cake while everyone else arranged themselves around the table. He was allowed to drink some coffee and take a bite of the cake before Mrs ffinch said, 'Esme says you want Matilda to do you a favour. Perhaps you would rather talk to her alone after we have had our coffee.'

'There is no need for that, Mrs ffinch. She may wish to discuss what I have to ask of her with you and it will save time if you are told at the same time.'

'Is there such a hurry?' asked Matilda sharply.

'I am going to see Roseanne, and I should like my answer when I come back, in about an hour.'

'What do you want?'

'Not what I want, Matilda,' he corrected her quietly. 'It is what Lucy wants.' He waited while Mrs ffinch refilled his mug. 'She has the mumps and very severely too. My housekeeper, who was also my nanny, is getting on a bit and although she is wonderfully kind and helpful she is tired. Lucy wants you, Matilda—no one else will do save her mother, and that isn't possible as you know. Would you consider coming for a few weeks? There is very little nursing and you will probably be bored but the child is so unhappy...'

'Well, of course I'll come if she wants me.' Matilda spoke impulsively as she so often did and then had second thoughts. 'But wouldn't your fiancée feel—well, perhaps she would rather be with Lucy?'

His 'no' was decisive and made it difficult to pursue the matter.

'Poor little girl,' said Mrs ffinch, 'of course she misses her mother, though I'm sure you do your best, Mr Scott-Thurlow.'

She glanced at her daughter, who frowned heavily and looked at the faces round the table. They all expected her to accept—somehow he had got them all on his side. She said crossly, 'Oh, very well, I'll come, just until Lucy is feeling better.'

'I wouldn't dream of keeping you a moment longer,' said Mr Scott-Thurlow. 'I know that she will be delighted. Now I must go. Could you be ready in just over an hour?'

'I haven't much choice, have I?' She was being rude and she didn't care.

When he had gone her father said mildly, 'You were rather ungracious, Tilly; he is after all doing his best for the child.'

Her mother added, 'Such a kind man, too.'

'Mother!' said Matilda fiercely, and rushed out of the room.

CHAPTER SEVEN

'I DON'T even know where he lives,' grumbled Matilda, flinging things into her case.

'Well, we can ask when he comes back.' Esme was sitting on the bed eating biscuits out of a tin and advising Matilda on what to pack. 'Don't put that old thing in,' she warned, 'it's only fit for the jumble. Take that flowery skirt and lots of tops. Will you have to do your own washing? I wonder what his house happens to be like. I know he's got a housekeeper, but lots of quite poor people have one—she's his nanny anyway, I dare say she lives there and looks after him in return for a home. She'll have her OAP anyway...'

'How you do run on,' said Matilda, who had been wondering the same thing. 'Shall I take the green dress?'

'Yes—you won't need to dress up if you have your meals with him, but if he has people to dinner or drinks you'll have to look decent. Can't you get another dress? I suppose you gave most of your wages to Mother—she'll let you have them back—'

'Certainly not. I don't expect to lead a social life, love, but I'll pack the green thing if you think I should.' She burrowed into her wardrobe. 'I'd better wear the patterned blouse and skirt.' She glanced at the clock on the mantelpiece. 'Oh, lord, he'll be here in ten minutes. Shut this case for me, there's a dear, and I'll get changed.'

She was thrusting pins into a severe French pleat when Esme asked, 'Do you suppose that Rhoda will be there? In his house...?'

'Probably,' said Matilda thickly through the pins. 'She is going to marry him after all.' It hurt to say that.

'I mean, does she live there?'

Matilda withdrew the pins from her mouth the better to speak clearly. 'I think it is very unlikely. Doctors and the like have to think of their reputations.'

'You'll be living there with him, though,' went on Esme, never one to mince matters.

'I shall be employed by Mr Scott-Thurlow, and that's quite different.'

'Why? I can't see...' Luckily she paused when she heard the car coming up the drive. 'He's here—I'll take your case. Come along, do, you can't keep him waiting.' As they went downstairs she hissed, 'Is he going to pay you?'

'I suppose so.'

'How much?'

Matilda quelled her with a frown and crossed the hall to where Mr Scott-Thurlow stood talking to her father and mother.

'You will want to know where you're going,' he observed in the mildest of tones. 'Lucy is in London with me at present, and as soon as she is well enough I thought you might go, the pair of you, to a cottage I have near Dartmouth—Stoke Fleming—the sea air will do her good.'

It would be more than two hundred miles from London, reflected Matilda. 'It sounds a splendid idea,' she said quietly. 'Whereabouts in London, Mr Scott-Thurlow?'

'Near Piccadilly and Oxford Street. Just off Orchard Street.'

'Isn't that near Wigmore Street?'

'Yes. Fifteen Blenheim Street. Your father has the address and the phone number.'

The rector nodded. 'We shall no doubt hear from Matilda once she has settled in. I hope that she will be of assistance to you and that the little girl will get well quickly.'

Everyone had gathered in the hall by now and Matilda began a round of goodbyes while Mr Scott-Thurlow shook her parents' hands and then waited patiently while she embraced her mother and father.

She twisted round in her seat to wave goodbye as they drove away and said with a snap, 'You're always in such a hurry.' She shot him a cross look and he said gravely, 'I'm sorry about that, Matilda. I promise you that I won't badger you once you are installed and I'll send you down to Stoke Fleming just as soon as Lucy is fit to travel.'

Why not? she thought unhappily, he—and certainly Rhoda—wouldn't want them at his London home. He was doubtless a good godfather and anxious to do his best for the child, but he had his work and more than that he had Rhoda.

He was silent for a while but presently he began to tell her about Lucy. 'She feels wretched, her throat is sore and she is feverish and cross, and above all she misses her father and mother. I'm hoping that you will be able to fill that gap to some extent. She seems very attached.'

The car phone interrupted him and he slowed his speed. He listened for what seemed to Matilda to be a long time, then said, 'I shall be an hour late, Henry. Let Theatre know and if possible get on with that last case yourself. The tendon. How's that boy? Good, I'll see him before I go to Theatre—be around, will you? Goodbye.'

'What boy?' asked Matilda, who liked to know things.

'A nice lad with a fractured spine; he was knocked down by a car last night—'

'Last night? You operated in the night and then drove down here to Roseanne and—and us?'

'Driving is very soothing,' he said smoothly.

'You ought to be in your bed.'

'I don't need a great deal of sleep and I promise I won't doze off over the wheel.'

'I am not in the least nervous, Mr Scott-Thurlow.'

'I suppose it's no use asking you to call me James?'

'No use at all...'

'May I know why?' He was driving fast along the A303 and despite the good weather the traffic was thin.

When she didn't answer he said, 'Ah, well, it is of little consequence.'

He drove on for a time and neither of them spoke. Presently he said, 'I'm afraid there isn't time to stop for lunch on the way—Mavis will have something for you when we get in. You must forgive me if I go straight on to the hospital. Perhaps we can talk this evening when I get home.'

'Very well.' She added impulsively, 'I do hope someone sees

that you have something to eat when you get there. You can't work on an empty stomach.'

He forbore from telling her how many times he had done just that and had hardly been aware of it. 'My theatre sister takes good care of me,' he said carelessly.

She sat quietly, watching the countryside flash by now that they were on the motorway, and now and again she stole a glance at his profile, very calm and rather stern, and at his large, well-kept hands resting lightly on the wheel. Her feelings were mixed; she longed for the drive to go on forever and at the same time wished it were over.

He slowed the car as they reached the suburbs, weaving his way through narrow streets until he came out into Millbank, then Whitehall, Trafalgar Square and thence into Pall Mall and St James's Street and so at last to Orchard Street and the narrow street leading off it. Blenheim Street was a cul-de-sac with what looked like mews at its further end. The houses on either side of it were narrow with bow-fronted windows and each had delicate fanlights over their pristine front doors. Early Regency, thought Matilda, peering out of her window, and charming. Mr Scott-Thurlow stopped his car, got out and opened her door and invited her to alight, and at the same time a door was opened and an elderly man, very neatly dressed, came down the few steps to meet them.

'Ah, Twigg, Miss ffinch has come to help us with Lucy. Matilda, this is Twigg, who runs my home with his wife. There's a case in the boot, Twigg; I'll come in for a moment but I must leave within minutes. See that Miss ffinch has lunch, will you?'

As he talked he had ushered her into the house and Twigg put down her case and opened a door in the small square hall. It was charming, red-carpeted, its white walls hung with paintings and lighted by wall brackets, and the room which they entered was just as delightful. It overlooked the street, its bow window draped with chintz curtains patterned in soft dim blues and greens and pinks, colours echoed in the magnificent carpet which covered the parquet floor. The furniture was a nice mingling of delicate rosewood cabinets and tables and comfortable sofas and chairs.

Matilda, taking one swift look, approved of it; it was exactly to her taste and despite its elegance it exuded an atmosphere of cosiness.

Mr Scott-Thurlow waved her to a chair. 'I do apologise for rushing you like this. As I said we can have a talk this evening; in the meantime Mavis and Twigg will look after you. But first I will take you up to see Lucy.'

They mounted a graceful curving staircase at the back of the hall to the narrow gallery above. There were several doors here but he turned down a narrow passage leading to the back of the house and opened one of the doors at its end. The room was large and light with a big window overlooking quite a sizeable garden. It was charmingly furnished with white-painted furniture and flower-patterned curtains and quilt and Lucy was sitting up in the bed, her small face rendered grotesque by the mumps, flushed and hot but instantly overjoyed at the sight of them. There were two dogs on the end of the bed, one of which was Theobald, and Matilda hardly recognised him, for he was now well fed and very clean, a happy tongue lolling out of his foxy little face. The other dog was a golden Labrador with a gentle face. They got off the bed and Mr Scott-Thurlow caressed them as he advanced to the bed.

'Your Theobald,' he said to Matilda, 'and this is Canada.' He bent to kiss the small girl holding her arms out to him.

'Here is our Lucy. Say hello to Matilda, darling; she has come to keep you company.'

Matilda bent to kiss the child and was held in a throttling embrace. 'I knew you'd come—Uncle James said you would. You're the next best thing to my mummy. Will you live here?'

'Well, until you're fit enough to go to school and by then your mummy will soon be home again.'

Mr Scott-Thurlow put a hand on her arm. 'Mavis will be here presently to show you to your room and answer your questions. Then you will have lunch of course.' He bent to kiss Lucy again, disentangling himself gently from her small arms and went to the door, where he paused, turned round and came back again.

'I haven't thanked you,' he told Matilda and bent his handsome head and kissed her too.

Matilda opened an indignant mouth to utter the scathing words on her tongue and then she thought better of it; Lucy was watching. 'Daddy always kisses Mummy when he has to go away,' she remarked.

Matilda conjured up a bright smile and stooped to pat Theobald. She looked composed when she lifted her head just in time to see Mr Scott-Thurlow disappear through the door, Canada at his heels.

'Why Canada?' she asked.

'She's a Labrador,' Lucy explained kindly. 'Didn't you think of that?' and then, 'You won't stay away for long, will you?'

The door opened then and Mrs Twigg came in, a stout elderly woman with small bright eyes in a round cheerful face. 'Welcome, Miss ffinch, and I hope you'll be happy with us. I'll take you to your room if you're ready to see it now and Twigg has laid a nice little lunch for you in the dining-room. Ever so glad we are that Lucy will have you. I've done me best, miss, but I'm not so young any more. She's a dear little girl and no trouble.'

She exchanged a beaming smile with Lucy and Matilda said, 'I won't be long, darling. Do you have a little nap in the afternoons?'

'Sometimes, but I'll read my book and wait until you come back—may I call you Matilda too?'

'Of course you may.'

Matilda was led away but not very far. Her room was in the corridor too, at the side of the house with a window overlooking a corner of the garden. It was just as pretty a room as Lucy's, furnished in some pale wood she thought might be yew. It had fitted cupboards along one wall and a bathroom, tiled in very pale pink and equipped with everything a girl might need.

'I hope there's all you want, miss,' said Mrs Twigg, 'and just you ask if there is anything at all that we can do for you.'

'It's lovely, Mrs Twigg. Would you like me to come down now for lunch? I can unpack later.'

She followed Mrs Twigg downstairs again and into a fair-sized room opposite the drawing-room where Twigg was waiting.

'A glass of sherry, Miss ffinch? You will take soup?'

She lunched with a good appetite; the food was delicious and Mrs Twigg was a splendid cook. Mr Scott-Thurlow might be a very busy man, she reflected, but when he wasn't being busy he had all the creature comforts he could wish for.

She went back presently and found Lucy hot and restless.

'Another nightie?' she suggested. 'And I'll bathe your face and hands, shall I? Then you'll feel cooler.'

Which she did and then shook up the pillows, gave Lucy a drink and suggested that she should read to her. The child looked ill and very feverish, and since there was a thermometer in a little jar on the dressing-table she took her temperature. It was over a hundred and one and after a little muddled arithmetic she decided that was over forty degrees Celsius. A bit high, but Mr Scott-Thurlow would certainly have been keeping a check on that. She settled down close to the bed and opened *The Lion, the Witch and the Wardrobe* and began to read.

Presently Lucy fell asleep and Matilda sat in the quiet room with no other sound but Theobald's gentle snores. After a while she got up silently and went to her room, leaving the doors open, and unpacked the few things she had brought with her and then went back to sit quietly again; when Lucy woke she would probably be cross and hot and thirsty.

She was all of these things and she wanted her mother. Matilda sponged her small swollen face, mopped her tears, gave her a drink and wrapped her in one of the light wool blankets on the bed before sitting her down on her lap.

'You shall tell me all about Mummy and Daddy, and if you want to cry go ahead, darling, and I won't mind a bit.'

Lucy sniffed mightily. 'You really don't mind? Rhoda says I'm a cry-baby.'

'Pooh to Rhoda. Tell me—is your Mummy pretty?'

Lucy embarked on a description of her mother, pausing for a little weep now and then. She was very hot and Matilda wondered if she should have left her in bed. At least the child was calmer now. She was wondering what was best to be done when there was a knock on the door and Mrs Twigg came in.

'A nice cup of tea,' she said in her soft voice. 'I'll put the tray on this little table so's you can reach it. There's ice-cream for Lucy too. Mr James said as how she could have that.'

'Why doesn't Uncle James come home?' Lucy wanted to know.

'He'll be here in no time, my pretty. Just you let Miss ffinch get her tea while you eat your ice-cream.'

'Her name's Matilda.'

Mrs Twigg looked at Matilda.

'No one ever calls me Miss ffinch...'

'Well, then, Miss Matilda, will that do?'

Lucy nodded a satisfied head and Mrs Twigg trotted off. Matilda longed for a cup of tea; it had been a strange day and she was getting tired. She hadn't phoned her mother yet, her hair was springing loose from its pins and she hadn't even gone round the house to find her way about the place.

Lucy ate her ice-cream and promptly went to sleep, leaving Matilda to clasp her in her arms and watch the teapot, trying to work out a way of reaching it without waking the child up.

The minutes ticked by and all Matilda could think about was how to get a cup of tea; the more she thought about it, the thirstier she became.

Ten minutes passed as slowly as ten weeks, then the door opened and Mr Scott-Thurlow came in. He took in the situation at a glance, and without speaking went to the bed, tidied it, rearranged the pillows, came to Matilda and scooped Lucy off her lap and tucked her into bed. She didn't stir as he took her pulse and felt her head.

'Drink your tea,' he advised Matilda. 'Has it been here long? Would you like a fresh pot?'

'This is quite all right. Do you want some?'

'I had a cup at the hospital.' He sat down in a chair opposite hers. 'How has she been this afternoon?'

'Hot and tearful but she cheered up and ate her ice-cream. She went to sleep all at once before I could get her back into bed.' She added, 'She's feeling wretched, isn't she, poor moppet?'

He leaned forwards and handed her a plate of small sandwiches. She took one and offered them to him. He looked hungry.

He took one and said, 'Now let us go over the routine for you.

You will be busy enough for the next few days but by then Lucy will be feeling better and you will have some time to yourself. Mavis will take over from you for an hour in the afternoon—not long, I'm afraid, but you can sit in the garden. Have you phoned your mother?'

She gave him a limpid look. 'No.'

He frowned. 'That was a silly question. Go and do it now as soon as you have had your tea. I'll stay here.'

So she finished her second cup and hurried downstairs and found Twigg to ask where she could phone. There were, it seemed, phones in almost all the rooms; she went into the drawing-room and found Canada lying before the open french window and bent to pat her, wondering when anyone had the time to take the dog walking. Her mother answered her when she rang but she didn't waste time gossiping. 'I'll write,' she promised. 'I must go back to Lucy now. Everything is fine.'

Lucy was still asleep with she went into the room, and Mr Scott-Thurlow was asleep too, lying back untidily in his chair, his long legs stretched out before him so that she had to step over them to get to her chair.

She sat and pondered as to whether she should wake him or not. He had said that he wanted to talk to her, tell her what her duties were; on the other hand he probably needed his sleep. She studied his face lovingly and was suddenly aware that he was watching her from half-closed eyes.

He began without preamble, 'Your duties are vague, I'm afraid—a surrogate mother is the nearest to them and you are, as far as I can make out, the only one whom Lucy fancies in the role.'

'Surely there must be aunts or cousins or—or what about Miss Symes?'

She shouldn't have said that. He said in a voice as bland as his face, 'Her aunts and cousins are scattered far and wide and I don't quite know why you should mention Rhoda.'

'Why shouldn't I mention her?' she snapped. 'She's going to marry you and I should have thought you would have asked her—she knows Lucy.' She gave him a fiercely defiant look, her insides quaking at the expression on his face. Ferocious was the only word for it.

'I do not think that you need to concern yourself with the whys and wherefores, Matilda. If you would be good enough to listen without interrupting, I will give you some idea of what you may expect from day to day while you are here.'

His voice was coolly civil as he outlined her duties. He was brief too and when he had finished he asked, 'Is there anything else you would like to know?' and when she shook her head, 'Then I suggest that you have a breath of air in the garden. I shall be here for half an hour or so.'

So she found her way out of the house through a small side-door and wandered up and down between the flower-beds, feeling miserable. She had been silly to have dragged Rhoda's name into it in the first place, it was none of her business anyway. She would have to apologise...

She went back presently and found Lucy awake and sitting on his knee, sharing one of her picture books with him, but as she went in he popped the child back into her bed.

'I'll be in my study if you should want me. Twigg will let you know when dinner is ready. Lucy has had rather an exciting day; I dare say she will eat her supper and go to sleep very quickly.'

He went to the door and Matilda followed him. 'I'm sorry I was rude,' she said, 'I can't think why I spoke like that.'

He smiled down at her. 'I have always understood that redheads have a habit of speaking before they think. You are no exception.'

After he had gone she busied herself getting Lucy washed and into a fresh nightie before her supper of soup and more ice-cream, and that done she fetched a book and began to read to the child. It was a favourite of Lucy's and of Matilda's too, *The Secret Garden*, and she stopped frequently to talk about it for they both agreed there could be nothing nicer than having a secret place where one might go, and at Lucy's suggestion Matilda undertook to accompany her when she was well again to see if such a place could be found.

'You're really very nice,' said Lucy and fell asleep, and ten minutes later Mrs Twigg arrived soft-footed.

'Twigg's just about to serve dinner, miss, if you'd like to go down.'

'Have I time to tidy myself, Mrs Twigg?'

'No need, miss, there b'ain't no guests this evening.'

So she went downstairs, rehearsing in her mind the kind of conversation she would have with Mr Scott-Thurlow. The weather was safe enough, and Roseanne's leg, Theobald and his grandparents—there were plenty of innocuous subjects.

'In here.' His voice came from the drawing-room and she went in, surprised to find him in a dinner-jacket. 'You have time for a drink,' he told her and offered her a chair. 'I'm dining out but Twigg will see that you have everything you would like.' He poured her a glass of sherry. 'I dare say you're tired; it has been a busy day for you.' He sounded uninterested.

'No busier than yours, I should think,' said Matilda, determined to be polite. 'I expect you have very little time to yourself.' Her eyes fell upon Theobald and Canada, sitting side by side, their eyes on their master. 'Whenever do you get time to take the dogs for a walk?'

He smiled a little. 'Before breakfast—Twigg takes them during the day and I walk them again before I go to bed.'

She drank her sherry too quickly. 'I expect you want to go out…'

'As soon as Rhoda arrives. You must stay a moment and meet her.' His voice held amusement and his eyes gleamed with it when she said,

'Oh, yes, that will be delightful.'

Rhoda came a few minutes later and Matilda, twiddling her empty glass in her hand, wished she hadn't tossed off her sherry quite so quickly.

Rhoda looked lovely, but then she always did. Vivid green satin under an enormous velvet cloak and Italian shoes with gleaming buckles. She pecked Mr Scott-Thurlow's cheek and said, 'Darling, you're actually ready. I'm so glad—the Mathersons' dinners are always such fun and one meets all the right people—prospective patients for you…' She laughed and Matilda watched the look of distaste hidden at once behind that bland mask.

He said, 'Matilda has arrived, you see. Lucy is delighted and so am I to be able to leave the child in such capable hands.'

Rhoda smiled across at Matilda. 'Can you nurse as well as cook?' she wanted to know. 'You really are a paragon.' She didn't hide her scorn.

To which piece of rudeness Matilda could find no answer. It was Mr Scott-Thurlow who spoke. 'Some day some lucky man will make her his wife.' He smiled across the room at Matilda as he said it and she smiled back, dully conscious that she felt suddenly shy, and Rhoda, watching them both, said quite sharply,

'Well, we had better be going, darling. Come back to my place after the Mathersons'—there are so many plans…'

She nodded at Matilda as she went out of the room, but Mr Scott-Thurlow paused by her chair. 'Breakfast is at eight o'clock,' he told her. 'I hope you sleep well. Goodnight, Matilda.'

She ate her solitary dinner presently under the kindly eye of Twigg. The food was delicious but she hardly noticed what she had on her plate. She was entirely occupied with the unsuitability of Rhoda as Mr Scott-Thurlow's wife. She would ruin him, or try to—turn him into a fashionable surgeon when really what he wanted to do was to use his skill upon anyone who needed it, never mind if they could pay or not. That he was a wealthy man was apparent to her now but she had the feeling that it was a matter of little importance to him. She wondered for the hundredth time why on earth he was going to marry Rhoda.

She thanked Twigg for his attentions and went back upstairs to find that Lucy was soundly sleeping and, since she had nothing better to do, she had a leisurely bath and went to bed herself.

She was up soon after six o'clock, roused by Lucy's small unhappy voice demanding a drink, to have her bed made more comfortable and someone to talk to.

Matilda pottered to and fro making the child comfortable, and since it was still so early suggested that she should go on with *The Secret Garden*.

'I'm thirsty,' declared Lucy, 'I'd like a cup of tea.'

Matilda quite fancied one herself. 'All right, why not? I'll pop down to the kitchen and make us some. I'll have to boil a kettle so don't expect me back for about five minutes.'

The house was quiet as she went downstairs, hoping that the dogs, who probably slept in the kitchen, wouldn't bark when they saw her. She went through the baize door at the back of the hall and crept into the kitchen. It was a delightful place with a well-scrubbed table and rows of polished pans on the walls and an old dresser with rows of plates. There was an Aga too but her eye fastened on an electric kettle.

She filled it, switched it on, peered around for the dogs, who were nowhere to be seen, and went in search of a teapot and cups.

She had made the tea, found milk and sugar and a tray and was on her way to the door when it was opened and the dogs came dashing in followed by Mr Scott-Thurlow in elderly trousers and a cotton sweater.

If he was surprised he didn't show it. His 'good morning' was polite and slightly questioning.

'Lucy woke early, she wants a cup of tea.' Matilda was very conscious of her hair all over the place and her dressing-gown, flung on without due regard to her appearance. She looked at the dogs, grinning at her from either side of their master. 'You've been out,' she said foolishly.

'Our usual morning walk. Is there a cup of tea for me?' When she nodded he picked up the tray and, accompanied by the dogs, they went upstairs.

Lucy was delighted. The dogs got on to the bed and settled down beside her and Mr Scott-Thurlow put the tray on a bedside table and sat on the bed too. 'Slept well?' he wanted to know. 'Stick out your tongue...'

Matilda poured the tea and sat down primly in a chair by the window to drink hers. When she was asked she said that yes, she had slept very well and that no, Lucy hadn't wanted anything during the night.

He finished his tea and got up to go. 'Breakfast at eight o'clock sharp,' he reminded her. He wandered over to the door and stood there looking at her. 'Get dressed first,' he said softly.

She dressed with ferocious speed, muttering crossly to herself, and scraped her glorious hair back into a tight French pleat, under a false impression that it made her look severe, whereas it made her look like a little girl whose hair had been pinned up out of the way ready for her bath.

When she went downstairs she went straight to the kitchen for Lucy's tray only to have it taken from her by a respectful Twigg. 'I will see that Lucy has her breakfast, miss—Maisie, here,' he nodded towards a young girl making toast, 'will come with me and stay with her until you have had your own breakfast. Mr Scott-Thurlow is in the dining-room already.'

So she went to the dining-room to find him there at the table, reading the paper. He got up when she went in, seated her and invited her to help herself to whatever she wanted.

'You don't find this too early?' he asked her politely.

'Not at all. Only shouldn't I be with Lucy?'

'No. I've been to see her again. Her temperature is down, which is a good sign, but I must warn you that as she improves she is likely to be peevish. I rely upon you to cope with that.'

He maintained a steady flow of small talk until they had finished the meal; he was, she conceded, a very good host although she found his reserve chilling. He got up to go presently with a word of apology. 'I seldom get home for lunch,' he told her, 'but I should be back rather earlier than usual this afternoon. Remember that you should get out for an hour after lunch. Mrs Twigg will sit with Lucy.'

He laid a hand lightly on her shoulder as he went past her chair. Long after he had gone she could feel the imprint of it there too.

That evening, strolling in the garden after her solitary dinner, she reflected that she had enjoyed her day despite the fact that just as they were sitting down to dinner Mr Scott-Thurlow had been called to the hospital, and now, two hours later, there was still no sign of him. Twigg had told her that this was often the case and there was no knowing when he would return, 'So just you enjoy your dinner, Miss Matilda, and take a turn in the garden; it's a splendid evening.'

She had been kept busy during the day with Lucy, who, just as Mr Scott-Thurlow had predicted, was inclined to be peevish, but she had devised games and read until her throat was dry and the child had settled down for a nap after lunch so that she was able to go for a quick walk in the quiet streets near the house while Mrs Twigg sat and knitted in Lucy's room. When she had returned there was just time to freshen up Lucy before her godfather, true to his promise, came home and they had tea together. He had looked tired, but he had set himself to amuse the child and the little meal was a happy one.

When it was quite dark she went indoors, made sure that Lucy was asleep and took herself off to bed. She was pleasantly tired but she didn't go to sleep—she lay awake listening for Mr Scott-Thurlow's return. It was one o'clock in the morning before she heard his quiet tread on the landing and the gentle closing of his door.

The days slipped easily into each other and by the end of a week Lucy was very nearly her old self again. She had the run of the house and she and Matilda spent a good deal of time playing duets on the piano in a small sitting-room at the back of the house. The child was talented and Matilda played with verve and a great many wrong notes and they enjoyed themselves hugely. They saw very little of Mr Scott-Thurlow for now that Lucy was out of her bed she and Matilda breakfasted after he had left the house. He himself had suggested it in a manner which led her to assume that he didn't wish for their company at that meal, and, since he came rarely to lunch at his own house and when he did dine at home his cool courtesy towards her successfully put a stop to any remarks she might make other than mundane ones about the weather, she rapidly reached the conclusion that he disliked her. If that was so, however, why had he asked her to come and look after Lucy?

Even that melancholy thought couldn't stop her loving him.

The days were warm now and she took Lucy out into the garden where they played clock golf, much hindered by the dogs. Nothing more had been said about their visit to Stoke Fleming and Matilda began to hope that he had decided not to send them away. Perhaps he would take a holiday himself and go somewhere with Lucy and Rhoda, for she herself wouldn't be needed for much longer—an opinion not shared by Rhoda, who arrived one afternoon shortly after Matilda had tucked Lucy up for her rest and then had gone downstairs to sit in the garden.

Her greeting was perfunctory. 'How can you bear to sit in the sun?' she asked, and arranged herself carefully in the shade of some artfully planted silver birch trees. 'Where's that child? Isn't she well yet? It's high time she was sent down to Devon; I absolutely refuse to have her tagging around any longer. James has his nose buried in that wretched hospital all day and half the night and I'm sick of making excuses for him. I'll talk to him and get him to send you both away, then perhaps he will be able to lead a more civilised life again. You can stay down there until she's due back at school...'

Matilda's eyes opened wide. 'Oh, that won't be possible; I came to look after Lucy until she was well again, and she is now, so I am free to go home.' She smiled sweetly. 'Why can she not go on holiday with you? I understood that she had been invited to spend the whole of her summer holidays with Mr Scott-Thurlow.'

'Who cares what you understood?' asked Rhoda rudely. 'He pays you so you'll do what he wants.'

'Perhaps he doesn't want me to go to Stoke Fleming...' Matilda's voice was pure syrup.

Rhoda laughed. 'We'll see about that...'

'What will you see about, Rhoda?' asked Mr Scott-Thurlow from the french window.

'Darling, how you startled me. We were discussing plans. Matilda is looking forward to going down to the cottage with Lucy—'

'No, I'm not,' said Matilda. She spoke pleasantly but her green eyes blazed.

Mr Scott-Thurlow lounged over to where she was sitting so that she felt obliged to look up at him looming over her.

'Now that is a pity,' he said gently, 'for I have arranged for you to go down to Devon in two days' time.'

CHAPTER EIGHT

MR SCOTT-THURLOW had an 'I told you so' look on his handsome features. 'I did mention that you would be going to Stoke Fleming as soon as Lucy was well enough and since you raised no objection I went ahead with my plans.'

Rhoda gave a brittle laugh. 'There, did I not say so? How lucky you are getting a holiday for free, Matilda. Darling, I'll cancel my engagements—where shall we go? Will you get tickets? Do be sure that the hotel is a good one—will it be too hot in the Bahamas?'

He had been staring at Matilda and she had been unable to look away for his gaze held hers but now he turned to Rhoda. 'I'm committed to a seminar in Leiden and a couple of lectures in Oslo and I must be back as soon as possible—I have a backlog of urgent cases...'

A speech Matilda heard with satisfaction and Rhoda with ill-concealed temper.

'What am I supposed to do?' she wanted to know. 'Don't think I'm trailing round Europe while you make dreary speeches about bones. The Burches asked me to go to Bangkok; I shall go with them.'

'It sounds delightful; there is no reason why you should get bored while I lecture. Besides, there would be little time to spend together; these sessions carry their quota of dinners and drinks parties and I'm ashamed to say that we all talk shop.'

'I suppose you're going back to that beastly hospital or rooms until midnight or longer. We're supposed to be at dinner with the Burches, or had you forgotten?'

'No, I phoned my excuses half an hour ago. They're expecting you and said they would get another man.'

Matilda, watching Rhoda, saw how her ill temper had made her quite ugly; it was a pity that Mr Scott-Thurlow hadn't seemed to notice that for he was smiling at Rhoda quite charmingly.

'I'm going,' said Rhoda coldly.

He went with her into the house and presently returned to where Matilda was still sitting.

'Have you nothing to say?' he asked. 'I feel sure that you are bottling up a number of searing speeches calculated to put me in my place.'

'Well, I am, but what would be the use?'

'None at all, so swallow your dudgeon and listen to me... You will be kind enough to get your things together tomorrow and Lucy's too, telephone your family by all means—I have already told your mother. I will be here by eight o'clock on the day after tomorrow, so be ready to leave then. We should get to the cottage by lunchtime. There is a housekeeper, my mother's cook, pensioned off—her name is Emma Truscott, and she will have everything ready for you both. Please get Lucy out of doors as much as possible but don't let her get tired. But I don't need to tell you this—you're a sensible young woman. In just over two weeks she must return to school, when your duties will end.'

'Why should I do this?' demanded Matilda. 'You come here without a by your leave—'

'It is my house,' he reminded her blandly.

'You know very well what I mean, Mr Scott-Thurlow; I feel as though I'm being—being trampled underfoot.' She glared at him and looked quite enchanting. 'Do this, do that, go here, go there! I don't know why I put up with it.'

'Yes, you do, Matilda.' He watched the colour flood into her face. 'But when you address me so severely as Mr Scott-Thurlow I realise what a despot I am.'

He sounded so meek that she wanted to laugh and did.

'That's better. Shall we have tea out here? Go and get Lucy and I'll tell Twigg.'

Lucy was enchanted with the idea of going down to Devon. She plied her godfather with questions while they had their tea until he said, 'I must get back to my rooms—I have several patients to see.' He got up and stopped to receive Lucy's hug and kiss. 'Remember to be ready to leave promptly,' he reminded Matilda. He hesitated, staring down at her, smiling wryly, but he didn't say anything, only nodded briefly as he went.

It was Twigg who told her that evening that Mr Scott-Thurlow had gone to Birmingham to operate at one of the hospitals there. 'Some tricky case, I'll be bound, Miss Matilda; he gets called all over the place, so he does.'

They were up early on the day of their departure and went down to breakfast soon after seven o'clock to find Mr Scott-Thurlow already at the table. His 'good morning' was genial and followed by the observation that he was delighted to see them up so promptly.

'Will you stay at the cottage with us?' asked Lucy.

'No, I shall have to come back here this evening; I'm going to Leiden tomorrow.'

'You will come down and see us though?' Lucy persisted.

'Well, we'll have to see about that. Shall we take Canada and Theobald with us?'

Matilda and Lucy chorused, 'Of course,' and two pairs of eyes gave him an indignant look. 'They don't see much of you anyway,' declared Matilda.

His smile was mocking. 'Sometimes I suspect that you would wish to change my life for me, Matilda.'

She choked over her coffee. 'Certainly not,'

She spoke with such vehemence that he laughed. 'You're not much good at telling fibs,' he told her.

They set off in good time with Lucy on the back seat, Theobald on her lap and Canada sitting very erect beside her. Matilda settled into her seat beside Mr Scott-Thurlow and cast about for harmless topics of conversation. She tried the weather, the charm of the country, the pleasure of driving early in the day and so on, then since she had received nothing but grunts and monosyllables in reply, lapsed into silence.

Presently he said, 'You have no need to make small talk with me, Matilda, I am very content to drive with you silent beside me.'

At which remark she drew a long, smouldering breath. 'If you will stop for a moment I will change places with Lucy...'

He answered her seriously, although she suspected that he was laughing to himself. 'No, no that won't be necessary. Have I offended you? I'm sorry; I haven't had much practice with pretty speeches.'

'Well, it's time you had,' said Matilda wrathfully. 'You'll have to change your ways when you get married.'

'I suspect that they will be changed for me.'

She frowned; it had seemed to her that Rhoda would be quite content with a husband who was absorbed in his work and left her free to live the social life she seemed to love. She uttered her thoughts out loud.

'Has she gone to Bangkok?' The words were out before she could stop them, but before she could do anything about it he answered her in an ordinary voice with no surprise in it.

'Yesterday. The Burches were delighted that she could go with them; I imagine that she will enjoy herself enormously.'

Matilda muttered a reply, very red in the face, and he, glancing quickly at her, smiled slowly and then said over his shoulder, 'I thought we'd stop presently, Lucy—would you like that?'

They were north of Salisbury by now, still on the A303, and it was after they had passed Wincanton that he said, 'Your mother suggested that we might stop for coffee,' and turned off on to a side-road. 'We can't stay long but you will have the time to collect anything you may want.'

'Thank you. May Lucy go into the sea?'

'If the day is warm and she stays only a short time. Do you wish to swim?'

'Yes.'

Then they didn't speak again until he drew up outside her home.

The entire ffinch family came out to meet them; Matilda wondered if Mr Scott-Thurlow was comparing the warmth and noise of their reception with the cool and perfect manners of Rhoda. It was impossible to tell from his expression and his own manners were too good to give her a clue. Lucy, instantly made much of, was borne away to the kitchen by Esme to be refreshed with cake and lemonade while the rest of the party strolled after them. The kitchen door was open and the sunlight streamed in to the comfortably shabby room, smelling of freshly ground coffee and newly baked cakes. Matilda saw Mr Scott-Thurlow's splendid nose twitch appreciatively.

'You're in a hurry,' said her mother, 'so I thought it better if we had coffee here—Tilly, you'll want to run upstairs and collect some clothes, I suspect. Hilary put everything out on the bed, ready to pack. If you'll just pick out what you're going to want, my dear.'

'I'll go now, while you're pouring the coffee. Thanks, Hilary...'

She flew upstairs and found the elderly zipper bag they all borrowed in turn in the bedroom and a couple of cotton dresses neatly pressed and folded. Her swimsuit was there too and some old sandals, just right for the beach. She packed the bag, added a thick sweater in case it turned chilly and went back to the kitchen, to find everyone there, some sitting at the table, the younger ones milling around, in and out of the garden.

Mindful of Mr Scott-Thurlow's wishes, she gobbled her cake, swallowed down her coffee and pronounced herself ready to leave, but another ten minutes was wasted while she made her protracted goodbyes and the dogs were rounded up and they were all stowed into the car once more.

'What a pity you can't go and see your grandparents,' said Matilda at the end of her polite speech of thanks. 'You practically pass their door...'

'No time. I'll call on my way back.' They were again on the A303 and he sent the Rolls forwards at the steady maximum speed allowed. They joined the A30 presently and then turned off on to the motorway south of Exeter. Here he could travel faster and the big car shot effortlessly ahead, eating up the miles, and so on towards Plymouth and to the road over Haldon and then the long straight stretch to Buckfastleigh and Totnes and all too soon—from her point of view—they were on the road to Kingsbridge.

'This is the long way round,' said Mr Scott-Thurlow, 'but it is by far the prettiest road.' At Kingsbridge he took the road to Torcross and then raced along Slapton Sands with the beach on one side of them and a charming lake on the other, and at its end he took the car smartly up the steep wooded road which led to the village.

Stoke Fleming rambled on either side of the road; small white and pink painted cottages with thatched roofs and gardens bright with flowers, and splendid views of the beach and sea below. He turned the car down a narrow lane and in through an open gateway and stopped before the open door of a traditionally pink-washed cottage, its thatched roof pierced by small lattice windows and surrounded by a fair-sized lawn and a wealth of flower-beds. He leaned over to the back seat and opened the door for Lucy and the dogs and got out himself to go round to Matilda's side.

'Why, it's pure heaven!' she told him. 'What a pity that you can't stay here too—you need a holiday.' She waved an arm. 'All this space and the view and this darling little house...'

She became aware that he was looking at her and smiling. As usual, she reflected crossly, she was allowing her tongue to chatter on. She looked away from him and said stiffly, 'This seems a charming place; Lucy will love it.'

The child and the dogs had rushed into the house; she could hear Lucy's voice, squeaky with excitement, and a moment later she came running out again, this time with a small round woman, grey-haired and rosy-cheeked.

She went straight to Mr Scott-Thurlow, who hugged her, kissed her soundly and told her in a voice Matilda had never heard before—it was so content—that she was prettier than ever. 'And this is Matilda,' he told her, 'come to keep this imp of mischief out of trouble and keep you company.'

Matilda smiled at the nice kind face as she shook hands; they were going to like each other. She said happily, 'I'm sure we're going to be very happy here.'

'No doubt of it, me love. And as pretty a maid as I seen for many years. Now just you come in and eat your dinners and you, Mr James, must have a nice lay-down before you go back. More's the pity that you have to go.'

She bustled them indoors, through a small hall and into a large, low-ceilinged room with a table set under the far window; the floor was polished and spread with thick rugs and the chairs were comfortable and well cushioned. A matronly cat sat in one of them, washing herself, taking no notice of the dogs pottering to and fro.

'You'll be wanting to tidy yourselves,' said Emma Truscott. 'Up the stairs and the first door on the right—don't be long, I'll be dishing up.' As she trotted off into the kitchen Matilda heard her telling Mr James to fetch the cases, do, and take them up to the bedrooms.

When they went downstairs again there was an old-fashioned soup tureen on the table and Mr Scott-Thurlow was ladling its contents into deep plates. Matilda sat Lucy at the table. 'Can I do anything to help, Miss Truscott?'

'Call me Emma, me love, and sit yourself down. Watercress soup I made myself and as nice a chicken as ever I saw to follow.' She cast Matilda an approving look. 'Enjoy good food, do you? You're a nice healthy shape—I don't hold with all this fancy eating; I like a woman to look like one. Don't you agree with me, Mr James?'

Matilda bent a red face over her plate. Mr Scott-Thurlow gave a serious reply but she had no doubt that he was amused.

The chicken was brought in, carved with the expertise expected of the carver, and eaten with the appropriate trimmings and followed by raspberries and clotted cream, while Emma enlarged on the various small events in the village. All too soon the meal was over and Mr Scott-Thurlow was preparing to leave.

'You'll not go, Mr James, until you've sat yourself down for ten minutes, quiet like. Dear knows what your insides will be like if you get straight into that car of yours and go dashing off.'

It surprised Matilda that he did as he was told and went to sit outside in a garden chair with nothing but the sea in front of him. Lucy climbed on to his lap and sat quietly while Matilda helped clear the table. At the end of ten minutes, he got to his feet, hugged the child and said in a voice which meant what it said that he was leaving.

'Well, if you must, you must,' grumbled Emma, 'but just you take care how you drive.'

He said 'yes' meekly, hugged her fondly, kissed Lucy and nodded to Matilda. However, halfway to the gate he paused and came back to her, put his hands on her shoulders and kissed her. It was a tender, lingering kiss and she thrilled to it, aware that if he had dropped his guard the kiss would have been quite different. She turned her back on good sense and kissed him back, knowing that she would regret it bitterly.

He said nothing at all but turned on his heel, got into his car, and with a wave of his hand, drove himself away.

She turned round to see Emma eyeing her thoughtfully. She said breathlessly, 'I expect he thought I was Rhoda...'

A silly remark which received a tart answer. 'You know and I know that he thought no such thing, love. Now you go and unpack your things and take Lucy down to the beach. There's a path down the cliff to the shore, through the wicket gate at the bottom of the garden.'

The sand was firm and clean, and they strolled along on the edge of the sea, their sandals in their hands, revelling in the warm air and the sound of the water splashing their feet. 'I wish Uncle James was here too,' said Lucy. 'I can't see why he can't have a holiday...?'

'He has to go to Holland, darling—he's a busy man.'

'Do you suppose he'll come and see us while we're here?'

'I don't think so.' Matilda sounded sad; if he had any time at all he would surely spend it with Rhoda.

'Well, I do,' said Lucy., 'he likes me and he likes you too—he kissed you goodbye.'

'Well, that was because he kissed us all, didn't he?'

'He took a lot longer over you,' said Lucy.

They went to bed early, bidden to do so by Emma in her soft West Country voice, so it made sense that they should be up early too, to spend a long day, shopping for Emma, doing a few chores around the house and then going down to the beach, this time with a bucket and spade for Lucy and wearing cheap straw hats to protect them from the sun. All the same Matilda had a sprinkling of freckles across her nose by the evening. She sat at her dressing-table that evening, rubbing them with a cream to remove them and which did no such thing. Not that she minded much; there was no one to see them, and by no one of course she meant Mr Scott-Thurlow. She jumped into bed and inspected her room with pleasure. The cottage was charmingly furnished with the right kind of furniture, pretty chintz curtains and soft rugs. It had been skilfully modernised but it still contrived to look cosy despite the porcelain ornaments scattered around the silver tableware and fine linen. It was, reflected Matilda, a home—a retreat. She wondered how often Mr Scott-Thurlow came to stay in it and if Rhoda had ever been with him. It was a pity that she couldn't ask Emma…

But she had no need; over breakfast the next morning Emma volunteered the information that Mr James, when he came to stay for a few days or a weekend, came alone. 'That Miss Symes he's supposed to wed came to visit one afternoon—she can't a-bear this end of the country; likes the bright lights or foreign parts. Dear knows how they'll sort that out when they marry, if ever they do.'

Matilda murmured vaguely, glad that Lucy had left the table to take the crumbs for the seagulls, and Emma went on chattily, 'You've seen quite a bit of Mr James, I dare say, what with the little dog and his granny and now little Lucy.' She cast a shrewd eye at Matilda. 'He's a good man, is Mr James, as well as being a gentleman born, and you don't often get the two together.' She obviously expected an answer.

'Yes, he's very kind…'

''Andsome too, and then all that money… There's been plenty of young women willing to have him and his money.'

Matilda reflected that she was willing to have him without a single penny piece; she loved him regardless of anything else, but love wasn't enough. She said in a small wooden voice, 'Well, he's found someone he wants to marry…'

She was piling marmalade on to a piece of toast and didn't see Emma's look. 'That he has, me love, and the sooner the better, he's been too long without someone to love him and be loved.' She was suddenly brisk. 'Now, if you'll go, the pair of you, to the butcher's and fetch some of his sausages we'll have toad-in-the-hole for our dinner and there's raspberries to be picked in the garden. You'll be going to the beach presently?'

Matilda got up with a sense of relief. Emma was a darling but her eyes were sharp and she seemed to know a great deal about James—well, of course she would, having been cook to his parents and then joining his grandparents' household until he had installed her as housekeeper in this cottage. He wasn't mentioned again that day and indeed no one mentioned his name during the next few days, which slid with pleasurable slowness into a week, during which the pair of them acquired a glorious tan and Lucy, under Matilda's patient guidance, learned to swim. They also developed healthy appetites. 'I shall get fat,' declared Matilda, helping herself to more clotted cream. They went for gentle strolls in the evenings once the supper had been cleared away and the dishes washed, leaving Emma to sit with her old-fashioned specs perched on the end of her nose, reading the paper, and on Sunday they all went to the village church before going back to Emma's splendid Sunday dinner. Quite perfect, thought Matilda, or almost quite—if James were there it would be...

The lovely weather showed no sign of abating. Matilda got up early while Lucy still slept and got into one of her rather elderly cotton dresses, tied back her hair and went downstairs to give a hand with the weekly wash. There was a washing-machine of course and she had engaged to keep it filled and emptied while Emma got the breakfast. With all the doors and windows open, and the morning already pleasantly warm even at seven o'clock in the morning, she went happily about the task. Emma had put the first load in earlier; Matilda piled the clothes basket, loaded the machine again and went off to where the clothes-line hung out of sight at the bottom of the garden. It was pleasant hanging up sheets and towels and pillowcases with no sound but the waves below, the seagulls on the look-out for breakfast and a car or two on the road, going down the hill to Slapton Sands, intent on finding a vacant parking space before everyone else got there. She finished ramming home the last peg, picked up the basket and went back to the cottage; Emma would have breakfast ready by now.

She put the basket in the scullery ready for the next load and went through the open kitchen door. Mr Scott-Thurlow was leaning against the wall, talking to Emma, frying bacon on the Aga. He was wearing an open-necked shirt and drill trousers and had the air of someone who had been on holiday for some time.

Matilda fetched up short, frowning fiercely because she felt the bright colour flood into her face, but she couldn't stop the happy sparkle in her eyes.

He studied her face for a moment. 'Good morning, Matilda.' His eyes left her face and travelled over her person, giving her time to regret the elderly dress. 'You look well—Emma's cooking, no doubt…'

'If you mean I've got fat—' she began wrathfully.

'No, no, nothing of the sort. You appear to me to be—er—exactly the right shape. And Lucy?'

'Is splendid—she's put on weight too and she looks marvellous.'

'That makes two of you.'

She didn't answer that. 'Have you just got here?' she asked politely.

'I got here about three o'clock this morning.'

'Three o'clock… But you ought to be in bed, you must be tired out.'

'Not a bit of it. I've given myself two days off so I hope that you—and Lucy—will bear with my company.'

She couldn't prevent the wide smile and when he smiled slowly too she actually took a step towards him, wanting to be near him, tell him how happy she was to see him. It was providential that Emma spoke.

'Bacon's done to a turn and there's the tatties fried up how you like 'em. Sit down, do, and eat your breakfasts.'

Matilda dragged her eyes away from Mr Scott-Thurlow's face. 'I'll fetch Lucy.' She flew out of the room and up the little staircase and found the child hanging out of the window. 'I heard some dogs barking, they sounded just like Canada and Theobald, but it's not of course. I was looking to see if there's anyone on the beach…'

'Come down and eat your breakfast, love,' said Matilda, and

laughed out loud when she saw the child's delight and surprise when the dogs came to meet them at the kitchen door.

Lucy burst into the room. 'Uncle James, you're here, it was Theobald barking and Canada!' She flung herself at him, talking excitedly, and it took a few minutes before they were all sitting at the table intent on breakfast.

Mr Scott-Thurlow ate an enormous meal, but then he was a very large man and probably he hadn't had his supper or stopped on the way down.

'Are you here for weeks and weeks?' asked Lucy.

'Two days, sweetheart, so tell me what you want to do most and we'll do it.'

He looked across the table at Matilda as he spoke, and because there was something in his face which she found disquieting she said quickly, 'It's going to be a lovely day.'

A silly remark, but he agreed with her, still staring at her until the slow lovely colour crept into her cheeks. He smiled then and looked away and Lucy broke the silence.

'I can swim, Uncle James—can we go down on to the beach and I'll show you? I do six strokes if Matilda is beside me.'

'I can think of nothing nicer. Emma, have I got some swimming gear somewhere?'

'In the airing cupboard, ready and waiting.' She beamed at him and offered more toast.

'Could we have a picnic lunch in the garden? All of us—sandwiches and so on. Would it upset your plans if we had our dinner in the evening? I'd hate to miss any of this wonderful sun...'

'Anything you say, Mr James,' said Emma. 'It's a treat to have someone in the house. I am going to miss you when you've all gone.'

'I promise you we shall come back again, Emma.'

Matilda, watching Emma's face, knew exactly what she was thinking—if Rhoda were to come she would prefer to be on her own, thank you.

Breakfast over, James astonished Matilda by doing the washing-up while she and Emma cleared the table and set the place to rights again and then went to make the beds.

'Don't be long about it,' he called after them. 'Lucy, feed the dogs, will you? Everything is ready on the garden table.'

So presently, their chores done and leaving Emma to have what she called a nice sit-down, they went down the path to the beach. The tide was on the turn and it was already warm. Matilda sat down against a convenient rock, rammed her wide straw hat over her bright hair and delved into the large straw bag she had brought with her. She had prudently got into her swimsuit and donned her dress on top of it, feeling shy of James, but Lucy's childish bikini was there, and so were three cans of lemonade, a bag of doughnuts, some Dettol cream and some Band-Aids. There was a paperback there too, but she didn't think she would have a chance to read. She hoped she wouldn't.

Her hopes were realised; Mr Scott-Thurlow was transformed from a rather unapproachable consultant surgeon to a godfather willing to do anything within reason. They built a tremendous sand-castle with a channel running down to the water and a moat around it and then they sat eating their doughnuts while the tide came in and washed it all away again.

'Time for a swim,' said Mr Scott-Thurlow and stripped off his shirt and trousers, caught up Lucy in a giggling bundle and waded into the water, leaving Matilda to peel off her dress and follow them.

Lucy had to demonstrate her swimming prowess and, that done, sat happily enough on the beach with the water washing around her feet while Matilda and Mr Scott-Thurlow swam strongly out to sea and back again, and once back they lay, the three of them, with the gentle waves washing over them, soaking up the sun. The tide was coming in, so they got up reluctantly and went to sit out of reach of the water, and presently at Lucy's insistence they built another sand-castle. Matilda, obediently filling buckets of sand and handing it over to the builders, thought what a splendid father he would make and lost herself in a daydream peopled by a horde of little Scott-Thurlows, herself and James, so that she was only aroused by repeated shouts for more sand.

They had their picnic in the garden with Emma and then lay about doing nothing until it was time for tea. After tea, in the cool of the late afternoon, they went walking. Down the hill to Slapton Sands, still packed with day visitors, to walk along the sands, barefooted, splashing along on the very edge of the sea. When they got back to the cottage they showered and changed and sat down to one of Emma's delicious meals. Garlic mushrooms, roast chicken with all the trimmings, a pile of roast potatoes and asparagus, creamed spinach and baby corn, and one of her fruit pies with a crust which melted in the mouth and loaded down with clotted cream.

They sat over the meal until Matilda gathered up Lucy, already half asleep, and bore her off to her bed. When she came down Emma had taken the coffee into the sitting-room and they sat over that too. Presently Mr Scott-Thurlow suggested that a stroll along the sand would be pleasant on such a splendid evening, so Matilda fetched a cardigan and slung it around her shoulders and accompanied him down to the beach once more.

'You really ought to go to bed early,' she told him. 'You shouldn't burn the candle at both ends.'

'Afraid I might let the knife slip? I have never met a girl who was so anxious to order my life for me, Matilda.'

His mocking voice hurt her and wakened her quick temper. 'Don't talk nonsense—I don't imagine there is anyone on this earth who can do that, and if there is it's Rhoda.'

'You are mistaken. Nothing and no one, save one person, will have the power to change my life.'

She had her mouth open to ask who the someone was and then snapped it shut; it wasn't her business, but did it mean that he wasn't going to marry Rhoda? She said in her best social manner, 'What a delightful evening it is; we're having a marvellous summer.'

He answered her with a hint of a laugh in his voice. 'Indeed, yes—the most marvellous summer of my life.'

Which wasn't quite the answer she had expected; she worked away at her small talk and he politely followed her lead and in a little while they went back to the cottage and said goodnight.

The next day followed the pattern of the previous one only there was no stroll in the evening, for after dinner, eaten a little earlier than usual, Mr Scott-Thurlow prepared to leave.

'Must you go?' asked Lucy tearfully.

'Yes, but I'm taking my two lovely days here back with me, aren't I? And who knows, I may come again before you go back to school. In any case I'll come and fetch you back to London and take you back to Miss Tremble's.'

He swung her up in his great arms and kissed her soundly and then hugged Emma. 'Dear Emma, thank you...' He kissed her pink cheek with affection. Matilda, standing a little apart, wondered if they should shake hands, or would he give her a friendly nod as he went?

He did neither; he put his hands on her shoulders and kissed her too, another gentle, lingering kiss which sent her pulses racing and took her breath, but not quite all of it for she kissed him back, flinging good sense to the winds again, never mind the future, never mind Rhoda, this moment was hers.

Mr Scott-Thurlow straightened his imposing height and then stood looking at her. He said nothing at all but bent once more and kissed her again, this time swift and hard.

They stood at the cottage door waving him goodbye. 'He kissed you twice,' said Lucy. 'I think Uncle James likes you very much, Matilda.'

'Bedtime, love!' said Emma. 'You uncle likes us all and what a lovely time you've had these last two days. Eaten us out of house and home, he has—tomorrow you and Matilda will have to go shopping for me. You can get the bus into Dartmouth.'

She bustled the child upstairs, which gave Matilda a few minutes in which to pull her disordered thoughts together and regret very bitterly that she had returned Mr Scott-Thurlow's kiss. It had been heaven, of course, but now she went scarlet with shame at allowing him to find out her feelings for him, for she had certainly made no secret of them. She frowned; his kisses had been rather more than friendly...

There was a letter from Esme in the morning, full of family news and bits of gossip about the village. One of the maids at the manor-house was going steady with the milkman's son, Lady Fox had a new and quite awful hat, Sir Benjamin had fluffed his lines reading the lesson on Sunday and Nelson the cat had caught a rat at the bottom of the garden. 'And I must tell you,' wrote Esme in her impetuous scrawl, 'who do you suppose came to see Mother the other day? That Rhoda woman who's going to marry our nice Mr Scott-Thurlow; she'd been to see Roseanne, who's almost well—and called in on her way back to London. Said what a lovely time she and he were having—parties and so on—I didn't believe half of it. Said what a pity it was that Roseanne wouldn't be able to be one of the bridesmaids since she and Mr Scott-Thurlow are getting married very shortly. I hate her.'

So do I, thought Matilda bitterly. His kisses hadn't meant anything, just a last fling before he married. She hoped that she would never see him again. She looked at the letter once more. Esme wrote that Rhoda had actually said that she would send Matilda an invitation to the wedding because she had been so kind and capable.

'Pah!' said Matilda with such force that Emma and Lucy both looked at her with astonishment.

The days, empty of Mr Scott-Thurlow's presence, went slowly by. They did the same things, went for the same walks, played the same games and spent a good deal of time messing about on the beach and in the water. Matilda made no mention of him and was outwardly cheerful as usual but Lucy observed a dozen times a day that she wanted him back.

'You're a very nice person,' she explained to Matilda, 'and so is Emma, but it's not quite the same.' Tears weren't far off. 'And it's almost time for me to go back to Miss Tremble's.'

'It's also almost time for your mummy and daddy to come home, love, only another week or two...'

There was no word from Mr Scott-Thurlow, not until their very last day when he phoned to say that they could expect him for lunch on the following day and they were to be ready to leave in the early afternoon. So Matilda packed their things and took Lucy down to the beach for their last morning bathe and, while they were gone, Emma, listening to Mr Scott-Thurlow's voice on the phone once again, chuckled comfortably at what he had to say.

The next day—the last, thought Matilda gloomily, alternately thrilled at the thought of seeing him again and still smarting from Esme's letter—they went down to the beach just once more. She had laid their clothes ready for travelling and left enough room to stuff their cotton dresses in at the last minute; she hadn't bothered about make-up either, or her hair, which she had tied back with a handy piece of string from the kitchen.

They were building a sand-castle to end all sand-castles when they heard the dogs—Canada's gruff unhurried bark and Theobald's excited yap. Coming towards them were three people: Mr Scott-Thurlow and a man and a woman.

Lucy flung down her spade. 'Mummy! Daddy!' she bawled, and tore to meet them.

CHAPTER NINE

MATILDA stood still and watched Mr Scott-Thurlow and the dogs coming towards her; he wasn't hurrying, which gave her time to get over the rapture of seeing him and stoke up her indignation at his behaviour, so that when he reached her she returned his cheerful greeting in a witheringly chilly, calm voice which sent his eyebrows up.

'Surprised you? Matt and Jean got back yesterday, several weeks earlier than they had expected. They'll stay here and keep Lucy with them—Matt has already spoken to Miss Tremble—and they'll take her with them when they go to Berkshire. You're ready to leave? Good. I'll take you back with me and drop you off at Abner Magna—I have to be back in town this evening.'

He didn't wait for her reply, which was just as well. 'Come and meet Jean and Matt...' He stood towering over her, smiling, looking, she reflected, a bit smug. 'I like the string,' he told her.

She gave him a haughty look. 'We weren't expecting you—we came down here for a last hour or two and naturally we couldn't wear the clothes we shall travel in.'

'Lucy won't be travelling. Anyway, I like that chemise thing you're wearing.'

She got rather pink; the white cotton dress she was wearing was sleeveless and with a scooped-out low neckline—a well-worn garment she had kept for messing around with Lucy, but before she could answer him he was introducing her to Lucy's parents and presently the whole party made their way back to the cottage. Once there, he made no attempt to engage her in conversation but wandered off into the garden, leaving her to gossip gently with Jean while Lucy sat between them bubbling over with happiness.

'We are so grateful to you,' said Jean. 'James says you're marvellous with children, animals and sudden mishaps—you've certainly been a fairy godmother to Lucy. He didn't tell us how pretty you are. No, not pretty—beautiful, and I love your hair.'

'I'm not very tidy, I'm afraid. I'd better go and change; I expect Mr Scott-Thurlow will want to leave directly after lunch and I mustn't keep him waiting. He's giving me a lift home.'

Jean gave her a nice smile. She was tempted to tell this delightful creature in her simple clothes just what James had said about her, but that would never do; besides, they had a long drive before them, ample time for them to talk. 'I'll unpack Lucy's clothes, shall I? I've brought one or two things with me.' She dropped a kiss on her daughter's head. 'Would you like to see them now, darling?'

So the three of them went upstairs and Matilda had a shower and got into the flower-patterned two-piece, stuck her stockinged feet into neat shoes, did her face and brushed her hair into its severe French pleat. Surveying her reflection, she thought that she hadn't looked like that for more than two weeks.

Mr Scott-Thurlow had meant what he said when he had told her that they would leave immediately after lunch. He stowed her case in the boot, whistled to the dogs, bade everyone a brisk goodbye and then waited with no sign of impatience while Matilda said her own farewells. Prolonged hugs from Lucy and promises to meet again, reiterated thanks from her mother and father and a rather tearful one from Emma, who pressed a dozen brown eggs and a pot of cream on her with the fervent hope that Matilda would come and see her again. A rare pity, she thought as she watched the beautiful Matilda get into the car, that her Mr James hadn't chosen to marry her instead of the haughty creature who, on her one visit, had ignored her completely.

They all waved at the departing car and Emma said, 'Ah, well, it's a nice long drive.'

Jean smilingly agreed; she had only met Rhoda once and she hadn't liked her either. She had no doubt that she and Emma were thinking the same thing.

It was Lucy who put their thoughts into words. 'It would be nice if Matilda and Uncle James got married,' she said.

If they had been in the car they would have had their doubts.

Matilda, sustaining a polite flow of small talk in a frosty voice and encouraged to do so by an amused James, was as unapproachable as a bed of stinging nettles. Presently he said, 'We have a long drive ahead of us—could you stop being so polite with your chit-chat and be you?'

She wouldn't look at him. 'I'm sure I don't know what you mean.'

'No? Ah, well—all in good time. Let us continue with our small talk. Did you know that Roseanne is getting married in September? The wedding is to be a very grand affair.'

It was on the tip of her tongue to ask him if his own wedding would be grand too; she couldn't imagine it to be otherwise with Rhoda as the bride. She checked the question just in time and was rewarded by his, 'A wedding should be a family affair with only close friends, do you not agree?'

'Well, yes. Everyone else only comes out of curiosity.'

The car ate up the miles in a well-bred fashion and he kept the talk undemanding, lapsing into long silences which strangely enough left her perfectly at ease with him. They also gave her a chance to think, and her thoughts were sad. This was probably the last time she would be with him; their paths were unlikely to meet in the future, and a good thing too for it was hard to maintain her chilly politeness.

They were nearing Montacute on the A303 and not far from Abner Magna now when he turned off into a side-road.

'You've gone off the road,' said Matilda unnecessarily.

'We are having tea at Grandmother's.' He glanced at his watch. 'It's barely four o'clock—just right. We're expected.'

'But Mother is expecting—'

'Around half-past five or six o'clock.'

Mackrell Cantelo basked in the afternoon sun and the village was quiet as he swept through it and turned in at the stone pillars. As they stopped before the house Slocombe came through the door to meet them.

'A pleasure to see you, Mr James and Miss ffinch. Your grand-parents are in the conservatory—I'll bring tea there in a few minutes. Perhaps you would like to freshen up, miss?'

Matilda smoothed her hair, applied more lipstick and tidied her already tidy person and then went back into the hall. Was she supposed to find her way to the conservatory on her own? she wondered. Apparently not; Mr Scott-Thurlow was sitting on the stairs waiting for her. She might have known that he would be; he was so thoughtful of other people. She hoped that Rhoda appreciated that.

His grandparents were sitting in peacock chairs overshadowed by palms, ferns and clinging greenery. The doors to the terrace were open but even then it was warm. The dogs made a beeline for the lawn outside and she envied them as she greeted her hostess and, obedient to Mrs Scott-Thurlow's request, sat down beside her.

'It is delightful to see you again, my dear,' said the old lady. 'Now you must tell me about your stay at Stoke Fleming. Such a dear little cottage, is it not?'

The talk was general and pleasant over tea and presently the old lady said, 'Why don't you two young people have ten minutes in the garden and take a little stroll before you go? My roses are glorious and you really must see them.'

Matilda was surprised when Mr Scott-Thurlow got up. 'A splendid idea—come along, Matilda.'

Her inclination was to refuse, but with the old lady's kindly eyes fixed upon her that would have been impossible. Crossing the lawn with him, the dogs wreathing around them, she said with some asperity, 'I thought you were in a hurry?'

'Oh, I am, but I have found that there is always time for something one wishes to do.'

'Oh, yes, the roses.' They had reached the end of the large garden where the rose-beds made a splash of lovely colours, the beds separated by closely cut turf paths.

He came to a halt, staring down at her with a faint frown. 'What is the matter, Matilda? When I was at the cottage I thought... Well, never mind that now.' He put his hands on her shoulders. 'You have always been frank and outspoken,' he smiled a little, 'too outspoken sometimes, but you are hiding something and I wonder why?'

'I don't know what you're talking about...'

She drew back from him and he let her go at once. 'In that case I'll not say what I wanted to say to you; I should have told you at the cottage.'

She said fiercely, 'Well, I'm glad you didn't for I don't want to know.'

He stared down at her thoughtfully, his face calm and unworried. 'No? If ever you should change your mind, Matilda, you know where to find me.' He smiled suddenly. 'And having admired the roses we had better be on our way.'

They made their farewells and the two old people came to the door with them and watched them drive away, the dogs once more on the back seat, Matilda sitting rather erect beside James.

'A dear girl,' remarked his grandmother. 'She will manage him very well.'

Abner Magna looked peaceful in the late afternoon sunshine and the rectory garden, untidy and a little neglected though it was, was full of colour. Their welcome was warm for everyone was at home and anxious to greet them, but Mr Scott-Thurlow, in a few well-polished sentences, made his excuses, bade them all goodbye and got back into his car, the reluctant dogs climbing in once more. He had said all the right things; Matilda had been of the greatest help and Lucy had grown very fond of her, in fact he was indeed very grateful and hoped that he hadn't hindered her in getting some more congenial job. He had wished her goodbye with a bland smile and eyes as hard as blue steel.

'A pity he couldn't stay for supper,' said her mother, 'but I dare say he wants to get back to town. Did Esme tell you in her letter that Rhoda Symes came here, Tilly? Full of her wedding arrangements, said to be sure and tell you because you'd be interested. I don't like her.'

'Now, now, my dear,' said the rector mildly, 'we must try and like everyone.'

For once his wife disagreed with him. 'You can't like someone you don't like,' she told him with female logic.

The busy, happy life at the rectory was soothing to Matilda. Just for a moment she had felt sudden happiness at the sight of the envelope addressed to her in James's illegible handwriting, which someone had put on her dressing-table. She had opened it with a shaky hand and found a cheque inside and a businesslike slip of paper, typed no doubt by his secretary and signed with his initials. She would have liked to have torn it into little shreds and sent it back to him, but for once good sense had the ascendancy over her red hair. The cheque was for a tidy sum; it meant football boots for the boys, a new hat for her mother, a longed-for book for her father and clothes for Esme, Hilary and herself. She had put it in her purse, sniffed away a great desire to cry and gone downstairs to her supper.

She had been home for a few days when her mother came back from the village. 'I met Lady Fox, Tilly—she had heard that you were back and Roseanne wants you to go and see her.' She glanced at her daughter's beautiful and sad face. 'I hope I did the right thing in saying you would go. She's coming home in a few days now but Bernard has had to go away and she's longing for company. Esme's too young and Hilary doesn't want to talk about anyone else's wedding except her own.'

Matilda rubbed butter into flour, intent on making an apple tart. 'I'll go tomorrow if Father will let me borrow the car.'

It was a quiet morning with the faint haziness of late summer in the air. She drove slowly while she thought. Once the boys were back at school and Esme back at her school, she would get a job, somewhere where there was no chance of meeting James, somewhere where no one knew him so that when he married Rhoda she wouldn't know about it, and then in no time he would become a memory, getting more and more vague until she couldn't remember what he looked like, and that would leave her free to marry some man who wouldn't rock her heart and send her pulses racing. Even as she thought it she knew that the very idea was nonsense; she would never forget him...

Roseanne was sitting outside on the hospital veranda and professed herself delighted to see Matilda, proudly demonstrating the fact that, excepting for a gutter crutch, she was well again.

'Of course, by the time we marry I shall be able to walk without the wretched thing. I must tell you about the wedding...' Something she did at great length; indeed she hadn't finished when she was interrupted—one of the sisters came through the open door on to the veranda and with her came Mr Scott-Thurlow.

He saw Matilda at once but his face remained impassive. Nothing could have been more polite than his 'good morning', uttered in a pleasant voice before he turned his attention to Roseanne.

'I'll go,' said Matilda, praying feverishly that he would say that she might stay. Only he didn't, merely waited until she bade Roseanne goodbye and then nodded and smiled at her, at his most urbane. The impetuous side of her nature longed to throw something at him but the loving side wept silently at his bland indifference.

The hospital was away from the main road, and Matilda started to drive back to Abner Magna along the network of country roads which would eventually take her home. They were quiet, used mainly by farm vehicles and people who had lost their way, and the villages were few and some miles from each other. The country here was open with splendid views and low, rolling hills. It was halfway up one of these that the engine coughed, laboured on for a few yards, coughed again and stopped.

'Now what?' enquired Matilda of the surrounding quiet and got out and looked under the bonnet—a useless exercise for she had only the vaguest idea as to what was underneath it. It looked the same as usual. She got back into the car and pressed the self-starter; nothing happened, and it was then that she saw that there was no petrol. 'Halfway up a hill, too,' she exclaimed. 'Now what?'

'What' materialised in the shape of a car coming with effortless ease up the hill. It came to a smooth halt a few yards ahead of her and Mr Scott-Thurlow got out. He walked unhurriedly to her car, stuck his head through the window and observed mildly, 'Not a very good place to stop, but no doubt you had your reasons.'

She bristled. 'As though anyone with any sense would stop halfway up a hill...'

He glanced at the dashboard. 'Out of petrol?' He shook his head in a particularly infuriating manner. 'And I thought you were such a sensible girl.'

'I *am* a sensible girl,' she snapped and tossed her fiery head at him. 'Anyone can run out of petrol.'

'Of course,' he said soothingly. 'One only needs to forget to fill up.'

Her eyes gleamed greenly. 'Don't let me keep you—someone will come along presently—or perhaps you would be so kind as to stop at Dunn's garage—it's a mile or so along this road, just before you get to Littlecote-sub-Magna...'

'I will be even kinder—I will put some petrol in your tank for you.' His smile mocked her. 'I carry a spare can or two.'

She might have known that he would; he was a man who was prepared for all eventualities. She watched him go back to his car, fetch the petrol, empty its contents into her tank and return the can to his own boot. He did it without haste and very tidily and then walked back again and opened her door. 'Move over,' he told her.

'Why?'

He glanced at the few yards between the cars. 'I don't want the Rolls to get bashed. So move over, dear girl; much as I would like to waste my time in your company I have to get back to town.'

She moved over. 'You had no need to stop,' she muttered crossly.

'That is one of the silliest remarks I have ever heard; a pity I haven't the time to tell you why.'

He drove her car up to the crest of the hill and stopped. 'Off you go,' he told her as he got out. 'And for heaven's sake drive carefully.'

A remark calculated to send her shooting along the narrow road as fast as she could. All the same, he overtook her at the bottom of the hill and soared away out of sight without even glancing at her as he passed.

She was still seething when she got home and the sight of Lady Fox sitting outside the drawing-room window hardly improved her temper. Her mother was there too and the coffee-tray and both ladies turned to look at her as she crossed the grass.

Lady Fox was all graciousness. 'Matilda—you have just returned from visiting Roseanne? Does she not look well? Such a splendid job Mr Scott-Thurlow has done on her poor leg.' She sighed loudly. 'Though I shudder to think of his bill. Still, one must have the best, must one not?' She took a good look at Matilda. 'I must say you are rather pale; surely you should have more colour after your lovely holiday in Devon? I heard all about it from Rhoda.'

Matilda accepted a cup of coffee from her mother. 'But she wasn't there.'

Lady Fox looked arch. 'Well, no—she dislikes the cottage, I believe, but Mr Scott-Thurlow spent a couple of days there, did he not? And naturally he would have told her all about it.' She added reprovingly, 'They are engaged, after all.'

'I wonder what will happen when they marry?' mused Matilda out loud. 'Will he spend his holidays at Stoke Fleming and Rhoda carry on with her round of parties?'

Lady Fox's formidable bosom swelled alarmingly. 'Really, Matilda, I don't think that remark is in the best of taste.' She looked away from Matilda's green stare. 'What do you intend to do next?'

'I've no idea, Lady Fox.' She finished her coffee. 'You'll excuse me?' She smiled at her mother. 'I'll get those beans blanched ready for the freezer.'

The two ladies watched her go. 'Such a sensible girl,' said Lady Fox. 'It must be a great worry to you that she is not yet married.'

Mrs ffinch smiled. 'Why should it worry me? Matilda could have married several times over but she is content to wait until she meets the right man.'

'Supposing she doesn't?' asked Lady Fox acidly.

'Oh, but she will, I have no doubt about that.' Mrs ffinch lifted the coffee-pot. 'Will you have another cup?'

Mrs ffinch might have had no doubts about her daughter, but Matilda was a mass of conflicting emotions. She longed to see James again but what good would that do? For when they did meet, she snapped at him and he—he laughed at her even when his face was placid. She must amuse him a good deal and she had been a fool to kiss him. He shouldn't have kissed her in the first place though...

She did her best to settle down into the bosom of her family, undertaking rather more chores than she needed to in and around the parish, helping in the house, cooking and gardening. None of these were enough to stop her thinking. She had been at home for just over a week when she told her mother that she had seen a job in the *Western Gazette* and intended to apply for it. 'Someone wants help with an old lady who has gone a bit dotty, I gather. In the Western Highlands...'

Her mother, beating batter, paused for a second and then went on calmly, 'It sounds a long way away, darling—and an old lady, senile at that—she would be very trying.' She saw the obstinate set of Matilda's gentle mouth and went on quickly. 'But I dare say a change would be pleasant. They say the scenery is magnificent.'

Matilda thought sadly she didn't care a button about the scenery; it was a long way from James. 'I think I'll write anyway,' she announced and drifted away to find pen and paper, sit down at the little desk in the sitting-room and then fall into a daydream where James came in through the door...

Esme came through the door instead. 'I say,' she said excitedly, 'have you seen this?' She waved the *Daily Telegraph* at Matilda.

'How could I have seen it?' Matilda, her daydream interrupted, spoke testily. 'You've got the paper.'

'Well, I'll read it to you. It says, "The marriage arranged between Miss Rhoda Symes and Mr James Scott-Thurlow will not now take place—"'

The paper was whipped out of her hand and Matilda read it for herself, and just to make sure she read it for a second time. He had wanted to tell her something at the cottage and she hadn't let him—he had told her that she would know where to find him if she were to change her mind and yet when he had stopped to give her petrol he hadn't said a word; indeed, he had been at his most tiresome...

'What are you going to do?' asked Esme.

'Do, what should I do? It's no concern of mine.'

Esme gave her a thoughtful look. 'You've been in love with

James for a long time, haven't you? The least you can do is tell him.'

Matilda looked at her with horror. 'Tell him? I'd sooner die.'

Which dramatic statement was ignored by her sister. 'Rubbish—you do love him, don't you, Tilly?'

'Yes.' Matilda got up so quickly that paper and envelopes flew in all directions. She darted through the door and into her father's study.

'Father, may I borrow the car? Just to get to Sherborne—I want to catch the London train.'

Her father studied her face, usually so serene, and saw that she was labouring under some strong emotion. 'Certainly you may, Matilda. How long will you be gone? I might need it in the meantime...'

'Oh, I hadn't thought of that. I don't know, I'm going to see James—Mr Scott-Thurlow—if—that is, I might come back later today—it depends.'

The Reverend Mr ffinch pushed his sermon to one side. 'Hilary will be back from Salisbury this afternoon; ask the station-master to tell her to pick the car up from the station yard. She can drive herself back here.' He glanced at the clock on the mantelpiece. 'You had better hurry, my dear.'

She dropped a kiss on to his thatch of grey hair and tore through the house and upstairs to her room, where she began rooting around in her wardrobe. It had become important that she look her best.

A glance at her watch told her that if she was to catch the train fussing around deciding what to wear wasn't to be considered. She got into the flowered two-piece; he had seen it often enough, but who cared?

She would have liked to have spent some time on her face and hair, but as it was they both received perfunctory attention. She crammed odds and ends into her handbag; at least she had some money...

Her explanations to her mother were garbled and vague, leaving that lady to sort them out at her leisure. She kissed her parent swiftly and ran out to the shed where the car was kept. Esme was there. 'You're wearing that again,' she said, 'but of course if James loves you he won't care if you're wrapped in a sack.'

'I don't know,' said Matilda wildly. 'Sometimes I thought...and then I was sure that he didn't...'

She got into the car and Esme leaned through the open window. 'Well, you'll soon know...' She glanced over her shoulder and luckily Matilda, bent over the ignition key, didn't see her face, wreathed in a wide grin. The Rolls was nosing its way through the open gate and came to a halt. 'Back carefully,' she told Matilda.

The car started up in a middle-aged fashion and Matilda began to back it out of the shed; there was plenty of room to turn at the side of the house. She gave a perfunctory glance in the mirror, gasped with fright and braked within a few feet of theRolls, which was effectively blocking her path.

Mr Scott-Thurlow had got out and so had the dogs. Esme, regretful that she was about to miss an interesting situation, whistled to them and took herself off, round to the back of the house.

Matilda didn't see her go and if Mr Scott-Thurlow did he gave no sign.

He walked without haste from his car to hers, opened the door and waited while she got out.

'Going somewhere?' he wanted to know.

She was trembling with the excitement of seeing him and the shock of very nearly backing into the Rolls. She said in a shaky little voice, 'I almost backed into your car. I could have damaged it.'

He had taken her hands in his. 'Rolls-Royce motor cars don't damage easily. Were you coming to see me?'

When she nodded he said, 'I thought that you might. You are a very obstinate girl, my darling—that is because of your lovely red hair, of course, but I do hope that, when we are married, you will listen meekly when I have something to say to you. Of course until this moment there has been very little opportunity.'

'Don't you love her?'

'No. And I never did. How delightfully direct you are, dear heart.' He smiled down at her. 'I love you, and deep in your heart you know that. I loved you the moment I saw you in church. I wanted to marry you there and then, but of course that wouldn't have been very practical, and besides I had to end my engagement to Rhoda. All the while I wasn't sure if you loved me.'

'How could you possibly know? I never said a word.'

He smiled slowly. '"There's language in her eye, her cheek, her lip..."'

'Shakespeare, *Troilus and Cressida*,' said Matilda, momentarily diverted. 'Then why didn't you—?'

He bent and kissed her very gently. 'Dear heart, when did you ever give me any encouragement?'

'You don't need encouragement,' she told him flatly. 'You know just what you're doing with your life; you're successful and nothing seems to disturb you—you're so calm.'

'My dear life, I can see that you know nothing about me at all. You will have years in which to discover just what kind of man I am.' He plucked her close and wrapped her in his great arms. 'There is one thing you must learn immediately. I do not care to waste time.' He kissed her then, and there was nothing gentle about it this time.

'Oh, my goodness,' whispered Matilda when she had her breath again. 'What—?'

'Marry me, Matilda. You can ask me anything you want once we are married, but there is one question. Do you love me?'

'Yes, oh, dear James, you have no idea how much.'

'I shall enjoy finding out, my darling heart. We had better tell your family, had we not? But first...'

He pulled her close to kiss her soundly and the ffinch family, watching unashamedly from a variety of windows, sighed their satisfaction. Her father went down to the cellar to fetch up a bottle of champagne he had been saving for some special occasion; her mother, arranging glasses on a tray, reflected with guilty satisfaction that Lady Fox was going to be put out and, as for Esme, she was dreaming up her bridesmaid's dress.

Not that any of these things mattered to the two people standing so close together in the drive; they had found their heaven and they were content.

A SUMMER IDYLL

by

Betty Neels

CHAPTER ONE

IT WAS QUITE ten minutes after a ragged chorus of church bells had tolled the hour of five before Phoebe tapped on the office door and when bidden, entered. Sister Evans was at her desk, looking as fierce as usual, and without glancing up she asked briskly: 'Yes, what is it?'

Phoebe didn't allow the eagerness she felt to sound in her voice. 'I've finished, Sister—I'm off at five o'clock.'

'Very well, Nurse Creswell.' It was a surprised Phoebe who heard Sister wish her a pleasant evening. She thanked her politely and whisked herself out of the office and back down the ward. Almost at the doors old Mrs James sat up in bed. 'Nurse, nurse—I feel sick!'

There wasn't another nurse to be seen. Busy in the sluice or the kitchen or even having a cosy chat in the linen cupboard—it was such a safe time on a medical ward, not time for evening medicines, far too early for the getting ready of suppers, a most unlikely hour for a houseman to do a round and Sister safe in her office. Phoebe sighed, nipped into the sluice room for a bowl and hurried back with it. Just my luck, she thought silently, proffering it and arranging a towel in a strategic place, just when she needed at least an hour to get ready before Basil expected her. A precious ten minutes went by before Mrs James decided that she felt better and consented to be tucked up once more.

The hospital, hedged in by East End streets lined with small grey houses, was old, added to from time to time, regardless of level floors or unnecessary staircases, so that Phoebe was quite out of breath by the time she reached her room in the nurses' home, a state not helped by the speed in which she flung off her uniform, showered and then began to dress. She had given a good deal of thought to what she should wear, Basil had mentioned casually that the party was being given by a cousin of his—a real swinger, he had called her, and possessed of stunning good looks. Phoebe, surveying her own very ordinary features in the mirror, wished wholeheartedly that the cousin would spare some of her good looks for her. There was nothing wrong with her face, she supposed, but it would never set the world on fire. And mousy hair did nothing to help, and since no one had ever pointed out that her eyes were beautiful grey and heavily fringed, she set no great store by them. She sat down and did her face and then her hair, twisting it up in a neat knot and pinning it carefully before getting into the new separates she had bought in the January sales, a pleasant shade of green and of a fine jersey, just right for a spring evening. She had only been out with Basil three times, and she was still secretly surprised that she was going out with him and that he seemed to like her. He was one of the most popular housemen and could have taken his pick of any number of girls far prettier than she. He was good-looking too, and never at a loss for conversation. Phoebe thought he was marvellous, and she had a perpetual daydream, in which he fell in love with her, married her and became a successful consultant with a Harley Street practice with her running a flat-fronted Regency house and entertaining his rich patients in a little something from Bellville Sassoon. Nonsense, she told herself firmly several times a day, while a tiny corner of her mind persisted in denying that.

She put on the plain court shoes she had saved to buy, found her velvet jacket and, with a couple of minutes to spare, made her way round to the car park at the back of the hospital where the staff kept their cars.

Basil's car was there—an elderly Triumph, its vivid red needing a good clean—but Basil wasn't; he was at the other end of the row of cars, leaning on the bonnet of a sleek Rover, talking to Staff Nurse Collins whose father was well-heeled enough to keep his daughter in a style quite inaccessible to a nurse living on nothing but her pay. Phoebe stayed where she was, not sure whether to join them or look as though she hadn't seen them. She decided on the latter, and presently was relieved to hear Basil's voice remarking that there she was and why hadn't she given a shout.

She mumbled something or other, bereft of words as usual when she was with him, although her smile made up for that, and when he opened the car door, she got in. She had hoped he would say something nice about her outfit, but he hardly glanced at it, merely said that they would have to step on it if they weren't to miss the best of the food.

The cousin lived miles away, near Croydon. What with Basil taking a wrong turning and all the evening traffic, the party was in full swing by the time he had found a place to park the car and they had walked back to the rather staid-looking house in a quiet street. Although neither the house nor the street were quiet; the din met them as they opened the old-fashioned iron gate and pushed open the half-open door.

The moment they were inside, Phoebe saw that she was dressed quite wrongly; there were dozens of girls there, wearing slinky black dresses with deep vee necklines and no backs worth mentioning, and those who weren't wearing black were in tight pant suits, glittering with gold and sequins. The girl who came to meet them was wearing black satin, skin tight and short; she wore one very large dangling earring and there were pink streaks in her dark hair. She flung her arms round Basil, kissed him with great warmth and then looked at Phoebe. 'Girl-friend?' she enquired, 'Basil, I can't believe it?'

The amused look she cast at Phoebe sent the colour flying into her cheeks, and it stayed there because Basil looked at her too with a faint derisive smile. 'Hardly that,' he said, but he took Phoebe's arm and squeezed it, and the smile changed so quickly that she thought that she might have imagined it.

The girl grinned, 'I'm Deirdre,' and when Phoebe said politely: 'How do you do? I'm Phoebe,' she said rather impatiently: 'Well, come on in and meet everyone.' Somebody went past with a tray of drinks and she caught him by the arm. 'Have a drink for a start.'

It tasted like sugared petrol, but Phoebe sipped it obediently, keeping close to Basil because she didn't know a soul there. True, he threw names at her carelessly from time to time, but faces came and went so rapidly that she never caught up with them. And presently she found herself against a wall and Basil at the other end of the room surrounded by a crowd of people all laughing their heads off. She had hidden her glass behind a great vase filled with lilac and was trying to look as though she was enjoying herself; not that that mattered, because no one noticed her. It seemed like hours later when Basil reappeared, a glass in his hand. 'Hullo there,' he began carelessly. 'Having a good time? I say, this is some party—haven't enjoyed myself so much in years.' He looked at her and frowned. 'You look a bit of a wet blanket, darling—it's not quite your scene, perhaps.'

She was anxious to please him. 'Oh, it's lovely,' she assured him. 'I came here just for a minute or two, to get my breath.'

He dropped a casual kiss on her cheek. 'Oh, good. There's masses of food in the other room, but I daresay you've had all you want.'

He slid away, leaving her with her mouth watering; she was famished, now that she came to think about it. Hunger sent her edging her way through the people milling round the room. She found a plate and collected tiny sausage rolls, smoked salmon on slivers of brown bread and butter, tiny vol-au-vents, a stick of celery—hardly a meal, but it would keep her empty insides quiet for a little while—then she found a chair in a corner of the room, and was surprised when presently she was joined by another of the guests. A thin, pale man, in a good grey suit, looking, she had to admit, as much like a fish out of water as she did.

'On your own?' he asked.

'No, but I've—that is, the man I came with has heaps of friends here—and of course he wants to talk to them.'

He gave her a long considered look. 'Not quite your sort,' he commented. 'Not mine either—a lot of layabouts with too much money and nothing to do. You look as though you earn your own living?'

It was hardly a compliment, but it was so nice to talk to someone that she felt no resentment. 'Yes, I'm training to be a nurse.'

'Good Lord—who did you come with?'

'Basil Needham. He's a houseman at St Coram's.'

Her companion said, 'Good Lord,' again, and gave her another faintly pitying look. 'I'd never have believed it of him.'

She misunderstood him and said earnestly: 'Oh, he's very clever—I expect he'll be famous one day.' Her eyes shone with delight at such a prospect and the man looked vaguely uncomfortable.

'Not very old, are you?' he observed.

'Twenty-two.' She looked around her. 'Are people beginning to go? I must find Basil...'

'Oh, they'll go to a night club.'

'Well, I'll have to find him just the same—we'll have to get back to St Coram's.' She added politely: 'It's been nice meeting you. I expect you're going to a night club too.'

He got to his feet. 'God forbid—I live here.' He walked away, leaving her gaping after him, and then she forgot him as Basil pushed his way through the people leaving.

'There you are. We're all going on to a disco...'

Phoebe wasn't listening. 'Who was that man?' she asked. 'He said he lived here.'

'Well, of course he does, you little idiot, he's Deirdre's husband. Get your coat—it'll be a bit of a squash in the car, but that won't matter.'

'We're going back to St Coram's?'

He gave her an impatient look. 'Good God, no! Do get a move on.'

Phoebe, a mild-tempered girl, didn't budge. 'I'm not coming,' she said mulishly.

'Don't be a fool! You've no way of getting back on your own.'

Which was true enough. She had thrust a handful of small change into her purse, probably not enough to get her back to St Coram's. Her mind boggled at the long walk ahead of her, even if she could get a bus for part of the way.

'If you could lend me some money for a taxi?' she suggested diffidently.

'No way. I'll need all I've got with me. Get a bus.' Just for a moment Basil looked uncertain. 'You won't change your mind?'

She shook her head, willing him to change his, but he didn't; he turned on his heel and left her without so much as a backward glance. After a minute or so Phoebe followed him, to find the hall empty. She picked up her coat for a moment, pausing, then put it on and went to the door. She was on the point of going through it when the man she had spoken to during the evening came into the hall.

'Everyone gone?'

'Yes. I'm just...that is...thank you for a nice party.'

'Not going to the disco?'

'Well, no. I'm going to catch a bus...'

He had come to stand beside her. 'I'll drive you back to your hospital.' He muttered something under his breath, it sounded like, 'It's the least I can do.' But she wasn't sure of that.

Phoebe said politely: 'It's very kind of you to offer, but you have no need.'

For answer he took her arm, banged the door behind them and crossed the pavement to a Mercedes parked at the kerb. Phoebe got in, since there seemed no point in protesting further, and was whisked across London without further ado. Her companion didn't say a word until they had reached the hospital, and when she thanked him he said carelessly: 'Not at all. I'd better go and look for my wife, I suppose.'

Phoebe couldn't think of anything suitable to reply to this; she murmured goodnight and smiled uncertainly. It surprised her very much when he leaned across to say to her: 'Give him up, my dear—he's not for you.'

He had driven away before she could think of an answer to that one too.

And it seemed as though he would be right. Phoebe didn't see Basil at all the following day—nor, for that matter, for several days to come. And when at last she met him face to face as she came back from the Path Lab he gave her a cool nod and would have walked right past her if she hadn't stopped him with a firm voice which surprised her as much as it surprised him.

'Didn't you worry?' she asked. 'Leaving me to get back on my own from that party?'

He flushed a little. 'Worry? Why should I worry? A sensible girl like you—you're hardly likely to attract unwelcome attentions, are you?'

His faint sneer made her wince, but all the same she asked: 'Why not?'

She knew the answer; she supposed that because she had thought that she was in love with him, it was going to hurt, however nicely he put it.

But he didn't bother with niceness. 'My dear girl, you're not silly enough to imagine you're pretty?'

'Then why did you take me out?'

Basil laughed. 'An experience, shall we say—a very unrewarding one, I might add.'

Phoebe didn't say anything to that: she stood on tiptoe in her sensible black shoes and smacked his cheek hard. She was appalled the moment she had done it; it was an unpardonable thing to do, she told herself as she bolted back to the ward, to find Sister irate at the length of time she had been away. She stood meekly before that lady, letting her run on and on, and then, impatiently dismissed, skipped back to the ward to her endless chores.

There was an auxiliary nurse off sick, which meant that there was even more to do than usual; she steadily trotted to and fro, getting hot and untidy, responding to her patients' wants, glad at the same time that she had so much to occupy her that there was precious little time to think. Only when she was off duty did she allow her thoughts to dwell on Basil—a broken dream, she admitted that honestly, and she had been a fool to indulge in it. He'd been amusing himself between girlfriends, she had no doubt—like eating a slice of bread and butter between rich cream cakes.

She sat down at her functional dressing table, took off her cap and studied her face. Presently she unpinned her hair and pushed it this way and that, judging the effect. It was no good—she remained, at least to the casual eye, uninteresting. In her dressing gown presently, she trailed along the corridor and joined her friends over tea and a gossip, while at the back of her mind the idea of leaving—going right away—was already forming. She could give a month's notice and start again at another hospital. It would be a wrench, because she had been happy during the last year; she was never going to be brilliant in the nursing world, but she was good with patients and kind and gentle. Besides, she was young enough to start again. The idea had solidified into certainty by the time she was in bed; a fresh start, and she would forget the hurt Basil had inflicted.

She slept soundly because she was tired, but when she woke she knew that her mind was made up. She would go that very morning and see the Principal Nursing Officer, something she hardly looked forward to, as that lady was known among the lesser fry at the hospital as the Tartar—a quite unsuitable name, as it happened, for she was by no means fiery in character, although her wooden expression, and the fact that she smiled only at Christmas and the Annual Ball, made her intimidating. But Phoebe, having decided, wasn't going to be put off by that. When the breakfasts had been served and Sister had come on duty, she knocked on the office door, ready with her request to go to the office at nine o'clock.

But the speech was unnecessary. Sister looked up as she went in. 'They've just rung through, Nurse—you're to go down to the office at once. Run along.'

Phoebe didn't run, mindful of Sister Tutor's remarks about fire and haemorrhage, but she walked very fast, wondering what on earth she'd done.

She put an anxious hand to her cap, knocked on the door and was bidden to go in. The Tartar's wooden features wore an expression which Phoebe could only imagine to be sympathy, although she spoke briskly enough.

'Nurse Creswell, your aunt, Miss Kate Mason, is ill. She has asked her doctor to send for you—apparently you are her only relative.' She gave Phoebe an accusing look as though that was her fault. 'She feels most strongly that your place is by her side so she may be nursed back to health. I should add, Nurse, that your aunt is suffering from chronic bronchitis and crippling arthritis and is unlikely to regain a state of health when she will be unable to do without your care. It means, of course, that you will have to give up your training for at least the immediate future.'

Phoebe stared at the Tartar's cold eyes while she digested this information. Here was help not quite what she would have wished for, but a loophole of escape. Aunt Kate was a holy terror; dictatorial and on the mean side, she had ignored her family for years and Phoebe, the last member of it left, hadn't seen her for some time. So like Aunt Kate, she mused, to turn a cold shoulder on the family and then demand help as though it was her right. But it was an escape...

'Am I to go at once, Miss Ratcliffe?'

'Naturally. I consider this an emergency and the doctor who is attending her stresses the need for nursing help as soon as possible. You will be given compassionate leave until your leaving date and you will, of course, receive payment until that day. You may go today, Nurse Creswell, and I trust that your year with us as a student nurse has given you a good grounding for whatever tasks you will need to undertake.'

Phoebe sorted this out. 'Yes, Miss Ratcliffe, I'll do my best.' She added rather shyly: 'I've been very happy here.'

The Tartar inclined her head graciously. 'I trust that your future will be as happy, Nurse. Goodbye.'

Very doubtful, thought Phoebe, speeding back to the ward to tell Sister. Aunt Kate lived in Suffolk, in a village which she remembered only vaguely—but even if it had been a large town, she doubted very much whether she would get a great deal of time to spare. All the same, she liked the country; she would use some of her savings to buy a bike, so that when she had an hour or so... She was already making the best of a bad job when she knocked once more on Sister's door.

Sister was surprised and flatteringly reluctant to let her go. 'Not that I can do much about it,' she grumbled. 'I quite see that if your aunt has no one else to look after her, there's nothing else to be done.'

Phoebe refrained from saying that Aunt Kate had sufficient money to employ a private nurse if she so wished.

'Well, you'd better go,' sighed Sister, 'and you were turning into quite a good nurse too.'

Phoebe bade her goodbye, announced her departure to the nurses on the ward, explained to the patients, and took herself off to her room, where she started to pack. She was about halfway through this when two of her friends came over to change their aprons. They listened to her with astonishment, heedless of returning to their wards, begged her to write, and promised to say goodbye on her behalf to her other friends.

'What about Basil?' one of them asked.

Phoebe bent over her case, ramming things in with some force. 'I've had no time to see him or let him know,' she said casually. 'I daresay we'll meet up some time.'

Her companions exchanged glances. 'Well, have fun, Phoebe—we shall miss you.'

She would miss them too, she thought, sitting in the train, gazing out at the flat Essex countryside, but perhaps she would make new friends in the village. It was quite a long journey, and by the time the train reached Stowmarket, she was famished. She put her two cases in the left luggage at the station, then went into a nearby café and had a meal of sorts before collecting her luggage once more and crossing the square to board the bus for Woolpit. It was a five-mile ride and Phoebe sat in the almost empty bus, watching the first signs of spring with delight. London's parks were all very well, but they couldn't compete with primroses and the bread-and-cheese in the hedges under a thin sunshine from a pale blue sky. The bus turned off the by pass, rattled down the narrow road to the village and stopped at one side of the village green. Aunt Kate's house was on the other side, beyond the village pump, a nice old house with sash windows and tall Tudor chimneys. Phoebe said goodbye to the driver and carried her cases across the green, put them down in the porch which sheltered the white wood door, and thumped the knocker. The Tartar had told her that she would telephone the doctor to say that Phoebe was coming at once, but she doubted if she was expected quite as soon.

The door opened cautiously and a girl of sixteen peered round it.

'Hullo,' said Phoebe, 'I've come to look after Miss Mason. May I come in? I'm expected.'

The girl smiled then. She opened the door wide, took one of Phoebe's cases from her and said breathlessly: 'Oh, miss, come in, do. I said I'd stay until you got 'ere, 'e said I was to, but now I can go 'ome.'

'Do you come each day?' asked Phoebe quickly. 'And what's your name?'

'Susan, and I come mornings, to clean and that—there's been a nurse, but she won't come no more—couldn't manage with Miss Mason's ways. Went this morning, early she did.'

Hence the urgency, thought Phoebe. The doctor, whoever he might be, must think of her as a gift from heaven. She could imagine his relief; being a niece of his troublesome patient, she could hardly pack her bags and leave.

'Well, I'm here now,' said Phoebe hearteningly. 'Just show me where my room is and where you keep everything. Is my aunt in bed? Asleep?'

Susan nodded. 'She usually has a nap till tea.' She added anxiously. 'We could be quiet like.'

Phoebe nodded in wholehearted agreement. Let her just have time to look around her and make a cup of tea, she prayed hopefully, and followed Susan down the hall.

She remembered the house well enough. The kitchen was at the right of the passage at the back, a roomy old-fashioned place, its only concession to modern times being the gas stove. Aunt Kate had never seen the sense in spending money on washing machines and the like when she could get a young local girl to do the chores for a small wage. All the same, it was a pleasant place as well as old-fashioned, and it was clean. Phoebe nodded understanding at Susan's pointing finger; the larder, the sink, the various drawers and the old-fashioned dresser. They went quietly out again and disregarded the sitting room and dining room doors, then crept up the stairs beside the back door. The landing was roomy and had four doors leading from it as well as a narrow stair leading to the attics. One door was closed; and they listened long enough to hear the snores from behind it and then crossed to one of the rooms at the front of the house. It was rather sparsely furnished and the curtains and bed spread were a depressingly dull green, but it overlooked the street and the pale sun made it cheerful. A vase of flowers, thought Phoebe, and her few bits and pieces scattered around, would make all the difference. She nodded to Susan, took off her coat and left it on the bed and accompanied her silently downstairs again.

'Tomorrow?' she asked.

Susan nodded. 'Ar past eight, miss, till 'ar past twelve.' She was putting on her coat. 'There's things for supper in the larder—eggs and that.'

Phoebe opened the door, wished her goodbye and closed it quietly. Tea first, she decided, and something to eat. She was famished again, and once Aunt Kate woke she would probably be kept busy.

She put the kettle on, found teapot, tea, a bottle of milk and the sugar bowl and half a packet of digestive biscuits, and presently sat down at the table. It wasn't much of a meal, but she felt all the better for it and after she had tidied up she poked her head into the larder and assessed its contents. Eggs, some fish on a plate—but only enough for one—bread in the bin, butter, some old cheese and nothing much else. She wondered what the nurse had had to eat, and what, for that matter, she was to eat herself. The cupboards yielded a good supply of flour and oats and rice and sugar though; given time she should be able to whip up some sort of meal for the invalid. She found a tray and put it ready in case Aunt Kate should wake. It was well after four o'clock and perhaps she should take a look.

There was no need, a bell tinkled urgently and Phoebe hurried up the stairs, tapped on her aunt's door and went in.

Aunt Kate was propped up in bed, swathed in a thick shawl and by no means in a good temper. 'So there you are,' she snapped between coughs. 'And high time too—when a body can't depend on her own kith and kin taking care of her it's a poor state of affairs. I don't know what the world's coming to!'

Phoebe didn't know either, and since Aunt Kate's remarks were exactly the same as the last time they had met, she said merely: 'I came as soon as the hospital had your message, Aunt Kate, I'm sorry you are ill.'

'Pooh,' said Aunt Kate strongly. 'Fiddlesticks—and don't think you'll get a penny piece from me, my girl—I've better ways of leaving my money.' She added quickly: 'Not that I have any money, living here on my own with no one to bother about me.'

'The nurse?' asked Phoebe.

'Bah—stupid woman, all she could think of was her meals.' She shot Phoebe a grumpy look, her dark little eyes half closed. 'Do you eat a lot?'

'Yes,' said Phoebe simply. 'Would you like your tea now?'

Aunt Kate had a fit of coughing. 'Yes—thin bread and butter with it. When I've had it I'll talk to you.'

It was hard to be sorry for the old lady; she was ill and crippled with arthritis, and Phoebe did her best to pity her as she went back to the kitchen. She made the tea, cut paper-thin bread and butter and at the same time made jam sandwiches for herself, since she was still hungry, and having settled her aunt against her pillows with the tea tray on the bed table, went down again to make another pot of tea to accompany the sandwiches. She had just finished the last of them when Aunt Kate rang the bell.

'You'll stay of course,' she began without preamble. 'You're my niece, my great-niece, and it's your duty.'

'I've been training as a nurse,' observed Phoebe mildly.

'Time enough for that after I've gone. I'll not last long that Dr Pritchard says I'm good for a few more years yet, but I know better.'

'What happened to Dr Bennett?' asked Phoebe, vaguely remembering a small neat man with a goatee beard who called Aunt Kate 'dear lady' and sometimes had stayed for tea.

'Retired, drat him. Now I have to bear with this little whippersnapper who takes no notice of me whatsoever.' Aunt Kate pushed the bed table away impatiently. 'You can take this; I'll have a bit of fish for my supper—done in milk, mind—and an egg custard.'

Phoebe took the bed table away and picked up the tray. 'Tomorrow,' she said with firm gentleness, 'perhaps you will give me some money and I'll buy some food. There's almost nothing to eat in the house.'

'My appetite's poor,' snapped Aunt Kate.

'I expect so, but mine isn't. If I'm to stay, Aunt Kate, then I shall want to be fed, and since I've no money of my own, I'm afraid you'll have to pay me a salary.'

The old lady's eyes snapped. 'My own niece demanding a salary?'

'That's right. After all, you had to pay the nurse, didn't you? Private nurses are very expensive.'

Aunt Kate mumbled something in a cross voice and Phoebe was given to understand that she would be given pocket money—the sum mentioned would buy toothpaste and shampoo and tights, but precious little else, but Phoebe was satisfied. It was, after all, a small declaration of independence; if she hadn't taken a stand then and there, she would have become a doormat.

She took the tea tray downstairs and went back again to wash her aunt's face and hands and make her bed, chatting cheerfully as she did so. The doctor, her aunt told her grudgingly, came in the morning after surgery; it was he who had insisted on her having a nurse after calling unexpectedly one afternoon and finding her out of bed and struggling to get downstairs to get herself a meal.

'Why not the district nurse?' asked Phoebe.

'Won't have her near me,' declared Aunt Kate, and Phoebe sighed; the old lady took fierce dislikes to some people and no amount of inconvenience to other people would alter that. 'Nothing more than a baggage, that nurse Dr Pritchard made me have. Always looking at herself in the glass, wanting time off, if you please, said she needed recreation.' Aunt Kate gave a weary little snort. 'As though she had anything to do here! Susan cleans the house.'

Phoebe held her tongue and then asked what time she wanted her supper.

'Half past seven, and no later. And mind you do that fish in milk.'

Phoebe left a bedside light on, laid spectacles, book, handkerchief and bell within reach and took herself off to the kitchen. The fish looked unappetising; a morsel of creamed potato might brighten it up a bit, and she could purée a few carrots.

She had just set the egg custard in its pan of warm water when the front door was opened. Susan couldn't have closed it properly and she hadn't bothered to look herself. It might be a neighbour, but she doubted that; Aunt Kate didn't encourage neighbours; she ought to go into the hall and see who it was, but if she did the custard might spoil if she didn't get it into the oven at once.

Her decision was made for her. The kitchen door, half open, was flung wide and a large man came in. He was tall as well as broad with fair hair, cut short; a handsome face and a decidedly brisk manner.

'So you got here,' he stated with satisfaction. 'Thought I'd make sure you had arrived, otherwise it would have been the district nurse and fireworks. What's your name?'

'Phoebe Creswell.' Phoebe frowned. 'What's yours?'

'Pritchard, George.' He held out a hand and smiled and she didn't feel put out any more; he had a smile which was nice, friendly and reassuring. 'I hope your aunt is pleased to see you.'

Phoebe closed the door gently on the custard. 'Well, yes, I think on the whole she is.'

He nodded. 'Good. She's ill, you know that.' His gaze swept round the kitchen and stayed on the fish. 'Her supper?' he wanted to know. 'What about you?'

She was touched that he had thought of that. 'Well, there's nothing much in the house—I can't think what the nurse had to eat. I'll make some toasted cheese.' The small nose twitched; she was hungry again. After all, she hadn't had much to eat all day—a good cooked dinner. Her mouth watered at the thought.

'I'm on the other side of the green. When I've done my rounds I'll send my housekeeper over to sit here while you have supper with me. No, don't argue, it'll give me a chance to explain your aunt's case to you and discuss medicines and so on.' He glanced at his watch. 'About eight o'clock. Right?'

Phoebe nodded happily. If this was Aunt Kate's little whipper-snapper then she liked him. She closed the door after him and went back to her cooking. Life was suddenly full of promise. She hadn't thought of Basil even once.

CHAPTER TWO

AUNT KATE, while showing no gratitude for her supper, ate all of it, reminded Phoebe that she would have a glass of hot milk at nine o'clock precisely and told her grudgingly that she might go downstairs and eat her own meal. But first she needed her pillows shaken up, her spectacles, glass of water, and the local newspaper. Only then did she add: 'At least your cooking is passable, and don't forget my milk.' She added: 'I shall be perfectly all right for an hour or so. When you've cleared up you can unpack your things.'

'Yes, Aunt Kate.' Phoebe spoke mildly, her thoughts on supper.

She had had the forethought to leave the front door on the latch, and before she had done more than clear the tray, a thin elderly woman came quietly in. She was dressed in a thick skirt and a grey cardigan, which, with her pepper-and-salt hair cut severely short and her pale face, gave Phoebe the impression that she was looking at an etching. They shook hands and she changed her mind. Mrs Thirsk had the bluest eyes she had ever met, and when she smiled her whole face lit up.

'Supper's on the table, Miss...'

'Call me. Phoebe, please, Mrs Thirsk.'

'Phoebe.' The smile came and went again. 'But I'll just see to these...'

'You leave them. The doctor said you were to go straight over.' She studied Phoebe's small, too thin figure. 'You look as though you could do with a good hot meal.'

'Oh, I could—there's been no time...'

'And nothing in the house, I'll be bound.' Mrs Thirsk went to the sink and filled the bowl with water from the kettle. 'I've brought my knitting,' she stated. 'Take your jacket, it's chilly.'

Phoebe nodded, slung her cardigan over her shoulders and went out of the house, across the green, to tap on the solid wooden door of the doctor's house. It was a good deal grander than her aunt's, of white bricks, with a tiled roof and Elizabethan chimneypots to match and latticed windows. She stood back to get a better view just as the door was opened.

'Come in,' invited Dr Pritchard, 'it's rabbit stew with dumplings—one of Mrs Thirsk's masterpieces.'

The hall was square, with a curved staircase to one side of it and several doors leading from it. The floor was of flagstones covered for the most part with rugs with a carved chest along one wall. A large black labrador pranced to meet Phoebe as she went in, sniffed her fist and barked cheerfully.

'Beauty,' said Dr Pritchard, 'I hope you like dogs?'

'Oh, yes, but I've never had one of my own.' She gave him a rather shy smile. 'I like cats too.'

'In the kitchen,' he said briefly, 'a basket full of them; Venus has just had kittens.'

He pushed open one of the doors and she went past him into the sitting room, a low-ceilinged, beamed and cosily furnished room, with chairs pulled up to the log fire in the wide hearth.

'You could do with a glass of sherry,' stated the doctor, and handed her one before she could answer. 'Do sit down.'

They didn't talk much as they had their drinks, only a few questions and answers; how long was it since she had been there? How far was she with her training? Did she intend to resume that later on?

To all of which she replied a little vaguely, since she hadn't really thought about it yet. And over supper the doctor kept the conversation on general topics while they ate with healthy appetites. It was only when they had carried the dishes to the kitchen, admired Venus and her kittens and taken the coffee tray into the sitting room that he started to tell her about Aunt Kate.

'Of course, she can't last out much longer,' he explained. 'She's worn out and her heart is already weak. I've done what I can, but she refuses to go into hospital or a nursing home and the nurse I arranged for was given short shift. How about you? You've not had much to say so far.'

'Well, I've not had much time to think about it, have I?

Phoebe's quiet face was turned to the fire. 'Of course, I shall stay even if Aunt Kate dislikes it, and she will in a few days, even though she insisted on my coming. She's never liked anyone in the family and I'm the only one left now. She says it's my duty.'

She glanced at the doctor watching her intently. 'There's nothing else to do,' she added simply. 'But I'd much rather not.'

'Any ties?' he asked idly, and when she looked puzzled. 'Boyfriends and so forth?'

Phoebe went pink. 'No.' She had the urge to tell him all about Basil and how coming to Aunt Kate's had solved that problem for her, but after all, she had only just met him. When she didn't say anything he said slowly: 'Well, that makes things easier, doesn't it? Now, as to treatment...'

He was all at once the doctor.

'When he had finished she said: 'I'll do my best, Dr Pritchard. Do you come every day to see Aunt Kate?'

'Oh, yes. Just a quick check up, you know.' He smiled at her very kindly. 'And don't forget to pass on any problems, however small.'

It seemed the right moment to go and he made no effort to keep her, but walked across the green to her aunt's door and waited until Mrs Thirsk opened it, said a few brief words to Phoebe and went back with her. Phoebe, closing the door slowly, watched them go, comforted by the fact that they were within shouting distance.

Aunt Kate was sitting up in bed reading. As Phoebe went in she looked up and asked: 'My milk—is it ready? It's more than time—and I have some pills to take.'

'Yes, Aunt, I'll fetch the milk now and your pills. Is there anything I can do for you before you have them?'

Aunt Kate rapped out a list of small wants. 'And mind you lock up properly,' she ended breathlessly 'I never trusted that other creature.' She fell into a fit of coughing and finally gasped crossly: 'For heaven's sake, Phoebe, don't just stand there!'

It took almost an hour to settle Aunt Kate for the night. When she was at last satisfied that everything had been done to her satisfaction, she lay back against her pillows, allowed Phoebe to shade the bedside light and declared herself ready for sleep. 'And don't forget that I like my tea at seven o'clock,' she commanded as Phoebe bade her goodnight.

There were chores to do downstairs, but presently she locked up and went to her room where she unpacked and undressed. The room looked better already with her own things scattered round it. Tomorrow she would get some flowers and look in the cupboard on the landing and see if there was a more colourful bedspread.

Aunt Kate was asleep, looking old and frail, so that Phoebe, peeping round the door, felt a pang of real pity. With any luck, she would sleep the night through. Phoebe crept into the bathroom on the other side of the landing and turned on the old-fashioned geyser and presently sank into a hot bath. The day had been long and eventful and she was tired. It was an effort to get herself out and into her bed, and once there she was asleep at once.

She was used to getting up early. She was downstairs in the kitchen in her dressing gown making tea when Aunt Kate rang her bell. Phoebe picked up the tea tray and hurried upstairs, to find the old lady irritable and impatient.

'Still in your dressing gown?' she wanted to know. 'I hope you're not lazy...'

Phoebe wished her good morning, sat her up against freshly shaken pillows and offered her pills and tea. 'I'll dress while you drink your tea, and then I'll freshen you up before breakfast.'

She prudently didn't wait for Aunt Kate to disagree, but whisked herself back to her own room, got into a grey wool dress which did nothing for her at, all, tied her hair back with a ribbon to save time, and went back to Aunt Kate.

Aunt Kate was as firmly against being washed and put into a clean nightie as Phoebe was determined that this was to be done. Phoebe won. A stint on Women's Medical Ward had taught her how to get round elderly ladies who wanted to do exactly the opposite of what was asked of them; calm, kindness and never-ending patience were three virtues she had acquired and she was by nature a kind girl. Aunt Kate, almost without realising it, found herself washed, clad in another of her old-fashioned nightgowns, her hair combed and pinned into a tidy knot, and then she was lifted into a bedside chair, where she sat watching clean sheets being put on her bed and wearily scolding at the extra washing which would have to be done. Phoebe popped her back into bed while she was still complaining. 'There,' she said, 'isn't that better? I'll get your breakfast.'

Coddled egg, thin bread and butter and a cup of tea, nicely arranged on a tray—even Aunt Kate could find no fault with that. Phoebe went back to the kitchen and boiled an egg, made some toast and a pot of tea and sat down at the table to eat her own breakfast, while she made a list of the shopping which had to be done. She hadn't finished when Susan arrived, accepted a cup of tea, and declared her intention of giving the kitchen a good going over. 'But I'll tidy up first, miss, only Miss Mason don't much like me in her room.'

'Then I'll do it—you see to the rest of the house, Susan, just as you always do. Dr Pritchard doesn't come until after surgery, does he? I'll go out as soon as I've seen to my aunt and do the shopping.'

Aunt Kate had eaten most of her breakfast. 'And what do you fancy for your lunch?' enquired Phoebe. 'I'm going to the shops presently. What about a morsel of chicken and potato with some mashed parsnips?'

'Chicken costs a lot of money,' observed Miss Mason.

'Cheaper than meat, Aunt Kate. And I'll get a marrow bone and make soup—that's nice with toast for supper.' She added carefully: 'I'll need some money.'

Aunt Kate put her hand under the bedclothes and withdrew a purse, she had sat with it in her hand while Phoebe had made the bed. 'I'm a poor old woman,' she said with mournful mendacity. 'We'll be starving at this rate.'

'I'm a good manager,' Phoebe assured her, 'but there really is nothing in the larder, and you need good nourishing food. The milkman called just now and said you only had a pint every other day; I asked him to leave a pint each day. I can make milk puddings and custards which won't cost much and will do you good.' She added cunningly: 'There's masses of rice in the kitchen cupboard, and semolina too—no need to buy those for weeks.'

'You'll use up everything there is,' demanded Aunt Kate, 'and not waste my money!'

Phoebe was nipping round the room with a duster; she could have written her name on the old-fashioned mantlepiece. Obviously the nurse had either not bothered, or Aunt Kate had refused to let her keep the room clean, let alone tidy. The floor could do with a good Hoovering, only she doubted if Aunt Kate had such a thing in the house. Oblivious to her aunt's complaining voice, she wiped down the ledges and the table tops, and collected newspapers, pacifying her aunt with the paper which had just arrived. Promising to be back to give her her elevenses, she got a jacket and let herself out of the house. It was only just after nine o'clock and the street was quiet, although there were several cars outside the doctor's house, Phoebe walked the short distance to where the shops were—the butcher's, the general store and Post Office, and tucked in between these, a bow-fronted window full of small antiques. She paused a moment to peer at these before opening the door of the stores. There was no one in the shop, but the old-fashioned bell at the door brought a small round woman from the door behind the counter.

'Miss Mason's niece,' she said with satisfaction. 'Susan said you was come.'

Phoebe offered a hand over the counter. 'Phoebe Creswell,' she said politely.

'Mrs Platt. Come to stock up a bit, 'ave you? By all accounts there weren't much in the house. Can't say I blame that nurse—not that I liked her, mind you—a stuck-up piece if ever there was one.'

She studied Phoebe's pleasant not quite pretty face and nodded. 'Now what's it to be?'

Phoebe studied her list. She had whittled it down as far as she dared, for Aunt Kate hadn't been over-generous with the housekeeping. Luckily Mrs Platt was sympathetic; Phoebe made her purchases, bought some stamps for herself and went to the butcher next door. He obliged with a piece of chicken, a large bone and two lamb chops, made the observation that it was a pleasure to have her for a customer, and bade her a cheerful good morning.

At least the people were friendly, she thought, and the morning was bright and the sky blue. Life could be far worse. Just for the moment she allowed her thoughts to dwell upon Basil, but only for a moment; he wasn't worth wasting time over. She went back into the house, watched, if she did but know it, by Dr Pritchard, pausing between patients. Only when she had closed the door behind her did he press his buzzer and turn an impersonally friendly face to his next patient.

Phoebe put away her purchases, made a neat list of what she had spent, and took it upstairs with her aunt's egg and milk. She listened to Aunt Kate's tirade over the cost of everything without rancour, handed over the change and observed that she was going to find out from Susan where she could buy vegetables. She slipped away before her aunt could argue.

Susan was a mine of information. Her own dad had a tidy bit of garden, she could bring anything within reason any time she was asked, she said.

So Phoebe made another list, argued prices with Susan and went back upstairs to ask for the money. 'Far cheaper than I could buy in a shop,' she pointed out cheerfully, 'and Susan will bring just as much as we need; there won't be any waste.' And this argument appealed to Aunt Kate, who produce the purse once more.

Susan had done her best with the kitchen. Phoebe shared the Nescafé with her, and, left alone, began on the lunch. She was peeling potatoes when Dr Pritchard came in. His 'Hullo,' was brisk and friendly. 'I never knock,' he advised her. 'Susan's always sweeping and dusting and I know my way around.' He gave her a quick look. 'Sleep well?'

'Me? Oh yes, thank you. Aunt Kate had a good night, she's got a very rapid pulse and a bit of a temperature; I've written them down upstairs. She ate most of her breakfast and took her pills.'

'Then we'll have a look at her, shall we?'

We waited while she washed her hands and then followed her upstairs.

Aunt Kate received him with a testy observation that she didn't need him, that she was feeling better and that if she wanted him to visit she would send a message.

To all of which he merely nodded his handsome head, observed that it was nice to see her looking so much better and that he would take a look at her chest now that he was there.

He was kind and gentle, waiting patiently while she coughed and grumbled, struggling for breath. He put his stethoscope away presently and sat down by the bed to enquire in a leisurely fashion just how she felt.

The old lady cast him a waspish look. 'None the better for seeing you, young man. I doubt you know anything about me—all I need is a bottle of tonic to get me on my feet and something to ease the cough.'

It was no good talking to Aunt Kate about antibiotics, Phoebe could see that, and Dr Pritchard didn't really try, he remarked that it was early days for a tonic to be of much use but that he would send over a bottle of something to help the cough.

Phoebe's eyes flew to the bottles already arranged tidily on the chest of drawers, some only half finished. She looked away and caught the doctor's eye, a limpid stare which forbade her to make any comments about the half-empty bottles. It was as they went downstairs and she was on the point of opening the door for him that he said: 'Your aunt forgets easily. Pop over to the surgery in about half an hour, I'll give you a bottle of linctus; keep on with the antibiotics. Her heart's weaker, but there's nothing much I can do for congestive heart failure at this stage.'

'I'll take care of her,' said Phoebe. 'You'll—you'll come if I'm worried? There's no phone...'

'I'll come.' He nodded and strode off across the green. Perhaps she should have offered him a cup of coffee, she thought, watching his broad back disappearing into his house.

Life settled itself into a routine, taking care of an increasingly querulous Aunt Kate, shopping as frugally as she was able and taking snatches of time off whenever she could. The highlight of her day was Dr Pritchard's visit—not that he wasted much time on her, merely giving her fresh instructions, enquiring casually as to her own welfare and urging her to get out into the fresh air as often as she could. 'Make a point of going for a walk before you do the shopping,' he suggested. 'Susan's in the house and she'll let me know if I'm needed in a hurry.'

His intent eyes studied her face. 'You're too thin and far too pale.' He grinned suddenly. 'Pining for the bright lights or a boy-friend?'

She was furious to find herself blushing. 'No, I'm very happy here.'

His grunt was unbelieving.

Days became weeks and March became April, and the early mornings were now a delight. She read letters from her friends at St Coram's and found herself glad that she wasn't there any more. There was nothing to do in Woolpit, and yet she was content with her dull life, nor did she look ahead. It was soothing to live from day to day, forgetting the past and paying no attention to the future. Aunt Kate took up more and more of her time, for she was becoming weaker and more difficult to nurse. She had no appetite now and Phoebe spent a long time with her nose in a cookery book, turning out appetising little meals which, as often as not, were not eaten. But ill though she was, Aunt Kate's tongue hadn't lost its sharpness, nothing was right. Phoebe spent too much money on the food, didn't answer the bell as quickly as she should, left her poor old aunt alone for hours on end…

She said nothing, because it was clear that Aunt Kate was getting worse. Dr Pritchard had taken to calling in twice a day now, never stopping for more than a few minutes, but it was comforting to know that he was very aware of the situation. Phoebe had been in Woolpit almost three weeks when Aunt Kate began to go downhill fast. Phoebe took to sitting up late and getting up very early and then, finally, getting into her dressing gown and sitting in a chair in Aunt Kate's room and dozing through the night, waking at the first cough or movement.

'Getting tired?' Dr Pritchard wanted to know. 'Hang on if you can—I don't want to upset her by bringing in a strange face. I'll come over about midnight. Would you like Mrs Thirsk to sleep here?'

Phoebe shook her head. 'No, thank you all the same. I'll be all right. If—if I'm worried I shall run over and fetch you?'

'Right, do that.'

Her aunt was weaker when he came that afternoon. 'Plenty to drink if she'll take it, and keep her comfortable,' he said and went again.

With the evening the house seemed very quiet. Phoebe saw to her patient, made herself some tea and finally got ready for bed. She longed to sleep, but although Aunt Kate was sleeping she looked much worse. She curled up in a chair just beyond the lamp's dim light and longed for Dr Pritchard to come. But that wouldn't be for another couple of hours.

He came long before then, opening the street door and calling softly as he came into the house. When he came into the room Phoebe got out of the chair. 'I am glad you're here,' she whispered. 'I don't think—that is, I think Aunt Kate's not so well…'

He had gone to bend over his patient. 'We won't disturb her. I'll stay—you can go to bed, you're asleep on your feet!'

'Is she…?' And when he nodded: 'I'll stay, she's my aunt.'

So they sat facing each other in the big bedroom while Aunt Kate slipped peacefully away. It was after midnight when the doctor stood up finally.

'You'd better sleep at my place,' he suggested gently.

'I'll be quite all right, thank you. Would you like tea before you go?'

'A good idea. I'll get the writing done while you are making it. You'd rather stay here?'

'Yes.' She went past him and down to the kitchen and put the kettle on. There was really a good deal to think about, but she was far too tired.

They drank their tea almost in silence, while Dr Pritchard did his writing, and she got up and went to the door with him when he'd finished. It was a chilly night and she shivered as she opened it, and not altogether with cold, although her thanks and goodnight were composed enough. He took the door handle from her. 'Mrs Thirsk will be over in five minutes,' he told her and was gone before she could argue.

Indeed, she didn't much want to argue. She was thankful not to be alone in the house despite her assurances to him, and the housekeeper's matter-of-fact presence was comforting. She waved away Phoebe's apologies, took the cup of tea which she was offered and sat talking about nothing much for a few minutes. Then she got up briskly, asked where the hot water bottles were kept, filled them, gave one to Phoebe and told her with brisk kindness to go to bed, 'And no getting up at crack of dawn,' she warned. 'I'll see that you're up in time for Susan before I get the doctor's breakfast.'

Phoebe hardly heard her. She said goodnight in a wispy voice and went upstairs and presently got into her bed, listening with childish relief to Mrs Thirsk's rather heavy footfall mounting to the room on the other side of the landing. The bed hadn't been made up, thought Phoebe sleepily, and closed her eyes.

When she opened them Mrs Thirsk was standing by the bed with a cup of tea in her hand. 'Plenty of time, Phoebe. Just you drink this up and then come down when you're ready. I've put everything out for your breakfast. I'll be off now—you'll be all right?'

Phoebe sat up in bed, her mousy hair a fine curtain round her still pale face. 'Oh, Mrs Thirsk, thank you! Yes, of course I will.' She hesitated. 'I'm not sure what to do...'

'Doctor will be over when he's had his breakfast—he'll know,' said Mrs Thirsk comfortably.

Things seemed so different now. The morning was bright and sunny and Dr Pritchard would see to everything. Phoebe dressed and got her breakfast, then opened the door to Susan, who in some mysterious way knew all about Aunt Kate. 'Poor ol' soul,' she observed in her soft courteous country voice. 'She'll be better off where she is. When's the funeral, miss?'

Phoebe shook her head. 'I don't know—I don't know anything at present.'

Dr Pritchard came then, and sat himself down at the kitchen table. 'The district nurse will be here in a few minutes,' he observed. 'Now listen to me...'

He had thought of everything. When he had finished he said, 'Mr Cole, your aunt's solicitor, will come here for the funeral—

you'll stay here for the time being, of course. Do you mind being in the house alone?'

'No.' She glanced at Susan, sitting between them, listening to every word. 'Susan and I could springclean.'

'You'll sleep here on your own?'

'Oh, yes.' She looked enquiringly at him and he said: 'You'll have it to yourself, Phoebe.' He started for the door. 'Borrow Mrs Thirk's bike and take yourself off for a ride round, and don't come back until after twelve.' He smiled. 'Doctor's orders!'

The next day or so went quickly enough. Susan came each morning and the pair of them scrubbed and polished and turned out cupboards and drawers, and Phoebe was too tired in the evenings to do more than tumble into bed. She saw almost nothing of Dr Pritchard, but he was there, on the other side of the green, and she was content with that.

It surprised her that so many people came to the funeral. The church was full, but only a handful of people came back to the house afterwards and they didn't stay long. And when the last one had gone Mr Cole sat down in the sitting room and opened his briefcase.

'Miss Mason's will is brief,' he began in his dry elderly voice. 'It was made some months ago, before you came to nurse your aunt.' He smoothed the paper in his hand. 'I will read it to you.'

Aunt Kate had left every penny she possessed, a not inconsiderable amount, to charity, and the house was to be sold and the proceeds of it given to a list of charities she named. 'I leave nothing to my sole surviving relation, Phoebe Creswell,' she had written. 'She is young and strong enough to make her own way in life.'

Mr Cole coughed and folded the paper carefully. 'I regret this, Miss Creswell—you could, of course, contest it.'

Phoebe shook her head. She supposed that in the back of her mind she had nurtured the faint hope that Aunt Kate had left her a small sum, but she wasn't surprised at the will and since Aunt Kate didn't want her to have any money, then she for her part had no intention of trying to get it.

'I can go back to nursing,' she pointed out quite cheerfully, 'and

I really didn't expect anything, Mr Cole. Aunt Kate didn't like me—indeed, we hardly knew each other.'

Mr Cole grunted morosely. 'I still regret it, my dear. You have, after all, interrupted your training in order to look after her.'

'Yes, but I daresay she didn't realise that. I can always start again.'

'There is, of course, no hurry for you to leave here. The place will have to be sold, but it will probably take some time and it will be all the better for someone living here. Have you any money?'

'Well, I can manage for a week or two, but I can't afford to pay Susan.'

Mr Cole looked thoughtful. 'Ah yes—well...it would be quite in order for the estate to settle her wages until such time as the house is sold. I can arrange that and I will see that she is told. You will remain for the time being?' Phoebe said yes, she would. A week or two would give her time to apply to be taken on as a student nurse—not in London, though. She didn't want to go back there, she didn't much care if she never saw London again, nor St Coram's, nor Basil. Certainly not Basil.

He arrived the next day, driving up in his flashy little car and hooting furiously in front of the house. Phoebe, upstairs sorting blankets, poked her head out of the window, and when she saw who it was, gazed down at him speechlessly.

'Hullo there—aren't you going to let me in?' He spoke loudly enough for the neighbours to hear—indeed, Dr Pritchard, on the other side of the green, heard him and turned a placid gaze on him through his surgery window. He had been about to ring for the next patient, now he took his hand off the bell and waited to see what would happen.

Phoebe withdrew her head and went down to open the door, to stand squarely in the doorway. She didn't invite Basil in. Not only was she aware that several people would be peering through their windows at her, but she really didn't want to see Basil. She realised this with great relief. She had got over him entirely—indeed, looking at him, she wondered how on earth she could ever have thought she was in love with him in the first place.

She said soberly, 'Hullo, Basil,' and waited.

'Well, aren't I to come in?' he asked, and flashed her his charming smile.

'No, I'd rather you didn't.'

He shrugged. 'I've driven all this way to see how you were getting on. How's that aunt of yours?'

'Aunt Kate died a few days ago.'

'Left you all her worldly goods and the house? Lucky you!'

'Aunt Kate didn't leave me anything.'

'The miserable old...' He stopped at the look on Phoebe's face.

'She was my aunt, she was entitled to leave her money to anyone she wished. I hardly knew her.'

'Hard luck, old girl. Coming back to St Coram's?'

Phoebe studied his face. Very good-looking, but there was something missing. 'No.'

'Oh, come on, now!'

'Why do you ask?'

He shrugged again. He wasn't going to tell her that he had had a bet with some of the other housemen that he would persuade her to return to St Coram's. 'Idle curiosity. I say, aren't you really going to ask me in?'

'No.' She added: 'I'm very busy. Goodbye.' She closed the door in his face.

Basil muttered to himself, got into his car and roared off, and Dr Pritchard, his face still placid, rang for the next patient.

When he had done his morning rounds he crossed the green and knocked on the door. Phoebe, still upstairs, poked her head out of the window again. She said with marked relief: 'Oh, it's you—I'll come down. Susan's just gone.'

She was very untidy and faintly grubby with it. Dr Pritchard eyed her keenly and went past her into the kitchen. 'Having a busy morning?' he wanted to know.'

'Well, yes, there is a lot to do. The whole house needs a good clean, and I'm making an inventory—in case someone wants to buy the furniture and things.'

'Not lonely?'

'No, Susan comes.'

'Your aunt didn't leave you the house?' The doctor sounded very casual.

Phoebe hadn't told anyone about the will. 'No—she left everything, this house as well, to charities. I'm just staying for a few days. Mr Cole said I could until they put the house up for sale, it'll give me a chance to apply for training somewhere.'

He leaned against the kitchen table. 'And that's what you intend to do?'

'Yes,' said Phoebe in a determined voice. She picked up the crockery spread on the table, ready to pack, and started to stack it neatly.

'Start all over again?'

'I'll have to, won't I?'

'Only if that's what you want.' He went to the door. 'You and I must have a talk. A pity I have to go out this evening. How about tomorrow morning? Before surgery? Say eight o'clock, we'll have half an hour. I've been having breakfast at half-past seven—have it with me?'

She hesitated. 'Thank you, but isn't that—I mean, isn't it rather an odd time?'

He grinned. 'I don't imagine anyone in the village could possibly weave a romance round breakfast at half-past seven in the morning, do you?'

Phoebe went pink. 'No, of course not. Aren't I silly... I'd like to come. What do you want to talk about?'

He was suddenly serious. 'Why, your future, Phoebe, what else?'

She went back to her sorting of the contents of the linen cupboard, wondering why he should show even a faint interest in what she intended to do. But it spurred her on to make some definite plans. When she had finished with the endless counterpanes, pillowcases and enormous linen sheets her aunt had favoured, she changed into the grey dress, did her face and tidied her hair and went down to Mrs Platt's shop. One end of the counter was stacked with weekly magazines and daily newspapers, but there wasn't a *Nursing Mirror* or *Nursing Times* among them. Phoebe bought some sausages for her supper, then crossed the street to the row of brick cottages where the district nurse lived. Nurse Wilkins was at home, getting her lunch and feeding her cats; she called 'Come in' in answer to Phoebe's knock and shouted: 'I'm in the kitchen, come through.' She smiled when she saw who it was, 'Hullo, love, feeling lonely?'

Phoebe shook her head. 'I've got too much to do—the house goes up for sale in a few days and I'm getting it ready.'

'Miss Mason didn't leave it to you? The village seemed to think she might, and she had pots of money.'

'Everything is to go to several charities.' And at the look of disbelief on her companion's face: 'It doesn't matter—I hadn't expected anything, she didn't have anything to do with the family for years and years.'

'Until she needed someone to nurse her. What are you going to do?'

'That's why I came. Have you any copies of the *Nursing Times?* I'll apply to start training.'

'But didn't I hear that you'd done a year already? Won't your old hospital take you back?'

'I don't want to go back to London. I'd forgotten how lovely it is living in the country. I thought I'd try a provincial town.'

Nurse Wilkins prudently refrained from pointing out that the country could be quite a long way from a provincial town large enough to have a training school for nurses. 'You'll find a pile in the sitting room—there are some *Nursing Mirrors* there too—take as many as you want. I'd ask you to stay to have a meal, but I popped back for half an hour from a midder case. I'm sorry you've had such rotten luck.'

'That's all right. Actually I've liked being here very much, and thanks.'

Nurse Wilkins waved her spoon at her. 'Any time.'

There were depressingly few hospitals offering vacancies. Phoebe made a careful note of them while she ate her lunch and then sat down to apply to each one of them. She couldn't expect to be taken on for at least a month, but she had a little money saved, so perhaps she could find a job in Stowmarket while she waited for the answers. She wrote her letters, and since she had no stamps and Mrs Platt was closed for the half day, put on her jacket and took herself off for a long walk. The house seemed very empty when she got back. She made tea, then sat in the kitchen at the table and worked out how long she would be able to manage on the money she had. The result wasn't very satisfactory. She went into the sitting room and settled down to washing the china in the cabinet opposite the window. While she was doing it she saw Dr Pritchard, splendid in a black tie, get into his Bristol and drive off. Somehow the sight of him made her feel lonelier than ever. She ate her sausages gloomily, then took herself off to bed and stayed awake a long time feeling depressed.

It was a relief to wake early to a lovely morning with the sun already streaming through the window. She got up and dressed in the grey dress once more, did her hair rather more severely than usual and at half-past seven crossed the green and rang Dr Pritchard's bell.

Mrs Thirsk opened the door with a cheerful good morning, and the news that she was on the point of dishing up the bacon and eggs and would Phoebe like to go straight into the dining room. 'Doctor had an early morning call, and he's having a shave, but he'll be down in a moment.'

'Oh,' said Phoebe, 'perhaps some other time—I mean, I daresay he's tired…'

'No, he's not, only ravenous. Good morning, Phoebe.' He had come down the stairs and caught her arm and whisked her into the dining room. 'Pour the coffee, there's a good girl.'

She did as she was asked, taking a quick look at him. He didn't look in the least tired and his manner was as unhurried as it always was.

Mrs Thirsk came in with their breakfast then, and beyond a word here and there for politeness' sake, he said very little. Only when they had got to the toast and marmalade and his third cup of coffee did he ask: 'Made any plans?'

'I've borrowed some nursing magazines from Nurse Wilkins and written to five hospitals to see if they'll take me in their training schools.'

'Posted them?'

Phoebe thought it a funny question. 'As a matter of fact, no—I hadn't any stamps.'

'Good. Tear them up, I've got a much better idea.'

She opened her grey eyes wide. 'You have? Whatever is it?'

'It seems to me to be an excellent idea if we were to get married.'

Phoebe's eyes almost popped out of her head. 'Married? You and me? But you don't and I don't...that is, we don't know anything about each other.'

'Oh, I know a great deal about you, quite enough to be sure you'll make me an excellent wife. As for me—well, I live here, don't I? I live in this house and intend to live here for the rest of my life. I like it here. I like to travel too. My mother is Dutch; my father died several years ago and she spends a good deal of the year in Holland—she has a home there as well as a house in Grantchester; naturally I visit her frequently.'

Phoebe closed her open mouth to ask: 'You're half Dutch?' A silly question, but it was all she could think of.

'Yes.' He smiled at her. 'I could practise there if I wished—I qualified there as well as in England.'

'Oh, yes, well...' She gave him a bewildered stare. 'But why do you want to marry me?'

I'm thirty-two and it's time I settled down. I haven't met a girl I wanted to marry, someone who would fit into my life—but you, you would. We could, of course, get to know each other better, have a long engagement, but what would be the point of that? You have no plans for the future, no money, no family, your heart is whole...'

Phoebe nodded. 'Yes, oh yes. But I'm not sure...I mean, would it work?'

'I can't think why not. We get on well, don't we? We might just as well get married now and get to know each other.' He smiled kindly. 'I won't rush you, Phoebe. We'll have a month or two of getting to know each other, just as an engaged couple would, only we'll get married for the sake of convenience.'

Phoebe was still bowled over. 'I—I must think about it—it's a bit of a surprise.'

He glanced at his watch and said matter-of-factly: 'Off you go, then. I must start surgery. Only promise me one thing—don't send those letters until you've made up your mind. Give it a couple of days' thought.'

'All right,' said Phoebe, 'I'll think about it, and I won't send those letters.'

'Good girl! I must fly.' He patted her shoulder and left the room as Mrs Thirsk came in.

'It was a lovely breakfast,' said Phoebe. 'Thank you, Mrs Thirsk.' She had no idea how agitated her face looked, nor did she see Mrs Thirsk's thoughtful glance. 'I must get on with the packing up,' she told that lady, and got herself out of the house.

'That's a right old shame that Miss Mason left all that money to silly old charities,' Susan greeted her. News spread fast in the village.

'Charities do a lot of good,' said Phoebe feebly. 'I wonder if the house is put up for sale yet?' She put a hand to her head. She must forget about Dr Pritchard for the moment, there was still a lot to do. Later she would sit down quietly and decide what was best. It would have helped a lot if there had been someone in whom she could have confided.

CHAPTER THREE

IT DISCONCERTED Phoebe very much not to see anything of Dr Pritchard for the next two days. For once quite unable to make up her sensible mind, she fought the urge to go across the green and bang on his door—an urge she suppressed until the evening of the second day. Then she suddenly flung down the curtains she was folding away into, the landing cupboard, opened the street door and hurried across the green to beat a tattoo on his knocker.

Mrs Thirsk opened the door, bade her enter and said comfortably: 'You'll be wanting to see the doctor? He's gone to Baxter's farm to see their youngest—measles, by all accounts. He'll be back in about ten minutes. Come in and sit down.'

Phoebe sidled to the door. 'No—no, thanks. It was just something...not important—any time will do.' She actually had her hand on the doorknob when Mrs Thirsk said matter-of-factly: Seeing as you're here, it makes sense to stay, otherwise he'll go across to see you when he could just as soon be sitting cosy by his own hearth.' She smiled suddenly and opened the sitting room door. 'He won't be above a few minutes.'

So Phoebe went and sat down in the smaller of the armchairs on either side of the hearth, and Beauty came and sat with her, pressed up against her legs, yawning into the log fire. It was pleasant room and peaceful, and somehow knowing that she was there sent her problems oozing away. She had been a fool to come in the first place, she decided. How did one seek advice about marrying someone when that someone was the person expected to give the advice?

The knotty point was settled for her by the doctor's quiet entry.

'You look quite at home sitting there, Phoebe.' He smiled at her and sat down in the big wing chair opposite her, and Beauty moved across to lay her head on his shoes. 'What's the trouble?' He shot her a keen look. 'Or is it just the pleasure of my company?'

'I like being with you,' said Phoebe ingenuously, and didn't see the gleam in his eyes. 'It's a bit difficult—you see, I want to talk to someone and ask their advice, only there isn't anyone—only you, and you're the person I want advice about.'

'I'll do my best to be impartial,' he told her gravely.

'Oh, good. It's like this…' She paused and asked hurriedly: 'Have you had your supper—am I keeping you from that? Or—or reading or anything?'

'Supper's an hour or more away, but we'll have a drink while we're talking.' He got up and poured her a glass of sherry and gave himself a whisky, then settled back comfortably in his chair.

Phoebe took a sip of sherry and then another one. 'Did you really mean that you wanted to marry me?'

'Yes, I meant it.'

'Do you think we would be happy? I mean, just being friends without being in love and all that?'

The corners of his firm mouth twitched. 'Yes, being friends is very important if you're married—you can love someone, or be in love with someone, and dislike them intensely.'

She nodded, thinking fleetingly of Basil. 'Yes, but suppose you fell in love with someone after we were married?'

'Or you fell in love, Phoebe, or someone fell in love with you?'

She shook her head. 'I don't think that's very likely. I'm not pretty, you must have noticed…'

'I can't say I had.' His voice was gentle. 'And as for me, I've had years in which to fall in love and marry, haven't I? I've fancied myself in love on countless occasions—you too, I daresay.'

She didn't answer him because it wasn't a question. 'You don't think that if I married you, I'd be doing it because it was easier than looking for a job?'

The doctor was taken with a fit of coughing. 'Er—no, the thought hadn't crossed my mind.'

'You really think it would work?'

'Indeed I do—but we'll make haste slowly, don't you agree? Get to know each other for a month or so.'

'You mean after we're married?'

'Yes. I'm quite sure that, given time, we shall become a happily married couple.'

Phoebe's grey eyes looked into the future. She liked him very much; she would miss him if she were never to see him again. He was a comfortable companion, and she, so shy and uncertain with people she met, had always felt as if she was at ease with him. She said slowly: 'If you're quite sure, I'd like to marry you. Will you let me share your life, though? I wouldn't want to stay at home all day—and you've got Mrs Thirsk. She might not like it...'

The doctor bent to stroke Beauty's head. 'Mrs Thirsk is my housekeeper, Phoebe, and will continue to be that, but you will run my home—she'll gladly show you how to set about it—and of course you'll share my life; help in the surgery if you like, answer letters...besides, I have a number of friends, and I hope they'll be your friends too.'

'I'm not much good at meeting people,' said Phoebe doubtfully.

'I think you'll find they'll be very easy to get on with.' He became brisk all of a sudden. 'Have you any family or friends you'd want to come to the wedding?'

'I haven't any family at all now, and no close friends at St Coram's.'

'Then we'll have a very quiet wedding here, shall we? Just a couple of witnesses and Mrs Thirsk. Quite early in the day, don't you think? I've a week or so holiday due, we'll go to Holland and you can meet my family.'

He thought for a minute. 'When is Miss Mason's house being put on the market?'

'Tomorrow.'

'Well, no one is likely to buy it at once, and if they do it will be a week or two before they can possibly move in. You can stay there until I can make arrangements for us to marry. We won't bother with the banns—I'll get a licence, you'll want to do some shopping, I expect. I'll drive you to Cambridge—I've got a half day on Friday. Have you any money?'

Phoebe did a few sums in her head. 'Enough to buy a new suit or something.'

He nodded. 'Good. You're quite happy about this, Phoebe?'

Strangely enough, despite their businesslike conversation, she was. It would need a bit of getting used to, of course, but it was lovely to feel that someone wanted her and didn't seem to mind that she wasn't stunningly pretty. It seemed strange that George—she must really think of him as George—with his good looks and placid charm, hadn't wanted to marry a really stunning girl. Of course, clothes would help, and a new hairstyle and make-up…

'Hey, come back,' said George softly. 'You're a long way away.'

She smiled at him. 'I was wondering why you'd picked on me—I mean, there must be dozens of girls…'

'Dozens,' he agreed placidly, 'but I haven't fancied any of them.' He grinned. 'Perhaps I'm not romantic.'

She had no chance to answer him, because Mrs Thirsk tapped softly on the door and put her head round it to ask: 'Will Miss Creswell be staying for supper, Doctor? There's a nice steak and kidney pie…'

'Indeed she will, Mrs Thirsk, and we'd like you to be the first to know that Miss Creswell and I are going to get married.'

Mrs Thirsk came right into the room, beaming. 'Well, I never did! If that isn't as good a piece of news as I've heard for I don't know how long!' She shook hands with them both. 'And won't the village be pleased! Took to you, they have,' she explained to Phoebe, 'just the wife for the doctor. When's it to be?'

'As soon as I can arrange it. And very quiet, Mrs Thirsk, just us and two witnesses and yourself.'

'I must get a new hat,' declared Mrs Thirsk, and marched off to the kitchen, humming the Wedding March in a surprisingly tuneful voice.

The doctor laughed gently. 'And will you have a new hat, Phoebe?'

She said seriously: 'Oh, yes, I think so, I mean, it's a wedding.'

He got up. 'Let's have supper,' and when she got up too, he took her hands and kissed her on the cheek. 'We shall be happy, Phoebe, you and I.'

She felt happy and content. Probably, she thought, she would wake in the small hours and panic, but there was no need for that

George wasn't the kind of man one panicked about; they would lead a pleasant life together, growing closer as the years went by and they got to know each other. She would enjoy being a doctor's wife and she wished for nothing better than to live in Woolpit for the rest of her life. It would take time to adjust, of course, but he had said he wouldn't hurry her. She would, she promised herself silently, be a good wife.

They ate their supper together, talking like old friends. She told him about her childhood, not realising how bleak it sounded; she told him about Basil too. 'Of course, it was silly of me,' she observed, 'only I was so pleased that he'd noticed me—I thought he really liked me, but of course he was only amusing himself.'

'You're sure of that?' The question was asked casually.

'Yes, perhaps when I first came here I hoped...but when he came the other day I knew at once that I never wanted to see him again.' She smiled across the table. 'Isn't it funny how one discovers quite suddenly that something—someone—that one thought mattered doesn't mean a thing?'

'And that acts the other way too—something that means nothing at all is suddenly all-important.'

They sat for a while talking after supper before Phoebe said it was high time that she went back. She felt faint disappointment when George made no effort to keep her, a disappointment mitigate to some extent by the kiss he gave her when they reached her doorstep. She hadn't much experience of being kissed; she'd enjoyed this one, although thinking about it afterwards she felt vaguely disquieted. George had kissed her with warmth rather like an old friend, but not, she considered, as a man who was about to marry her. But why should she expect more? she argued as she undressed. They were only friends, after all, he had never once mentioned being in love with her—but then he wasn't was he? Basil had kissed her several times and called her darling and declared that she was a wonderful girl, but he hadn't meant a word of it. George, she felt sure, would only say things like that if he meant them. She sighed a little wistfully and fell asleep.

The postman came while she was getting her breakfast. She had overslept and hadn't hurried over her dressing, and it was almost nine o'clock. The house agents were sending Mr and Mrs James over in half an hour to view the house and would she be good enough to show them round? She had planned a walk, but instead she gobbled her breakfast, made her bed and tidied the already spotless house, and was waiting in her grey dress again to open the door when a large Mercedes drew up before it.

A thin, sharp-faced man got out first, followed by a tall stout woman who overshadowed him completely. It was she who rapped on the door knocker and answered Phoebe's polite 'Good morning' with a condescending nod, and an impatient: 'Well, come in, Arthur!'

They went slowly round the house, making disparaging remarks about the worn curtains, the rather nice furniture Phoebe had so carefully polished and the old-fashioned wallpaper. Susan was in the kitchen, cleaning the sink, and the woman paused to stare at her. 'Who's she?' she asked.

'This is Susan, she lives in the village and comes here every morning.'

Mrs James sniffed. 'I'll engage my own servant, she observed, and ran a finger along one of the shelves and examined it for dust.

They went at last, and Phoebe made coffee for Susan and herself. 'Let's hope they don't buy the house,' she said. 'I don't think they'd be very happy in the village.'

'Not likely, they wouldn't, miss.' But Susan didn't waste time on the Jameses; she wanted to talk about the wedding. In some mysterious way she had known about Phoebe and Dr Pritchard getting engaged, and she assured Phoebe that the whole village knew anyway. 'And we're all that pleased,' she told her. 'What will you wear?'

More people came in the afternoon, pleasant elderly couples who said very little and went away without expressing any wish to buy the house. Phoebe had her tea rather late and when she was at last free to do so went for a walk. She hadn't seen George to speak to; he had gone off in his car in the morning, and although she had seen him getting into it again after lunch, he hadn't as much as looked her way. She walked back briskly, deciding what she would cook for her supper, and met George on her doorstep.

'Hullo,' he greeted her with his usual placid friendliness. 'Surgery's finished and I've only got a couple of calls to make, so come over when you're ready and wait for me.'

'Yes, all right—I was just going to get my supper…'

'Whatever for? You'll have supper with me each evening—it's about the only time we'll get to talk.' He patted her on the shoulder with a large hand and went back across the green, then got into his car and drove away.

Phoebe changed the grey dress for a brown one, almost as dull. In a day or two, she told herself happily, she would go shopping. She had written to the bank and asked them to transfer her account to Stowmarket. Provided the house agents left her in peace she could catch the bus there one morning and draw out most of her savings. She had always bought her clothes with an eye to their durability, but now she would let herself go…

Mrs Thirsk opened the door to her, led her to the sitting room and informed her with satisfaction that the village, to a man, were delighted to hear that she and the doctor were to marry. Having said which, she took herself off to the kitchen, leaving Phoebe to sit and sniff appreciatively at the fragrant smells coming from it.

The doctor arrived presently, with Beauty at his heels.

'Oh, I wondered where she was,' said Phoebe. 'Does she go with you on your rounds?'

'If I haven't many visits, yes. Have you had anyone to look at the house?'

She told him while they had their drinks. 'Well, you can't sit around all day,' he observed. 'I'll phone the agents in the morning and tell them to send people either morning or afternoon which suits you best?'

'Afternoon, I think. Would they mind?'

He looked surprised. 'Perhaps, but if you weren't there they would have to send a clerk each time, you know.'

Phoebe didn't argue; it was wonderful to have someone who bothered about her. They spent the rest of the evening planning their wedding, and although George's kiss was exactly the same as the last one—an old friend's—she had found it somehow very comforting. The more she saw of him the more she was sure they would be happy together—no high-flown romance, perhaps, but genuine regard for each other.

She went for a walk in the morning, shopped for her lunch and sat down to wait for any possible viewers. An elderly couple came first. She found them pleasant because they didn't make remarks about anything. The second couple found fault with everything, told her that she hadn't a hope of selling a dump that had no central heating, no double glazing and no plumbing for a washing machine. They called it plain speaking, but she found them downright rude. She made tea after they had gone; it was well past four o'clock and it wasn't likely that anyone else would come before five now.

She was washing the tea things when the door-knocker was thumped. She sighed and went to answer it. There was a youngish man on the doorstep, dressed in leather, his hair hanging untidily round his neck. A vast motorbike had been parked on the verge and he was taking off his helmet.

'House for sale?' he asked, and gave her a grin

'The agents sent you?' asked Phoebe.

'Course they did. I'll have a quick dekko, love.'

He had pushed past her and was in the hall before she could answer and he had gone ahead of her into the sitting room. Phoebe, not much liking him, recited her short rigmarole about size and furniture and coal fires and all the rest of it and led him into the kitchen. He wasn't very interested; he glanced at the pantry, the scullery and the garden from the window and asked: 'Upstairs love? Got a bathroom?'

She led the way, opened the doors of the bedrooms and the bathroom and stood on the landing while he went from one to the other. She remembered uneasily that her aunt's silver treasures were spread out on the bed in the smallest bedroom. They were waiting to be wrapped and packed away. She had got them out before tea and had cleaned them and had intended to wrap them carefully and put them in the locked cupboard in her aunt's room. The man was there now, picking up the silver trinket boxes, the brushes, the heavy mirror and the small silver vases. He glanced over his shoulder at her.

'Nice bit of stuff here—worth a bit,' he remarked softly. 'Can't say I think much of the house, but these will do me.'

'Put them back!' said Phoebe sharply. 'And get out of this house!'

'Before you call the police?' He laughed nastily. 'No phone either, is there, and you'll never get to the door, love. I'll take what I fancy and go quiet-like and no sneaking when I've gone or I'll come back and break your jaw!'

Phoebe could feel her knees wobbling, but rage sent her into her bedroom to slam the door in his face and put her head out of the window and screech 'George!' at the top of her voice. For all she knew he wasn't even home, but if he was and he'd heard her, she knew he would come.

She wasn't given the chance to find out, though, for the door behind her was flung open and the man stood there, the nasty smile back on his face just staring at her. And now she was frightened. She turned her head and opened her mouth to shout again, but he pushed past her and banged the window shut. It gave her an opportunity to kick his shins, something she did with a kind of desperate satisfaction. The slap he gave her sent her head swinging sideways and the tears starting up to her eyes, but she got in another kick before he caught her roughly by the arm and pushed her on to the landing. 'You asked for it,' he called her a vile name and she said in a choking voice: 'Don't use that kind of language to me. Get out of the house before someone comes!' Her eyes fell on his loaded pockets. 'And put everything back on the bed.'

He leaned against the wall, just looking at her and saying nothing, and she wondered what he was going to do next. Her heart had sunk to her boots. George hadn't heard her—worse, he couldn't have been at home. The front door, she remembered, had shut behind the man as he had come in and would have locked automatically. She took a breath and gulped back her fear; someone would surely see the motorbike presently and wonder whose it was. 'What are you going to do?' she asked.

He took a hand from a pocket and showed her the flick-knife. 'See this, love? You're no beauty, but even a plain face can be made plainer...'

Phoebe thought she would be sick; a Victorian Miss would have swooned and at least delayed matters, but she was a remarkably healthy girl who had never fainted in her life. Her mouth was so dry that she couldn't speak, only stare back at him defiantly. At last she said in a whisper: 'You're like something nasty under a stone...'

He laughed loudly at that—a good thing, because he didn't hear the faint creak of the stairs as the doctor came up them two at a time. The laugh came to an abrupt halt as his chin came in contact with a huge fist and he slithered to the floor, Aunt Kate's silver falling and tumbling around him in a silvery shower.

The doctor stepped over him and plucked Phoebe from the windowsill she had been clinging to, and held her close. 'My poor girl—I came as fast as I could, but I had to go round the back and through the kitchen window. Has he hurt you?'

She lifted a pale face to his; the slap had left an angry red mark on one cheek. 'He slapped me,' she said in a shaky voice, 'but I kicked him.' She began to cry in earnest. 'Oh, George, suppose you hadn't come...'

'But I did come,' he said in a comforting voice, 'and I shall always come when you want me, Phoebe—don't forget that.' He bent and kissed her gently. 'Brave girl, but I think this is the end of you staying here alone. I'll get hold of Nurse Wilkins—you can stay with her.'

He bent over the man lying on the floor, still keeping an arm round her.

'Now run across and phone the police—ask them to come here.' He touched the supine man with the toe of his shoe. 'I'll stay here until they come.'

His voice, placid still, brooked no arguing, only at the door she paused. 'You'll be all right? He's got a knife—George, be careful.'

'Has he indeed.' The doctor had sat himself down on the side of the bed. He smiled faintly. 'I'll be careful.'

Phoebe raced away to bang on the door of his house, give a rapid and rather incoherent account to Mrs Thirsk and ring the police. That done, she turned to the housekeeper, standing right by her. 'Do you think the doctor will be all right?' she wanted to know urgently. 'That man might attack him…' At which Mrs Thirsk laughed comfortably.

'I'd like to see him try—just you set your mind at ease, Miss Phoebe; Doctor'll take care of himself. Now you just come with me and I'll bathe that cheek and make you a nice cup of tea—a proper nasty shock you've had.'

Being fussed over made Phoebe feel a whole lot better. All the same, as she sat sipping her tea, she worried about George. Suppose the man attacked him? Stabbed him? She imagined him lying on the floor bleeding and could bear it no longer. She put her cup and saucer down and started for the door, to be halted by the quiet arrival of a police car.

She watched from the window—the police officer being admitted by George, their return with the man, who was put into the car with the other officer, and their unhurried approach to the doctor's front door. She had just the time to fly back to her chair by the fire and assume an expression of calm she didn't feel before they came in.

Short work was made of her statement. She answered questions in a level voice and left the doctor to discuss the outcome with the police officer. Presently he went away, and George gave her a drink, poured himself a whisky and sat down opposite her.

'Feeling better?' His voice was kind and concerned and she stopped worrying. 'That settled it—you'll not stay in that house any longer. You can sleep at Nurse Wilkins' and spend your days here. We'll collect what you need for the night, and you can pack tomorrow morning. The agents can send a man with anyone who wants to look over the place.'

He got up and came to bend over her, examining her reddened cheek. 'My poor dear, does it hurt much?'

She shook her head. 'Thank you, George—I was so frightened.'

He smiled. 'I'm not surprised, I'd like to keep you here, but I have my reputation to think of.'

Phoebe looked at him and saw that he was laughing softly now, and for no reason at all she laughed too; it was nice to feel so safe.

George went with her presently to fetch an overnight bag, going upstairs and sitting on the bed while she rummaged round collecting what she needed. 'I'll see Susan in the morning,' he told her, 'and tell her not to come any more for the moment; she'll go on being paid and probably when the house is sold, the new people will be glad to have her back. You'll move all your things out tomorrow, Phoebe. Mrs Thirsk will go with you while you do that and then the house will be locked up, I'll attend to the agents for you. They can make their own arrangements.'

To all of which Phoebe happily agreed. It was as they walked the short distance to Nurse Wilkins' cottage that George said: 'Come over to lunch tomorrow, Phoebe, we'll get the wedding fixed up and I'll let John Matthews, the vicar, know. I'm free in the afternoon, we'll do your shopping if you like.'

'I'd like that... at least, I've still got to go to Stowmarket—my money's being transferred there, so could we go there first?'

'Waste of time—you can pay me back later. I haven't another half day until next week, and by then we'll probably be married.' He spoke so matter-of-factly that she felt no surprise. Until that moment, although they had discussed the wedding, no dates had been suggested, and she had thought vaguely of several weeks ahead, but now she was glad that it was to be so soon. She said happily: 'Oh, will we? You'll be sure and tell me how much I owe you, won't you?' She stopped suddenly. 'George, I've unsettled you such a lot since I came—you're still sure?'

He took her hand and walked on. 'Quite sure. Indeed, I quite like being unsettled.'

He didn't stay long at Nurse Wilkins' cottage, only took her case up to the small bedroom at the back of the landing, thanked Nurse Wilkins for her kindness, dropped the lightest of kisses on Phoebe's cheek and left.

'See you at lunch,' he said as he went.

There was no question of going to bed, because Nurse Wilkins wanted to know just what had happened. They sat in the tiny sitting room while Phoebe told her over a pot of tea.

'Knocked him out, did he?' commented Nurse Wilkins. 'Tied him up too—did the police mind?'

'I don't know. Shouldn't he have done that? The man could have escaped...'

Nurse Wilkins nodded. 'He could too, and done the same thing to some other poor soul. Lucky Dr Pritchard heard you scream.' She poured them both more tea. 'Now, what are you going to wear for your wedding?'

Phoebe still had no idea about that as George parked the car in Cambridge. She had spent a dreamless night, packed her things in Mrs Thirsk's friendly company, and then had lunch with George. She had been accepted into his household without fuss, indeed she was beginning to feel she had known George for years, so relaxed was he in her company. Which was, she told herself, entirely satisfactory, although right at the back of her mind there was the unwelcome thought that it would have been even more satisfactory if he had displayed more interest in her as a person. It seemed to her that he accepted her as an old friend of many years' standing, nice to have around but incapable of exciting him in any way. He took her arm now. 'Wedding clothes first? There are some good boutiques...'

They strolled along, looking in shop windows, until he came to a halt outside a small elegant shop window. 'That's it,' he said. 'Do you suppose it'll fit?' He measured her with his eye. 'You're rather small and too thin.'

Phoebe studied the outfit in the window; a fine wool crêpe in a deep honey colour, a pleated skirt, straight jacket and a patterned silky top.

'It'll cost too much,' she suggested soberly, 'and I've got quite a lot of other things to buy.'

To which prudent speech George made no answer, merely urged her through the door.

It could have been made for her, the fit was so perfect, and there was a narrow-brimmed hat which matched it exactly. In her excitement she forgot to ask how much it cost, and it wasn't until George was writing a cheque that she remembered to ask. The sales lady told her in a sugary voice, and Phoebe felt her cheeks pale. There would be almost nothing left of her money and she still had things to buy, things she simply had to have. George had handed over the cheque by now, and in any case, it would be difficult to do anything about it now. She waited until they were outside on the pavement: 'George—George, you don't understand, when I've paid you back for that outfit I won't have enough money to get some things I just must have!'

He sounded very matter-of-fact. 'Suppose you buy all you need now and when we get back home we can settle the matter. You'll be getting an allowance once we're married; you can pay me back from that.'

'Oh, well, if you don't mind...' She felt relief surge through her.

'So what comes next? Shoes, gloves, purse? Something pretty for visiting? Friends will call, you know, and we'll get asked out. Let's look around.'

Phoebe ended up with a Jaeger suit, several sweaters, two pretty dresses which George assured her were absolutely essential to her wardrobe, a jersey dress in sapphire blue, and shoes—smart brogues for the suit, brown court shoes and a purse to go with them for the wedding, high-heeled sandals for the dresses and because she had paused to admire them as they left the shop, a ridiculous pair of bedroom slippers, pink satin and high-heeled.

After this orgy of spending Phoebe did her best to call a halt. 'If I could just slip into Marks and Spencer,' she suggested.

'Undies?' asked George placidly. 'Tights and so on? This shop will do.' He gave her a gentle push towards the door. 'Get all you want and I'll come in and pay when you're ready. At least three of everything,' he told her gravely with twinkling eyes, 'and no cheeseparing!'

Well, thought Phoebe, inside the shop, staring at the delicate wisps of garments on display, this was no place where one could pare cheese. She would be the rest of her life paying George back, but in for a penny, in for a pound. Obediently she bought three of everything, revelling in the reckless extravagance. It was only when the bill was made out and she saw the total that she had qualms. But it was too late now; she went to the door and George came in, made out a cheque without a muscle of his face changing and then collected her numerous parcels.

'You told me to buy three of everything, and I did,' said Phoebe. 'It's the most wickedly expensive shop I've ever been in—I almost came out without buying anything.'

'I'm glad you didn't. Let's have tea somewhere and make sure you've got everything you need.'

He took her to the University Arms and gave her teacakes, hot and dripping with butter, and then ticked off the items she had bought.

'Raincoat?' he wanted to know. 'Wellington boots—for when you come with me on my rounds and we have to walk through muddy farm-yards...'

Phoebe went delicately pink. 'Oh, may I come with you sometimes? I'll like that.'

'Of course you'll come with me if you want to. Dressing gown?'

She bit into a teacake. 'My mac isn't really old—I haven't any wellies, though. I've got a dressing gown...' She paused. It was a useful garment, designed for warmth and hard wear and a quite unsuitable covering for the nighties she had bought.

'Right, we'll get those next.' He cast an eye at the pile of elegant carrier bags. 'There's time before the shops close.'

So she found herself the possessor of the latest Burberry raincoat and a matching hat and scarf, wellies and, lastly, a pink silk quilted dressing gown which George, when asked, told her to buy. On the way back to Woolpit Phoebe tried to add up how much she had spent; it was an astronomical sum.

Indoors, sitting in the sitting room with George, she broached the subject once again, and was told with kind firmness to wait until they were married and she had her allowance paid into the bank.

'Yes, but it's hundreds of pounds!'

'And I never spent them with greater pleasure.' He got up and went to the small rent table under the window and opened one of its drawers. 'If you don't like this tell me and we'll find something more to your taste. This was my grandmother's, and I'd like you to have it.'

It was a very beautiful ring; old-fashioned rose diamonds and rubies set in gold. Phoebe gave a gasp of delight and held out her hand. It fitted exactly. 'It's gorgeous,' she told him, 'and I like it very much. I'll take such care of it.'

He smiled at her. 'It suits your hand. You have pretty hands, Phoebe, has anyone ever told you that?'

She thought for a moment. 'No. I'm glad you think they're pretty, perhaps that'll make up for my ordinary face.'

'I can see that it's time someone told you that's a load of nonsense.' He leaned down and pulled her out of her chair. 'Let's have supper, then I'm going to walk you down to Nurse Wilkins'—I've got some work to do later on.'

Phoebe accepted that tranquilly. She had no illusions about their life together; she would learn to fit in to his way of living and learn not to mind if his work came between them. If she had loved him, she supposed, she would mind very much. As it was, she was quite prepared to take a back seat, be an understanding friend, there when wanted, but able to efface herself if it seemed the right thing to do. She hadn't seen the intent look he had bent on her when she had spoken, watching to see if she were disappointed.

Over their supper they fixed the date for the wedding the following week; Thursday morning at ten o'clock. 'And we'll come straight back here, Phoebe, I've got an appointment at Stowmarket Hospital in the afternoon which I can't miss, but I've fixed up a week's holiday—we'll go over to Holland on the Saturday and you'll be able to meet my mother and the family.'

She agreed readily, hiding twinges of uncertainty. Suppose his mother didn't like her? Suppose his family cold-shouldered her? She hadn't the faintest idea what they would be like. Of course, if they were all like him, that would be all right. She cheered up at the thought and presently declared that she was more than ready to go to Nurse Wilkins'. There was still a lot of the evening left and she would have liked to have spent it all talking to George, but instead she would unpack her parcels and try everything on for Nurse Wilkins to see. She made no attempt to linger, but wished him a quite brisk goodnight with the observation that she wouldn't delay him further, and went into the cottage and shut the door. The doctor walked back to his own house, his shoulders shaking with laughter. He had enjoyed his afternoon, he felt sure he was going to enjoy the rest of his life. Patience would be required, of course, but he had plenty of that.

CHAPTER FOUR

PHOEBE HAD ARRANGED to meet George at the church door. Mrs Thirsk would already be there, waiting for them, and Andrew Powers from Stowmarket, the doctor with whom George exchanged duties from time to time, would be there too. And at the last minute Nurse Wilkins, who had arranged her rounds to fit in. Phoebe walked to the church with her, feeling self-conscious in her new outfit, although as it happened there was no need, because there was no one about. At the church door George was waiting, sitting on a tombstone. He had taken surgery as usual but she was glad to see that he had dressed for the occasion. Indeed, she could find no fault with his, grey suit; it was exquisitely cut and faultlessly tailored. She said hullo shyly and scarcely saw Nurse Wilkins slip past into the church.

George unfolded his length and took her hand. 'You look just as a bride should,' he observed. 'Let's go in, shall we?'

In the porch he reached for a small posy of flowers, lilies of the valley, early roses, hyacinths and freesias, put them into her hands and pushed the inner door open.

The church was full; the entire village must be there, thought Phoebe confusedly. If it hadn't been for George's hand on her arm, she might have turned and run away, but as it was, she walked down the short aisle beside him to where John Matthews was waiting for them.

She hardly heard a word of the short service. She heard her voice, a little high, giving the right answers, and George's deliberate tones; she watched him put the ring on her finger in a kind of dream, signed the register and then walked out of the church, her arm tucked into his, looking half smilingly at the rows of faces in the pews.

At the church door she asked in a whisper: 'Did you know, George?'

'I suspected something.' He gave her arm a small squeeze. 'When you think about it, it was a pretty nice thing for them to do.'

'Yes. Where do we go now?'

'Oh, a drink with John and Andrew, and then we'll take ourselves off for lunch. It's our wedding day, you know, even though I've got surgery this evening. Mrs Thirsk and Nurse Wilkins will see that your things get brought over this afternoon, because of course you'll come back with me now.'

They had strolled down the church path and now most of the congregation had caught up with them and they were engulfed in congratulations and goodnatured greetings—even more good-natured when George caught sight of the pub's landlord and asked him to see that the drinks were on him for the rest of the day.

Presently they were free to walk on once more, to find that Mrs Thirsk, Nurse Wilkins and the two men were waiting for them. They drank champagne, discussing the wedding, until presently George said: 'Phoebe and I are off now—take any calls, Andrew, won't you? I'll be back for surgery.'

They went to Wetheringsett Manor, not too far away, a nice country house standing in twenty acres, so that after lunch they were able to stroll around undisturbed. It was a splendid day for a wedding, as George pointed out; a blue sky and a sunshine bearing the early warmth of promised summer. They found a seat in a sunny corner and sat quietly, admiring the view, not talking much, but quite content with each other's company. Once or twice Phoebe looked at the ring on her finger and reminded herself that she was now Mrs Pritchard, although she didn't feel any different. They wandered back presently and had tea at the hotel, then got into the car and drove back to Woolpit.

While George was in the surgery, she unpacked her things in the pretty bedroom waiting for her. There was a bathroom beside it and George's bedroom on the other side, and presently she went exploring, to open two more doors on to two rooms at the back of the house, one very large, furnished with a pale wood she didn't recognise. The bed was covered with a quilted spread which matched the curtains and the carpet was soft and deep. Perhaps she and George would share it one day, but first, as he had said, they must get to know each other. Easy for him, she thought, hanging her new clothes in the roomy built-in cupboard lining one wall; he only had to get to know her, there wasn't anyone else, whereas she would have to meet his mother and his family, and in another country too. The thought was daunting and at the same time a challenge too. She paused in her unpacking and went to study herself in the long pier glass; clothes certainly did something for one, and as soon as she could, she would go to a good hairdresser and get her hair done.

She went down to the sitting room presently, feeling rather shy, to discover that George was still in the surgery. But Mrs Thirsk came from the kitchen, smiling broadly, to follow her into the sitting room and ask if she wanted anything. 'Doctor won't be long, Mrs Pritchard, he said I was to see that you had all you wanted.'

Phoebe said quickly: 'I'll wait for the doctor, Mrs Thirsk,' and then: 'Did you enjoy the wedding?'

'That I did, and so did everyone else.' She chuckled: 'Your face—so surprised you were! You looked very pretty too—you make a fine pair, you and the doctor, Mrs Pritchard.' She went to the door. 'I'd better be back in my kitchen—it's dinner you're having tonight, on account of the wedding—champagne too.'

George came presently: 'You look as though you've been here all my life,' he told her. Phoebe wasn't sure if that was a compliment, it made her feel like his favourite chair or a comfortable pair of old slippers, but she smiled and murmured something and accepted a glass of champagne that he offered her.

She murmured something too when he toasted their future, suddenly afraid that she had bitten off more than she could chew.

But George seemed to have no such qualms. He talked about the wedding, invited her to go round the house at her leisure and decide if she wanted any alterations in the furniture or decorating, and lastly mentioned casually that they would be going over to Holland in two days' time.

'Andrew Powers will take over my patients for a couple of

weeks. We'll take the car and drive around so that you can see something of the country.'

'Shall we stay with your mother?' she asked.

'For some of the time, yes. I phoned her this morning early, and she's delighted at our news and looking forward to meeting you.' He refilled her glass. 'Can you drive a car, Phoebe?' She shook her head. 'No matter—you shall have lessons as soon as we get back. I'll run you into Stowmarket after I've done my morning round—I can spare an hour. You only need to go to the bank.'

'Yes—I'll be very quick. Should I close my account and open another one at your bank?'

'Yes, do that, will you? We'll discuss your finances at our leisure.'

Mrs Thirsk appeared then to tell them that dinner was waiting, and a splendid meal it turned out to be. The table held a centrepiece of flowers, and the silver and crystal glasses Phoebe had admired the very first time she had stayed to supper shone and gleamed. They began with hors d'oeuvres, went on to chicken à la king with asparagus and baby peas, and finished with a magnificent trifle. And when Mrs Thirsk came in to the room with the coffee, George told her to fetch a glass and the three of them finished the champagne. It was a pity that the doctor should have been called out to visit an urgent case before they left the table. Phoebe helped Mrs Thirsk clear and then went to sit with a book picked at random from the well stocked bookshelves in the small library behind the sitting-room, but she didn't read for more than a minute or two; she had a lot to think about. She was a practical girl; she decided that when they went to Stowmarket in the morning she would get herself some wool and knitting needles—she was quite good at following advanced patterns, she would get something really complicated which would keep her occupied. She would have a chat with Mrs Thirsk too, because she couldn't sit idle all day; there must be several small chores she could take over without upsetting the housekeeping. How fortunate that they liked each other.

She sat on, oblivious of the time, until Mrs Thirsk came in to ask her if she would like more coffee.

Phoebe looked at the clock and saw that it was already half-past ten. George had been gone a long time. 'I'll wait up for a bit,' she said. 'Do you usually go to bed if the doctor's not here?'

Mrs Thirsk nodded. 'He could be out till all hours. I'll lock up everything but the front door and take myself to bed. You'll be all right, Mrs Pritchard?'

'I'm not sleepy yet—I'll wait a bit longer and then go up. What about the morning, Mrs Thirsk?'

'I'll call you at seven o'clock, ma'am—breakfast at half past so that the doctor has time to read his post and that before surgery. Is that too early?'

'No—I had to get up at half-past six in the hospital, I shan't mind at all.' They wished each other goodnight and Mrs Thirsk went back to her kitchen, and presently Phoebe heard her deliberate tread on the back-stairs.

She read for a while after that and was surprised to find that an hour had gone by. She was sleepy now and closed the book and her eyes with it, so that she didn't hear George come quietly into his house. She did wake up, however, as he came into the room. The look on his face startled her. He was standing in the doorway, frowning, looking so stern that she sat up straight in her chair.

'My dear girl, it's after midnight—you should be in bed!'

She found herself apologising. 'I'm sorry—I went to sleep over my book.' She added, in the hope that it might put things right: 'I didn't mean to wait up for you.'

His cool voice chilled her. 'No? I hardly expected you to be a wife who expects to check every breath her husband takes.'

His words hurt her so much that she could have wept, but that wouldn't help matters; she said pleasantly: 'I can promise you I won't do that.' She got to her feet and put the book carefully on the lamp table. 'My goodness, I'm asleep on my feet—it's been a long day hasn't it? Goodnight, George.'

She gave him a bright smile and went upstairs and into her room. Once there, she undressed in a fury of haste, jumped into bed and for no reason which she could think of, had a good cry.

She was at the breakfast table next morning only minutes after

George, wished him a good morning, exchanged the same with Mrs Thirsk, and applied herself to coffee and toast.

George glanced up from his letters. 'That's an inadequate breakfast,' he pointed out. 'I hope you'll do better tomorrow.' He studied her rather pale face. 'You slept well?'

'Like a log,' she assured him cheerfully, and buttered more toast.

George put down his letter. 'I do apologise for last night, Phoebe, it was unpardonable of me.'

'That's all right; I expect you'd forgotten that I was here. I daresay I shall take a bit of getting used to.'

He said seriously: 'Yes, I think I must agree with you there. All the same, I'm sorry. It wasn't much of an end to our wedding day.'

She thought of several replies to that, none of them suitable. 'What time do you want me to be ready this morning?' she asked.

'Oh, around twelve, I should imagine.' He glanced at the clock. 'I must go; I've got one or two matters to attend to before I start work.' He got up and as he passed her, paused and put a hand on her shoulder. 'Friends?' he asked.

She smiled up at him. 'Well, of course, George.'

After he had gone she poured herself another cup of coffee. There would be pitfalls ahead; to be expected, of course, but she would have to be prepared for those. Even though they liked each other, felt as though they had known each other for a long time, they still didn't know much about each other. She finished her coffee and carried the tray out to the kitchen where Mrs Thirsk was cutting up rhubarb at the table and Susan, of all people, was getting ready to wash up at the sink.

'Why, Susan!' cried Phoebe. 'Good morning—how nice to see you.'

Susan grinned, but it was the housekeeper who answered. 'There weren't no chance to tell you yesterday, ma'am, but the doctor suggested that I might like to have Susan mornings now she's not wanted across the green. And that reminds me, I'm to go with you and help you pack up. When shall that be, ma'am?'

'When you've got time, Mrs Thirsk. And is there anything I can do?'

'Well, this morning, there's not much else than the flowers, Doctor, he likes flowers round the house and there's plenty in the garden, but if it suits you we could go now to Miss James's house...'

'That suits me fine. It'll only take me twenty minutes or so.' The pair of them started for the door. 'And while I'm doing it, will you tell me your routine for the day and tell me how I can best help?'

'That I will gladly.' Mrs Thirsk rolled down her sleeves and got a cardigan from behind the door. 'The key's on the hall table,' she observed.

Aunt Kate's house felt chill and unlived-in as Phoebe unlocked the door. She was glad to hurry upstairs and get her case and start to pack the rest of her clothes while Mrs Thirsk peered into drawers and cupboards to make sure that nothing was left behind. 'Let's hope a respectable nice couple will buy the place,' she observed as Phoebe shut the lid. She picked up the case and followed Phoebe downstairs.

'Now if you like to put these things away, ma'am, I'll get the coffee ready—the doctor likes a cup when he finishes surgery and there weren't many patients this morning—the evening is always busy when the men have finished work. Will you want lunch at one o'clock, same as usual?'

'I expect so, Mrs Thirsk. We're going to Stowmarket as soon as the doctor's done his visits but we'll only be there for a very short time. I expect we'd better ask, hadn't we?'

By the time Phoebe had put away her things, surgery was over, She could hear George's voice downstairs and when she went down it was to find him in the sitting room, sitting on the edge of the Pembroke table under the window with Beauty at his feet. He was his old placid self, she saw with relief, and smiled. 'Shall I get the coffee, or does Mrs Thirsk bring it?' she asked.

'She'll bring it. You've fetched your things?'

'Yes, I've been putting them away.'

He nodded. 'Can you be ready by twelve sharp? Half an hour will be time enough in Stowmarket, won't it?'

'Oh yes.' It looked as though she wouldn't have time to buy wool and needles unless the bank business was dealt with quickly.

As it turned out, it took barely ten minutes. Phoebe skipped down the street found wool, needles and a pattern complicated enough to keep her busy for days on end, and hurried back to where the car was parked. George was at the wheel, his face calm and patient. 'Five minutes to spare,' he said as he opened the door for her 'Everything all right?'

'Yes, thanks. It'll take about a week, they said.'

He was already driving out of the town, back to Woolpit. 'Well, there's no hurry, I've opened an account for you at my—our bank, and your allowance will be paid in each month. Mrs Thirsk has always kept the household accounts and given me the bills at the end of every month; she's hated that side of housekeeping—do you think you could cope?'

'I'd like to. She'll show me what to do?'

'Yes, of course, and when I've got an hour or two, I'll give you some idea of how much you can spend on housekeeping. We'll go on paying the bills each month, but you can do it instead of me.'

He glanced sideways at Phoebe's expressive face and smiled a little. 'You look pleased,' he observed.

'Well, I am—I mean, there must be several things I can do to help you and Mrs Thirsk.' She paused, 'It was nice to see Susan in the kitchen. She would have been out of work…'

He made no answer. Presently he asked if she had all she wanted for their trip to Holland. 'We'll go via Harwich tomorrow evening,' he told her. 'We'll be gone for about ten days; if you need any more clothes we can get them while we're there.'

'I've got enough, I'm sure, only I haven't got a dress for the evening, but I don't suppose I'll need one.'

He glanced at her, very smart in her new outfit and shining shoes. 'Well, we might go dancing one evening. John Matthews is taking his wife to Bury St Edmunds tomorrow morning—she has to go to the dentist—he'll give you a lift and you'll be back before lunch.'

Phoebe thought of the few pounds in her purse; her account wouldn't be cleared yet and hadn't she handed her cheque book in that very morning and she wouldn't get the new one in time. She was wondering what to say when he went on: 'I'll let you have some cash.'

'Yes, well—thank you, George, but I owe you an awful lot of money already.'

'Ah yes—we'll have time to sort that out when we're on holiday, won't we? He named a sum that shocked Phoebe.

'My goodness, that's far too much!'

'Then get two dresses.' He swept the car to a halt before the house and they got out.

She asked carefully as they went indoors. 'Do you want me to pack for you, George?'

He stopped, his hand on the surgery door. 'Er—don't bother, my dear. I'll throw a few things into a bag tomorrow. Lunch in five minutes? I must phone...'

Phoebe packed after lunch, all her lovely new things, glad at least that her case wasn't too shabby. But she would have to get an overnight bag in the morning if they were going on the night boat. She sat down and did sums on the back of an envelope and found that she was hopelessly in debt to George; probably it would take her months and months to pay him back.

He gave her the money casually while they were waiting for their supper that evening, and all she could do was to thank him; something in his face stopped her from saying anything else. Later on, when she felt quite at ease with him, she would ask him how he would like her to repay him.

She didn't suppose he was too badly off, but he had the house to maintain and Mrs Thirsk to pay and the car to run, and she couldn't help but see that he wore beautifully tailored clothes which must cost a good deal. But even if he lived comfortably, she was an extra expense now, and she had no intention of being a burden on him. She made a careful note of her debt and stowed it away in her handbag so that when a suitable moment cropped up, she would be ready.

The Reverend John Matthews collected her the next morning at nine o'clock. He had his wife with him, miserable with toothache but all agog, just the same, over the wedding. It was the sole topic of conversation until they reached Bury St Edmunds, where they set her down near the shops and promised to wait for her in the car park. 'But not later than half past twelve,' she was warned.

'I'll be there at twelve at the latest,' she promised.

She didn't know the town, but the shops looked satisfactory. She bought her overnight bag and then studied the windows of several boutiques, and with an eye on the clock chose one. She was fortunate in her choice; the turquoise blue crêpe dress she tried on fitted her to perfection. It was suitable, she felt, for a first meeting with George's mother, as it was simply cut and had style. There was enough money over for her to buy a dark green taffeta skirt and a chiffon blouse to go with it. She was aware that her purchases were perhaps a little old for her, but she was, after all, a married woman. She resolutely refused to try on the more youthful clothes the sales lady showed her and found her way back to the car park, arriving, most luckily, at the same time as the Matthews.

George wasn't back from his visits when she went into the house. She packed the dress and skirt and blouse, added some last-minute odds and ends and sat down to wait for him.

'Find what you wanted?' he asked when he got home.

'Yes, thank you.' The doubt at the back of her mind showed through and he gave her a quick glance, although he said nothing, but over lunch he observed that he hadn't given her a wedding present yet. 'We'll go shopping, and you can spread yourself.'

'But I've already done that,' she protested. 'I've never had so many new clothes!'

'No? Well, I've a great many friends and acquaintances, Phoebe, we shall go out quite a bit, you know, so you'll need clothes.'

She agreed meekly and wondered what he had thought of her dull dresses. Too late, she wished she had agreed to the sales lady's advice in the boutique and bought one of the more spectacular dresses she had been shown. On the other hand, she wanted most desperately that his mother should like her, and she might be a lady who had conservative ideas about dress.

It wasn't a great distance to Harwich. They left after George had done his evening clinic and conferred with Andrew Powers. To Phoebe, on tenterhooks to be gone, George seemed almost too casual, and yet they arrived at the quay in plenty of time. She hadn't been out of England before. The Customs and passport procedures were strange and exciting; she watched her passport being stamped and quite expected that her case would be opened and inspected. But no one did anything, so they went on board, parked the car in the car deck and climbed the stairs to the decks above. She hadn't known what to expect; certainly she had had no idea that George would have got everything so well organised. They were taken at once to their cabins, where she had laid out what she needed for the night, and then, in response to George's knock, accompanied him to the restaurant, where they had had a late supper and then gone on deck to watch the last of the lights from the fast receding shore.

She slept like a top, had eaten an early breakfast with George and then had gone to hang over the side to watch the ferry docking. And George had been very patient and kind, explaining everything to her and then taking her down to the car.

There was no hold-up going through Customs, and they were away, driving away from the Hook, in no time at all. It was only then that Phoebe said: 'I don't really know where we're going.'

'Hilversum—an hour more or less on the motorway. We'll be there for coffee.'

'Your mother lives in Hilversum?'

'Yes, she has a house there, left to her by my grandfather—my Dutch grandfather. She spends part of each year there. It's a pleasant town and the country round it is charming, wooded and peaceful, not at all like this.' He nodded at the flat water meadows they were passing, with the black and white cows scattered thickly and the farms with their great barns lying back from the road. 'This is the Holland people always expect to see, but although it's so small, the north and the part we call the Veluwe are quite different. I'll drive you there, at this time of the year it's delightful.'

Phoebe turned to look at his placid profile. George, do you feel more Dutch than English?'

He laughed. 'I suppose when I'm in Holland I feel Dutch, but in England I'm as English as the next man. But don't worry, Mother speaks excellent English and you'll have no difficulty in the shops—Dutch isn't an easy language to learn, so most people take care to learn some English at least.'

They were going through Rotterdam by now Phoebe wondered how he could find his way so easily through the busy streets, but presently they were free of the city, racing along towards Utrecht.

'It's a pity the motorways bypass the towns and villages,' observed George, 'but I promise you we'll take the side roads when we go on a sightseeing tour. There's Gouda to the right and there are some rather pretty lakes a little further on.'

They were going so fast that she barely glimpsed them, and in no time at all they were at the roundabout outside Utrecht, not going into the city but taking the road round it and then striking north. The country was green and wooded now, and presently as they reached the outskirts of Hilversum, the trees crept down to the verge of the motorway, opening into a wide, tree-lined road taking them into the town.

The road was lined with solid mansions standing in well kept grounds, each with a wide gateway leading up to the house. The road seemed to go on for ever, and Phoebe asked: 'Is this Hilversum? There's no town...'

'It's a short distance ahead.' George swept the car between stone pillars and into a gravel drive leading to a magnificent house standing well back from the road. Phoebe caught her breath. 'Is this it? Is this where your mother lives?'

'Yes, it's home to me too when I'm in Holland. He undid her seat-belt and leaned across to open her door and got out himself. She was glad of his friendly hand on her arm as they went up the wide steps to the massive door. She said nervously laughing a little: 'It's the kind of door you expect a butler to open, and then gave a gasp as it was thrown wide by a tall, reedy man, no longer young, dressed in a black jacket and striped trousers.

'Phoebe, this is Ulco, who has been with the family since I was a very small boy. He is also one of my greatest friends.' George's voice was very kind. 'Ulco, this is my wife.'

Phoebe held out a hand and smiled from a flushed face. 'How do you do, Ulco—I'm sorry, but I can't speak any Dutch.'

'I speak a little English,' Ulco told her gravely 'and I am most happy to welcome you, Mrs Pritchard.' He smiled at her then and her own uncertain smile widened. 'Mrs Pritchard senior is in the drawing-room, Mr George.'

He led the way across the wide high-ceilinged hall, with its polished wooden floor scattered with rugs and its panelled walls hung with portraits. Phoebe, still firmly held by George's hand, had no time to take it all in. She felt like someone leaving the dentist's waiting room for the dental chair, only worse. But not for long. The double doors they were approaching were suddenly flung wide and a comfortably plump lady darted out. She was no taller than Phoebe and although elegantly dressed, exuded an air of cosiness which Phoebe found distinctly heartening. She cried: 'George, dear George!' and stood on tiptoe to embrace him before turning to fling her arms round Phoebe. 'And Phoebe—so exactly as George has described you! Welcome, my dear, I'm so very happy to meet you.' She said something to Ulco and led the way into the drawing-room, a vast apartment, furnished with a nicely balanced mixture of comfortable sofas and easy chairs and quite beautiful antiques. George had taken his hand from her arm with a little chuckle, and it was his mother who led Phoebe to a handsome velvet-covered sofa and sat her down, then sat beside her, leaving her son to settle himself in the great winged chair opposite.

The next few minutes were taken up with questions about their journey and how was Woolpit and Mrs Thirsk and what had they done with Beauty while they were away; and was George's practice flourishing, and could Phoebe bear it if her mother-in-law invited herself for a week or two later on? 'I've a house in Grantchester,' explained that lady. 'I live there quite a lot, you know, but I'd love to stay with you both.' She broke off as Ulco came in with the coffee tray and then rattled on happily about various members of the family, her friends, people George knew… 'I'm giving a party for you both,' she told them, 'next week—we'll have a few friends and the family to dinner and everyone else can come later on.' She turned to Phoebe and smiled, her eyes as startlingly blue as her son's. 'I want you to meet them all,' she told her, 'I'm so proud of having a daughter-in-law.'

Presently she took Phoebe upstairs, mounting the grand sweep of the staircase with the lightness of a girl. The gallery above the hall was wide with a number of doors leading from it as well as several corridors. Mrs Pritchard opened a door and ushered Phoebe inside. 'Here you are,' she said happily. 'There's a bathroom through that door and George is next to that. Ring for anything you want—everyone in the house speaks a little English, and George will help, of course. I expect you'd like to tidy up after that long journey, but come down as soon as you like, my dear.'

Left alone, Phoebe looked around her. The room was large, furnished with great taste and luxury, and the bathroom was equally splendid. She went to look out of the window at the formal garden below, bright with spring flowers, the lawns like velvet. After a few minutes she washed her hands and face and sat down to do her hair and put on fresh make-up. That done, she made no effort to move, but sat there, staring at her reflection in the big winged mirror. When someone tapped on the door, she said, 'Come in,' without bothering to look round, and only when George sat down on the side of the bed did she look at him.

'Why didn't you tell me?' she asked.

He didn't pretend not to understand her. 'Oh, several reasons—you see, Phoebe, this is my home as well as England. I spent a good deal of my boyhood here—school holidays and so on. My father was happy here too, you know. I suppose to you it seems a little grand, but to me it's just my second home. I hope you'll come to love it too.'

She asked quietly: 'George, is your mother rich?'

'Yes. Father had money and she comes from an old Dutch family—Thyss van Linke. She's a baroness in her own right and has, even for these days, a sizeable fortune.'

Phoebe opened her mouth to speak, but he didn't give her the chance. 'I have a good deal of money too, my dear, but I've never let it influence my life. I hope it won't make any difference to you, Phoebe.'

'Well, no, it won't once I've got used to it. Only I wish you'd told me before—before we got married.'

'Then you might not have married me.' He smiled at her and got up from the bed. 'Come downstairs, Mother's dying to talk to you. Are you tired? You can have a nap if you'd like to.'

She looked astonished. 'Tired? Not a bit.' She laughed a little. 'Only grannies take naps...' She pinkened.

'And you're not a granny yet,' finished George smoothly.

The day passed pleasantly. After lunch, Phoebe was taken on a tour of the house and then with George strolled round the large garden. The boundary bordered on woods, pine trees mostly; there was a little wicket gate which opened out on to a bridle path, and George told her they could walk for miles if they felt so inclined. 'But not today a quiet evening and early bed for you, Phoebe, it's been a long day.'

'But a lovely one,' said Phoebe, and then, worriedly: 'I do hope I've got the right clothes.'

He took her arm. 'I think we might go shopping tomorrow. Ask mother what you should wear—is it the party you're worried about?'

She thought how kind he was to bother himself about it. 'Yes. I bought a dress—I thought it would be suitable for a doctor's wife.' She didn't see his smile. 'But when I went to the party with Basil, the girls were wearing very smart dresses or trouser suits, perhaps they're very smart here, too?'

'Well, I daresay the younger women will be,' observed George placidly, then added: 'I dislike trouser suits.'

'Well, I won't buy one, then,' conceded Phoebe, 'I might not have to buy anything, your mother might think the one I've got is quite suitable it would be an awful waste if I don't wear it. I've got a skirt and a blouse too.'

His lips twitched. 'Well, shall we see what Mother says?' he suggested.

Phoebe changed into one of the pretty dresses she had bought in Cambridge for dinner that evening, and was relieved to find that Mrs Pritchard was wearing something similar. They finished dinner and were in the drawing room drinking their coffee when visitors arrived an elderly man and woman and a pretty girl, older than Phoebe but beautifully turned out. Old friends, explained George, shaking hands and then kissing the girl: Mijnheer and Mevrouw van Renkel and their daughter Corina. They were offered coffee and sat drinking it, speaking English but occasionally switching over to Dutch, only to stop and apologise to Phoebe because she couldn't understand a word. Corina, she noticed, did that more often than anyone else, smiling at her with a kind of sly amusement. She was glad when the van Renkels got up to go and then put quite out of countenance when Corina declared that she was going to stay for a little longer, explaining that her parents could call for her on their way back from a visit to friends. Neither Mrs Pritchard or George showed anything but pleasure at her decision, and they sat around talking, carefully including Phoebe, until Mrs Pritchard suggested that if Phoebe was going shopping in the morning, they had better go upstairs and look at her dresses. Phoebe followed her out of the room, reluctant to leave George with Corina, aware that she was being foolish and quite startled at her strong feeling of annoyance. But she didn't let Mrs Pritchard notice that, but followed her obediently to her room, where she took out the blue dress and, when encouraged to do so, put it on.

'A very pretty dress, my dear,' pronounced Mrs Pritchard, 'but it doesn't do you justice. You're too thin, of course, but you've got a lovely figure and some of the clothes these days are charming for the young. Get something with big sleeves and a lower neckline, and you're slim enough to wear one of those lovely full skirts. What else have you got?'

Phoebe produced the skirt and then the blouse. 'You have good taste, my dear, but you're far too young to wear anything like that. You shall go with George tomorrow—and mind you take his advice!'

They went downstairs presently and found Corina still there, a fact which Mrs Pritchard remarked upon in her friendly way. 'Shall I get Ulco to drive you back?' she suggested. 'George and Phoebe have had a long day...'

Perhaps it was fortunate that Corina's parents returned at that moment, because Phoebe was sure that George was on the point of offering to drive the girl home himself. As it was, Corina was swept away after ten minutes or so and Ulco, without being asked, came in with more coffee. The three of them sat talking for another half hour or so until George said abruptly: 'You're already almost asleep on your feet, my dear. Go to bed.'

'Of course you must,' agreed Mrs Pritchard, 'especially as you're going shopping tomorrow. George, Phoebe needs quite a few things—take her into Hilversum. There's Gig's boutique and Haan's and de Cuyp, one of them should be able to fit her out.' She took Phoebe's hand and said kindly: 'That's a Jaeger suit hanging in your closet, isn't it? My favourite—and always in such excellent taste.' She leaned forward and kissed Phoebe. 'My dear, don't think I'm patronising you—you're so sweet, and just the daughter I would have so loved to have had.'

Phoebe kissed the beautifully made up cheek. 'If you don't mind,' she said shyly, 'I'd like to think of you as Mother. I can hardly remember my own, you know.'

She said goodnight and George opened the door for her and dropped a kiss on her cheek as she paused there. 'Sleep well,' he said in his kind voice.

There was no reason why she shouldn't have done just that. Instead, she lay awake for a long time in her luxurious bed, beset by doubts. The biggest doubt, for some reason she couldn't fathom, was Corina.

CHAPTER FIVE

TWENTY-FOUR HOURS later, Phoebe was back in bed again, but with far different thoughts. It had been an exciting day and a very happy one, and she hadn't given Corina van Renkel a single thought. Now she lay, determined not to go to sleep until she had gone over every minute of it. They had left the house shortly after a leisurely breakfast and driven the short distance to the centre of the town. She had been surprised to find it so modern, but she had liked it at once. With the car parked in Het Hof Holland hotel car park, they had had coffee, booked a table for lunch and gone in search of the boutiques. She hadn't expected George to take such an interest in what she bought; indeed, he picked out several dresses which she had looked at longingly but considered too much in the forefront of fashion for herself. He had insisted, with a placid determination she couldn't ignore, that she tried them on, and when she paraded in them, observed that they suited her very well. They were certainly like nothing she had ever worn before—the materials silky and gorgeous colours, cut so cunningly that she had to admit that they did something for her. She felt a different girl, looking at the transformation in the enormous mirror.

They took the dresses back to the car and Phoebe said diffidently, 'Shall I find a hairdresser and have something done to my hair?' She had been very surprised at George's quite emphatic refusal.

'Your hair is exactly right,' he told her, 'and it suits you. Have it washed and so on if you like, but don't dare have it curled and waved.' They had been strolling along, glancing in shop widows, and he had stopped to look at a silvery-grey dress, cast negligently over a gilt chair in a boutique window. 'Now that,' he had told her, 'is just made for you. Let's get it.'

So she had acquired yet another dress, a dream of a dress, she mused; soft silky pleats and a gorgeous belt. The had had lunch after that and he had suggested that they should drive round for a while. He had taken her to Loenen along the country roads and down the River Vecht, with its country houses bordering the river, and crossed to the other side and gone through Maarssen. They drove slowly so that she could see the lakes, and so to Tienhoven, past the airfield and on to Hilversum, where George had parked the car once more and had taken her to an elegant little teashop, where she had eaten an enormous cream cake and, when pressed, a second.

'I'm greedy,' she observed, 'only they are sheer heaven.' She plunged her fork into the mountain of delicate pastry. 'I shall get fat, and it will serve me right!'

George had laughed. 'You're very satisfactory as you are, but a few more pounds wouldn't come amiss, and it's delightful to be with a girl who doesn't pick at dry biscuits and lettuce leaves.'

She had paused, the fork halfway to her mouth. 'Oh—did you go out with girls—a girl, who did that?'

He had laughed again. 'Oh, several.' He added. 'That was a long time ago, Phoebe.'

A very satisfactory answer. She smiled sleepily and closed her eyes.

There were uncles and aunts and cousins coming to lunch the next day. It was a chilly, blustery morning and Phoebe wore the Jaeger suit, and was rewarded by George's smiling approval and his mother's, 'Charming—how well it suits you, my dear.' But before the guests arrived she put on a raincoat, tied a scarf over her head and went for a long walk with George through the wicket gate and into the dripping woods behind the house. It was very quiet there, the trodden earth paths soft and damp underfoot.

'We might as well have our little chat about ways and means,' George observed. He had put a hand on her shoulder and slowed his stride to fit her smaller steps. He talked calmly for some time and she listened carefully, for he was explaining how his family had become wealthy. It went back a long way. His father's forebears had been what Phoebe privately called landed gentry and had invested wisely in the first railways. There had always been doctors in the family, he explained, who had done well and added to the family fortunes, and his mother—well, her family had made its fortune in the Dutch East Indies in the seventeenth century and prudently added to it over the centuries. 'And of course there aren't so many children nowadays. Once upon a time the money had to be divided between a dozen or more, now the family is large enough, but half the size it was a hundred years ago. So there's more money for all of us, if you understand me.'

'Yes—well, I suppose I'll get used to that.'

Her companion's face expressed faint arrogance. 'Naturally you will. You said you would like to help with the practice. I should be glad of that—of course there's Nurse Wilkins, but just lately I've been wondering if I should take on a nurse for the surgery. It would save a good deal of time-injections, bandaging and so on, holding babies, soothing anxious mothers... Would you like to do that? It would still leave you plenty of time to do what you wanted, and I doubt if I should need you at evening surgery.'

Phoebe felt a wave of pleasure. 'Oh, I would like that. I'm not trained, though I learnt to bandage and I can give injections and that kind of thing.'

'That sounds just right. Shall we give it a try?'

She agreed happily, and they retraced their steps.

They reached the house a few minutes before the first of the family arrived. Oom Charles and Tante Beatrix came first; a baron and baroness, Phoebe guessed from Ulco's announcement, although they didn't look like the part. Oom Charles strongly resembled his nephew, although his hair was grey and he stooped a little, and his wife was small and mouselike. She had barely exchanged polite nothings with them when two young women and a youngish man came in.

'Cousins,' murmured George in her ear. Juliana, tall and imposingly built and dressed rather strangely in an enormous cloak, a wide-brimmed felt hat and a vivid green dress; Sibilla, a smaller, paler edition of her sister and dressed, like Phoebe, in a classic suit, and lastly Cornelius, bearing a strong family likeness to George although he was shorter and more solidly built. Juliana was an artist, which might account for her rather startling clothes, thought Phoebe. Her sister did nothing; she was engaged to be married and invited Phoebe and George to the wedding, an invitation which George accepted at once before Cornelius joined them.

Ulco was offering drinks when the last of the guests arrived—another aunt, Mrs Pritchard's sister, and very like her in appearance, accompanied by her daughter and her husband, and a tall white-haired old lady, very upright and dignified. 'Grandmother,' said George in Phoebe's ear. 'She doesn't go out much, she's come to look you over, my dear.'

She couldn't be worse than Aunt Kate, thought Phoebe as she stood quietly while the old lady's blue eyes examined her slowly.

'You may kiss me, Phoebe,' said George's grandmother.

Phoebe planted a light kiss on a nicely made up cheek and smiled, because she couldn't think of anything to say to fit the occasion. It seemed to have been the right thing to do, for the old lady nodded her stately head, offered a cheek to her grandson and said something to him in Dutch. He answered in the same language as they both looked at her. 'It's all right,' he explained. 'We're agreeing that you'll make me a very good wife.'

He smiled as he spoke and took her hand and held it quite unselfconsciously, and Phoebe, for the first time since they had married, felt wholly happy, although she had no idea why.

Lunch was a lengthy meal with a great deal of talk, almost all of it in English. Phoebe, sitting beside George at his place at the head of the table, with an uncle on either side, enjoyed herself. True, it was rather like being in a dream, but it was a nice dream, and she supposed, with her usual calm, that she would get used to living in the lap of luxury in time—after all, everyone else there took it for granted. Besides, even if George was rich, his home in Woolpit, although the ultimate in comfort, was... Her thoughts were interrupted by George saying quietly: 'This is delightful, isn't it, Phoebe, but I have a great fondness for my own home in Woolpit.'

She turned surprised grey eyes on his. 'How did you know what I was thinking?' she asked.

'Your face is very expressive. I think I shall always know.' He told her.

The afternoon was spent pleasantly. One by one the aunts and uncles and cousins came and sat by Phoebe and cross-examined her in the kindliest possible way, always finishing by saying that George must give himself another holiday soon and bring her over to Holland for a long visit. They all lived in different parts of the country; Groningen, in the north, near the Hague, and at Rhenen on the Rhine. Grandmother lived in Friesland, they explained, by herself, if you discounted the companion who had been with her for ever. And Phoebe had an invitation from the old lady too, before she took her departure with a good deal of ceremony, driving away in an elderly Daimler driven by an elderly chauffeur. 'You'll visit me,' Phoebe had been told. 'George shall bring you over as soon as he can arrange it.' She had held Phoebe's eyes with a piercing stare. 'I am devoted to George, as I am sure you are also, my dear.'

Phoebe had the extraordinary feeling that a large bubble had burst somewhere inside her. She went very red and found that she hadn't enough breath. Something had just been made very plain to her. She was devoted to George too—more than that, she was besotted, hopelessly in love with him, and how was it possible that she hadn't discovered it until that very minute?

She went on staring at the old lady, while colour rushed into her face and then ebbed away, leaving it very pale. George's grandmother said nothing for a moment. 'I can see that we agree, my dear.' She offered a cheek to be kissed as George came towards them. She took his arm and went out to where her car was waiting.

When everyone had gone, they went for another walk. It was much easier, Phoebe decided, to walk and talk without having to look at him most of the time. They discussed his family in a mild sort of way, a subject which took them comfortably back to the house for a late tea.

'A quiet evening at home,' observed George with satisfaction, his eyes on Phoebe's face.

Only as it turned out it wasn't that at all. They were still sitting idly long after the tea tray had been taken away, when they heard a car turn into the drive and stop at the house. George didn't move, and Phoebe, taking a quick look at him, could see no change in his expression; all the same, it seemed that he was annoyed.

He said quietly. 'Kasper—were you expecting him, mother?'

His mother frowned slightly, 'No, dear,' then turned her head as Ulco came in to inform them all quietly that Mijnheer Kasper Thyss van Linke had arrived. He opened the door a little wider to allow the young man behind him to enter the room.

There was only one description that fitted him; tall, dark and handsome, for he was all three. What was more, he was smiling with such charm that he would have wrung equal smiles from the most ill-natured.

Something George was not. He got to his feet, topping their visitor by several inches. 'An unexpected pleasure, Kasper.' His voice was placid and he was smiling too, as his cousin crossed the room to kiss Mevrouw Thyss van Linke's cheek. 'You must meet my wife—Phoebe, this is Kasper, another cousin.'

Phoebe shook hands, going a little pink under the frankly interested gaze of his dark eyes, and wondered if George was going to enlarge on his rather uninformative introduction. Apparently not. She withdrew her hand, held a little too long, and regained her usual calm, despite her pink cheeks.

'How do you do? George, what a large family you have!' She smiled across the room at him and caught his curiously intent look. I wish I didn't blush, she thought, like a silly schoolgirl.

She didn't want to meet that dark gaze again, but she had to, for Kasper was speaking.

'But not so many of us that we cannot welcome such a charming addition to the family.' He glanced at George. 'My congratulations, George. What a pity your wedding was so quiet—I would have enjoyed being your best man. Are you staying here for long?'

'A few days so that Phoebe can meet as many of us as possible. And isn't it about time we danced at your wedding, Kasper?'

It was then that Phoebe realised that George didn't like him. There was nothing in his manner to betray it; she supposed that when you loved someone you acquired an extra sense which made you aware of their feelings even if they were well hidden.

'Time enough, George, though now that I've met my new

cousin, I'm full of regret that I didn't see her first now I have lost my heart too late!'

He thumped his chest so dramatically that Phoebe giggled. He was joking, of course—but all the same a small sneaking wish that George would lose his heart too, and not as a joke, crept into her head. She suppressed it at once as being disloyal, and felt relief when George laughed and his mother smiled.

'You'll stay to dinner, Kasper?' she asked, and George followed that with: 'What about a drink?'

'I hoped you would ask me. I'm on my way to Rhenen.' He turned to Phoebe sitting quietly, her colour once more normal. 'I live there. You must come and see it one day—it's on the Rhine and the country is charming.'

And Phoebe, anxious to return to a casual conversation, said readily: 'Oh, yes, weren't there bishops there once upon a time?'

He looked surprised. 'You've been there? You know Holland?'

'No, but when I knew we would be coming here I read one or two books.'

She accepted a glass of sherry from George and felt relief as he swept them all into an easy conversation with apparently no effort at all. And presently his mother went away to tidy herself for dinner and Phoebe went with her, wanting to stay with George but anxious to get away from Kasper, who unsettled her so. She was quite sure she didn't like him, but he certainly unsettled her.

'I shall change,' declared Mevrouw Thyss van Linke. 'Put on one of your pretty dresses, child.'

Phoebe took great pains with her face and her hair. Surveying her person in the lovely old pier-glass in her room, she felt almost content with her appearance. True, she had no looks to speak of, but she had made the most of what she had, and surely George would notice…

She went slowly downstairs and found no one in the drawing room but Kasper. He came to meet her as she crossed the room and took a hand and held it between his own.

'That's a lovely dress, and a lovely girl in it,' he told her.

Phoebe tugged to free her hand, but he didn't let go. 'It's kind of you to say so, but I'm not lovely.' Her voice was tart. 'Besides,

I don't think I like that kind of compliment.' She gave another tug. 'And I'd like my hand back.'

He paid no heed to her, looking over her shoulder and smiling. 'George, my ego is crushed—I don't think Phoebe likes me.'

He let her hand go then and she said quietly, not looking at George: 'I have to know people before I like them.' She smiled as she said it because Kasper was undoubtedly charming and she didn't want to hurt his feelings.

He didn't appear to be in the least put out. 'You've known each other for a long time?' he asked casually.

George caught her eye and smiled faintly. 'Oh yes, although I must point out that time doesn't have much to do with it, does it, my dear?'

Phoebe wished with all her, heart that she was his dear as she agreed fervently and crossed the room to slip a hand into his. Its large firmness closed reassuringly round it, but only for a moment, for his mother joined them and he went to pour her drink, leaving her to sit rather uneasily and talk nothings until Ulco announced that dinner was served.

It was during dinner that Corina's name cropped up. 'Seen anything of Corina?' asked Kasper casually. 'Always great pals, weren't you? When I saw her a month or so ago, she was babbling on about paying you a visit.'

'Corina was here yesterday. A pity you missed her—the girls had a chance to get to know each other. I daresay we shall see her again before we go back.' George spoke with lazy good humour, and Phoebe seethed; she hadn't thought about Corina all day, and here the wretched girl was, popping up again into her head to nag her. But that was all that was said about her; Kasper was amusing as well as charming and a clever talker, and they were all laughing by the end of the meal. All the same, she was glad when they left the table. Kasper had been sitting opposite her and each time she had looked up, his dark gaze had met hers. George, sitting at the head of the table, had his eyes on her too, but she didn't know that.

Later, sitting in the drawing room over coffee, she listened to his slow, deep voice and felt she would burst with love. It would never do to give him an inkling of her feelings. In her efforts to hide them, she was alternately silent or too chatty; it was a relief when Mevrouw Thyss van Linke declared it was her bedtime and she was able to make her own excuses and go with her. She bade Kasper a pleasant goodnight, replied suitably to his renewed invitation to visit him, offered a cheek to George and followed his mother to the door. They were leaving the room when Kasper called to her: 'I'm going very shortly, Phoebe—I won't keep George from you.'

Phoebe didn't answer, but when they reached the gallery at the top of the staircase George's mother paused.

'Do you like Kasper, my dear?'

Phoebe paused to think. 'I'm not sure that I do—only he's fascinating, isn't he? You don't mind me saying that?'

'Not in the least. I asked a question and you gave an honest answer.' She kissed Phoebe's cheek and just for a moment Phoebe thought she was going to say more than that. 'Goodnight, my dear.'

In her room Phoebe undressed slowly and sat for a long time brushing her hair. She wasn't thinking about Kasper, her head was full of George—dear darling George, who liked her enough to marry her, but showed no signs of loving her. 'I must do something about that,' muttered Phoebe as she got into bed, prepared to stay awake until she had hit on a solution, but it had been an eventful day; she fell asleep at once.

Mevrouw Thyss van Linke never came down to breakfast; she and George ate it together in a small room at the back of the hall while they discussed what they should do with their day. 'Well,' said Phoebe, 'it might be dull for you, but I like being here. I mean just for a day, you know, to get my breath.'

'Then that's what we'll do. Suppose we walk into town? There's a quiet path across the road and through the woods; it's a long way round but pretty. We might see something to take back for Mrs Thirsk...'

'And Nurse Wilkins and Susan.'

'Of course. You do realise that we'll have to pay family visits before we go home? We'll space them out so that you're not too overwhelmed.'

'I shall like that. They all come from different parts of the country, don't they?' She added shyly: 'I liked your grandmother.'

'We'll go there first. It'll be a pleasant drive, we can stay for lunch and have dinner on the way back here. Tomorrow?'

She nodded. 'Oh, yes.' She filled his coffee cup. 'Your mother won't mind if we go out each day?'

'Not in the least. We're a close-knit family, you know.'

Except for Kasper, she thought silently. She supposed they would visit him too, and she had to admit that it would be—well, interesting to meet him again. To be admired so openly was soothing to a girl who had precious little to be admired. She smiled at the thought and George said:

'You're pleased? Good. Put on some sensible shoes and we'll be off.'

The walk through the woods was delightful. The paths were sandy and they met few people; dog owners and one or two horse riders. Once at the shopping centre, they had coffee and then strolled along looking, not very seriously, for suitable gifts to take back with them. It took quite some time before Phoebe saw a leather handbag which she thought was just right for Mrs Thirsk, and presently a couple of silk headscarves which would be just the thing for Susan. That left Nurse Wilkins. 'She's got her own home,' mused Phoebe, 'so china or something like that...' They found a Delft blue cup and saucer and plate, prettily boxed, and well satisfied, they started back home, very much at ease with each other. They reached the house far too soon, thought Phoebe, parting from George in the hall to go to her room and tidy herself for lunch, for her—although she took heart at the thought that George had enjoyed her company.

They left early the next morning, and since it was almost like a winter day Phoebe wore the Jaeger suit again. She was glad about that when she saw George's approving eyes at breakfast; it had been well worth getting up earlier than usual so that she had had time to do her face and hair really well. They set off in high good humour and drove north, at first along the motorway through

Nijkerk and Harderwijk and then to Zwolle, where they stopped for coffee, but after that George left the main roads and took a country road to Steenwijk and then on to the highway to Leeuwarden. Just short of the town he turned off into a narrow road which in turn led to a brick road running along the top of a dyke: the fields were wide here, well stocked with black and white cows wearing sacking coats, and in the distance Phoebe caught a glimpse of water.

'Surely not the sea?' she asked.

'Lakes, all connected by canals and rivers—we're almost there.'

Sure enough there was a cluster of houses round a church ahead of them. George slowed to go through its small centre and took a lane leading to a clump of trees. A moment later he had turned into a gravelled drive and she saw the house. Flat-faced with a ponderous door flanked by wide windows, it rose for two storeys with a highly ornamental balcony running across the first floor and rows of windows above it. Phoebe didn't say anything; perhaps old Mevrouw Thyss van Linke had more of her family living there with her…

A stern-faced woman admitted them and then led them across the wide hall to double doors at one side. She said something to George as she tapped on the door and smiled at him as she opened it. Before they went in George said, 'Phoebe, this is Marthe, who housekeeps here.' He spoke to the woman too, and Phoebe held out a hand and was relieved to see the housekeeper smile again.

George's grandmother was sitting very upright in a small armchair near a log fire, almost lost in the huge fireplace with its great hood and coat of arms above it. The room was large, very light by reason of the wide high windows, and richly furnished. Phoebe, once greetings were over, found time to look around her, sitting quietly, not taking a large part in the conversation. But presently the old lady began firing questions at her, a state of affairs which lasted until they were bidden to lunch. This was eaten in another large room, its walls hung with family portraits, the dining-room table large enough to take a dozen people in comfort.

'I'll take a nap,' declared Mevrouw Thyss van Linke when they had had their coffee. 'Take Phoebe round the house, George.'

So they wandered off, peering into any number of rooms, all looking as though they were in constant use. 'Does your grandmother live here all by herself?' asked Phoebe.

'For a good deal of the time, yes. The family gather from time to time.'

'It's rather large…'

'The first Thyss van Linkes to live in it had ten children, and since then there have never been less than six. Grandfather was one of eight, Grandmother was the youngest of five. She married young and Grandfather was some years older than she; there's no one left now, just her, but she wouldn't dream of leaving. It's been home for too long.'

They went into the garden presently and through a small gate into the little wood beyond. It was still chilly and overcast, but as far as Phoebe was concerned it could have snowed.

They left after tea, with his grandmother's wedding gift, a silver tea service, securely packed in the boot. 'You'll do very nicely,' the old lady had said as she kissed Phoebe goodbye. 'Come again whenever you like.'

'A lovely day,' sighed Phoebe, eating a splendid dinner at the Grand Hotel Wientjes. 'George, what a large family you have!' She didn't mean to sound wistful, but he said at once: 'Enough for two of us, my dear.'

They were off again the next morning, this time to The Hague to see Tante Beatrix and Oom Charles. They lived on the outskirts of the city in a pleasant wooded area between it and Wassenaar. Another enormous house, thought Phoebe, but quite different from the one in Friesland. This one was of red brick with a good deal of ornamentation over its windows. It had a steep tiled roof and two little turrets at either end and there were steps to climb to the front door, opened by a very correct manservant. Phoebe was glad it was warm and sunny enough for her to wear a rather dashing two-piece. Six months ago she would never have dreamed of wearing anything quite so chic, but it was astonishing how quickly she was getting used to it. They were welcomed warmly, and Phoebe found that the Baroness expected her to answer all the same questions as George's grandmother. It was a relief when they were offered drinks and presently went in to lunch, a lengthy elaborate meal in an intimidating room, heavy with solid furniture, and yet more ancestors glaring from the walls. She preferred the drawing room even though it was furnished in the same heavy style.

'Well?' asked George as they drove home.

'They were awfully kind,' said Phoebe, and added carefully, 'but I liked your grandmother's house better.'

'Me too. Tante Beatrix is far too grand for me.'

That, coming from George, struck her as very amusing, although she didn't say so.

They stayed at home the next day, walking a little, talking a great deal to George's mother, and although they had intended to go to Groningen on the following day, a phone call made them alter their plans. Lena, George's cousin, was ill with 'flu and they were advised not to go. 'So we'll go to Rhenen instead,' suggested George. 'Kasper's still home—I'll give him a ring.'

He was looking at Phoebe as he spoke and she found to her annoyance that she had pinkened. The calm of his face didn't change. 'I'll suggest dinner, shall I?'

'Whatever you like.' Her cheeks were cooling, thank heaven; she hoped he hadn't noticed, and her voice was quiet and just sufficiently interested. All the same, she didn't want to go.

They spent the next day walking in the woods and then sitting about talking, lounging in the comfortable chairs, listening to the radio, watching TV, until it was time to dress for the evening.

She put on the dress George had chosen, its silken folds falling gracefully, its magnificent belt showing off her small waist. George would surely be pleased that she was wearing it. She took a final look in the mirror, caught up the wide mohair wrap she had bought in Hilversum, and went downstairs.

George was in the hall, his hands in his pockets, rather remote and austere in a beautifully cut grey suit. He looked handsome and very large and self-assured; Phoebe thought fleetingly that he was just as good-looking in the slacks and thin sweaters he'd been wearing each day at home.

He turned round as she reached the bottom stair, staring at her so intently that she said uncertainly: 'Is there something wrong? I wore this dress—it's the nicest of them all...'

'It's delightful,' he said slowly. 'You should make a lasting impression.' Which wasn't quite the answer she had hoped for.

It wasn't a long drive and George took the side roads. It was a light pleasant evening and the country was tranquil. Phoebe felt like talking, but presently she gave up. George, always polite and beautifully mannered, wasn't in a chatty mood; she contented herself with sitting quietly, watching his hands on the wheel, weaving day dreams which, as far as she could see hadn't a hope of coming true.

Kasper's house stood well back from the road just before the small town of Rhenen. It was a fair-sized house and thatched and the garden around it, encircled by trees, was full of colour. A solid middle-aged woman opened the door to them and was brushed aside by Kasper, who greeted them with wide smiles and a further flowery speech about Phoebe's charming appearance. She wished him good evening and at the same time wished she didn't feel so awkward about his compliments but she could think of nothing to say; she had had little enough practice, after all. She glanced at George, standing beside her, wearing a bland expression which for some reason annoyed her, so that when Kasper took her hand and said, 'Come along—there's plenty of time before dinner for a drink,' she smiled at him and went down the hall and into a big room that ran the width of the house at the back. It wasn't like any of the other rooms she had seen during her stay; it was ultra-modern, sparsely furnished with curious tubular furniture, the walls hung with a flame-coloured paper. There was someone sitting on a hideous sofa—Corina.

CHAPTER SIX

PHOEBE WOULD HAVE paused in the doorway, but Kasper had a firm hold of her hand. 'Surprise, surprise!' he cried. 'I decided that three was the wrong number for a dinner party, so I got Corina to come along; which means that I can get to know you better, Phoebe darling, and she and George can renew their old friendship.'

Corina got up and strolled to meet them, and Phoebe was conscious of a variety of strong feelings jostling for expression. Dislike for Corina for a start, fierce jealousy because she and George were old friends—and that could cover any number of things—and fortunately for her, stronger than these, an intense satisfaction that her dress, so different from Corina's narrow-skirted, backless black satin, was a great deal more becoming. She said coolly: 'Hullo, Corina, what a surprise, how nice to see you again,' and summoned a smile which at least looked genuine. A smile when she managed to keep in place as Corina flung her arms round George's neck and kissed him.

The evening went on for ever. Dinner, in a dining room as ugly as the drawing room, all uncomfortable chairs and a glass-topped table, was a splendid meal, quite wasted on Phoebe. Even if she had stolen a march on Corina's outfit, she couldn't hope to compete with her undoubted talent for holding everyone's attention, so she smiled and laughed and said little, and she didn't look at George at all. And when Corina began to talk about people she didn't know and times long past, before Phoebe had known George, she suddenly cast good sense to the winds and encouraged Kasper's more than cousinly attentions. He was being rather silly, she thought, but at least it helped her to ignore Corina making a dead set at George, who should, she decided severely, know better.

The lengthy meal came to an end at last, and they went back to the drawing room for coffee. Phoebe, peeping at the modern clock on the overmantel, made out that it was almost ten o'clock; surely they would go soon? But George appeared to be in no hurry, nor did he seem to mind the way Kasper was monopolising her Phoebe, made aware of strong feelings she had never experienced before, responded halfheartedly to Kasper's talk and wished they could end the evening.

Which they did some hour or so later and not entirely to her satisfaction. George, it seemed, was willing to give Corina a lift, and since she begged to sit in front by George because on the back seat she always felt car-sick, Phoebe found herself sitting lonely behind the two of them. Even Kasper's soft: 'A delightful evening, Phoebe darling, the beginning of a close friendship—England isn't so far away, you know.'

He had kissed her hand, which rather pleased her, even though she didn't much like it.

Corina talked almost without ceasing until they reached Hilversum and when George stopped the car and got out to open Phoebe's door and open the house door for her, begged her sweetly to visit her. 'There's an awful lot you should know about George,' she said lightly 'and I'm the best one to tell you.'

Phoebe went back to the car and poked her head through the window. 'I think I'd rather find out for myself,' she said gently. 'Goodnight, Corina.'

Her goodnight to George was glacial as she went past him into the house.

Corina lived with her parents in Baarn, only a few miles away. Phoebe got ready for bed and went to sit by the window until she saw the car coming up the drive again. At least George hadn't done more than drive the girl home—there hadn't been time for more than that.

She got into bed, fuming, and went to sleep at once to dream of George and Corina and Kasper, so that she woke in the early morning not sure what had been dream and what had been reality.

A condition not helped in the least by George's matter-of-fact good morning when she got down to breakfast. 'I fancy you didn't enjoy yourself overmuch at Kasper's,' he observed blandly as she poured coffee. 'I have a great many friends, Phoebe, old friends who I have known for many years—I hope that they will be your friends too when you have got to know them.'

She wasn't going to let him see that she minded; she said in a rather high voice: 'Actually, the evening was delightful, only I'm not quite used to compliments and—well, the kind of joking talk. I daresay I'll get better at it.'

'Kasper has really fallen for you—aren't you flattered?' He smiled at her across the table and she itched to throw a plate at him.

She said airily and with no truth at all: 'Yes, I suppose I am—I'm not used to it either, you see.' At his quizzical look she added hastily: 'I'm not sure that I like being flattered.'

'A good thing,' observed George placidly, 'for I don't think I'm much good at it.' He buttered some toast and she passed him the marmalade. 'Would you like to go anywhere today?' He glanced up and smiled at her. 'Only three more days, you know.'

Phoebe looked out of the window. 'Unless you want to go somewhere... I'd love to just potter around—your mother wouldn't mind?'

He gave her a pleased look. 'She'll be delighted. She's been longing for a long gossip and tomorrow she'll be rather occupied making sure that everything is just as it should be for the party.' He took the cup of coffee she was offering him. 'If you're sure that's what you want to do, I'll drive to Leyden to my old hospital and look up a few men I know.'

He spoke casually, his eyes on her face.

She bent her head and busied herself with what was on her plate.

'What a good idea,' she said brightly. 'You trained there? It's one of the oldest medical schools isn't it?'

Of course he wouldn't want her with him, she would be in the way if he wanted to talk to his former colleagues, but all the same, she felt hurt. But wild horses wouldn't drag that from her. She listened to him talking about Leyden, without hearing what he was saying, her smile as bright as her words had been.

Actually, she spent a very happy day with his mother. While there wasn't much to say about her own family, since she had none, Mrs Pritchard had several dozen members to discuss, so when she had exhausted the Dutch side, she began on the English relations of her husband. 'All in Cumbria,' she observed, 'but now and again they come down to London and we have a grand get-together—and there's a niece who's married and lives in Cornwall—a dear girl with five—no, six children—so unfashionable, but so happy,' She peeped at Phoebe. 'You like children, dear?'

'Very much.' Phoebe had been expecting that and her voice was composed. 'I expect that's because there haven't been any in my family for such a long time.'

'Ah well,' Mrs Pritchard sounded pleased with herself, 'that's something that can be remedied, and how fortunate that George has the means to care for half-a-dozen children.'

Phoebe mustered a smile and agreed.

George was back shortly after they had had tea and the rest of the evening passed pleasantly enough, what with his account of how he had spent his day and Mrs Pritchard's plans for the next day's party.

'Will there be a lot of people coming?' asked Phoebe, 'and do we dress up?'

'About thirty or so, and yes, I think we might dress up, Phoebe. There will be a buffet supper and dancing; it's a chance for even more family and our friends to meet you.'

It was their last day. Phoebe got up and looked out of the window with real regret; she had loved every minute of her stay and she had got to know a good deal more about George too. She dressed and went down to breakfast, to find him already there, and when he suggested a walk through the woods she agreed happily.

'You've liked it here?' he wanted to know as they took a sandy path away from the house.

'Oh, yes, George—I love it. And I do so like your mother.'

'And she finds you exactly the kind of daughter-in-law she wanted.'

'Does she? Does she really? Well, I'm glad. You know, you seem quite a different person here, George—I mean, I wouldn't have guessed the half of this, just knowing you in Woolpit.'

'That's why I wanted us to come here. In a couple of days I'll be a village GP again.' He smiled wonderfully at her and tucked her arm under his. 'And you'll be a GP's wife, answering the phone and the door and taking messages.'

'I shall like that.' She beamed at him, 'I hope your mother comes to stay with us soon.'

'She will.'

They walked on in a companionable silence until Phoebe asked: 'Have you known Corina a very long time?'

'Oh, years and years.' His voice was dry. 'You find her pretty?'

'Very—and very attractive.' There was a faint question in her voice which he didn't answer, so she changed the subject hastily. 'That dress we bought in the Hague—the one with the long bodice and the chiffon skirt—would that be too grand for this evening?'

'Certainly not. I should think it would do admirably—you are, after all, the belle of the ball.'

'No, I'll never be that,' she said soberly, 'although it's kind of you to say so.'

All the same, when the evening came and she put the dress on, she had to admit, even to her critical eye, that it really was something. She hadn't dared to query its price, but it was undoubtedly haute couture; the dropped bodice, apricot silk embroidered with silver thread, merged into a swirl of silk chiffon skirts, and when she had dressed her pale brown hair high and applied an extra special make-up, she couldn't help but be pleased with her appearance. She was preparing to go down to the drawing room when there was a tap on the door and George came in. He closed the door, behind him and stood looking at her. 'Very nice,' he commented, studying her at his leisure, and then he strolled towards her. He took at once a hand out of a pocket and she saw the shimmer of pearls. 'Will you wear these? My father's mother's pearls—he left them to me for my bride, and tonight seems a fitting occasion on which to wear them.'

It was a three-stranded, pearl choker with a diamond clasp, and Phoebe took it in her hands, touching the pearls gently. 'They're beautiful,' she whispered. 'You're sure you want me to have them?'

He smiled. 'Are you not my bride?' And when she looked at him uncertainly, 'And I want you to have them, my dear.'

He fastened them and she turned to look at them in the mirror. They were exactly right with the dress. She turned back, one hand on the pearls. 'Thank you, George—it's the most beautiful thing I've ever seen...'

He bent his head and kissed her lightly. 'I'm glad you like them. Shall we go down?'

Mrs Pritchard was already in the drawing room, its furniture set against the walls so that later on anyone who wished could dance. She was wear-ing black velvet and a discreet sprinkling of diamonds, and Phoebe was on the point of exclaiming how very nice she looked when Mrs Pritchard forestalled her. 'Phoebe—but how enchanting, and the pearls are just right. That's an exquisite dress, my dear. George, aren't you proud of your wife?'

'I've always been that—I'm utterly charmed as well.'

Phoebe blushed and wished with all her heart that he had really meant that. Of course, he was being kind, putting her at her ease, making her feel beautiful when she wasn't. She said shyly: 'Thank you, Mrs Pritchard, you look lovely.'

Mrs Pritchard twinkled. 'Mother of the bridegroom,' she laughed. 'I always promised myself I would deck myself out in black velvet and diamonds—so dignified and suitable.' She smiled at her son and Phoebe looked at him too. He was handsome and distinguished and she wanted to say so, but she couldn't get the words out. His eyes held hers and she might have gone on gazing at him for ever if Mrs Pritchard hadn't observed matter-of-factly: 'There are sandwiches in the sitting room—supper will be late and we'll be famished...'

She led the way across the hall and Phoebe and George followed her. Halfway across the hall he stopped, caught her by the hand and kissed her. She stared up at him wide-eyed. 'Oh, why did you do that?'

'One day I'll tell you.'

It was exasperating when his mother paused ahead of them and turned round, and disappointing that George didn't look in the least put out.

The guests began to arrive presently. Phoebe had met a good many of them already and she began to enjoy herself, sometimes with George beside her, sometimes the centre of his friendly family. She felt they liked her and she blossomed out under their kindly chatter. She was standing talking to a circle of the younger guests and a sprinkling of cousins when Corina and her parents came in—they were late, but she guessed that it was deliberate on Corina's part so that she might make an entry. Which she certainly did. She looked magnificent in vivid emerald green, a slinky tube of a dress, slit up the side, an enormous bow on one hip making her appear even slimmer than she was. She greeted Mrs Pritchard perfunctorily, leaving her parents to do so in a more leisurely way, and crossed the room to where George was standing with a group of guests. Phoebe couldn't hear what she said, and anyway it was in Dutch, but she laid a hand on his arm and smiled up at him in a way to make Phoebe seethe with rage, a rage by no means mitigated by George's smile and laughing rejoinder. Phoebe turned a shoulder and pretended that she hadn't noticed, and when Corina and George appeared at her elbow managed to look both delighted and surprised.

'How nice to see you, Corina,' she uttered insincerely, 'and what a gorgeous dress.'

Corina's eyes took in every inch of Phoebe. 'I see you've wrested the pearls from George. I always rather fancied them, though they are not quite my style.'

Spiteful cat, thought Phoebe, and felt jealousy turn a sharp knife deep inside her—was she implying that George had once upon a time offered them to her? Aloud she said in her pleasant voice: 'You don't need pearls, Corina, you're pretty enough without.' She smiled around the circle of faces. 'What about supper? Shall we see what there is to eat? I believe we're going to dance presently...'

She felt her hand taken from someone behind her and turned to see Kasper smiling down at her. 'Hullo, beautiful cousin.' He nodded at the others. 'Did I hear you mention food? I'm famished, let's attack the buffet.'

He urged everyone towards the dining room, still holding Phoebe's hand, laughing and joking, calling over his shoulder: 'See you later, Corina—and George.'

Perhaps, thought Phoebe uneasily, she and George would have been expected to go in to supper together, but it was too late to do anything about that now. She found herself surrounded with a laughing cheerful crowd, with Kasper still close, his hand on her arm.

'You look terrific,' he whispered, 'and I've never seen Corina look so vulgar.' He got her a plate of food and all of them sat down at-one of the tables arranged round the room. 'To our very own fairy on the Christmas tree,' cried Kasper, and raised his glass to her.

It wasn't George, but just to be admired by someone, even if she didn't like him at all, was soothing to her pride. And Kasper, give him his due, was expert at keeping up the party spirit. Presently they all went back to the drawing room where someone had already started the music, and Phoebe found herself swept on to the floor. Kasper danced well and she, although she had never had much chance to dance, instinctively good at it, and when the music changed to pop, she fell to twisting and twirling as though she had done it all her life.

'I say,' said Kasper, 'you're pretty good—is this another of your hidden talents, Phoebe?'

'I didn't know I had any.' She swung round and found herself face to face with George, who whisked her away to the edge of the room where it wasn't so crowded. 'Having fun?' he wanted to know.

'Oh, yes.' She made her voice enthusiastic; it was already breathless because she was with him. 'It's a wonderful party,' she added. 'Isn't it?'

She glanced at him and then quickly away, so that she didn't see his thoughtful eyes on her face. 'I'm glad you're enjoying it. You'll find life dull when we get home.'

She didn't look at him. 'Oh, George, no! It will be lovely.' She paused, remembering how he had smiled at Corina, and added deliberately and recklessly: 'I shall miss Kasper, though, he's such fun.'

'Then we must ask him to visit us,' said George at his most placid. 'Be sure and do so before he leaves.'

She had already regretted it: 'We can always write.'

He had danced her round the room and come to halt by the French windows. 'Oh, that's not the same.' He turned towards the dancers and lifted a hand to Kasper, dancing past with Corina.

'Phoebe wants to have you to stay,' he said easily. 'Fix up something between you.' He beamed warmly at them both and danced off with Corina.

'Well, well,' murmured Kasper. 'If I didn't know you were newlyweds I might be getting ideas!'

Phoebe pinned a bright smile to a stricken face. 'Pooh, what nonsense—George would like you to come and see us too. Are you a busy person? I mean, what do you do?'

'Absolutely nothing,' declared Kasper. 'I'm the black sheep of the family, we all have far too much money, but I'm the only one who idles away my life, spending it.' He smiled beguilingly. 'I'll come when you want me to, little cousin.'

'Well, it's lovely in England in the early summer—June...'

'June it shall be. Shall I be bored with the rustic life?'

She looked surprised. 'I don't know. You see, I'm never bored, and I don't think George is either. But there's some lovely country round and about Woolpit, and you can always drive up to London if you can't bear it any more.'

'It's a deal. I'll come at the end of June—I'll bring the car so that we can explore a bit while George has his handsome nose to his stethoscope or whatever.'

He bent and kissed her cheek. 'A bargain sealed,' he explained at her look of surprise. 'I can't see George—probably in a quiet corner explaining things to Corina. Let's dance.'

'What do you mean?' asked Phoebe in a quiet little voice.

'Oh, nothing sinister, darling. The dear girl had her claws into him the moment she'd left school, and she's not one to take no for an answer.'

And if that wasn't a word of warning, what was? thought Phoebe.

She changed partners presently, and it was some time before she found herself dancing with George once more.

'Fixed things up with Kasper?' he wanted to know placidly.

'Yes. The end of June. George, you and Corina...were you ever engaged? I mean, she seems—that is, she's a very old friend...'

His voice became even more placid. 'Oh, a very old friend. But no, we were never engaged. Why do you ask?'

'Oh, no reason...' She tried to sound nonchalant. 'She's very pretty.'

'Very.' They danced in silence then, and Phoebe, to her shame, had the hardest job in the world not to burst into tears, a circumstance which gave her heightened colour and a very bright pair of eyes.

People began to leave round about one o'clock. She kissed aunts and uncles and family friends goodbye, exchanged wishes to visit, accepted invitations and gave them, and finally found no one left but Kasper, the van Renkels and Corina and a rather tart old aunt who lived nearby in Hilversum. Phoebe helped her on with a vast number of shawls, topped with a fur coat, while the old lady mulled over her evening.

'Very pleasant,' she observed in her stilted, quite perfect English. 'You will be an asset to the family, my dear. George has taken his time to find himself a wife, but I see he has chosen wisely.' She shot a beady-eyed look across the hall, to where Corina was talking to George and Kasper. 'Such a relief!'

George joined them then to take her out to her car and stow her carefully into the back seat, and by the time he came back the van Renkels had said their goodbyes and Kasper was preparing to leave too.

They all went through the door together and George went with them, and Phoebe and Mrs Pritchard went to the sitting room and sat down. Ulco had set a tray of coffee and a plate of sandwiches on a small table and Mrs Pritchard went to pour out. They had almost finished their first cups when George joined them.

'Kasper having a last-minute chat?' asked Mrs Pritchard.

George accepted a cup of coffee and took a sandwich. 'No—Corina, nattering on about this and that.'

He sat down opposite Phoebe and she took care not to look at him, giving her whole attention to her coffee.

'I thought her dress was most spectacular,' remarked Mrs Pritchard in a carefully expressionless voice. 'Has she got designs on Kasper?'

'They don't like each other.' George sounded faintly bored.

'Oh, really? Then I wonder for whose benefit she wore that very vulgar dress?' Mrs Pritchard didn't wait for an answer, but went on: 'I thought your cousin Sibilla looked charming.' She turned to Phoebe. 'That was the dark-haired girl who came with my sister, dear, such a sweet girl...'

They sat talking for some time until Mrs Pritchard glanced at the great Friesian wall clock and exclaimed at the time. 'Good gracious, it's past two o'clock! I shall have my breakfast in bed—and you do the same if you want to, my dear. Have you done your packing?'

Phoebe shook her head. 'But that won't take long and we don't go until the afternoon, but I think I'll come to bed too.'

And when George got up she offered him a cool cheek for his kiss and wished him an equally cool goodnight.

Just before they left the next day an enormous bunch of red roses was delivered. The card that came with it read: 'To my favourite cousin, *tot ziens*.'

George put the flowers carefully on the back seat. He didn't appear to mind about them in the least, a fact which Phoebe found very disappointing. If only the silly man knew that I'd rather have a weed from the garden as long as he'd picked it and given it to me, she thought.

Hard on the thought came the much more disquieting one that perhaps he had sent red roses to Corina.

Their journey home was uneventful. Mrs Thirsk was waiting for them with a nicely laid table and a late supper ready. She accepted her presents with pleasure, told George that his post was on his desk in the study, and assured Phoebe that there were no worries since she had been away. Then she had departed to dish up supper while Beauty dashed between the study and the sitting room, beside herself with delight.

Half an hour later, sitting opposite George, eating Mrs Thirsk's delicious omelette, Phoebe felt as though she had just wakened from a dream. Only it hadn't been a dream; there were red roses, arranged in a great glass vase, to prove her wrong.

The evening had gone by the time they had finished. They sat for a while over their coffee but presently George went back to his study and she, after a word with Mrs Thirsk, went up to her room and unpacked. Hanging her lovely clothes in the enormous clothes closet, she wondered when she would wear them again; they weren't really suitable for Woolpit and she didn't think that George was a man to spend his few free evenings living it up in London. She lay for a long time in a very hot bath, pondering the events of the last few days or so. She had liked his mother—more, she was fond of her, and she liked his family, although she wasn't quite sure about Kasper. Corina was the only cloud in her sky and unfortunately she was a large one, looming dangerously. Perhaps George was in love with her; she wasn't sure of that, his face gave nothing of his feelings away, and Corina would have made him an unsuitable wife. Even if he loved her desperately, he would have admitted that; anyone less likely to make a village doctor's wife would be hard to find. Whereas she…'Most suitable,' she said out loud, 'able to answer the phone, talk to patients, do a little bandaging on the side and probably sit on a variety of village committees…' She licked away a tear. 'And happy to wear simple sensible clothes.'

She lay there until the water cooled around her, dried herself, slapped cream on to her flushed face, and got into bed. She had been there for some time, still wakeful, when she heard George's quiet footfall crossing the landing. It was only then that she fell into a troubled sleep.

She didn't look her best in the morning; her eyes were a little puffy and she was too pale, but when George, already at breakfast, remarked on her looks with some concern, she brushed it aside. 'It was a long day, yesterday,' she pointed out. 'Would you like me to help in the surgery this morning?'

He shook his head, 'Take Beauty for a walk, if you like. Andrew will be over presently—there are one or two patients we must check over together. See you later for coffee, perhaps.'

So Phoebe went for a long walk with an ecstatic Beauty, to get back home just as Mrs Thirsk was carrying in the coffee tray. She had coffee with the two men, sitting between them while they discussed their work. Now and again they remembered that she was there, and Andrew asked her how she had enjoyed herself in Holland, and George wanted to know if she had enjoyed her walk, but she suspected that she was surplus to their needs at the moment, and presently, with a murmured excuse, slipped away. It wouldn't be like that all the time, she told herself bracingly.

And it wasn't. At breakfast the next morning she was invited to put on a white overall and go along to the waiting room. Dr Pritchard was back; the word had gone round the village, and patients who had put off paying a visit to the surgery because he was away had been ringing up, making appointments. 'If you'd take names and get their cards out for me,' suggested George, 'it would save a great deal of my time.'

Phoebe was delighted; at last she was being of some use. The waiting room was filling up fast when she got there, although the surgery wasn't open for another ten minutes or so. Indeed, George was in the garden with Beauty, she could see him as she stood at the filing cabinet. She had the time to put old Mrs Owen's notes on his desk before he went into his surgery through the garden door. And after her there was Billy Pearce, with one of his regular sore throats and his rather bad-tempered mum, and Mrs Platt from the shop with what she called a nasty sharp pain inside. Just where inside was she was reluctant to say, although she informed the occupants of the waiting room that it was something cruel and she hadn't had a wink of sleep. She was almost immediately eclipsed by Mrs Foster with an even worse pain in her leg. Phoebe, searching for their cards and notes, made soothing noises, ushered them in one by one and made appointments for those who would need to come again. It was quite a busy morning and well past eleven o'clock before she poked her head round the surgery door.

'That's the last,' she told George cheerfully. 'I've taken two calls; one from Mappit's Farm and one from a Mr Westcott, both in bed with what sounds like bad chests, though neither of them were very clear about symptoms.'

He looked up from his writing. 'That will be the Mappit boy—

he's an asthmatic—and Mr Westcott has chronic bronchitis.' He leafed through the notebook on his desk. 'I've another four or five calls to make—would you like to come with me?'

Phoebe's eyes sparkled. 'Oh, please, George. Coffee first?'

And when he nodded, she went along to the kitchen and then raced upstairs to re-do her face and find a cardigan.

Mappit's Farm was several miles out of Woolpit, but they didn't talk much; she guessed that George's mind was on his patients, so she kept quiet, content to sit beside him. Really this was much better than the parties and outings they had had in Holland. Those had been fun too, of course, but here at home, they were doing something together.

He wasn't long at the farm, although most of the other calls took longer. She sat in the car, not impatient, dreaming of the perfect future she longed for and which was so unlikely. But she couldn't help but dream, all the same.

They took Beauty for a walk after lunch and came back to one of Mrs Thirsk's splendid teas, eaten hurriedly on George's part because he had a call to make before they had even finished. Phoebe took the tray out to the kitchen, had a pleasant gossip with Mrs Thirsk and went to tidy herself. By the time she was downstairs it was almost time for evening surgery and George wasn't back. The waiting room already held several patients; she found their cards and put them ready on the surgery desk, passed the time of day with this patient and that and went away to take another phone call—an agitated voice this time, asking if the doctor could call. 'Grandma's a very nasty colour,' said the voice, 'I don't like the look of her.'

It took a few moments to get the patient's whereabouts and another minute or two to reassure the caller. Luckily the address was one of the cottages at the end of the village street, and as she put down the receiver she heard the car at the door.

George, primed with her details, drove off at once and she went back to the waiting room to explain the delay. It seemed that Grandma was a well-known member of the community, and an interesting discussion as to her chances of survival kept everyone interested until George got back.

The evening surgery went smoothly enough after that. It was while she was tidying the waiting room when the last patient had gone that Phoebe asked: 'Was she all right, the old lady?'

George turned off his desk light and got up. 'Indigestion,' he said. 'She's eighty-eight and as sound as a bell, but she will indulge her fancy for pickled onions. What's for supper? I'm famished!'

A lovely day, thought Phoebe, curled up in bed a few hours later. If they could all be like that, life would be—if not quite perfect, then getting on that way; no Corina, no Kasper… Holland was a long way away. She thought to herself sleepily and she had George alone here. She was dozing off when the tiresome thought that perhaps he might find life with her a little dull flashed through her mind. She tried to remember what they had talked about during the evening. Nothing very interesting—indeed, he had read the papers for a good deal of the time while she sat opposite him, knitting. Compared with Corina in her lovely clothes, laughing her tinkling laugh, she was deadly dull. As from tomorrow, she would change into a pretty dress each evening and do her best to make witty conversation so that he would laugh at her as he had laughed at Corina. She closed her eyes again; perhaps tomorrow would be as nice a day as today had been.

CHAPTER SEVEN

TOMORROW, Phoebe was delighted to discover, was every bit as good as the previous day had been, and so were the succeeding days. And as the days lengthened and the weather settled into a promise of summer, they began to get invitations to visit George's friends. He seemed to have any number of them, scattered round the countryside, making their evening drives an added pleasure; more than that for Phoebe, it was heaven to sit beside George as he drove, listening to his desultory talk about his day, asking her opinion of this and that, laughing with her over some amusing incident. And his friends were nice. She had been scared before the first invitation, but afterwards she had to admit to herself that she had enjoyed every minute of it. George's friends had been youngish, with children and a comfortable untidy home and they had made her welcome and accepted her. Then after that she looked forward to their other visits, wearing the dresses George had chosen for her in the Hague and taking great care about her hair and make-up.

'We'll have to give a dinner party ourselves,' observed George, driving back through the still light evening. 'Shall we start with four? The Mansells and the Prices—they get on well together, and the Gregorys and the Normans a little later on.' He glanced sideways at her. 'It had better be on a Saturday or Sunday evening, we've got more chance of being free then.'

Phoebe said worriedly: 'I've never…I'm not sure I'll know what to do.'

'Just be you, Phoebe—they all like you, they won't be looking for faults, you know. You and Mrs Thirsk put your heads together and see what you can cook up between you. It's my weekend off in ten days—shall we decide on Saturday and see if the others are free then?'

'Yes, all right. Do you want me to write to Maureen and Leslie?' She added: 'Leslie's such a super cook...'

He laughed. 'A good reason for you and Mrs Thirsk to outshine her!'

A remark which made Phoebe decide to take a cookery book with her to bed each night; not that she would have to do the actual cooking, she thought comfortably. As things turned out, she was wrong. Having decided on a menu with Mrs Thirsk, the flowers, the table linen, the silver, Phoebe, relieved that everything was settled, occupied her days happily enough; as well as helping George in the surgery when he needed her, there was the garden, presided over by a taciturn old man who, once he had got used to the idea, raised no objection to her pottering alongside him, flowers to be arranged, shopping to do, occasional coffee mornings to attend, and the accounts to do—her days were nicely filled and she was happy. It was the day before the dinner party that Mrs Thirsk went down with 'flu. Sitting up in her bed, in an old-fashioned white nightie and a substantial bedjacket, she peered at Phoebe's anxious face from fever-bright eyes.

'You'll need to start today, Mrs Pritchard; it's all written down and everything's in the fridge. Do the watercress soup first. The lamb's coming this morning—Jim will have prepared the crown roast, the veg will be easy enough—new potatoes, like we said. As for the pavlova, that's easy...'

Phoebe agreed faintly; she had eaten pavlova when George had taken her out, but how to make it was a mystery she must solve. Mrs Thirsk was in no state to bother with such details. She went to the kitchen and looked over the contents of the fridge. At least she could get the soup ready. She peeled potatoes, cut them up and boiled them, added almost all the watercress, black-peppered it carefully and hopefully pushed the lot into the *mouli-légumes*. To her delight it came out looking like soup; she poured it carefully into a bowl and put it into the fridge. She would only have to reheat it at the last moment, add the cream and the watercress sprigs, and the first course was dealt with.

Quite cook-a-hoop as she was, it seemed the right moment to tackle the pavlova; the filling she could do just before the dinner party, but the meringue would keep fresh in the freezer. She followed the recipe painstakingly, getting rather hot and bothered before finally getting it into the oven. It was rather a pity that Susan should choose that moment to cut her finger. Not a bad cut, but it needed attention and, Susan being Susan, needed a cup of tea so that she could pull herself together again. What with one thing and another, Phoebe forgot the meringue. The ultra-crisp remnants which she took from the oven some time later were consigned to the dustbin. She would have another go after lunch, she decided. Now it was time to get a meal for George, who would be home from his morning rounds at any minute. Omelette, she decided, and a salad, and thank heaven there was a treacle tart in the fridge. She managed to have everything on the table as George swept into the house, although she hadn't had any time to tidy herself.

George threw her a quick glance. 'Busy?' he wanted to know cheerfully. 'How's Mrs Thirsk? I must see her presently.'

Phoebe observed that the housekeeper was feeling rotten and hadn't fancied anything for lunch but some soup. It would be too much to hope, she thought wistfully, that George might make some sympathetic remark about her busy morning. She stifled a wish to tell him how clever she'd been about the watercress soup and what a mess she'd made of the meringue for the pavlova, and she assured him cheerfully that she had no problems about their dinner party.

So, after lunch, with Susan enlisted to clear away lunch and wash up, Phoebe had another go at the pavlova, this time with success, mainly because she stayed glued to the kitchen for an hour until the meringue was exactly right. But at least she filled in the time mashing bananas and brandy to fill it later on, and when that was done getting down to making the saffron rice, a slow business with its half a dozen ingredients and all the stirring, but at last it was finished. She added the petits pois, the butter, the nuts and the little bits of apple and got out the crown of lamb and began to cover the top of each rib with foil, much encouraged by Susan's ohs and ahs of admiration.

She had to stop then and get the tea. George had gone into

Stowmarket, but he would be back around four o'clock. There was no surgery, it being a Saturday evening, although there was always the chance that he might be called out. Phoebe sent Susan home for her own tea and gave her strict instructions to be back by half-past seven, since she was to provide background help in the kitchen and wait at table, and then she took up a tray to the housekeeper. Mrs Thirsk was feeling a little better. Phoebe listened thankfully to last-minute instructions and went downstairs in time to welcome George.

'Had a pleasant afternoon?' he enquired, coming into the kitchen to carry in the tea tray.

'Oh, very.' Phoebe's voice sounded a little hollow, although she smiled cheerfully.

She enjoyed arranging the table. The cloth was a shining starched damask, the silver shone and so did the crystal glasses—George had beautiful things in his home. She had arranged a flower centrepiece in a low bowl and decided against candles in favour of the delicate chandelier hanging above the table. By the time she had everything to her satisfaction it was time to dress. She showered and put on one of the dresses George had chosen—pale green with a wide satin belt—and then hurried over her face and hair; it was time to put the crown of lamb in the oven.

She wasn't sure how she managed to be in the drawing room a minute or two ahead of their first guests. She was flushed from the heat of the Aga and her hair had come a little loose, and George gave her a long look as she came into the room. His placid, 'You look nice', more than made up for her hectic day.

On the whole, the evening went well; true the foil had somehow fallen off the tops of the ribs and they had got charred, but she had covered them with the cutlet frills and prayed that no one would take them off, and they hadn't. And even if the saffron rice didn't taste quite as delicious as it would have done if Mrs Thirsk had made it, it looked very nice.

Maureen and Leslie both declared that she was a splendid cook and they drank her health too. 'You must have been hard at it all day without Mrs Thirsk to give you a hand,' observed Leslie kindly, and Phoebe felt a pleasant pang of satisfaction at the surprise on George's face.

It was after everyone had gone, and Susan, replete with the remains of the dinner party, her evening's earnings clutched in a hand, had gone home too, that George said: 'That was a splendid effort, Phoebe, you must be tired to death. Go on up to bed, we can clear up in the morning.'

Phoebe had had a quick look round the dining room. The table was just as they had left it and when she peeped into the kitchen, there seemed to be a mountain of saucepans and dishes. Susan had stacked everything neatly before she had gone, but they would have to be washed.

She said brightly: 'I'm not a bit tired. I'll just clear the dining room; it'll be far worse if it's left until the morning.'

They began on the table, and it was almost cleared when the phone went.

George put down a pile of plates. 'I'll go,' he said, and glanced at the clock. It was well after midnight.

'The Bissett baby—sounds like croup.' He was already on his way to the study to fetch his bag. 'Don't wait up, my dear.'

Phoebe gave a tired snort as he closed the door quietly behind him. It was likely that she would be a long time clearing away the mess. She set to work on the dining room and when she had cleared it, put the kettle on, made a pot of tea, let Beauty out into the garden, kicked off her very expensive kid shoes and put on an apron.

The tea revived her and she set to, feeling more cheerful, going slowly because the silver had to be rubbed with Mrs Thirsk's special cloths and the glasses, hundreds of them, it seemed to her, needed precise polishing. She put them away in the big glass-fronted cupboard in the dining room, laid the silver carefully in the baize lined box, then started on the plates. It was striking one o'clock when she began on the saucepans, and half an hour after that when George came quietly back into the house. She heard him go into his study and then lock the street door and tread down the hall and into the kitchen. He said softly: 'Good God, my poor dear,' and took the tea towel from her and put his arms round her, and she buried her face in his waistcoat, wanting very badly to burst into tears. If he kissed her, she wasn't sure what she'd do...but he didn't, only patted her shoulder and said kindly: 'Now off with you—I'll finish this little lot,' and when she would have protested, 'No, not a word—bed for the cook, my girl.'

There didn't seem to be anything to say to that, Phoebe murmured goodnight and did as she had been told, and once in bed had a nice refreshing weep before she finally slept.

They laughed about it over breakfast in the morning, and it wasn't until that meal was over that Phoebe, making some remark about the Bissett baby, discovered that George had been out again at four o'clock in the morning, this time to drive the small sufferer and his mother to Stowmarket hospital. 'But you've had no sleep!' she cried worriedly. 'Thank heaven it's Sunday.'

'You don't want to go anywhere?'

'No. It's a lovely day, we can sit in the garden and read the papers. After church,' she added hastily. George, she had quickly discovered, was very firm about going to church on a Sunday. She enjoyed going down the village street to the morning service, and liked the sound of George's deep voice booming away at the hymns and the way he sat, listening to every word of John Matthews' sermon. Afterwards they went back home and had coffee and then took Beauty for a walk before Phoebe took a tray up to Mrs Thirsk, now almost herself once more. When she got back to the kitchen it was to find that George had put things haphazard on to a tray and carried it out to the garden, and they had a picnic in a rough-and-ready fashion, reading the Sunday news-papers while they ate. Afterwards George went to sleep, lying out on the smooth lawn, his firm mouth very slightly open and uttering the faintest of snores. Phoebe sat and watched him, her face alight with love, but presently she got up silently and carried everything back indoors. The washing up would wait. She went outside again and sat down close to George with Beauty's head in her lap. Just for a little while she was utterly content.

Mrs Pritchard phoned later in the day; she would be coming to England for a couple of months, probably in August. 'And I'll come and stay with you for a few days if you'll have me,' she told them, 'before I go to Grantchester. I can't come sooner. Your grandmother isn't very well—nothing serious, the doctor says, but she's asked me to stay in Holland until she feels herself again.'

They spent the evening discussing her visit and exchanging views on the Sunday papers, and Phoebe cooked a mixed grill, not quite Cordon Bleu, but George ate it, which was all she wanted.

Mrs Thirsk was so much better in the morning that she had to be restrained from getting up and going down to her kitchen. 'After lunch,' said Phoebe persuasively. 'There's nothing much to do. Susan's here seeing to the house, and I'll get a cold lunch for us; the doctor's got to go to Cambridge directly after his visits and won't be back until tea time at least.'

'I'll cook supper,' declared Mrs Thirsk obstinately.

'Oh, please do,' said Phoebe. 'You've no idea how much we've missed you.'

A remark which caused the housekeeper's rather stern features to relax into a pleased smile.

A week went by, a very pleasant one, although at the end of it Phoebe had to admit to herself that nothing in the least exciting had happened to enliven it. Indeed, she had been busy almost all day, what with helping in the surgery, pottering round in the house and garden and taking Beauty for her walk. She had taken over all the shopping now, too, and the accounts, so that she had little time in which to sit and laze. As far as she was concerned she would be happy—well, almost happy—to go on like that for ever. The summer stretched ahead of her and anything could happen.

But not quite what she dreamed of so constantly. It was after a busy Monday morning surgery, soon after George had driven off to the first of his visits, that a black Mercedes nosed its way down the village street and came to a halt outside the house. Phoebe, walking up the main street from the butcher's shop, her basket over her arm, wondered idly whose car it could be—someone too late for surgery, perhaps? She hurried her footsteps and arrived at her front door just as the front door of the car opened and Kasper got out, and after him, Corina.

Phoebe stood, her mouth slightly open, unable to believe her own eyes. Kasper's cheerful, 'Hullo, little cousin,' only made it worse. She looked from him to Corina, a glowing picture in a trouser suit and a camisole top. She found her voice then.

'What a surprise! I expect George forgot to let me know...'

'He doesn't know—we decided we would give you a real surprise. We wanted a holiday, and where else to go but to our so English George and his charming wife?'

Phoebe shifted her basket to the other arm, one part of her mind reminding her that she would have to go back to the butcher's and get more steak. 'Well, do come in—George is doing his morning visits, but he'll be home, for lunch you'll stay, won't you?'

Corina let out a peal of laughter. 'Stay? Of course we'll stay—there's room enough for the two of us, I imagine, and we hadn't planned to go anywhere else.' She looked around her. 'I must say it's quiet—a real English village.' She turned to Kasper. 'Bring in the cases, Kasper—I'm dying for coffee!'

Phoebe, bereft of words, opened the door and led the way in. 'If you will go into the sitting room,' she suggested, 'I'll get Mrs Thirsk to get the coffee.' She went along to the kitchen, trying not to notice the suitcases that Kasper was bringing into the hall—enough for a month's stay, she decided, her heart in her shoes.

In the kitchen Mrs Thirsk was podding the young broad beans Susan had brought with her. She took a look at Phoebe's face and said at once: 'What's wrong, Mrs Pritchard? What's the matter?'

'We've got unexpected guests, Mrs Thirsk—the doctor's cousin from Holland and—and an old friend. They want to stay. Could we possibly have coffee?' She put her shopping basket on the table. 'I'll go back for more steak presently, and perhaps Susan could do some more vegetables. The two rooms in the back wing have beds made up, don't they? They'd better have those.'

Phoebe sounded so unlike her usual self that the housekeeper said quickly: 'Don't you worry about a little thing, Mrs Pritchard, the rooms are quite ready. Susan can slip down to the butcher presently—there'll be four for lunch? You see to them and I'll be along with the coffee in five minutes.'

She was as good as her word. Phoebe, sitting uneasily exchanging nothings with Corina and listening to Kasper's lighthearted remarks about their journey, welcomed the diversion, while Mrs

Thirsk took her time setting the tray on a side table while her sharp eyes took in the visitors. She had responded distantly but suitably to Phoebe's introductions, and when she had gone Corina said: 'Bad-tempered, is she not?'

Phoebe was quick to defend her trusted helper. 'Good heavens, no—what makes you say that? She's marvellous and runs the house so beautifully, and she's a splendid cook. George and I think of her as a friend as well as a housekeeper.'

Corina threw up her hands in mock dismay. 'I seem to have upset you. It was only my impression. I have not seen her before—last time I came she was on holiday.'

Kasper sat drinking his coffee and smiling to himself. Phoebe, glancing at him, wondered what she had found attractive about him in Holland. Here he was thoroughly out of place, so for that matter was Corina, so disrupting the even tenor of their lives..

Corina put her cup down, 'I'd like a shower before lunch. Where am I to sleep? Last time I had a big room at the side.'

'Come upstairs and I'll show you—if Kasper would bring up your case?'

He laughed. 'You mean cases! Corina never travels without at least a month's supply of clothes.'

Phoebe led the way upstairs. 'Oh, God—at the back of the house,' observed Corina crossly. 'Poky rooms, and I suppose I can't have a bathroom to myself?'

'Afraid not,' said Phoebe politely. 'It's just next door to your room, though, and only you and Kasper will be using it.'

'There's another bathroom, though, as well as the one I suppose you and George use.'

Phoebe heard the lies tripping off her tongue and she, a truthful girl, felt no shame. 'Sorry, but the plumbing needs attention—it's not in use for the moment.' She had gone into the bedroom with Corina and cast a quick eye round to see that everything was just so. 'We lunch at one, so come just when you're ready.'

She went back downstairs, glad to be away from Corina's ill humour, to discover Kasper sitting at his ease, a glass of sherry at his elbow.

'Taken you by surprise, haven't we, Phoebe? Corina has these sudden fancies and nothing will shake her out of them or make her change her mind—besides, I must confess that I wanted to see you in your role of housewife.' He grinned. 'Perhaps it's nearer the truth to say that I wanted to see you, full stop.'

Phoebe eyed him coldly. 'Do help yourself to a drink,' she said crisply. 'I must see about lunch.'

She went into the dining room and started to lay the table, just as she always did. She didn't hurry about it because she wanted to be in the hall when George got back. She glanced out of the window and saw the Mercedes still there, and hurried back to Kasper.

'Will you move your car; there's a lane a few yards along the road—you can put it there for the moment. We leave the front free for George.'

'If you say so, darling Phoebe.' He drank the rest of his sherry and went out of the door, and Mrs Thirsk came into the dining-room and stood watching him with Phoebe beside her.

'Will it be a long stay?' she asked softly.

'I don't know.' Phoebe felt a childish desire to burst into tears. 'I daresay they'll tell the doctor. We'd better ask Susan if she would pop up each evening and give you a hand with the washing up and tidying the kitchen. It won't be too much work for you, Mrs Thirsk? I'll help as much as I can, and perhaps they won't stay for more than a day or two.' She broke off. 'Here's the doctor.'

She got to the door as George opened it, but before she could say anything she saw him look over her shoulder and heard Corina's voice from the stairs. 'Surprise, surprise, darling—I thought you'd like it if I came to cheer you up for a bit.'

George's expression, his usual expression of placid good humour, didn't alter. He paused just long enough to drop a brief kiss on Phoebe's cheek and then he went past her into the hall.

'Who brought you?' he asked blandly.

Kasper—I made him. He's here somewhere.'

'I asked him to put the car in the lane,' explained Phoebe in a wooden voice, and watched Corina fling her arms around George's neck and kiss him. The girl had changed into a stunning outfit—

white linen with a vivid green sweater, her make-up was faultless and so was her hair. Phoebe, without the chance to do things to her face and hair, felt positively dowdy.

George took Corina's arms from his neck. 'Well, now you're here, come and have a drink.' He glanced at Phoebe and smiled faintly. 'Lunch?'

'In about ten minutes. I was just going to see how Mrs Thirsk was getting on.'

'Really George,' drawled Corina, 'Phoebe is almost too good to be true.'

He agreed blandly and turned to meet Kasper, strolling into the house, just as though he owned it, thought Phoebe furiously, as she went to find Mrs Thirsk.

That good lady wisely said nothing; lunch was ready and she had found time to prepare shrimp cocktails. 'I'll take them in now, Mrs Pritchard, and we'll have the rhubarb tart and cream for afters. I'll make a creme caramel for this evening—they'll be here for dinner?'

'It seems as though they will, Mrs Thirsk—I'll let you know as soon as I can.'

'Well, don't you fret yourself, ma'am, but we'd better do something more than the omelette we'd planned—will you and the doctor be going to that concert?'

Phoebe had forgotten that. 'Oh, lord—perhaps we can get two more tickets. We must go because the doctor promised—it's for the League of Friends and we were specially invited.'

She went back to the drawing room, accepted a glass of sherry from George and started a conversation with Kasper, since Corina was deep in conversation with George, and since they were speaking Dutch, it made it difficult to join in. She sat listening to Kasper's amusing talk, not hearing above half of it, since she was trying to understand what Corina was saying; and she was rescued with Mrs Thirsk's announcement that lunch was on the table. It was during that meal that George observed mildly: 'Corina and Kasper plan to stay with us for at least a week, Phoebe.'

She hoped that her horror at the news didn't show on her face.

She said: 'How nice—we must think up a few trips while they're here. The country is so pretty...'

Corina gave her tinkling laugh. 'Oh, country—how boring! All right for you, Phoebe darling—you're a country girl at heart, aren't you? I want to do some shopping and visit a restaurant or two.'

'Well, we can start with this evening.' George's voice was so placid as usual. 'Phoebe and I have an invitation to a concert which we have no wish to break. I'll get two more tickets.'

'What kind of concert?' said Kasper idly.

'Orchestral and piano.'

Corina looked horrified. 'Piano?—No pop? Isn't there a disco somewhere?'

'Probably. I've never enquired,' said George, still placid. 'But I'll make enquiries and you and Kasper can go along and dance the night away.'

Corina pouted prettily. 'That isn't what I meant. Why don't you come too, darling George?'

He turned a bland face to her. 'I prefer my home—besides, I'm a busy man and I enjoy our quiet evenings.'

Corina's eyes sparkled. 'Oh, we'll have to change all that, won't we, Kasper?'

'We can always try! What about you, Phoebe?'

Phoebe said quietly, not looking at George, 'I like doing whatever George likes doing.' She smiled brightly round the table. 'Shall we have coffee in the drawing room?' Only then did she look at George. 'You're not in a hurry, George?'

She saw him shake his head. 'A couple of calls, but I can spare half an hour still. I'll see about those tickets.'

While they drank their coffee Corina kept the conversation firmly in her hands, talking about people Phoebe didn't know, recalling occasions when she and George had been dancing or dining. If only he'd mind, thought Phoebe. If she had to go on smiling much longer her face would crack. It was quite a relief when George got up to go, refusing quite firmly to take Corina with him. 'You'll be here when I get back,' he said casually, 'and the only person I take with me is Phoebe—she's a nurse, you see, and gives me a hand if I need one.'

Corina professed herself bored the moment George had driven away. 'I'll unpack,' she declared, 'and have a nap someone can bring me a cup of tea at about four o'clock.'

'I'll let you know when it's teatime,' said Phoebe. 'We have it in the sitting room.'

Corina flounced off, leaving Kasper lolling in his chair, still smiling. Phoebe got up. 'I've got things to do; there are some pleasant walks if you'd like to go out—I'll see you at teatime.'

His eyes widened with laughter. 'I do believe you don't like having us here!'

She stood in front of him and gave him a straight look. 'Since you ask, no, I don't, but you're George's guests, so I shall do my best to see that you enjoy yourselves.'

'Well, well, my little cousin has a sharp tongue! Let's hope George doesn't come under its sting.'

'George doesn't need to.'

In the kitchen Mrs Thirsk was tackling a mountain of dirty dishes. 'Susan will be back soon,' she explained, 'when she's had her dinner—she wanted to go home for it—she's a good girl.'

'Indeed she is, I'll dry, and while I'm doing that we can plan the meals for tomorrow. Our guests will breakfast with us, Mrs Thirsk—probably Juffrouw van Renkel will ask for her breakfast in bed, but I'm afraid, as they arrived unexpectedly, they'll have to fit in with the doctor's mealtimes I'll not have him inconvenienced.'

'Indeed not, ma'am.' Mrs Thirsk sounding approving. 'How about a nice piece of fish for tomorrow? There's that trout in the freezer—new potatoes and peas and a nice sauce. And an upside-down pudding for afters, the doctor likes them.'

'That sounds splendid. What about this evening? We'll have to eat at seven o'clock sharp—the concert is at half-past eight.'

'Tomato soup,' said Mrs Thirsk promptly lamb chops and a green salad ice cream for afters. Would that do?'

'Admirably. Do you want any extra help, Mrs Thirsk? A week is a long time…'

The housekeeper stole a look at Phoebe's unhappy face. 'Gone in a flash,' she said bracingly 'specially if you take one day at a time. Me and Susan will manage very well, the lady and gentleman can look after themselves when you're in the surgery with the doctor—I daresay they'll go for a walk. They're not…?' she paused expectantly.

'No, I don't think so, Mrs Thirsk, but I really don't know. They've known each other a long time, though.'

Mrs Thirsk made a strange muffled snorting sound and muttered something Phoebe didn't hear and decided not to notice. She didn't blame Mrs Thirsk for being put out.

In bed that night Phoebe came to the unhappy conclusion that the evening hadn't been a success. Corina had kept them waiting for dinner and had appeared, a vision in vivid pink, to keep them waiting still further because she simply had to have a drink before they sat down. Then she refused the lamb chops and asked for an omelette, so that by the time they were ready to leave, it was late. It was fortunate that they only had to go to Bury St Edmunds, no distance at all; all the same, they barely had time to take their seats. Phoebe sat up in bed and pummelled her pillows in a sudden rage. Corina had contrived to hang back, so that Phoebe found herself with Kasper beside her, and Corina between the two men. She sat, not hearing any of the concert, reflecting that she might just as well not have gone. It had helped a bit when the concert was over, for George had taken her arm and let the other two go on ahead.

'You enjoyed the concert?' he wanted to know.

'Oh, very much—they were all splendid, weren't they? I liked the concerto.'

'What are we to do with our guests tomorrow? Have you any ideas?' They were walking very slowly and a throng of people separated them from Corina and Kasper.

'Well, no. Would they like to go for a country walk?'

He let out a rumble of laughter. 'Corina in four-inch heels? Very unlikely. Besides, I've several babies coming for their triple injections and I could do with your help—they'd better go off on their own in the morning.' He smiled at her so kindly that she had felt tears crowd her throat. She smiled back at him, suddenly almost happy again. Only it was shortlived; Corina had turned back impatiently and slipped an arm into George's, wanting to know if there was somewhere lively where they could dance for an hour.

He had said no very decidedly. 'You forget that I'm a working man,' he had reminded her. His answer had consoled Phoebe; it was a small consolation, but it helped.

She got up heavy-eyed after a troubled night's sleep and went downstairs to find George already at the table. His, 'Good morning,' was brisk, and as soon as she had sat down he went back to his post. Presently he looked up. 'What about Kasper and Corina?' he asked.

'They had early morning tea and they know breakfast is at half-past seven.'

He leaned back in his chair. He said with a slow smile: 'You know, my dear, I fancy you have depths that I haven't yet plumbed.'

Phoebe didn't answer that but poured coffee buttered toast and began on her breakfast. Ten minutes later Kasper appeared. He wasn't at his best in the morning, she decided; his face looked puffy and there was no sign at all of all that charm. She made polite enquiries as to his night's sleep, put his toast near, poured his coffee and offered him a boiled egg.

'I looked in on Corina,' he observed grumpily, 'She's still in bed.'

'Too bad,' said Phoebe tartly, and refused to meet George's surprised look. 'I'll be in the surgery, Kasper, for the next hour or so. We usually have coffee after that, but if you two want to go out would you let Mrs Thirsk know, then she'll know what to do about lunch.' She smiled pleasantly. 'And now, if you'll excuse me, I must just go and see Mrs Thirsk in the kitchen…'

When she got back, George had gone to the surgery and Kasper was still at the table smoking. 'They'll be coming to clear the table,' she told him sweetly. 'The papers are in the sitting room.'

Kasper laughed. 'And Corina's breakfast?'

'I'm sorry, but you must see that we have to keep to a strict timetable unless George is on holiday. I daresay she'll be down by the time we have coffee.'

She whisked away, donned her overall and went along to the

waiting room, where she dealt with her usual calm with the patients, handed forms, wrote up cards, undressed a couple of babies and helped old Mrs Oakes to unwrap the layers of clothing she always wore, winter and summer, so that George could take a look at her painfully wheezing chest.

Surgery took longer than usual and then there was the clearing up to do while George sat at his desk, filling in forms and making notes. He didn't have anything to say and Phoebe, already regretting her sharpness at breakfast, held her tongue. Presently they went together back to the sitting room, where pacing up and down like a beautiful caged tiger they found Corina. Kasper was lounging in a chair, reading the papers.

'Well, I must say—' Corina began, and broke into a torrent of Dutch, ignoring Phoebe.

George answered her in English. 'I daresay you didn't quite understand, when you decided to visit us, that I have a working day just like anyone else who earns his living, and since Phoebe helps me, there's precious little time to do anything else.' He sounded matter-of-fact and added: 'Here's coffee—why not go for a stroll through the village? Phoebe has to shop, I daresay, and get the lunch. Perhaps this afternoon...'

'I'll come with you when you do your visits.' Corina was smiling again.

'No.' He looked at Phoebe. 'Will you pour the coffee, my dear?'

The day passed uneasily. Corina refused to go for a drive with Kasper but sat about the house saying nothing, only when George came back did she become animated. A wretched day, Phoebe decided, getting thankfully into her bed.

She did her best the next day, still conscious that she had been less than hospitable to her unwelcome guests. She persuaded Kasper to drive them to Cambridge, showed them as much of the city as possible, took them to lunch at the University Arms and possessed herself in patience while, Corina went in and out of various shops, only to return empty-handed.

'I must be taken to London,' she declared crossly.

Phoebe did not comment.

They took a disastrous picnic into the country the next day, and it rained, and the following day Phoebe, unable to think of anything else to do, suggested going to a film in Cambridge. It was all very well for George, she thought vexedly, he was hardly ever home, and the only time Corina was animated and smiling was when he got back in the evenings.

She sat after dinner, trying not to notice how Corina was charming him while she herself lent an inattentive ear to Kasper. The week was nearly up and no one had said a word about leaving. For two pins I'll leave myself, she thought, and heard George say carelessly: 'By the way, we've got a measles epidemic on our hands. Nasty thing, measles, and easily caught. It's not too bad with children, but there are two mothers with it already, and it hits hard with adults.'

Corina lounging gracefully on the sofa sat up smartly. 'I've not had measles. Is it spots? Is it dangerous George?'

'Well, hardly fatal, but the rash is nasty and one is liable to get chest infections and bad eyes, hair falling out and so on.'

'I will not stay here with this measles, however much you beg me. Kasper, you will drive me to London tomorrow.' She darted a look at George. 'These patients—do they come to the surgery with this measles?'

He shrugged. 'Bound to—they don't always recognise that they have the symptoms.'

'We shall go after breakfast.' Phoebe, listening and not saying a word, had never heard such good news in all her life.

CHAPTER EIGHT

THE REST OF the evening was taken up with discussions; patient and goodnatured on George's part, amused on Kasper's and pettish on Corina's. Phoebe contributed little to the talk, as a good deal of it was in Dutch and she felt sure that anything she might have to say would bear little weight with Corina. She offered more coffee, undertook to see that both her guests would be called betimes and asked diffidently if she could help Corina to pack.

Corina had refused. 'There's no room for two in that poky bedroom,' she observed waspishly, and had turned her attention on George once more.

'You must come up to London,' she urged. 'We haven't had any fun—I want to dance and have supper at a decent restaurant.'

George had smiled gently. 'Kasper dances far better than I do, and he knows all the best restaurants. Besides, we can't get away.'

Corina slid a malicious glance towards Phoebe. 'Tied by the leg?' she asked, and laughed.

Watching the Mercedes driving away the next morning, Phoebe thought that she had never been so happy—a happiness mitigated by an uneasy feeling that she had been less than a perfect hostess. But then Corina had needled her unmercifully and it had been hard to take her lighthearted jibes meekly. She went back into the house and met Mrs Thirsk coming from the dining room. 'Nice to be back on our own again, Mrs Pritchard,' she observed. 'How about a cheese soufflé and asparagus for lunch? and Susan's brought some strawberries…'

'Oh, lovely, Mrs Thirsk!' Phoebe danced upstairs and began to strip the beds; the day, already bright and warm, promised to be golden indeed.

She realised, when George rang the surgery bell for her to give him a hand, that she had hardly spoken to him while Corina and Kasper had been there—not alone, that was; they had had no chance, either one or other of their guests had been there and she had had to spend a good deal of time behind the scenes, organising meals and tidying rooms. She put on her overall and went through the waiting room to the surgery, to find George there with a weeping mother and a small screaming boy.

He said unhurriedly: 'If you would hold Ronnie, my dear, while I take a look for Kopek's spots.'

Phoebe smiled at the young woman and lifted the kicking small boy off her lap and set him on her own. Despite the fact that she was small she was strong; she held him firmly, his arms imprisoned against her, while George prised open his reluctant mouth and inserted the spatula.

'Yes, it's measles, I'm afraid, Mrs Watt. Take him home and put him to bed—and take care not to let him go near the baby. I'll be along later with some medicine and then I'll take a look at the baby at the same time.'

When Mrs Watt had led a tearful Ronnie away, he said: 'That's the third this morning—nine cases since Thursday. Thank heaven most of the children here have had their jabs. Send in the next patient, will you, Phoebe?'

Surgery finished, they spent twenty minutes or so, he at his desk, she clearing away whatever had been used, and tidying the waiting room. Finished, she said, 'Coffee when you're ready, George,' and went back to the sitting room where Mrs Thirsk had already put the coffee tray.

'It seems quiet without our visitors,' observed George as Phoebe poured out.

'Yes, and dull for you.' She hadn't meant to say that, but somehow it had popped out.

'Dull?' His voice was silky.

'Well, Corina is...well, she's so alive and amusing and pretty to look at, and Kasper is amusing too.'

'You think so? I had the impression from time to time that you thought the opposite.'

She put down her cup with a hand that shook just a little. 'Oh well, I expect that was because I was thinking about meals and—and that sort of thing.'

'I don't seem to have seen much of you,' he said mildly.

Phoebe felt a rare ill temper taking possession of her. 'I don't suppose you did,' she snapped. 'I expect if I were an experienced hostess I could have taken everything in my stride, but I'm not; you have no idea—and why should it bother you anyway? What a problem it is to think of meals, and the extra housework—beds to make and rooms to dust, and making coffee at all hours; and all the extra washing up and having to sit there, talking nothings while you know you should be laying the table or making a salad!'

George put down his coffee cup and she was furious to see that he was laughing. 'My poor Phoebe, and I quite thought you would enjoy some young company. I'm afraid I never thought about all the chores.'

It was really too much! She got to her feet and bounced out of the room and ran upstairs. There were still beds to make and perhaps if she had something to do she would feel better. He shouldn't have laughed, she told herself, and allowed the held-back tears to trickle down her cheeks.

Over lunch, again calm and freshly made-up, she enquired politely about the measles, mentioned an invitation to dine with some friends of his in a nearby village and remarked on the quite beautiful day.

To all of which George replied with a bland calm which she suspected hid amusement. They had almost finished when he said casually: 'How about an evening in town? We could meet Kasper and Corina and have dinner and dance. A small reward for all your hard work during the last week, Phoebe.'

The rage which she had so carefully mastered came racing back, almost choking her. The wretched pair had only been gone a few hours and here he was suggesting that they should race after them—probably he and Corina had arranged it; hadn't the girl been nagging at him to take her dancing?

'I can think of nothing more enjoyable,' she declared mendaciously. 'When do we go?'

George looked at her from under half shut lids, his eyes very intent. 'Saturday? We can arrange to meet somewhere—the Savoy, perhaps?'

'Very nice,' said Phoebe in a wooden voice. 'Will you be in for tea? I thought I'd go and see how old Mrs Down's getting on—she's worried about her cat.' At his enquiring look: 'He's off his food, if he's ill I'll ring the vet and get him to take a look.'

'You're happy, Phoebe?' asked George suddenly.

'Me?' She smiled in his general direction without meeting his eyes, 'Yes, thank you, George.'

'Why thank me?' he asked blandly. 'I hardly feel I deserve thanks. You don't feel that... You don't regret marrying me?'

Phoebe was thankful that she could answer that with perfect truth. 'Heavens, no! I love living here, it's a lovely village and everyone is so kind—it's so nice to feel wanted.'

George was looking at her and she frowned a little because it had been a silly thing to say. 'People tell me about their children and grannies and things like that, and then there's the surgery most days, and the house. I never have a dull moment.'

'You're content?'

It was on the tip of her tongue to shout no, she wasn't anything of the sort, she would never be until he loved her as much as she loved him, and that wasn't in the least likely. 'Quite.' That sounded bald; she added: 'And I'm fond of your mother.'

There didn't seem any point in adding to that, so she muttered: 'Mrs Down...' and smiled briefly as she went.

It would be splendid, she thought as she made her way to Mrs Down's cottage, if she could catch the measles. Then George could go to London on his own.

She had never felt better; she put on the dress she had worn for the party in Holland, took pains with her hair and face and joined George in the hall ready for their drive to London. She had prayed all day that some emergency would arise which would keep him busy; not that she wished harm to anyone, and it was George's weekend off anyway, so even an emergency would have been transferred to one of the other local doctors, but a suspected appendix or a fractured femur in the village would have been providential—held him up for long enough to make it too late to drive to London. However, the village remained healthy to a man, and

Phoebe got into the car, feeling guilty because she had hoped otherwise.

It was a beautiful evening and the roads were quiet. They made good time and parked at the Savoy exactly on time. They hadn't talked much on the way, casual remarks about nothing in particular, the easy chat of old friends. She had hoped that George might have made some remark about her appearance, but beyond a casual: 'That's a pretty dress,' he had said nothing. Phoebe wondered unhappily if he had even looked at her long enough to notice that she had altered her hairstyle. I'll tint it red, she thought crossly, and wear it in spikes—not that he'd notice.

Kasper and Corina were in the bar, and the first thing Corina said was: 'Hullo, darlings—Phoebe, you're wearing that dress again—of course you don't have much chance to dress up, do you?' She gave Phoebe a sugary sweet smile and kissed George, which made it easier for Phoebe to put up with Kasper's lingering salute.

She smiled back at Corina and said gently: 'Well, of course, if we had a really big date, I'd get something new.' She allowed her gaze to linger on Corina's vivid pink sheath. 'Haven't you been shopping yet?' she asked gently. 'Of course you haven't really had time.' She smiled at Kasper. 'I'd love a drink—gin and tonic, please.'

It was a drink she had never sampled; she disliked the smell of gin for a start, it reminded her of petrol, but so many people drank it there must be something about it…

When it came she sipped it. It was as disgusting as she had imagined it would be, but since George was watching her, a half-smile on his face, she took another sip and murmured: 'Very nice,' for his benefit.

They sat a while over their drinks before going through to the restaurant, and Phoebe, determined not to enjoy herself, found it difficult not to feel a thrill of pleasure at its grandeur. If she had been alone with George she would have exclaimed with delight, but since the other three took their surroundings as a matter of course, she did the same, prudently choosing a cold mousse to start with and thankfully, at George's suggestion, agreeing to Supreme de Turbotin Walwska to follow. Sherry trifle seemed a safe bet after that, a delicious sweet which she ate with pleasure, ignoring Corina's impatient pecking and complaints about the food. Phoebe, watching her push away the *mille-feuille* she had chosen, wondered what on earth she had thought of the far simpler meals she had had while she had been staying with them. No wonder the girl was as thin as a beanpole, and what a waste of good food and money. They had been drinking champagne. Now Corina demanded another bottle and pushed back her chair. 'Come on, George, I want to dance.'

Phoebe didn't look at him as he got up and followed Corina towards the dance floor. She hoped that one or other of them, even both, would twist an ankle, then felt horrified at her thought.

'Want to dance?' asked Kasper.

'Not yet—I'd like some coffee, please.'

He ordered it and sat back, looking at her and smiling. She wished he didn't smile so much. 'How long are you staying in London?' she asked.

'Oh, a few days, I suppose. It depends on how much shopping Corina wants to do. Or how long we can put up with each other's company.'

Phoebe turned surprised eyes on him. 'But you're old friends…'

'So I'm told. I endeavour to remember it.' She poured the coffee and handed him a cup. 'Are you happy, Phoebe?' he asked.

She busied herself with the sugar. 'Yes,' she said steadily, 'very!' She smiled briefly at him. 'Why do you ask?'

He shrugged. 'George took a long time to settle down, I suppose I thought that he was happy enough leading a bachelor existence; after all, there are compensations.'

She said quietly: 'I expect there are—you could say that about any state in life, I suppose. Do you come here a lot? It's magnificent, isn't it?'

'I've been put in my place,' Kasper laughed softly. 'I do wonder what goes on behind that calm face of yours, Phoebe.'

She didn't answer that but put down her coffee cup. 'I'd like to dance,' she told him.

The dance floor was fairly crowded, but she saw George and

Corina at once. George wasn't talking but Corina was, looking up into his placid face, laughing a little. Phoebe looked away and concentrated on her dancing.

When they got back to their table George and Corina were there. George was drinking coffee, but Corina was still at the champagne. She waved and giggled as they sat down. 'What do you say to going on to a nightclub? I know George wants to take me, only he says you aren't keen, Phoebe. I don't suppose you are—I daresay you've never been to one, have you? All the same, I want to go. Kasper can drive you back to that village of yours.'

'You've had too much champagne,' said George levelly. 'You've no idea what you're saying—and a good thing too, because you're being offensive. I've no intention of taking you anywhere; I'm going to dance with my wife and then we shall drive back to "that village of ours'. Kasper knows all the best night spots; he'll take you.'

'I don't want to go with Kasper.'

'Give her some coffee,' suggested George, and got up. 'Phoebe, shall we dance?'

Phoebe allowed herself a few blissful moments with George's arms around her, his elegant shirtfront against her nose. He danced well without effort and with no fussy mannerisms, and she floated round with him, not speaking.

'Enjoying yourself, Phoebe?'

What a nice voice he had, she thought, deep and rather slow and warm.

'Oh, yes, fabulous, isn't it? I've never been anywhere like this before.' She made herself look up at his quiet face. 'George, if you want to go on to a night club I don't mind.' She added apologetically, 'I've never been to one,' and when he didn't answer at once: 'I wouldn't like to spoil the evening for everyone.'

'As far as I'm concerned, it's already spoilt, Phoebe.'

There was no answer to that one. They danced in silence while she tried to think of something to say, and at the same time wonder exactly what he had meant. Had she spoilt the evening? She had done her best, but she hadn't really improved since that disastrous party with Basil; she was still shy and uncertain and she had been rude to Corina. The beastly girl had been rude to her, but apparently if one was pretty and amusing enough one could get away with anything.

The dance ended and when they went back to their table Kasper and Corina had their heads together, laughing softly and whispering. They looked up and smiled widely. 'We're going on to a night spot,' said Kasper. 'Corina has decided that if she can't have George she'll make do with me.'

George stood looking at them both, smiled a little and said: 'Enjoy yourselves. Let us know when you're going back to Holland.' He kissed Corina's cheek. 'A delightful evening.' He shook Kasper's hand and stood patiently while the two girls pecked the air by each other's cheeks and Kasper kissed Phoebe with unnecessary deliberation. They parted company at the table, leaving George to pay the bill, turning to wave carelessly as they left the restaurant.

Phoebe preceded George a few moments later after he had paused to speak to the restaurant manager. George, she reflected with satisfaction, was the kind of man who merited such attention; he made no fuss, never raised his voice, and yet he commanded attention without effort.

She got into the car beside him and sat quietly while he drove through the quiet streets. The theatres had disgorged their audiences long since and there weren't many people about. They were past Tower Hamlets, making for the Chelmsford Road, before George spoke.

'It's a pity those two don't marry each other,' he observed placidly. 'They have a lot in common. Of course, they've known each other for such a long time, so there's no novelty—besides, Kasper's more than half in love with you.'

Phoebe, who had been curled up cosily, sat up straight. 'What do you mean? What nonsense why, I might just as well say you're more than half in love with Corina!'

She could have bitten off her treacherous tongue. She added lamely: 'It's just as absurd.' And when he didn't say anything, her tongue took over again. 'She's more than half in love with you.'

She could detect nothing more than amusement in his voice.

'Corina is more than half in love with every man she knows.' She heard him chuckle. 'I should feel flattered that the idea should even enter your head.'

Phoebe muttered something. He was treating it as a joke, but it was no joke to her. She would have liked to have given vent to her rage and fright and misery, but she couldn't, not without him wondering why she, usually so composed, should exhibit such strong feelings.

'Nothing to say, Phoebe?' he asked silkily.

She summoned a hollow laugh. 'It was a silly idea, wasn't it? It must be all the excitement of the evening.' Anxious to get the conversation on to a more impersonal note, she went on: 'I had no idea that the Savoy was so grand. Have you been there very often?'

'Off and on, yes. But now the practice is so large that I've rather given up the bright lights.'

'You miss them?'

'Not any more, although I must confess that in the right company they still hold some attraction.'

Here we go again, thought Phoebe; it was as if Corina was sitting between them in the car. If only the girl would go back to Holland and stay there! No, Holland wasn't far enough—Australia would do, or the wilds of Brazil. She was a challenge, of course, but Phoebe wondered, just for a moment, if she would have married George if she had known about her. Only for a moment, though. Just to stay married to George she was prepared to take on a dozen Corinas.

They were clear of Chelmsford now and the country was quiet under the moon. 'It's going to be a fine day tomorrow,' said George quietly. 'Let's spend it at home doing nothing.'

She agreed with such fervour that he glanced at her. Her profile, clear and visible in the moonlight, looked sad despite her words. He dropped a hand on to her knee. 'You looked very pretty this evening,' he told her.

Her 'thank you' was a whisper, while she wondered if he meant it or if it was a kindly and probably remorseful attempt to cheer her up.

'I meant that,' he said, and stopped the car. Phoebe was quite unprepared for his sudden hard kiss, but she had no need to say anything, because he drove on again at once, and when he spoke next it was a mundane remark about taking Beauty to the vet the next week.

They went together into the quiet house. The hall looked welcoming with the shaded lamp on the wall table, and in the sitting room Mrs Thirsk had left a tray with cups and a thermos jug of coffee. George glanced at his watch. 'It's late, perhaps you're tired, but we've seen very little of each other lately. Shall we have a cup of coffee and talk?'

Phoebe wasn't in the least tired, and perhaps if they could sit together for an hour and talk they might get back to their first friendly footing—only of course it could never be quite that again for her, but George need never find out. She wondered how she would have felt about Corina if she hadn't been in love with him.

She curled up in an easy chair and kicked off her slippers while he poured their coffee, then went to sit opposite her with Beauty pressed up against his legs.

'Let's hope there won't be any more measles cases until Monday morning,' he smiled at her. 'That's wishful thinking, of course. At the least the children who haven't had jabs are turning up for them. It needs a mild epidemic to remind the mums.'

'None of the children are bad, are they?'

'No, although I hope none of the toddlers get it. We must ask Susan if she's had them, she's the eldest of four. How is she settling down with Mrs Thirsk?'

'They get on famously.' Phoebe was glad to have such a mundane subject to discuss, for she suddenly felt shy of George, sitting there, elegant in his dinner jacket and somehow remote too. He had wanted to talk, but surely not about measles? Was he going to tell her that their marriage wasn't turning out quite as he had hoped? She dismissed this idea at once, they hadn't been married long enough to give it a fair trial. Perhaps he wanted to explain about Corina, but she didn't think it could be that either, since he had no reason to explain anything. They hadn't pretended that they had loved each other when they married, so he wasn't being disloyal; it was just bad luck that Corina should have come back into their lives…

She was searching round for something else to talk about when George said blandly: 'You'd like to know about Corina, wouldn't you?'

Phoebe said a little wildly: 'No, I wouldn't,' and at the same time wanted to deny that. 'I'm not in the least bit interested. Anyway, it's all so obvious. I mean, she's an old friend, isn't she? You must enjoy meeting her again.' Her tongue ran on quite ridiculously. 'She's so pretty and…it's all such a waste of time, isn't it? and I think I'm tired after all.'

She whipped off the chair and skidded across the room on her shoeless feet and ran upstairs at a great-rate, just as though she expected George to run after her. Only he didn't.

And the next morning at breakfast he behaved just as though they hadn't parted so awkwardly. He made pleasant conversation about this and that, and when they got up from table observed that he would take Beauty for a walk before joining her in the garden. Phoebe longed to go with him, but she knew that he wouldn't ask her to—besides, she had made a complete idiot of herself. The chance of them getting back to their old friendly footing seemed more remote than ever, and all because she had been a fool.

She pottered round the house after he had gone, getting in Mrs Thirsk's way until she finally fetched her knitting and went into the garden. It was a glorious morning and the sun was brilliant. She perched herself on the edge of a garden chair and tried to look unconcerned and relaxed—not very successfully, though, because the knitting became confused and a jumble of stitches, and she was busy unpicking it when George returned.

He had Beauty with him and the Sunday papers were under one arm, as he stretched himself out in a lounger beside her.

Phoebe, rewinding wool at a great rate, said: 'I'll get the coffee.'

'Mrs Thirsk's bringing it, she saw me coming out here.' He closed his eyes and Beauty spread herself on the grass between them. They must make a cosily domestic group, thought Phoebe, and saw that Mrs Thirsk thought just that as she crossed the lawn towards them.

'That's right,' said that lady, 'you enjoy a nice sit-down—there's nothing like an hour or two with the Sunday papers, I always say.' She beamed at Phoebe. 'It's a nice cold chicken salad for supper, ma'am.'

'Oh, thank you, Mrs Thirsk,' Phoebe strove to look the part of a contented housewife. 'And if your nephew comes early do for heaven's sake leave the washing up, won't you? It's such a lovely day that you mustn't miss any of the rest of it.'

Mrs Thirsk went on smiling. 'Oh, I'll get finished on time,' she said comfortably, 'and I've got my key. It's little Jane's birthday, so I daresay I'll be back a bit late.'

George opened one eye. 'There's a small parcel for little Jane on the hall table—and go easy on the Guinness, Mrs Thirsk.'

She chuckled. 'Now, Doctor, you know as well as I do that I hate the stuff.'

He opened the other eye. 'That's why I do tell you to go easy with it.'

Phoebe poured the coffee and presently he went to sleep, lying on his back, looking, thought Phoebe severely, far too handsome for his own good. She went on doggedly with her knitting and presently gave way to the warmth of the sun and closed her eyes. When she opened them, half an hour or more later, it was to find George sitting up, looking at her over the top of his paper.

'Oh, lord, was I snoring?' she demanded. She didn't wait for him to reply but picked up her knitting and raced along a row, concentrating fiercely.

'No. I was watching you sleeping.' He smiled with such charm that her heart stopped and then beat so fast that she had no breath. 'It's the first time,' he pointed out. 'You're always wide awake and bent on filling the shining hour with as many jobs as you can fill in.'

She steadied her breath. 'You find that annoying? You see, I've always had things to do, and now that I don't need to do them, I feel guilty…' She added, anxious to seem keen to please, 'I'll change, really I will.'

'Don't you do that, my dear. You're very nice as you are.' He rolled over and picked up the paper again. 'By the way, I took your slippers upstairs and left them in your room.'

Phoebe blushed. 'Oh, thank you. I—I'm sorry about last night.'

George glanced quickly at her hot face and turned back to his reading. 'So am I, but for entirely different reasons, I imagine.'

She would have liked to have asked what those reasons were, but he was absorbed in the sports page. She went back to her knitting; perhaps things weren't as bad as she had thought. Corina had come and gone and probably they wouldn't see her again for a long time, time enough for her to get closer to George. She wasn't sure how to do that, because she had no sexy little tricks and she wasn't anything special to look at. She could only rely on being there, as well dressed as possible, a good companion and hostess to his friends, handy in the surgery when she was needed, and ready to listen to him when he wanted to talk.

The rest of the day passed in peaceful leisure. Mrs Thirsk, wearing her best summer hat, departed with her nephew to drive to Bury St Edmunds, and the old house was quiet. They sat in the garden again, reading and lying in the sun doing nothing, not even talking, and presently Phoebe went into the house and made the tea and George carried the tray outside again, cucumber sandwiches, cut paper thin as only Mrs Thirsk could cut them, china tea and a walnut cake.

'As far as I'm concerned this particular Sunday afternoon can go on for ever,' observed George. 'I'd better take Beauty for her walk before church.'

He didn't suggest that Phoebe should go with him and she didn't ask, although she had hoped that he might since they seemed to have become good friends again. While he was gone, she set the supper table, made sure that the meal was ready for them when they got back, then went upstairs to shower and put on something other than the sleeveless cotton dress she had worn all day. She heard George come in and go to his room while she was still getting ready, donning a pretty patterned silky dress and a plain straw hat, gloves and a clutch bag. She surveyed her person with some satisfaction when she was ready; she looked every inch a doctor's wife, and it was satisfying too to see her own opinion reflected in George's glance when she joined him in the hall. She did her best to listen to the sermon, but it was hard not to be gratified by the glances of approval cast in her direction from the surrounding pews.

George went to his study after supper and she cleared away, set the table for breakfast, then went to the kitchen to wash up and leave everything tidy for the morning, and since George showed no signs of joining her she tapped on the study door, put her neat head round it, wished him goodnight and went upstairs. She could always read in bed.

The waiting room was full the next morning. Phoebe had taken a quick peep after they had left the breakfast table, taken the plates and silver out to the kitchen and got into her overall. George had gone into the garden with Beauty before going to his surgery and she started on the patients' cards. Mr Maggs was back again, puffing and blowing and a nasty colour with it. Phoebe sympathised with him because he looked a bit lonely and frightened—as well he might be; a widower living on his own and no family to keep an eye on him. She found his card, assured him that he would be first in, and passed on to Miss Stokes, complaining loudly of her rheumatics and telling everyone who would listen that the world was coming to something when a body couldn't have the doctor to visit her decently at home.

'Well, if you were unable to come,' Phoebe pointed out reasonably, 'the doctor would be round at once.'

There was a murmur of approval from everyone else there. George was liked; he was dependable and kind and very clever as well. Phoebe, hearing various voices raised in his praise, beamed with pride.

She sent Mr Maggs in when George buzzed and went unhurriedly from chair to chair; small boys with cuts and bruises, two little girls with their mothers, both suspiciously spotty, a teenage boy from one of the farms with a septic finger, the butcher's wife with a burned hand... It was a couple of hours before the last of them went into the surgery. Phoebe rushed around now she was on her own tidying magazines, straightening chairs, opening the windows. She would see to George's surgery when they had had coffee and then dash upstairs and make the beds before nipping down to the stores. She was waiting, her usual calm self, by the time George came into the sitting room.

'I can't think how I managed before you married me,' he told her in his calm way. 'You did a splendid job this morning, Phoebe.' He took his coffee cup and sat down in his big chair. 'If it gets too much for you, let me know and I'll get a nurse-receptionist.'

She said 'No!' so fiercely that he stared at her, so that she went pink and stammered a little. 'What I mean is, I enjoy the work and I've got almost nothing to do in the house with Mrs Thirsk and now Susan...' She added rather desperately: 'I don't want anything to change.'

George's face didn't alter at all, but she had the impression that he was angry—perhaps disappointed was more like it, and she wondered why, then dismissed the thought as imagination on her part, because he went on talk placidly about his mother's visit later in the summer.

For the rest of the day she hardly saw him. It was one of those days when half the village required his services, even as they were finishing their supper he was called out to one of the outlying farms, and although he wasn't long away he had no sooner got indoors than the phone rang and he went to his study to answer it. He left the door open and Phoebe, leafing through a magazine, couldn't help but hear that he spoke in Dutch. She went to the kitchen to speak to Mrs Thirsk because if she stayed, she was afraid she might try to understand what was being said—only a word here and there, and she would probably get them wrong.

When she got back George was in his chair again, reading a medical journal, and although he looked up and smiled he didn't tell her who the caller had been. Surely if it had been his mother or one of his Dutch friends he would have said? She stayed staring down at the pages of her magazine and wondered if it had been Corina.

There were so few patients for the rest of the week that Phoebe wasn't needed in the surgery. She picked fruit in the garden for

Mrs Thirsk's jam-making, did the flowers and polished the silver. She was perched on a stepladder, carefully wiping the chandelier in the sitting room, when George came through from the surgery a few mornings later.

'Finished already?' She wobbled a bit and he went to hold the ladder.

'Yes—we'll have time to talk before I go out. There's something I must tell you, Phoebe.' The ladder wobbled again, this time because she was shaking with sudden fright that he was going to tell her something she didn't want to hear, and he stretched up to lift her down. His arms were round her when the front door was pushed open and Phoebe's ear caught the squeak of the old-fashioned latch and looked over her shoulder through the open sitting-room door. Corina was in the hall walking towards them.

CHAPTER NINE

PHOEBE FELT George's hands tighten round her waist and then lift her without haste to the ground. His easy, 'Hullo, Corina, what brings you here?' was uttered in a voice that betrayed neither surprise or annoyance.

Corina flung herself at him, wreathed her arms round his neck and kissed him. Only then did she say carelessly: 'Hullo, Phoebe,' before turning her attention to George once more. 'I got bored with Kasper—I sent him back to Holland; I decided I'd come and visit you again…' She began to talk in Dutch, and although George had removed her arms from around his neck, he listened with a half-amused smile. When she paused for breath he said over his shoulder to Phoebe: 'Can we put Corina up for a few days, my dear?'

Phoebe said from a dry mouth: Of course—there's a room ready. How nice to have her back again.' She added for good measure: 'For as long as she likes to say she can stay.'

George's firm mouth quivered very slightly. 'How did you get here?' he asked Corina.

'Oh, train and a taxi—it's still outside.'

He went out to see about her luggage and she called after him: 'Be a darling and pay him, George,' before she turned to Phoebe. 'Have I surprised you?' she asked. 'Probably not, you must have guessed that I don't give up easily.'

Phoebe crushed an impulse to slap the girl's face. 'Do come up to your room,' she said sweetly. 'Did you manage to buy any clothes? I'm afraid they'll be wasted here; we're all a bit old-fashioned.'

Corina, following her upstairs, giggled. 'George isn't—or hadn't you discovered that yet?'

A remark to be ignored. Phoebe opened the door of the room

that Corina had had previously. 'Come down when you're ready,' she invited, 'the coffee will be just about ready by then.'

She met George in the hall, surrounded by expensive luggage.

'Rather a surprise,' he observed placidly.

She paused. 'For me, yes, but not, I imagine, for you.'

She saw his face become a bland mask. 'Will you explain that?' he asked her silkily.

'You had a phone call in Dutch—you didn't tell me who it was. Now I know.'

She went past him to the kitchen, ignoring his thunderous look.

Mrs Thirsk tut-tutted when she told her. 'More lamb chops,' she said at once, 'and there won't be enough peas.'

'I'll go down to the village as soon as I've had some coffee,' promised Phoebe. 'The doctor's not busy this morning—Juffrouw van Renkel won't be lonely.'

Her tone was so waspish that Mrs Thirsk paused in what she was doing to take a look at her. 'I can send Susan,' she suggested.

'No, I'll go—Susan's got the dining room to turn out, hasn't she?'

Phoebe picked up the tray and went back to the sitting room and plonked it down on the table by the window. George had gone out into the garden, Beauty at his heels, and she went into the hall when she heard Corina's voice.

'Send George up with my overnight bag, Phoebe, will you? I must do something to my face.'

'He's in the garden. Your stuff is in the hall, why not come down and get what you want? We're going to have coffee, so don't be too long.' Phoebe added gently: 'I don't suppose it matters too much about your face—it's only us here.'

She went back into the sitting room, not listening to Corina's cross mutterings and her indignant footsteps on the stairs.

Phoebe, looking at a portrait of one of George's ancestors, said softly: 'I'm behaving in the most shocking manner, and I'm not a bit sorry.'

The ancestor gazed back at her from eyes as blue as George's, and for one bemused moment Phoebe could have sworn that he winked at her. Imagined or not, it heartened her for George's return. 'Would you like to wait for your coffee?' she asked him pleasantly. 'I don't suppose Corina will be long.'

He stared at her and her insides went cold at the icy anger in his face. 'In that case, I'll wait.'

'OK. You won't mind if I pop down to the village? We need more chops, you know, and a few other extras. I'll be back by the time Corina is ready.'

She had no intention of hurrying back. She sauntered along to the butcher's, purchased her chops, added peas and cream from Mrs Pratt and lingered to look in the antique shop; there was a charming little footstool she fancied. Old Mr Briggs, who owned the shop, was in the window arranging a French secretaire in one corner, and they smiled and waved to each other before she walked on. It was her birthday in a few days' time and she thought wistfully that birthdays for her had never meant much, with no family to send her cards, besides she had always avoided telling her few friends at the hospital for fear that they would pity her. George certainly didn't know, although she knew the date of his; his mother had told her. It would be nice to see Mrs Pritchard again.

She had taken longer than she should have done. She took her purchases to the kitchen and went along to the sitting room to apologise and drink her coffee. 'The freezer is being de-frosted,' she explained, 'so we've only got the minimum of food in the house for a couple of days.'

She realised as she spoke that Corina couldn't have cared less. She said: 'How boring for you,' and turned back to George. 'You cannot be busy all day,' she explained. 'Besides, I am your guest, and you must entertain me.' She opened her lovely eyes wide and added: 'Oh, George, you always used to entertain me.'

'Did I? I've forgotten.' He got to his feet. 'I'm off. I'll be back for lunch, Phoebe.' He bent and kissed her cheek, lifted a casual hand towards Corina and went away.

Which left the two girls facing each other over the coffee cups. 'Have you any plans?' asked Phoebe politely. 'There's not much to do, I'm afraid.'

'I will be all right.' Corina smiled widely at her. 'I will be—how do you say?—one of the family.'

The rest of the day was a nightmare to Phoebe, with Corina's ceaseless chat about clothes and make-up, only interrupted when George came home, when she transferred her attention solely to him. Phoebe, eyeing the cases lying around in Corina's bedroom, thought gloomily that her stay was going to be a long one. Corina had given no hint as to how long it might be, and since she had only just arrived, it would hardly do to enquire. She resolved to ask George when she had a little time with him.

Something easier said than done. He went to his study on the plea of work to be done after dinner that evening, and since by eleven o'clock he hadn't rejoined them, there was nothing to do but to suggest to Corina that they might go to bed. Something which she didn't want to do, but since Phoebe showed no sign of going upstairs without her, she gave in ungraciously enough and they went together, wishing each other an insincere goodnight at the head of the stairs. Phoebe, her ears stretched as she got ready for bed, heard George come up much later and go to his room. Even then she lay awake for another hour or more, listening to the familiar sounds of the old house settling for the night; creaks and rattles and the trees rustling against the side of the house, but nothing else. She slept at last, to wake early and go downstairs and make tea before Mrs Thirsk was up.

Corina didn't come down to breakfast. Mrs Thirsk, clearing the table once George had gone to the surgery, paused in her work.

'Would you be wanting me to take a tray up to the young lady?' she asked. 'Susan's not coming until ten o'clock and I've the lunch to see to…'

'No, there's no need', said Phoebe firmly. 'Juffrouw van Renkel knows when we have breakfast and I explained that if she didn't come down, there would be coffee when the surgery was over.'

Mrs Thirsk nodded briskly: 'Just so that I know, madam. You'll be going to help the doctor?'

'Yes, I think I'd better, the waiting room is pretty full. I'll make the beds afterwards and Susan can tidy upstairs when she comes.

If Juffrouw van Renkel comes down before I get back into the house, will you tell her there are chairs out in the garden if she'd like to sit there.'

She hurried into the waiting room and started on the cards. George had found the first two or three for himself, but there were another half dozen for her to find. He thanked her politely when she got them and took them in, then asked her to dress a varicose ulcer and make several appointments; all in his pleasant manner, just as he had been pleasant at breakfast, a nasty cold pleasantness which had left her uncertain and miserable.

She dealt with the ulcer, made the appointments and went back into the waiting room. Well, two could play at that game, she told herself crossly. The moment the tiresome Corina took herself off—and let it be soon—she would have it out with him. She had thought she would be able to cope, loving him and hiding her feelings and behaving as before, but she could see now that it wouldn't work out. At least, not with Corina in the house. She took in the last patient's card and went back into the house, to find Corina strolling round, looking cross.

'I've had no breakfast,' she complained, 'and that woman said I'd have to wait for coffee. Really, I should have thought someone would have brought me a tray to my room.'

'Then you thought wrong,' said Phoebe sharply. 'Mrs Thirsk has enough to do in the mornings without carrying trays upstairs, and I'm busy in the surgery. I'm afraid if you can't come down to breakfast, you'll just have to wait until we have coffee.'

Corina opened her eyes wide. 'Why, Phoebe, how cross you sound! Anyone would think you don't want me here.'

Phoebe said unforgivably: 'Well, I don't remember inviting you,' and went off upstairs to make the beds. When she got back again, George was in the sitting room, noting his visits, and Corina was perched on the side of the rent table, with her legs swinging. That she had been talking about Phoebe was obvious from the look of triumph she shot at her as she went into the room. She said at once in a little girl voice: 'You see, George, how cross

Phoebe looks. She doesn't want me to stay—she said she hadn't invited me…'

He looked up briefly: 'You've already said that, Corina, and I'm quite sure that if Phoebe did say that she didn't mean it. My wife would never be inhospitable to our guests.' His voice hardened. 'And if she did, I'm sure it was inadvertent and she'll apologise.'

Phoebe stood very still looking at him. He meant it, and she couldn't for the moment think of anything to do other than that. She said in a voice totally devoid of expression: 'I'm sorry—I have no wish to be inhospitable, but perhaps Corina will understand that carrying trays up to her bedroom is a little difficult. Mrs Thirsk is far too busy. Of course, I could leave the surgery while Corina is here. That's up to you, George.'

She glared at him and was struck by the ridiculous idea that he was laughing at her behind his bland face. 'I'm sure Corina will fit in with our busy mornings,' he said smoothly. 'And how about that coffee?'

He didn't seem in the least put out. Phoebe, handing cups, would have liked to have thrown something at him. And at Corina, smiling a satisfied little smile.

The next few days passed in an uneasy truce. Corina made no more efforts to have her own way, but she needled Phoebe whenever she had the chance. Then she criticised the food, always with a deprecating smile, complained gently that she couldn't sleep at night, that it was too hot to sit in the garden, too boring to go for a walk, too tiring to read. Phoebe made suitable replies and forbore to suggest that her guest might find life more exciting if she went back home. Almost a week had gone by and there was no mention of her leaving; almost a week in which Phoebe had had no chance at all to have George to herself. The only time they were alone was at breakfast, when he was immersed in his post, checking his visits and his diary, and interspersing this with a few polite remarks about the weather, calculated to reduce her to tonguetied silence and the briefest of monosyllables. This was a George she hadn't known about. Gone was the placid friendliness and ease of old friends; the cool politeness with which he treated her was more than she could bear. If they could have had just half an hour in which to talk—but somehow Corina was always there, taking the conversation into her own hands, begging prettily to be taken in the car when he paid his visits and pouting just as prettily when he refused.

'Well, since you are so disagreeable about it, George, I shall not ask you again, but at least you can take me somewhere interesting. I heard you say you were free on Saturday. Take me to Cambridge, I want to buy things and this funny little village of yours has nothing, and there is a restaurant there, Kasper told me about it—the Oyster Tavern. We'll lunch there and I'll shop, and in the evening we'll dine and dance.'

They were sitting in the garden after tea. Surgery was still an hour away and George was lying back, doing nothing, and so was Corina. Only Phoebe was sitting upright, knitting away like the furies.

'What do you say to that, Phoebe?' asked George. He spoke casually, but he had his eyes set on her face.

Before she could answer Corina spoke. 'Phoebe will be glad to have the house to herself for a few hours—besides, three is a horrid number.'

George had taken no notice of her at all. 'Phoebe?' he asked.

'I think it sounds fun, I'd like to go—we haven't been out much lately.'

Corina gave him a very direct look. 'Is there anyone we could rustle up for Phoebe?'

George's mouth twitched. 'Not offhand—all our friends are happily married and like to go out together.'

'Well then, we won't go,' declared Corina sulkily.

'But of course we'll go. You'll like Cambridge and there are some beautiful buildings—the colleges, you know.'

Corina said something in Dutch and got to her feet. 'I'm too hot, I shall sit indoors.' She got to her feet and said something, still in Dutch, to George. Her voice, Phoebe had to admit, was very beguiling.

'No, thanks,' said George, 'I'm very comfortable here.' He closed his eyes as she spoke and she flounced away.

'Phoebe,' said George, and his voice was so gentle that she dropped her knitting in a muddled heap to look at him. 'Phoebe, darling Phoebe...' and then, 'Oh, damn!' as the telephone rang.

He got up to answer it, leaving her to pick up her knitting and muddle through a row while she digested the fact that he had called her darling. A slip of the tongue? A softening up so that she would agree to stay at home on Saturday? She could hardly wait for him to come back so that she could find out.

Only he didn't return, except for a few seconds to say that he was going out to Pake's farm. 'Old Mrs Pake had a coronary. Don't wait supper—I'll have to go with her to the hospital. Tell any of the patients who come to surgery to please come back later.'

His voice was brisk and he went away again without a backward glance. Perhaps she had dreamt the whole small episode.

He wasn't back for supper. It was after nine o'clock when he got in and there were several diehards in the waiting room, determined to be seen even if they waited all night. It was another half hour or so before he came into the house, and Phoebe handed him a whisky before going to the kitchen, to return in a moment with the soup tureen and Mrs Thirsk following with cold beef and jacket potatoes and salad. Corina, who had sulked for most of the evening, followed her into the dining room and sat down beside George at the table, breaking into a flow of light chatter. 'Poor George—why do you do such a dreary job when you could live so comfortably without doing anything at all? All these sick people!' She made a little face and Phoebe looked away. She knew how George felt about his work; he would cheerfully give up every penny of his wealth if it were a question of that or his job. She wasn't surprised to hear his noncommittal grunt, and it cheered her enormously.

He was tired. She looked at him lovingly, seeing the lines etched on his calm face. She asked quietly: 'Were you in time?'

He nodded. 'I hope so. Old Pake's badly shaken.'

'I'll cycle out there in the morning, if you think that might help?'

'Will you? I think it might. There's a daughter coming tomorrow about midday.'

'I'll stay till she comes. I can go directly after surgery.'

He nodded and then turned courteously to Corina, who was asking him something in Dutch.

'Oh, no, no fear of that. I'll still have Saturday free—Andrew takes over for me.'

Mrs Thirsk came in with fresh coffee and Phoebe helped her clear the table while the others went into the drawing room. When she joined them, George was in his chair, going through his afternoon post, and Corina was sitting on one of the sofas doing nothing. Perhaps, thought Phoebe hopefully, she would go to bed.

But she didn't. She stayed there, rather silent for once, making conversation difficult, until George said: 'What about an early night?' and stood up and wished them a cheerful goodnight which they couldn't ignore.

Morning surgery wasn't busy. Phoebe did what was necessary there and got on her bike. It was a couple of miles to Pake's farm and a flat road all the way. Once she was there, she was kept busy, making up a bed for the daughter, getting old Mr Pake some kind of late breakfast, reassuring him about his wife, and then preparing some sort of a meal against the daughter's arrival. She was tired as she cycled slowly back home; the daughter had arrived, a nice, sensible woman who thanked her while she was putting on an apron. 'We'll be fine now, Mrs Pritchard, I've no doubt the doctor will be out to see us some time.'

Phoebe played a game with herself all the way home, pretending that Corina would be gone by the time she got there, but it was only a game. The girl was still there, all right, curled up on the sofa, doing nothing as usual, magazines scattered round and an empty coffee cup on the floor. Phoebe picked it up, wished her good morning and went to confer with Mrs Thirsk about lunch.

George had been his usual calm self at breakfast. Crumbling toast opposite him, Phoebe had waited hopefully for him to call her darling once again, but he hadn't, only made some prosaic remark about the Pake family and gone into the surgery. There was no sign of him now and this afternoon he had a meeting at the hospital at Bury St Edmunds. She sighed, seeing no hope of talking to him.

He was back for lunch but away again directly they had finished, taking no notice of Corina's grumbles that she was bored with doing nothing. 'I mean to say,' she said pettishly, 'Phoebe hasn't got a car, she can't even drive.'

'She's hardly had the time to learn,' George pointed out reasonably. 'What's wrong with a bike?'

Corina hunched a shoulder. 'In this heat? Besides, where would I go?'

'I'll be back for evening surgery,' said George, and went.

The afternoon lasted for ever; Phoebe thanked heaven for a full waiting room after tea to keep her busy until supper time.

To her surprise Corina joined them for breakfast the next morning, dressed ready for their trip to Cambridge—a sleeveless dress of wild silk and a little jacket to match, calculated to take her through the day—without the jacket the dress would be just right for dinner and dancing. Phoebe, still in a cotton dress, mentally assessed her wardrobe to see if she could do better.

'We'll leave at ten o'clock,' said George, and went to his study, while Corina disposed herself carefully in a chair in the sitting room and Phoebe cleared the table and then went upstairs to change her dress.

She had plenty of clothes to choose from. She chose a pale blue crepon, very plain and very understated chic. She did her hair and face once again, found a little blue cashmere jacket to go with the dress and went downstairs as George came out of the study.

He didn't say anything, but crossed the hall to kiss her quickly and then, still not speaking, opened the house door. Phoebe, a bit flustered by the kiss, went to say goodbye to Mrs Thirsk and Susan and then went out to the car. It was too much to expect that Corina would have got into the back of the car. She was already curled up beside George.

They were a bare five miles from Woolpit, on the main road travelling fast, when the car phone buzzed. George slowed and picked up the receiver and then stopped, listening intently. Finally he said, 'I'm on my way,' turned the car and went back even faster than they had come.

'Why have you turned round?' demanded Corina. 'We're going to Cambridge. You promised!'

He took no notice of her. Over his shoulder he said: 'That was Andrew—he's out on a baby case and he can't get back. The two Arkwright boys, Mrs Biggs' youngest and little Tracy Bunting have eaten Laburnum seeds. Mrs Bunting found some in Tracy's hand.'

He didn't expect an answer, and Phoebe didn't speak, thankful that his bag was in the car. It was Corina who broke the silence. 'George, I want to go to Cambridge. You don't have to go back; it's your day off...'

They were going down Woolpit's main street and he didn't answer her but stopped outside a row of cottages at the end of the village, reached for his bag and got out of the car. The door of the end cottage was open and there was a group of women outside it. George went past them through the door and Phoebe followed him; four small children, all most likely very ill and three mothers besides themselves—he would need help. She smiled a little at the women clustered round the door and found George in the small front room, made even smaller by his bulk and the four little creatures lying on their distraught mothers' laps. He was already bending over Tracy. 'Get the syringes out of my bag, Phoebe,' his voice was calm and unhurried, 'then get the other three on to their sides—we must try and make them sick and clear their airways.' After a moment he said: 'When you've done that get on the phone. I want two ambulances here, fast. Someone may have phoned—if so hurry them up.'

No one had phoned, they had all been too panicky; someone had had the sense to ring the surgery and it was Mrs Thirsk who had passed the message on to Andrew. Phoebe met her coming down the street as she ran over to the Post Office and banged on the door. Saturday morning, and most of the village off to Stowmarket for shopping and Mrs Pratt not opening the shop at all.

'The phone,' said Phoebe breathlessly when she opened the door, and darted past her.

The children were semi-conscious. The two boys had been sick and looked decidedly better, but Tracy and Mrs Biggs' little boy looked dreadful. Phoebe did the things George bade her to while Mrs Thirsk went to the kitchen and made tea for the mothers, and they had barely finished it when the ambulances arrived. 'I'll go with Tracy and Benny Biggs,' said George. 'You go with the Arkwrights. The mothers had better come too.' He called to Mrs Thirsk: 'Make sure someone looks after the other children.'

He picked up Tracy and went out to the ambulance, handed over Benny to the ambulance man, urged the mothers in and got in himself.

Phoebe did the same, vaguely aware that Corina was calling angrily for George from the car, but far too preoccupied to listen.

At the hospital the children were whisked away and Phoebe sat down to wait for George. He came half an hour later, shepherding the three mothers. 'Now to get back home,' he said cheerfully. 'They're all right—a few days here and they'll be home again. I'll see if I can get a taxi.'

But there was no need; the car was outside in the forecourt with Mr Platt at the wheel. 'Mrs Thirsk told me to come after you, sir. I hope I did right…'

'Indeed you did, bless you both. It'll be a squeeze, but I daresay we can manage. You three ladies get in the back; Phoebe in the front between us.'

It was a squash, but no one minded. Mr Platt and the three women got out at the bottom of the village and George drove on up to his own house.

They could hear Corina as they went in and she came racing down the stairs as they stood in the hall. 'I won't stay another minute here!' she screamed at them. 'Look at you, Phoebe—you're filthy—your dress, it's disgusting—don't come near me! Of all the beastly ways of living...' She rounded on George, standing quietly an arm on Phoebe's shoulder.

'I never want to see you again!' she screeched. 'I thought it would be fun to get you away from Phoebe, but you can have her! You can bring my bags down, there's a taxi coming for me, I can't get away from here fast enough.' She glared at Phoebe. 'You smell abominable!' she snapped.

George laughed. His arm tightened round Phoebe and he bent to kiss her flushed face. 'Go and get cleaned up,' he suggested. 'I'll see our guest off the premises.'

Phoebe heard Corina's outraged gasp as she sped upstairs, to find Mrs Thirsk already there, running a bath and arranging a pile of towels. 'All ready, Mrs Pritchard, and just you give me that dress, it'd better go into the dustbin, it's past saving. Still, what's a dress...they're all right, the children?'

'Yes, Mrs Thirsk.' Phoebe was tearing off her clothes. 'Is Juffrouw van Renkel really going? Has she packed?'

'Lord bless you, Mrs Pritchard, that she has—got me to get a taxi for her too. Going home, she told me, never wants to come here again.' Mrs Thirsk came out of the bedroom and poked her head round the bathroom door and addressed Phoebe's head sticking out of the bath water. 'In a bit of a taking, if I might say so. Shall I lay out some clothes for the doctor?'

'Please, Mrs Thirsk, he's just as filthy as I am. Do you suppose we could have some sort of meal? I know we're supposed to be out, but is there anything cold—sandwiches, perhaps?'

'Leave it to me, ma'am,' said Mrs Thirsk, and bustled away.

Phoebe, fresh from her bath, her mousy hair washed and hanging loose to dry, put on a sleeveless dress and some rather dashing sandals and went downstairs. Corina must have gone by now and she supposed George was in his room. There was no one in the sitting room, nor in the dining room, and the drawing room was empty. For an awful moment she stood in the hall, not allowing herself to think that George had perhaps driven Corina to wherever she wanted to go. She went slowly to the house door and opened it to look out. The car wasn't there and she let out a small wailing: 'Oh, George!'

She gave a squeak as his arms went round her. 'Still determined to think the worst of me?' he asked softly, and twirled her round to face him.

She stared up at him. 'Yes—no—that is, where's Corina?'

'Gone. I forgot to ask her where.' He added tenderly: 'What a goose you are, my darling. I was always under the impression that a girl knew when a man was in love with her—you're the exception to the rule.'

'How would I know?' she said with a snap. 'No one's been in love with me.' She suddenly burst into tears. 'Oh, George, I wish you were...' She gave a great gulp. 'Oh, I didn't mean to say that.'

'But you said it, and you can't unsay it. Lord, I began to think we were destined to be good friends for life—I couldn't have kept it up much longer.'

'Kept up what?'

'Why, the pretence of being just a friend, when I've been in love with you for ever—since we met, at any rate.'

Phoebe felt a pleasant tingle of excitement. 'You never said...' she began.

'Of course not, you would have turned tail and run away.' He bent and kissed her. 'Dear heart.'

No one had ever called her that before, it made her feel a little dizzy. All the same, she said severely: 'What about Corina?'

'I've known her most of my life and not liked her overmuch, but our families were friendly and we went out and about—oh, years ago. And when she turned up at Mother's house, it seemed to me to be a good idea to make you jealous.'

'Oh, I was, and when she came here with Kasper...and then coming again like that, I thought that you—that she...that phone call.'

'No, my love, I don't care two straws for her. And the phone call was from Grandmother. I didn't tell you because I was angry that you took it for granted that it was Corina.'

He caught her very close so that she could barely breathe. 'My dear darling, we shall be so happy, you and I and a houseful of children. You won't find it dull?'

'Dull?' said Phoebe. 'Dull? Oh, George, how could it be dull with you?' She kissed him gently, already savouring the delightful future stretching endlessly. She smiled up at him and he kissed her back, not gently at all, so that she trembled with the delight of it.

Mrs Thirsk, crossing the hall on the way to the sitting room with a tray of coffee, came to a soundless halt, turned on her heel and went back to the kitchen. At Susan's look of enquiry she said happily: 'They won't be wanting coffee just yet, they've got other things to think about. And don't you dare go into the hall, my girl, not till I say so.'

Susan peeled another potato. 'Happen they're in love,' she said.

'Happen they are.' Mrs Thirsk smiled broadly. 'And high time too.'

0702/73/MB45

Betty Neels Ultimate Collection
Official Prize Draw Rules

NO PURCHASE NECESSARY

Each book in the Betty Neels Ultimate Collection will contain details for entry into the following prize draw: 4 prizes of a signed Betty Neels book and a weekend break to Amsterdam and 10 prizes of a signed Betty Neels book. No purchase necessary.

To enter the draw, hand print the words "Betty Neels Ultimate Collection Prize Draw", plus your name and address on a postcard. For UK residents please send your postcard entries to: Betty Neels Ultimate Collection Prize Draw, PO Box 236, Croydon, CR9 3RU. For ROI residents please send your postcard to Betty Neels Ultimate Collection Prize Draw, PO Box 4546, Kilcock, County Kildare.

To be eligible all entries must be received by **July 31st 2003**. No responsibility can be accepted for entries that are lost, delayed or damaged in the post. Proof of postage cannot be accepted as proof of delivery. No correspondence can be entered into and no entry returned. Winners will be determined in a random draw from all eligible entries received. Judges decision is final. One mailed entry per person, per household.

Amsterdam break includes return flights for two, 2 nights accommodation at a 4 star hotel, airport/hotel transfers, insurance and £150 spending money. Holiday must be taken between 1/8/03 and 1/08/04 excluding Bank holidays, Easter and Christmas periods. (Winner has the option of accepting £500 cash in lieu of holiday option.)

All travellers must sign and return a Release of Liability prior to travel and must have a valid 10 year passport. Accommodation and flights are subject to schedule and availability. The Prize Draw is open to residents of the UK and ROI, 18 years of age or older. Employees and immediate family members of Harlequin Mills & Boon Ltd., its affiliates, subsidiaries and all other agencies, entities and persons connected with the use, marketing or conduct of this Prize Draw are not eligible.

Prize winner notification will be made by letter no later than 14 days after the deadline for entry. Limit: one prize per an individual, family or organisation. All applicable laws and regulations apply. If any prize or prize notification is returned as undeliverable, an alternative winner will be drawn from eligible entries. By acceptance of a prize, winner consents to use of his/her name, photograph or other likeness for purpose of advertising, trade and promotion on behalf of Harlequin Mills & Boon Ltd., without further compensation, unless prohibited by law.

For the names of prize winners (available after 31/08/03), send a self-addressed stamped envelope to: For UK residents, Betty Neels Ultimate Collection Prize Draw Winners List, PO Box 236, Croydon, CR9 3RU. For ROI residents, Betty Neels Ultimate Collection Prize Draw Winners List, PO Box 4546, Kilcock, County Kildare.